Born in London to a Swedish mother and English father, Anita Griffiths spent her childhood moving between the two countries. She met her husband when she was eighteen and they laid down roots in sunny Dorset to raise their four children. With the children now grown and flying the nest, and the family expanding, Anita divides her time between tracing her ancestral roots across Ireland, England and Scandinavia, and writing in her nature filled garden with her cats.

Also by Anita Griffiths

Beyond the Ironing Board – an autobiography about motherhood and life in the real world.

COBBLED STREETS
&
TEENAGE DREAMS

Anita Griffiths

Copyright © 2017 Anita Griffiths
First Edition

All rights reserved. This book or any portion thereof may not be reproduced or used in any manner whatsoever without the express permission of the author except for the use of brief quotations.

This is a work of fiction. Names, characters and incidents are the product of the author's imagination and any resemblance to actual persons, living or dead, is entirely coincidental.

Any reference to places or events is purely from a personal opinion.

ISBN 9781521082317

Cover by
Dan Van Oss,
Covermint,
The Book Cover Designer

Dedicated to
My family, Team Griffiths
You are my driving force.
Love you all
Xxx

A huge debt of gratitude to
William Shakespeare
Who has influenced my world
Since I was very young

Chapter One

"Thanks so much," Alice smiled gratefully at the cashier as she retrieved her credit card from the card reader by the till, and stuffed it back into her floral, Cath Kidston purse. Then, taking the proffered receipt, she dropped both things into one of the two bulging shopping bags, and headed for the door.

"Bye then!" she called, turning back to acknowledge the cashier; her chestnut brown, floppy fringe momentarily covering her face before she flicked her head back again. Pausing at the shop door, she surveyed the donkey laying in front of her, blocking the doorway completely, with eyes closed and legs tucked under in absolute contentment. He was a regular feature at the village convenience store, and well loved by locals and tourists alike. Alice had been born and bred in Brockenhurst, in the New Forest; equines had been such a normal part of her childhood that she had become indifferent to their appeal, and she barely even noticed them. This one however, she couldn't really miss. She had already stepped over him on her way in, but that was before she had bags full of shopping.

"Shoo! Shoo!" she encouraged, swinging a bag towards him. The donkey opened his eyes, lifted his head and blinked at her.

"That's it, shoo! Go on!" she urged, but he looked away and lazily twitched his ears, then rested his head back on his leg. He clearly had absolutely no intention of moving.

Sighing heavily, Alice held both bags with one hand, stretched her free arm out to grab hold of the door frame on the far side of the donkey, then steadying herself by leaning her other elbow on the adjacent wall, with the bags dangling precariously above the donkey's head, she extended her right leg over his body and twisted round slightly to steady herself.

"This is like some bizarre yoga move," she muttered, then pushing her weight through her right leg to bring her left leg over, she managed to land with a half skip, half stumble, on the other side of the threshold. She turned, expecting to see the cashier laughing at her endeavour, but there was now a queue at the till and nobody seemed to have noticed her ungainly exit. Re-arranging her thin, short-sleeved cardigan, and brushing back her fringe, she quickly regained her composure.

The main street was busy - as it always was in late July - with a steady stream of holiday makers ambling along the pavements, stopping to snap photographs of the pretty shop fronts, and the fearless ponies that wandered in family groups amidst the slow-moving traffic. Cheerful bunting had been strung across the street, drawing attention to the red brick, and black and white buildings, that made up the small row of village shops. A crowd gathered further up the street to watch a herd of Highland cattle amble through the village. The cattle, renowned for their lack of road sense, had caused the traffic to come to a stand-still, affording a perfect opportunity for eager photographers. Their massive, long horns and distinctive shaggy coats, delighted the tourists thirsty for encounters with the animals that epitomised the New Forest.

As Alice glanced to the left before stepping out to cross the road, she caught a glimpse of someone familiar out of the corner of her eye, walking towards her. At that moment, he looked up, and their eyes met for just a second. She looked swiftly to the right and crossed the road towards the car park, still focusing to the right, as if she hadn't noticed him. Her straightened back told a different story. It was as if she were bracing herself for something to happen.

"Alice?"

A voice from the past called her, bringing memories flooding back. She faltered for a second. Her heart started to pound as she stood for what seemed like an age, the bags growing heavy in her clammy grip. She closed her eyes momentarily, knowing she would have to respond; he was so close now, she could almost feel his breath on her back. She turned, steadying her breathing, and smiled.

"It *is* you, I thought so!" he exclaimed, a wide smile stretching across his handsome, rugged face. She noticed wrinkles that hadn't been there before and his stubbly chin, which was once clean shaven, aged him somewhat. There was a smattering of grey throughout his tidy, short, black hair.

"Hello, Elliot," she said demurely, her voice barely a whisper. It was the moment she had once dreamt of for so many nights, and now that it was here, she could hardly believe it was happening.

Instinctively, he reached forward, offering to relieve her of the bags, still smiling. She felt a surge of emotions welling up inside her as the intimate familiarity he displayed in that one simple action, took her by surprise. It seemed like only yesterday, she thought.

"I can't believe it's been eighteen years," he said, echoing her thoughts. She looked up and stifled a gasp at the intensity of his stare, his eager smile encouraging her to respond. Anger crept through her like a red-hot flame; how dare he even speak to her, after everything that had happened. She tightened her grip on the bags, muttering,

"It's okay, I can manage."

He stepped back, his smile fading.

"Of course, I just thought …" he paused. "So, how are you, what's been happening? I heard you moved away, I didn't think you'd ever leave the village." He spoke quickly and she was almost pleased to notice he looked uncomfortable.

"Yes, I did," she agreed. "I come home to visit quite often though. You?" she asked, trying to sound casual. She already knew the answer. She had always known where he was and what he had been doing. Her 'best friend' had made sure of that.

Alice would never forget it; the betrayal, the absolute desolation she had felt, when the one person she had trusted - her flatmate and confidant, Mary - had told her she was leaving town. With him. He had been in love with Alice, he told her he couldn't live without her, and they had spent a perfect seventeen months together. Then one day, without warning, he disappeared. Leaving Mary to tell her of their deception. Nothing could have prepared Alice for that. Nothing.

She looked at him now, desperately wanting to find something abhorrent in his face or his manner, but failed to do so. A prickly sensation started across the back of her neck and she nervously rubbed her hand across it. He watched through narrowed eyes, and half smiled. Nodding to her heavy load, he asked,

"Feeding an army?"

She nodded.

"Something like that, yes. A party, actually."

What was she doing? She chastised herself, but couldn't resist. He raised an eyebrow,

"Really? Anybody I know?"

Oh, this was too easy.

"No," she said with a definite tone. "No, you don't know her. You should do though," she continued, as she started to walk on, leaving him standing on the curb. With a backward glance, she added,

"It's an eighteenth birthday. Your daughter's."

A single gunshot to his heart would have been easier but this felt better, so much better. She straightened up and walked on, smiling.

"You did *what*?" Alice's mother and aunt exclaimed in unison, as they stared open-mouthed at her. The two sisters had been bustling about in the kitchen, laying out platters of party food and unpacking the last-minute supplies of crisps, biscuits, and drink that Alice had just bought. Physically, they were very similar: both small-framed, and both blue-eyed, but that was where the similarities ended. Celia dyed her short, dark blonde hair to preserve its natural colour, whereas Roz dyed hers a silver-white, banishing her greying blonde, and had it styled in a short, messy bob. She was the less conservative of the two and the more dominant personality. Hot-headed and forthright, she outshone her younger sister, who in turn, towed the line and used her calm nature to maintain peace and harmony within the family.

Roz sat down at the kitchen table opposite her niece, clutching a packet of Skips to her chest. She looked at her sister, wide-eyed, and then back at Alice.

"We didn't keep it a secret for all these years for you to just blurt it out on a whim! Why on earth did you do that?" She put the packet down on the table and rested her head in her hand, rubbing her forehead slowly, shaking her head in despair.

Alice leant back in her seat defensively and dropped the biscuit she had been nibbling at onto the table, rubbing crumbs from her fingers. She felt cornered. She felt like a teenager. She responded like one.

"Well I'm sorry, but he was stood there, looking all … handsome … in his smart suit, with his steely blue eyes and his … 'come hither' smoulder going on … and I thought, 'no, I'm not going to fall for that again, however lovely and handsome you are' … so I had to stop him." She picked up the biscuit again, blatantly ignoring her aunt's look of disbelief.

"It did the trick," she added defiantly. Then glancing across at the work tops piled high with plates of food, and overflowing bowls of crisps, she distractedly asked,

"Did we really need more crisps? You've got more than enough here to feed an army." She stopped short as she heard herself repeating Elliot's words.

Roz was up on her feet again, noisily getting glasses from the cupboard. She wagged a finger at Alice.

"He'll be after you now; mark my words," she warned. Alice snorted in exasperation.

"No, he won't. The last thing he would want is commitment, of any kind. I scared him off, well and truly."

"You did no such thing! He won't let go," Roz's voice rose in pitch. "He's a Barraclough; they never let go." Close to tears, she looked over at Celia, who gave her a consoling smile before turning back to the fridge to pull out a jar of pickled onions, and another platter of cheese.

"What does that mean?" Alice asked, feeling irate, and bemused by her aunt's outburst. She looked at her mother for an answer. Celia just shrugged her shoulders.

"No, no, I saw that look between you – what's going on?" she demanded to know.

"Nothing," Roz stated firmly, with a sniff.

Just then the doorbell rang. A young voice shouted excitedly from upstairs,

"I'll get it!"

"I think we have guests," Roz announced as she left the room, avoiding eye contact with Alice.

"Mum, what did she mean?" she asked urgently as they followed Roz into the hall. She caught hold of her mother's arm to slow her down. Celia turned, letting out a resigned sigh.

"Well dear, she means ... you're not the only one who slept with a Barraclough!"

Alice stopped in her tracks, dumbfounded. Her mind was racing and so many questions were formulating in her head, but she knew, frustratingly, that now was not the time. Forced to shelve it until later, she put on a bright smile and joined Celia and Roz at the foot of the stairs.

"Here she is!" Roz cooed as Ellie hurriedly descended the stairs and jumping from the third step up, landed with a flourish and a twirl, awaiting their approval.

Of medium height and build, like her mother, Ellie was a bubbly, vivacious teenager and was clearly adored by her grandmother and great aunt; the feeling was mutual. She did another twirl to show off her freshly curled hair, which bobbed about her shoulders. On top of her curls perched a plastic, silver crown, adorned with sparkly bits of fluff, stars, and glitter. The number '18' flashed on and off, changing colour as it did so. Her paisley-print vest top, denim hot pant shorts over navy tights, and purple, Doc Marten boots, defined her unique style. She had her mother's chestnut brown, wavy hair and open smile, but unlike Alice's dark brown eyes, Ellie's were a steely blue. Like her father's.

The doorbell rang again. Ellie jumped up and down, clapping her hands and giggling in girlish delight as Roz ushered her to the front porch to greet the guests, and they hung back in the inner hallway. Ellie pulled open the solid oak door.

"Ta-da!" She waved jazz hands at the figure standing there, then stopped and laughed a little awkwardly.

"Oh ... hello? You're not my uncle! Sorry I was expecting somebody else," she gushed, brushing a fallen lock of hair from her face and tucking it back under her crown.

"Sorry, um ... I was looking for Alice. This is the right house, isn't it?"
Elliot stepped back and checked the house number plate, screwed in to the brickwork on the side of the door.

"Yes, yes, it is." Ellie nodded, "Just a sec, I'll fetch her."

She turned to find her grandmother and aunt shaking their heads furiously: her mother, wide eyed and ashen, staring at the floor. She turned back to Elliot, smiling apologetically.

"Oh, that's right, sorry. I forgot. She went out. To the shop. Who shall I say dropped by?" Her heart sank as she could hear how unconvincing her lie sounded, but she held her smile and met his gaze. It struck her how familiar he looked; she was sure she had seen him somewhere before.

"I'm Elliot," he smiled and stretched out his hand to shake hers. Laughingly she accepted, nodding in acknowledgment.

"Alice and I used to know each other, a long time ago," he explained.

"Oh okay. Cool!" Ellie's smile widened, "Well I'm Ellie, her daughter. And it's my birthday!" she laughed, pointing at her crown.

Elliot looked down at his feet for a moment and drew in breath, realisation hitting him; Alice had been telling the truth. A pain spread across his chest and gripped his throat. Gulping hard, he lifted his head to look at his daughter. Concern flickered in her eyes at his changed expression, but he forced a laugh, and pointing at her flashing crown, said,

"Congratulations, Ellie! That's a pretty name; what's it short for?"

Ellie laughed back, relieved that the briefly awkward moment had passed.

"I get asked that a lot. Mum always says it's short for Amazing Ellie. But it's just Ellie," she grinned.

"Well, 'just Ellie', a real pleasure to meet you," he nodded. "Can you tell your mum I'll call back some time tomorrow, please?"

"Okay, will do."

She was about to say goodbye but hesitated, then leaning towards him, said,

"Actually, we're having a party later on: just family and a few friends, but you're more than welcome. Grandma has got tons of food; I think she worries we'll all starve!" She raised her eyebrows questioningly, watching his response.

"Mum will definitely be here by then," she added, a little mischievously. Elliot smiled; they both knew that her earlier attempt at deceiving him had failed.

"See you at seven, then?" she prompted, then happy with his affirmative nod, waved goodbye and shut the door. Leaning back on it, she gave a low whistle.

"Oh my God, he's gorgeous! Who *is* he?" she asked incredulously. Three pairs of eyes were staring at her.

"Ellie!" her grandmother remonstrated.

"Don't worry, he's too old for me," she gave her aunt a conspiratorial wink, "I was thinking he's more Mum's type."

Alice laughed abruptly and shot her mother a pleading look. Celia put her hand on Ellie's shoulder and guided her into the kitchen.

"I can't believe you just invited him to your party like that, dear," she lowered her tone, "did you ask your mother if she wanted him here? I'm not even sure who he is," she added, glancing at Alice who was once again sitting at the kitchen table, staring intently at a plate of sausage rolls, her mind racing. Ellie swung round to look at her.

"Oh my God, Mum ... is he your Facebook stalker?" she gasped.

"What? You have a stalker?" Celia was full of concern. "On the face book?"

Alice rolled her eyes back, shaking her head. Roz interjected,

"It's just called Facebook, Celia, not *the* face book. My goodness, get with the times!" she joked, trying to lighten the mood. "Alice?" she prompted.

"No, I don't have a stalker; thank you Ellie," she nodded pointedly at her. "It's just ... one of my students has a bit of a crush on me, that's all. He's a teenager: these things happen," she waved her hand in a dismissive gesture. Celia shook her head,

"Oh, that's not good, dear. Before you know it, he'll be banging on your door with a gun ..." her eyes were wide, imagining the scene. Alice interrupted her,

"Mum! I live in Stratford-upon-Avon, not New York. It's absolutely fine, there's nothing to worry about," she smiled, trying to placate her mother.

Ellie plonked herself down in the seat next to Alice and reached across her to grab a sausage roll. Looking sideways at Alice, she smiled.

"Good, that's sorted then. The gorgeous, mysterious, 'old friend' Elliot is fine to come to my party," she stated authoritatively, taking a big bite and in so doing, sprayed flaky pastry across the table.

By seven o'clock, the house was full of teenagers and adults alike; loud music and chatter filled the air. Roz and Celia were in their element, fussing about with plates of food and jugs of Pimms, and guiding the older guests in the direction of 'something a little stronger', from the well-stocked drinks cabinet in the corner of the lounge. Alice leant against the door, drink in hand, surveying the room. She was wearing a strappy, vintage style, wine-coloured, crushed velvet dress that hugged her top-half, then flowed out softly from her waist, stopping just above her knees. Teamed with black, strappy heels to give her a little extra height, she looked the picture of understated sophistication. Her hair hung loosely above her shoulders, the grown-out bob cut glinted auburn in the dimmed lights. She shivered slightly in the summery evening breeze that wafted in through the open French doors.

Family had been arriving in dribs and drabs throughout the afternoon, starting with her older brother, Andrew, his wife, Laura, and their three children. They lived nearby in Winchester, just over half an hour's drive away. Both of Alice's paternal aunts, with their husbands, children, and teenage grandchildren, had turned up an hour previously: all local to Brockenhurst, so had taken a leisurely stroll through the village to get there. Ellie was in her element now, centre of attention and talking nineteen to the dozen with her cousins. Their mobile phones were out and they scrolled through YouTube to share clips with each other, and every few minutes, would erupt with laughter, doubling over in the process.

Alice loved them all dearly and it hit her suddenly how blessed she was to have such a strong, close-knit family unit. They had all pulled together when her father had contracted cancer, and after he died, they all shared the burden of grief. Her mind turned back to Elliot. Now that the shock of seeing him again after eighteen years, had subsided a little, the knowledge that she would have to protect Ellie from the truth, was taking over. She was also beginning to feel something else: was it guilt, nagging at her? Had she been wrong to deprive Elliot of this, of family life? Not happy with the way her mind was wandering, she reminded herself that he had made his choice: he would have to live with the consequences.

Andrew appeared from behind her and put his arm comfortingly across her shoulders. A good six inches taller than her, he had the same chestnut brown, wavy hair, and the same deep brown eyes. It was clear they were siblings.

"You okay?" he asked quietly. She turned to look up at him, tears in her eyes. He nodded knowingly.

"It's not the same without Dad, is it?" he acknowledged. Alice shook her head, feeling a little guilty that he assumed her tears were just about their father, although he had more or less hit the nail on the head.

"No, it's not. I was just thinking: the last time we were all together like this, was for his funeral last year. I love coming back home but I think my visits will always be tinged with sadness. I constantly feel like there's something missing," she said, taking a sip from her wine glass.

They stood in mutual silence for a moment, reflecting on the past. Their house had been in the family for three generations; their father's maternal grandfather had been a property developer and builder at the turn of the 20th

century. It was a great time of change throughout the country, with more and more grand country estates being demolished, and Alice' great grandfather, already fronting a successful business, had seized the opportunity to invest in land. It was the making of him, and his business went from strength to strength. He then laid down roots and built their family home in Brockenhurst. When his daughter, Alice's paternal grandmother, was widowed during the second world war, she moved back to the family home to raise her young children. The house, and a substantial estate, were passed on to her when her parents died, and she in turn, left the house to her only son, Reggie - Alice's father. She bequeathed it to him on his wedding day, and she moved in to a small cottage further down the road, staying close to her three children but enjoying her independence.

It was a home built with love and made for a growing family. Over the years, it had been adapted somewhat; the large stable block to the side of the building had been converted into office space, which was rented out to local companies and provided Celia with a modest income. The solid brick house, covered in climbing roses and clematis, was far too big for her needs now but she refused to give it up. It was their home, their heritage, and besides, she loved to be in a position to have her extended family come visit anytime they wished.

'And she's right', Alice thought, as she moved to the other side of the room to refill her glass, 'this is just perfect for mum.'

She had her back to the door but she sensed Elliot before she even saw him. That same prickly feeling across the back of her neck. Turning, she caught her breath at the sight of him in the doorway, impeccably dressed in a steel grey suit, pale pink shirt, a lighter grey tie with pink stripes running through it, and tied loosely, with his top button undone. He was holding a bouquet of flowers and a card. Despite his confident attire and self-assured stance, Alice could see a vulnerability in his eyes as he held her gaze across the room. Instinctively, she gave him a smile, then lowering her gaze, negotiated her way across the room to his side. He watched her progress, not taking his eyes off her for a second. She nodded a greeting, a little stiltedly.

"Hello, you made it then," she tried not to stutter, knowing how awkward she sounded. It was a struggle to not look at him; she knew he was staring intently at her.

"Of course I did, Alice," he started. She interrupted, pointing at the bouquet.

"That was sweet, buying her flowers. She loves flowers. Shall I?" She held her hand out to relieve him of them.

"Actually, these are for you," he said, putting them into her hand. She looked at him, startled.

"But…why?"

"Because I remember how you love flowers too, and because…" he drew in a steadying breath and leant closer to her,

"And because you have just given me the best news of my life," he whispered. Her heart started to pound erratically, for the second time that day, and she felt giddy. He was so close that she could smell the clean tang of his aftershave, drawing her in, like a magnet. She needed to move. Stepping away and clearing her throat, she gestured with the flowers towards the kitchen, intimating he should follow her.

Reaching for a vase from the cupboard, she moved over to the sink to fill it with water, shooting an anxious glance around the kitchen. They weren't alone. Why did she even think they would be; the kitchen was where all the food was. Alice tilted her head towards a quiet corner by the back door and once there, looked Elliot straight in the eye.

"Please don't tell her who you are. Not yet, not here," she paused, "I'm sorry about earlier, what I said. How I said it. I'm really annoyed with myself," she patted a hand to her chest to emphasise the point.

"Don't be, it's okay," Elliot's voice was sincere, encouraging almost.

"No, no, it's not," she insisted. "It's just … coming home is tough since Dad died and …"

"I was really sorry to hear about your dad," he interjected, and put his hand on her arm, sending tiny shockwaves up it. She nodded appreciatively, trying to steady her breathing.

"And then, it's Ellie's eighteenth birthday, you know, and I was remembering the day she was born, and there you are all of a sudden, in front of me, and … and … I shouldn't have blurted it out like that, I'm sorry." She lowered her head, fighting back the inevitable tears and failing. He was still holding her arm, and with his other hand, carefully wiped away the tears from her cheek. She could feel herself starting to cave.

"Alice, it's okay, I get it. An emotional day, an emotional time for you. But what I don't understand is, why? Why didn't you..." his voice was urgent, his eyes imploring. Ellie appeared at their side just then, interrupting him in mid flow. She beamed at them both, her sharp eyes noticing Elliot's hand drop swiftly from Alice's arm.

"You came!" she greeted him happily. He smiled warmly at her.

"Yes, I did, and thanks for inviting me. This is for you," he announced, offering her the envelope, then sticking his hand in his jacket pocket, he carefully pulled out a small, square box.

"And this is also for you. I hope you like it, I had to phone my niece for some advice on what to get an eighteen-year-old," he explained. Ellie grinned excitedly.

"I wasn't expecting a present!" she laughed, "But thanks!"

Elliot nodded, enjoying her surprise.

"Ah well, I was always taught that you never go to a party empty handed, and you should always bring the host's mother some flowers," he gave Alice a reassuring look and nodded at the flowers she was still clutching. She had got as far as filling the vase but not actually putting the flowers in it. Elliot took the bouquet from her and efficiently arranged them in the vase.

Ellie opened the box and stared in delight, letting out a quiet, "Oh wow!"

She held up a silver chain with a delicate, silver crescent moon, encrusted with a single ruby. Her birthstone. She beamed at Elliot,

"This is beautiful, thank you! Oh my God, it's just so 'me', isn't it, Mum?" she said, then impulsively hugged

Elliot, and clasping it around her neck, happily patted it in to place. Elliot shot a look at Alice: one of pride and with a hint of embarrassment. She quickly looked away.

Ellie tapped Elliot's arm and leant against Alice in a playful manner. Eyeing them both, she asked curiously,

"So how do you two know each other?"

Elliot inclined his head towards Alice but as she drew breath to answer, he spoke for her.

"Well actually, we're both from Brockenhurst and went to the same school but never even knew each other until we met at Uni, did we?", he explained, looking at Alice. She nodded.

"What, you mean York University?" Ellie laughed incredulously. "Wow, what an amazing coincidence!" she chuckled, shaking her head in disbelief.

Alice looked away from Elliot and glanced around the room, searching for a distraction. Not such a coincidence, she thought, remembering how she had struggled to persuade her parents to let her move so far away from home. They had been adamant that there were plenty of excellent universities in the South that offered English Literature as a degree course, and could not understand why she had chosen York. The reason was Elliot Barraclough, quite simply. Not that she would have ever told them that.

Elliot had been her secret crush for as long as she could remember. A year older than her, and the youngest son of their local G.P., he had always seemed so confident yet kind with it. Not a swat, but clever at everything he turned his hand to, be it studies or sport. He had a way of embracing life, and Alice adored him for it. He however, didn't even seem to know she existed, apart from a brief nod if he passed her in the street and even then, she was convinced the acknowledgement was aimed at her pretty friend, Julie, not her. So, when she discovered that Elliot had been accepted at York University to study History, she applied for a place there for the following year, and focused all her efforts into obtaining the necessary grades. She intended to reinvent herself from the shy teenager that she was, and make him notice her. It had worked.

"Penny for them?" he softly prompted, snapping her back to reality. Blushing slightly, she shook her head.

"Nothing really," she dismissed him, turning to Ellie and trying desperately to think of something to say to draw the conversation away from the past. Right on cue, Andrew sauntered into the kitchen and spying them, held up a hand in greeting.

"There you are! I was wondering where you had slunk off to!" he admonished his sister, then turning politely to Elliot, sudden recognition spread across his face in a huge grin. He grabbed Elliot's hand to shake it warmly, in a delighted greeting.

"My god, Elliot! How great to see you! Crikey, it's been years, how are you? Still playing cricket?" he enthused, beaming at his old friend. Elliot laughed, a little taken aback.

"Not much time for it these days, Andrew," he started. Andrew interrupted him and turning to Alice and Ellie, he jabbed a finger at Elliot's arm, stating,

"This young chap was our hero on the team. A devil with the cricket bat. And the bowling, well … out of this world!" he gushed. Alice raised her eyebrows slightly, spying Andrew's empty glass. She seized the opportunity, taking it from his hand.

"Let me get you a re-fill, Andrew, while you two catch up. Elliot?" she enquired, waving the glass at him.

"Yes please: whiskey, if you have any," he nodded. As Alice left the room, she heard Ellie asking them both how they knew each other. It was making her nervous, she knew she was treading on thin ice. It was only a matter of time before Ellie would somehow start putting two and two together, and find out the truth.

By-passing the drinks cabinet, she put Andrew's glass down on a side table, stepped out through the French doors and breathed in the night air. The heady smell of jasmine and warm rose reminded her so much of her childhood, and as she strolled down the garden path, she cast an appreciative eye across the flower-filled borders, picturing her father tending his plants. Bending down, she deftly pulled a stem of lavender from the overgrown bush that hugged the edge of the slate paved path. Squeezing it to release its smell, she breathed deeply, instantly feeling calmer. A bat swooped above her head and disappeared into the shadows of the trees that framed the lawn. As she followed its progress, she felt a sudden surge of sadness and regret.

'How frail and fleeting life is,' she thought, 'and what a complete mess I've made of it.'

"I miss you, Dad", she whispered, holding the lavender close to her nose and inhaling it once again.

Rubbing the back of her neck, she turned to find Elliot watching her from the patio. He walked down the path towards her.

"I came in search of whiskey," he prompted, then indicating back to the house, said,

"She's a fantastic girl, Alice. You have done an incredible job. I can't begin to tell you how ... how overwhelming this is," he spoke earnestly. "And she's so bright! She told me all about her A-levels. The English Literature was no surprise or, to be honest, the History, but Psychology as well," he enthused, "Wow!" He kicked a stray stone from the path, falling silent. Alice stood still, not sure what to say. She didn't trust herself to speak right now but felt she needed to break the silence. Elliot looked up,

"I was quite taken aback when she told me she's going to study History at Uni. Does she know that's what I did?" he wondered. Alice shook her head.

"No, no she doesn't," she confirmed. "She doesn't know anything about you, Elliot - well, that is, she didn't until today," her voice started to break.

Elliot breathed out slowly, calculating his next words.

"I'd like to get to know her. Please," he urged as Alice was about to protest.

"I'm only here for a couple of days. I don't want to dig up the past but you must see, I can't just ignore this. I can't." He watched her expectantly, waiting for her response. She shifted slightly, then turning round, she walked further up the path towards the old wooden swing seat, tucked under the shade of a silver birch. It was dusk now but solar lights, dotted along the path, lit the way. Elliot followed and sat next to her, pushing with his foot to slowly rock the seat. Alice was acutely aware of his proximity and tried desperately to stop her stomach from churning like a spin cycle, and to resist the urge to lean against him. She was suddenly overwhelmed with tiredness and the need to rest her head. There was a lump in her throat and she took a moment to swallow hard before speaking.

"I'm sorry, but we're going away tomorrow," she explained. "Ellie's big adventure, as I call it. She missed the school trip to the war graves, in Ypres, last year, due to chickenpox." She laughed at Elliot's surprised face.

"Yes, I know! It by-passed her at primary school but caught up with her eventually," she laughed lightly. "She'd really been looking forward to the trip, partly because she's fascinated with anything to do with the world wars, and partly because we have family who died in both. So, I'm taking her tomorrow, with Mum and Auntie Roz," she informed him.

They sat in silence for a while, swinging slowly back and forth, absently gazing at the emerging stars. Elliot took her hand and squeezed it, sending not just little shocks this time but a massive bolt of electricity, up her arm and across her chest.

"She is so like you, it's uncanny," he said quietly.

"More confident than I ever was though," she noted. Elliot laughed softly.

"Oh, I don't know, you had your moments." His tone was deep and intimate. Alice blushed profusely, turning away so that he couldn't see just how much he was affecting her. He tightened his hold of her hand, nodding slowly as he mulled over the day's events. Taking her chin with his other hand, he gently turned her face to his and looked deep into her eyes, holding her gaze for what seemed like an eternity. She felt helplessly trapped but at the same time, was not wanting to move. The depth of emotion in his eyes was mesmerising, and feelings she had long kept buried, were starting to stir. He smiled, sensing her thoughts.

"Thank you," he whispered. Then slowly letting go of her face and hand simultaneously, he stood up, causing her to rock abruptly on the seat.

"Good night, Alice," he nodded, and disappeared back down the path towards the house, without a backwards glance. Alice steadied the seat and sank back in it, dumbfounded.

"What the hell was that all about?" she asked herself out loud. She stared up at the stars, searching for an answer. There was none.

Chapter Two

The next day dawned fair, with the promise of warmer weather to follow. A quick click onto her weather app on her phone, confirmed this. Checking over her suitcase, stored in the corner of her room, Alice was grateful that she'd had the foresight to pack the previous morning; before the events of, what turned out to be, a tumultuous day. Brushing her teeth vigorously, she determined to put yesterday on hold and focus on the forthcoming road trip. She could deal with everything else at a later date. It was boxed away for now.

Roz had been adamant that Alice receive counselling after she had given birth to Ellie.

"Just to make sure you are coping ok," she had insisted. It turned out to be hugely beneficial, Alice had to admit. She had learnt how to pigeonhole emotions and when she was feeling overwhelmed, to 'box it away' and shelve it in the back of her mind until she was ready to deal with it.

Staring at her reflection as she wiped away toothpaste from her mouth, she noted the dark rings around her eyes. Ellie bounded in to the bathroom, singing, and noisily kissed her mother's cheek in morning greeting. She grinned at Alice through the mirror, as she gathered up a bag of cotton pads and make-up wipes from the side.

"Wondering if he'll come along and sweep you off your feet?" she joked, invading her thoughts, then seeing Alice's startled reaction, gasped in amazement.

"Oh my God, did I actually just read your mind, Mum?" Alice bristled, caught unawares.

"Yes well, stop reading! You've got it all wrong anyway," she frowned defensively.

"Okay," Ellie nodded airily.

"Don't 'okay' me like that, young lady," she chided lightly.

"Okay," Ellie grinned and skipped out of the room with a little laugh.

Downstairs, Celia and Roz were busy lining up their bags by the front door, Andrew leaning wearily against the wall, nursing a cup of coffee. As she walked back and forth, Celia was issuing him with a list of instructions. He raised his eyes in mock resignation as Alice came down the stairs.

"I know, Mum, it's all in hand," he assured her. "You're only gone for a few days. We'll clean up here after last night's debauchery," he winked at Alice as Celia tutted loudly.

"Honestly, Andrew! I just want you to make sure you ..."

"Feed the cats and water the plants, yes I know!" he finished her sentence and pushing himself away from the wall, sauntered into the kitchen in search of Paracetamol.

"Oh, Alice", Celia beckoned her over conspiratorially, "there's a letter for you."

She nodded to the console table across the hall. Alice picked it up, instantly recognising Elliot's handwriting. It had been hand delivered, presumably in the early hours, she thought. Going back upstairs, avoiding her mother's inquisitiveness, she sat on the edge of her bed and stared at the envelope.

"So much for boxing it away," she muttered and carefully ripped the envelope open with her finger.

'Morning A.,
I still can't believe what happened yesterday.
Seeing you again and meeting our daughter has left me speechless. Forgive me.
Have a safe trip and please let me know when you get back.
I <u>have</u> to see you again.
Text me, please.
E.'

Alice tapped her teeth with her thumb nail as she stared at the mobile number at the bottom of the page. She re-read the letter. What did he mean by 'forgive me'? Forgive him for what? For being speechless? For creating a child with her? The fleeting anger subsided; she knew that wasn't what he had meant at all. Just by the way he had reacted to Ellie, she knew to accuse him of regretting her existence, was wrong.

She looked at the missive again, at the way he had used their initials instead of their names. They had always left little notes for each other, dotted around the flat or occasionally, she would find one slipped in between the pages of a book she was reading.

'Just to say, I Love You xxx E'.
They never signed their full name.

"Who needs a name when we know who we are," Elliot would say, "There's only one 'A' for me."

Drawing in a decisive breath, Alice reached for her phone and composed a text to Elliot's number. Reflecting over his parting words the night before, she typed simply,

'Thank you. A'

Her finger hovered over the 'send' icon, pausing as she debated. Quickly changing her mind, she added the remaining letters of her name, Alice.

"Too soon," she told herself, clicking 'send' and folding the letter back into the envelope, she buried it deep within her handbag and went back downstairs.

The trip to Ypres and Arnhem had been planned meticulously by Alice. She took pride in her organisational skills and had enjoyed researching the two main cemeteries they wanted to visit: Tyne Cot, in Belgium, and Arnhem Oosterbeek, in the Netherlands. Upon her initial investigations, she had quickly realised the extent of the battlefields, memorials and cemeteries, so picked out a route that could also incorporate a trip to the Normandy beaches, the Bayeux cemetery in France, the Airborne Museum 'Hartenstein' in Oosterbeek, and on to visit the Anne Frank Museum, in Amsterdam. They would do a round-trip, starting at Calais via the Euro Tunnel, across to Ypres, over to Arnhem and Amsterdam. Then back to France and on to Normandy, coming home via the Cherbourg ferry.

Alice had booked self-catering accommodation in Zonnebeke, on the outskirts of Ypres, also in Arnhem, and Normandy: printed off guides, and found information on the three graves they were looking for. She had planned for an overnight stay in Zonnebeke, and Normandy, but had booked two nights in Arnhem, allowing them a day for the cemetery and military museum, and a day in Amsterdam which was an hour's drive away.

Celia and Roz's grandfather had lost his brother at Passchendaele, in 1917, and Alice's grandfather had been killed at Arnhem, in September 1944 - three months after his younger brother lost his life during the Normandy landings. Alice's father, Reggie, was born in the October so had never known his father, who in turn, perished without knowing the sex of his expected child. Reggie had been named Reginald Albert Greene, in honour of the two brothers. Alice knew this was going to be an emotional trip; although essentially planned for Ellie, it was a pilgrimage that her father had always intended to make but never did. Just before his death, he asked Celia to make the trip on his behalf, and lay a wreath for the father he never met.

They left Brockenhurst just before six and made excellent time, arriving on the outskirts of Ypres by early afternoon. Stopping briefly to purchase a wreath of poppies, and supplies for their overnight stay, they followed the signs from Zonnebeke to Tyne Cot cemetery. They travelled along narrow, country lanes, edged with modern houses, and surrounded by acres of green and yellow fields that stretched out beyond the horizon; the skyline only punctuated by silhouettes of church spires in neighbouring towns. It was hard to imagine that these peaceful fields were once the scene of such devastating carnage during the battle of Passchendaele, and a living hell for those that endured it. Ellie peered out from the passenger seat window, avidly drinking in the scenery, remembering war footage she had studied at school, and trying to visualise its place in the passing landscape.

They pulled up into an understated, busy car park, and she scrunched her nose up, a little dismayed.

"It's not what I expected," she said to the others, "I thought it would be more impressive, more of a feature." She looked across at an uninspiring, wooden billboard by the carpark entrance, advertising the Passchendaele memorial museum, three kilometres back the way they came, in Zonnebeke. There was little else to capture the imagination in the bleak car park. Alice locked the car and took Ellie's arm, trying not to laugh at her deflated expression.

"It's a car park, Ellie! What *did* you expect?"

A coach had arrived minutes before they had, and the large, organised group headed in the direction of the visitor's centre. Alice ushered her small party to follow them. As they approached the box-shaped building, a voice could be heard over a speaker system, slowly reading out the names of those fallen, and commemorated, within the cemetery. Roz looked ahead of her, gauging the number of people filing in through the small door. She turned to Alice.

"Maybe we should come back later when the crowd has died down. We could go straight to the cemetery first, couldn't we?" She hated queueing for anything, and the monotonous voice was filling her with a sense of doom, and that was even before they had reached the cemetery.

They turned and followed a small crowd from the car park, down a path running alongside a long, stone wall that masked the cemetery from the outside world. It carried on for some distance, a good indication of the size of the plot. A gentle breeze could be heard rustling through the crops in the adjacent fields; the whispered sounds carrying in the air.

Eventually reaching the entrance and going through the gateway into the cemetery, Ellie stopped short and held her breath, awestruck at the sight that greeted them. Row upon row, upon row, of white, Portland stone, rectangular gravestones, stood glinting in the sunlight, stretching as far as the eye could see. They were spaced with a military precision, like soldiers standing to attention. Honouring the dead. The thousands and thousands of slaughtered, young men.

"It's endless," Celia whispered, clutching a hand to her chest, moved by the stark beauty of it as she struggled to take it all in.

It was eerily quiet, even the few trees among the graves seemed devoid of birds. They walked along the narrow avenues of the dead, respectfully looking at each dedication chiselled into the stone, occasionally reading out to each other, in hushed tones.

"My first pride, my first joy, My darling soldier boy. Mother."

"One of the best that God could lend, A loving son, A faithful friend."

"A soldier of the Great War, known unto God."

"My only son."

Alice blinked, hit by the simplicity of the three words that held a world of grief.

"Oh, Mum, look at this one: Far from the home of his childhood, sleeping his last long sleep."

Ellie stood for a while, contemplating the words.

"They were all so far away from home, weren't they. Away from family, from routine, home comforts. I can't imagine what it was like; ending up in these fields, blindly fighting a war they barely understood." She reached for Alice's hand, needing to feel the comfort of her mother's touch. She found it hard to fathom the enormity of it. Reading about it, watching films about it, didn't compare to actually confronting it. Having the scale of loss confirmed, in a patch of field, in the heart of foreign countryside.

"And this is just one cemetery," she murmured.

It soon became apparent that to look at every stone throughout the whole cemetery would take more than one day. Celia and Roz walked on slowly, in search of their great uncle, studying the print-out of directions to his grave, leaving Alice and Ellie to take their time. Ellie crouched by a grave, reading the inscription. With tear-filled eyes, she looked up at Alice.

"He was my age, Mum. Eighteen. Just eighteen. How did they let this happen?" she questioned, her voice thick with despair, imagining her own friends being sent off to war. She stroked the grass surrounding the gravestone, gently touching the petals of the rose in full bloom. She felt an urge to hug the stone, to hug the life that had been snatched away and now lay beneath the ground in cold eternity. Alice offered a hand to help Ellie back to her feet.

"I can't move," she shook her head. "I feel like the ground is literally dragging me down with the weight of grief that it holds." She looked to the side of her, and behind her.

"Look at it, Mum, there are thousands of them. And each one symbolises a life, a person. Not just a name or a regiment, but somebody's son, somebody's husband, somebody's dad. And they never got back home." She pulled the hem of her top up to wipe tears from her face, in the absence of a sleeve. Alice dug around in her bag and passed over a pack of tissues. Grabbing Ellie's arm, she helped her to her feet, and they stood holding each other; no words were needed. Ellie chewed on the corner of her tissue, sniffing repeatedly, feeling wracked with helplessness as her eyes took in the scale of the consequence of war.

They joined Celia and Roz, and after laying their wreath, stood sombrely in contemplation of their fallen uncle.

"Daddy always wanted to come here, didn't he?" Roz commented softly. Celia nodded.

"Yes, so did Reggie. But they were ruled by their jobs, weren't they? Every time I wanted to get something done, Reggie would say, wait until half term, dear." She shook her head, remembering. "And of course, half terms came and went, and before you know it, it's too late," her voice broke slightly. Alice rubbed her mother's shoulder comfortingly.

"He was such a handsome chap, Daddy's uncle Cyril," Roz commented, "Remember that lovely army photo Daddy had of him?" she reminded her sister.

"I remember that too!" Alice agreed, "And it has always struck me how they all looked older than they actually were. I remember thinking to myself, 'I know your face so well, but I know nothing about you'," she said.

"Reggie spent his whole life wondering what his dad would have been like. That must be awful!" Celia continued. Ellie turned away.

"It is," she muttered quietly.

Her hushed words rang out loud, rebounding off the white stones, echoing in the air. Roz shot a look at Alice's stricken face. The moment passed quickly as Ellie pulled out her phone and took some photos of the grave, but Alice was acutely aware of what had just happened; the significance of Ellie's weighted comment, concerned her. She knew what was brewing.

It was a sober meal they shared later that evening; a combination of travel fatigue and an emotionally draining afternoon, led conversation to run dry as they sat deep in their own thoughts.

"Right", Ellie announced putting four glasses and the bottle of Disaronno that she had persuaded Alice to buy earlier, on the low coffee table in front of them.

"Truth or Dare time, I think!"

Alice, Celia, and Roz stared blankly at her.

"Whatever do you mean, dear?" Celia asked. Alice shook her head at Ellie.

"Come on, that's a game for kids, Ellie, not us," she chided, "What's going on?"

Ellie sighed and sat down on the sofa next to her, turning to face her.

"I don't know, I just feel … today, it made me think about things. There's so much we don't actually know about our family, about each other even. And all those lost lives, all that wasted youth, wasted love. Because of war.

Because somebody wanted to rule the world, or whatever. And thousands died as a result." She looked round earnestly at each of them.

"And I was thinking: how many secrets died with them, how many loves were lost, how many hearts were broken?" she sniffed, as sad tears clouded her eyes. Alice drew her in for a hug, and soothingly stroked her hair.

"I know, it's tragic. I know, Ellie," she acknowledged softly. Ellie sighed, then asked lightly,

"What made you call me Ellie?"

"It was the first name that came to me the moment I held you in my arms," she smiled maternally, realising too late how her honest answer could be construed. Ellie nodded thoughtfully, then looked away, staring out of the window. Alice turned helplessly to her mother and aunt, sitting together on the opposite sofa. Celia widened her eyes and nodded slightly but Roz looked uncomfortable and following Ellie's example, stared silently out of the window.

Alice leant forward and grabbing the bottle, opened it and poured the amber liquid into the glasses. Pushing two towards Celia and Roz, she handed one to Ellie, and raising her own glass, said,

"To Ellie! Welcome to adulthood and to your first, legal, alcoholic drink," she winked with a grin. Ellie smiled but still looked troubled. Celia sniffed her glass cautiously, eyeing the unfamiliar liquid, then taking a sip, made an appreciative noise and raised her glass to Ellie, smiling.

Alice took a gulp, placed her glass back on the table and shifted slightly away from Ellie, looking at her earnestly. She reached over and taking her hand, studied it intently for a moment.

"Ellie, you know I have always wanted to be enough for you," she started.

"You are, Mum, you know that. But I just feel …" Ellie gushed nervously, "I just feel that to understand *me* I need to understand *you*. And I need to know where I come from; I hate the thought that I was a fling or whatever, you know, a drunken fumble!"

Alice stared at her in horror.

"You weren't. Absolutely not, Ellie. How could you even think that?" she implored, "I told you before, I was in love but as it turned out, he wasn't," she explained, echoing words she had already said in the past. "He wasn't the person I thought he was," she concluded.

Ellie nodded, still sniffing and brushed a hand across her cheek.

"I know. But I *need* to know who he was," she looked at Alice, her eyes questioning yet defiant.

Alice gulped. 'This is it,' she thought: the moment she had dreaded. Her palms felt clammy and she started to tremble.

"Mum, I need to know. I'm eighteen now, I'm an adult. Tell me," Ellie insisted.

Alice took a deep breath, closing her eyes for a moment, summoning up the courage to say the words. Opening them again, she gave a brief smile of defeat. Or was it relief she was feeling? Relief that the secret was finally being unlocked.

"It's Elliot. Your father is Elliot Barraclough."

Ellie nodded frantically, acknowledging her mother's confession, tears cascading down her face. She half laughed.

"I knew it! I knew, the moment I met him!" she gabbled, "There was this ... this kind of recognition, a connection. I just felt like I knew him," she continued, nodding and laughing.

"He knows, doesn't he?" she asked. Alice nodded,

"Yes, I told him literally ten minutes before you met him on the doorstep," she admitted. Ellie shook her head, her mind racing.

"No wonder he looked so stunned and awkward," she said, "I honestly thought he was going to cry at one point!" she laughed. Then throwing herself at Alice and hugging her tightly, she mumbled,

"Thank you Mum; you have no idea how happy this has made me."

They all sat in silence for a while, each one sniffing alternately, and Celia passing round tissues. Ellie refilled their glasses and snuggled into Alice.

"So, tell me all about it," she demanded happily.

Upon reflection, hours later, Alice had found it incredibly cathartic relaying her story. In the knowledge that she no longer needed to be cagey, she could revisit a part of her life that she had carefully kept under wraps for so many years. She told them of her childhood fascination with Elliot, which over time, grew into an overwhelming need to be with him. Hence her choice of University.

"I knew it," Celia butted in, nodding, "I said to your father, there's a boy behind all this, didn't I Roz?" she looked to her for agreement. Roz nodded slowly.

"And your father said, 'well then, my dear, we need to let her go. Let her find her path'," Celia smiled wistfully. "He could be so infuriating at times!" she added, then gestured for Alice to continue with her story.

Incredibly, Alice and Elliot had got together within hours of her arriving in York, on her first day of university life. Once she had waved her parents off late that afternoon, after they had deposited her bags and boxes into her tiny room within the Uni Halls, she and her new fellow flat mates trailed behind their Student Rep on a tour of the campus. This was followed by a 'welcome' drink at one of the many pubs in the centre of York. Having spent her whole life in sleepy Brockenhurst, surrounded by trees and ponies, the city of York seemed like another world to her caged soul, and she embraced it with such a passion. The students and their Rep made their way through the Medieval city, admiring the famous Shambles with its quaint, crooked buildings, tightly packed together, and in stark contrast, the magnificent, solidly built, York Minster. One of Europe's largest cathedrals, it stood proudly at the heart of York where it could be seen for miles, particularly when floodlit after dark.

A cacophony of live music could be heard from nearby pubs, one of which was their destination, in Stonegate, just yards from the Minster. As Alice gingerly stepped into the dimly lit 17th century pub, entering an unfamiliar realm, her stomach churned with excitement. Looking up, the first person she locked eyes with, was Elliot. His surprise mirrored her own, and he slid from his seat, abandoning his friends, and coming over to greet her.

"Excuse me, aren't you Andrew Greene's sister, Alice?" he had asked awkwardly. She nodded, grinning. He grinned back, and bought her a drink. And another.

And that was the start of their beautiful relationship. Alice skipped telling her mother, aunt, and daughter, the part where, a few hours later, they had emerged from the pub, stumbling along the cobbled streets, arms wrapped around each other in drunken joy. Or how she had fallen against him, murmuring, 'You smell like freedom', before kissing him passionately, unleashing years of pent-up longing. Or how they had hurried back to his place, and spent a night of unabated ecstasy, losing themselves to each other completely, both mentally and physically. Or how they had spent every waking moment, and every sleeping moment, in each other's arms from then on in.

Alice refilled her glass and took a thoughtful sip, smiling apprehensively at her daughter before continuing her account, mindful that the next instalment would not be easy for Ellie to hear. Each sentence was laced with the betrayal and hurt that she had felt, so, so deeply. At times, Alice had felt like giving up, ending it all, if it weren't for the tiny being growing deep within her. That tiny speck of life, which, in the eyes of the church, had been borne from illicit love, had indeed been her salvation.

Her perfect bubble of happiness burst half way through her second year of studies. She and Elliot had both been home to Brockenhurst for the Christmas holidays, and as the previous Christmas, had spent time with their individual families rather than together. Alice had wanted to keep their life in York separate from their lives in Brockenhurst. She was the vicar's granddaughter; her father was the lay reader alongside his day-job as a college lecturer, and she felt very uneasy about revealing the extent of her relationship with Elliot to them. So instead, she didn't tell them about him at all. Not that she thought it was wrong in any way but it felt more precious, more heightened, by keeping their relationship private.

When she had moved out of Halls at the end of her first year, Elliot had wanted her to move in with him but she opted to flat-share with one of her course mates, Mary O'Shea. As it was, they divided their time between the two flats anyway, completely inseparable. Week-days were spent at Alice's and weekends at Elliot's. He had a bedsit within a shared house, affording more privacy, but it was further away from their lecture rooms. The routine suited them and they remained profoundly happy, the initial intensity of their relationship never waning, only growing deeper. They were meant to be.

It was coming to the end of January, and Elliot was working on his dissertation. He had, on occasion, chosen to study alone in his bedsit but would always end the day with Alice, professing he couldn't sleep without her. She came home from afternoon lectures that fateful day, and lightly dropped a bag of shopping for their evening meal on the kitchen table before turning to fill the kettle at the sink. In so doing, she caught sight of a note, pinned to the fridge with a faded Take That magnet. It was Mary's handwriting:

'Alice, I don't know how else to tell you this – Elliot and I are having an affair.

It's been going on for a while now.

As soon as he finishes Uni, we will be leaving York together.

You can't even see what has been going on under your own nose!

I suggest you leave us now, before it gets too ugly.'

Alice was knocked sideways, completely stunned. Unable to believe it but dreading its truth, she sat at the kitchen table for the next three hours, waiting for Elliot to arrive. To explain it to her. But he didn't turn up, and neither did Mary. It was dark outside and it had started to snow again. Forcing herself to move, she walked the short distance to Elliot's house, her frozen hands pushed deep into her coat pocket. The usual, comforting glow from the Minster, seemed to cast eerie shadows across her path as she hurried past it, adding to her sense of foreboding.

She rang his private doorbell four or five times but he didn't answer. Peering through the letterbox, it was clear nobody was home; the hallway was in complete darkness. It wasn't uncommon for the house to be empty on a Friday night; Elliot's housemates were usually all at the pub. She headed there and surreptitiously peered in through the door and sure enough, there they were. However, Elliot was nowhere to be seen. At a loss, she carefully made her way back to her own flat through the settling snow and once again, sat at the kitchen table, numb with shock.

She woke the next morning with a start, her head resting heavily on the hard, pine surface. She was still wearing her coat. Getting up to check Mary's room, she could see, instantly, that she hadn't returned home in the night. Grabbing her bag, Alice once again retraced her steps to Elliot's house, but to no avail. She rang one of the other doorbells, waking his housemate who, bleary-eyed and worse for wear, confirmed that Elliot was not there. In fact, he hadn't been home all night and nobody knew where he was; they had assumed he was with her.

The full horror of the situation was sinking in and she felt desperately sick. Returning to her flat, she packed a small suitcase and headed for the train station. Four hours later, she arrived at her auntie Roz's house in Stratford-upon-Avon, exhausted, empty, confused and in desperate need of a hug.

Roz proved to be fantastic, mentally and physically scooping Alice up and patching her back together, without questioning or judging her. When Alice discovered two weeks later, that she was in fact three months pregnant, it was Roz who organised everything. She informed the university that Alice would have to leave due to personal reasons, she arranged pre-natal care locally, and she contacted Celia.

Celia was by Alice's side within hours and between them, the sisters agreed that Alice should stay in Stratford with Roz. She had plenty of room in her comfortable cottage, which was attached to her art studio. Going back home to Brockenhurst was not an option, they concluded, for a number of reasons. Elliot, it was decided, had made choices that effectively eliminated him from Alice's life and consequently, his baby's. Celia returned home and broke the news to her husband but it went no further. The rest of the family would find out in due course about the baby, but the baby's father was never to be named.

Roz was concerned about Alice's mental wellbeing; she had become a shell of her former self, and spent her time sitting at home, crying. Then the crying stopped and was replaced by deafening silence, until one day, Alice shouted from her bedroom for Roz to come quickly. She was clutching her stomach, tears streaming down her face. Roz, in a rare moment of panic, ran to fetch the phone, fears of a miscarriage racing through her mind. Alice grabbed her arm to stop her and forced Roz's hand onto her swollen stomach. She felt a definite nudge against the flat of her hand. She stared at Alice, who was smiling through her tears.

"Life!" Alice whispered, "This is my new life."

That first kick proved to be her turning point: she pulled herself together and got herself back on track, well ahead of her baby's arrival. Ellie was delivered on time, in late July, and was quite possibly the most loved baby on the planet. She flourished and thrived amidst her doting family, leaving Alice to continue with her studies. She finished her degree, at a slower pace, through the Open University, tending to Ellie during the day and studying in the evenings, in-between feeds. Once Ellie started primary school, Alice also returned to school, to do teacher training, then further to complete an M.A. in English Literature. This in turn, led to her much longed-for job as lecturer of English Literature, at Birmingham University.

Alice blew her nose and looked expectantly at her captive audience.

"Blimey," she laughed, "not a dry eye in the house!" She slid the tissues across the table to her mother and turned to Ellie expectantly, trying to gauge her reaction. Ellie widened her eyes and grimaced.

"Well, when I said tell me about it, I didn't expect *that*! You really are amazing, Mum, and I'm sorry if I don't tell you enough," she leant over and kissed her cheek and hugged her.

"So, you both always knew who my father was?" Ellie asked Celia and Roz. They nodded, sheepishly.

"Yes, dear, we did," Celia admitted, "although I didn't know the bit about your mother following him to York. I had thought they met there by chance. It's quite sweet really, isn't it, Roz?" Celia enthused, then catching Roz's pained expression, stood up and disappeared to the bathroom, muttering that the drink had gone right through her.

Alice eyed her aunt, remembering her mother's revelation on Ellie's birthday but felt too spent to probe further. Standing up and stretching, she asked,

"Tea, anyone?"

Chapter Three

Ellie was up first the next morning. Alice awoke to find her dancing round the small kitchen, headphones on and singing along to one of her favourite tracks. Eggs were bubbling in the pan, and she had laid the table for breakfast. She greeted Alice with a joyful hug and ushered her to the table, saying,

"I thought we could do with a decent breakfast; it's going to be a long day."

She wasn't wrong. They packed up swiftly and hit the road, ahead of the morning traffic. It was a straightforward route to Arnhem, and the car purred along as Ellie chatted happily about her expectations of University, and what the rest of her summer holiday would entail. Roz and Celia dozed in the back seat and as Alice glanced at their reflection in the rear-view mirror, she selfishly wished that Ellie would follow suit. She was so desperate to have a chance to think over the events of the previous night and what the consequences would be. She had opened the door to a part of her life that she had, until now, refused to revisit, and had surprised herself by wanting to linger over those memories - the happy ones. It unsettled her, and she needed some time alone, to understand why. But there was no let-up in Ellie's euphoria.

The cemetery at Arnhem Oosterbeek was not as overwhelming as Tyne Cot; partly because they were now prepared for the effect it would have, and partly because of its smaller size. However, there were similarities: the same regimental lines of the same, brilliant white, Portland stone, and the same, towering, Cross of Sacrifice - again of Portland stone, with a bronze inlay. The large, rectangular Stone of Remembrance, bearing the same, poignant epitaph: 'Their name liveth for evermore'. The same aura of quiet reverence.

Contained within a rectangular patch, and completely hemmed in by lofty, compactly planted trees, the 1,700 graves seemed less stark compared to the 12,000 graves of the day before. When Ellie remarked on this, her mother pointed out that this relatively small loss was chiefly as a result of just one battle, lasting nine days, whereas the casualties at Tyne Cot, had been from three battles on an epic scale. It suddenly made the cemetery very intimate; these fallen soldiers were more likely to have been known to each other, their brief military lives more intimately entwined and somehow, their loss more personal. Or maybe Alice was just feeling that, because for her, visiting her grandfather's grave was definitely more personal.

Reginald's grave was easy to find, and they once again, stood in respectful silence, each sending up a prayer of remembrance. The wind shook through the trees, as if whispering a thousand names with one, trembling breath. Prompted into action, blackbirds called to one another, their tuneful communication piercing the air, encouraging the higher, sweet notes of neighbouring birds to join in. The sounds reminded Alice of home, and she imagined her grandfather waking up to those same sounds in his youth.

Ellie read out the inscription, admiring the regimental badge of the Airborne Infantry, meticulously chiselled into the stone.

"R.A. Greene
Parachute Regiment
Army Air Corps
19th September 1944 Age 28
A devoted family man
My true love
We shall miss you till the end of time".

Celia reached for her tissue, tutting softly at the words.

"Of course, I knew that was the inscription but to hear you read it, here, Ellie, makes it so very real," she said.

"How did you know it, Grandma?" Ellie wondered, looking at the neighbouring headstones, noting their similar dates of death.

"Well dear, Reggie's mother composed it. And she then embroidered it onto a little cushion, which she stuffed full of lavender, and kept it on her bedside table next to a framed photo of him. And she had their wedding photo hanging above her bed. After she died, I kept them safely in the glass cabinet, in Reggie's study."

"Oh, yes, of course!" Ellie exclaimed, recognition dawning. "I've looked at that lavender cushion a hundred times but never realised its significance. I wish I could remember her," she added wistfully.

"Well, you wouldn't, dear, she died when you were only three," Celia replied, remembering how blessed, Edith - Reggie's mother - had felt, being surrounded by her young, great grandchildren.

"She made the trip out here, a year after the war, you know," she told them. "There was a big ceremony to commemorate the second anniversary of the battle of Arnhem, and she came, with Reginald's parents. She had thought that visiting his grave would put her mind at rest, enable her to move on with life, but all it did was make her realise what a pointless death his was. So many died that day, that week, and for what? She said it made her feel angry and resentful. Of course, this was long before any of these beautiful headstones were put up; it was a muddy field, full of shallow, mounded graves, marked by makeshift, wooden crosses." Celia looked out across the cemetery, at the neat planting, and lush, green grass.

"She told me that the hardest thing was, leaving again. Leaving him behind in Arnhem, not able to bring him back home to where he belonged. She could never get over that. It felt so wrong to walk away from him. She said *that* was more painful than getting the telegram to say he had been killed in action. She wished she hadn't gone to his grave, and she never went back." Her voice dropped, almost inaudible.

"I think that's why Reggie never made the trip, I think he was scared of how it would make him feel, having seen how it affected his mother." She gestured to the vast expanse of white.

"All those poor wives, and mothers: how did they cope?" Her throat was thick with tears. She took a moment to blow her nose before unwrapping a large, collage frame with four photographs, which she had been carrying in a canvas bag. She held it up, satisfied with the result, and carefully placed it against the stone. An arching branch from the adjacent rose bush, rested its red blooms across the top of the frame. A black and white wedding

photo of Reginald and Edith, his brothers, and both sets of
parents: a studio portrait of a young Reggie and his sisters,
May and Lucy: a colour photo of Reggie, holding Ellie and
Rachel as toddlers, balanced on his lap. And finally, a
whole group family photo, taken just after Reggie became
ill with cancer. It was their last photo all together.

Completely unprepared, Alice stumbled backwards, as
if winded, as if somebody had forcefully punched her in
the chest. She let out a sound like a wounded animal and
fell to her knees, sobbing uncontrollably. Ellie crouched
next to her, consoling her, the roles reversed from the day
before. Alice gulped for air, shocked by her own reaction.
Her head was so crowded, and her chest heavy with a
potent mix of emotions that screamed to be released. The
image of her father as a young boy and then, years later,
proud grandfather, hit a nerve so hard. The realisation of
how quickly time had passed - time that could never be
regained - shook her. And the knowledge of how much she
had deprived both Ellie and Elliot of, filled her with a panic
that she couldn't shake off.

The atmosphere was definitely even more sombre that
evening, after the heightened emotions of another heart
wrenching day. They sat in unified silence after their meal,
and grabbing the half empty bottle, Alice poured them
each a drink and settled on the sofa. Despite the change in
venue, they had automatically sat in the same way: Alice
and Ellie on one sofa, and the two sisters on the other,
opposite them. There was a television in the corner of the
room, but after a quick flick through the channels, Ellie
determined that Dutch TV didn't amount to much. Sinking

back into the cushions, Celia sighed deeply and stretched her legs out.

"I'm glad we've done this. I could feel Reggie with us today, I really felt close to him," she nodded, welling up. Roz gave her hand an affectionate squeeze.

"It struck me though, that I never really appreciated how he felt, growing up without a father. It didn't really occur to me what it must have actually been like for him," she continued, "I mean, I listened to him and everything, and I sympathised but I didn't *actually* think about the full weight of it. To never see your parent, not once. To know you never would. I think that's why Daddy had so much time for him," she turned to Roz, "he must have sensed that Reggie was a little lost without a father." She wiped her nose and then horrified, saw how Roz's face crumpled and she started to weep, unable to stop. Alice and Ellie stood up in shock and rushed to her side, passing tissues and rubbing her arm. Alice looked at Celia.

"What's happened?" she mouthed. Celia shrugged her shoulders, concern etched across her face.

As Roz's sobs subsided, Celia passed her a glass and encouraged her to take a drink.

"I'm sorry Roz, I really am," she whispered. Roz shook her head, blowing her nose.

"It's ok, Cee-Cee, it's just been a bit much today," she muttered, using the affectionate childhood nickname for her sister. Lifting her head up and breathing in deeply, she smiled apologetically at Ellie and Alice, then raising her glass, said,

"Cheers girls. Life, eh!"

Alice knew she should leave it at that but as she watched the aunt she had grown to know inside out, she felt that Roz was needing to open up. She could sense she was drowning. Something huge was weighing her down. She perched on the edge of the coffee table, and took hold of Roz's hand.

"Roz," she said quietly, "What did Mum mean the other day, when she said I wasn't the only one to have slept with a Barraclough?"

Ellie's head snapped round, eyes wide and questioning but didn't say anything, although it was evident her favourite expletive was playing on her lips.

Roz breathed in and looked steadily at Alice, about to speak but then turned to Celia, imploring her to step in. Nodding, Celia placed her glass in front of her, twisting it round on the coaster for a moment, formulating words in her head.

"Roz had an affair, a long time ago, with Elliot's uncle, David Barraclough. It was before you or Andrew were born. Anyway," she paused, choosing her words carefully, "David was older, by ten years. And married." She paused again, seeing the shock on Alice and Ellie's faces, and appreciating the effort it took for them not to exclaim out loud. Neither dared look at Roz, they focused completely on what Celia had to say.

"His father was ... oh, he was a tyrant. He was some big shot surgeon at Southampton hospital, and insisted, or rather bullied, his two sons into going to Med school. Anyway, their affair had been going on for nearly four years when he found out about them, and threatened to tell our father about it. He said he would ruin Roz, and shame her out of the village. Horrid man!" she scowled at the memory. Pausing to take a sip of her drink, she was about to continue when Roz butted in, her voice quiet and heavy with emotion.

"It was love at first sight for both of us, and not something either of us had expected. We weren't looking for love but as soon as we met, we knew," she said, her smile trembling at the memory. Nobody spoke, they sat attentively, waiting for her to carry on with her story.

"I had just finished my A-levels and couldn't decide whether I wanted to go to Art School in London, or go travelling, across France and Italy. I'd studied Art, French, and English Literature and wasn't sure which direction to go in next. So, I took a job at an Art Gallery in Southampton, which fed my creativity and lined my pocket. I decided to save up until I could decide, and continued painting in my spare time. And then one day, David came into the Gallery, and changed my life. Suddenly, nothing else mattered. I stayed at the Art Gallery and spent every free moment I could, with him." She swallowed hard, trying not to cry again. She looked at the three of them and shrugged.

"I knew it was wrong but it felt so right. His was a loveless marriage. His wife spent most of her time, and his money, in London, with her jet setting friends. He suspected she wasn't very faithful to him anyway - not that that's an excuse - but I could see how desperately unhappy he was. But even though it was the Sixties, divorce was still a taboo subject in certain circles. He was trapped," she nodded, "trapped by convention and trapped by his father." She put a hand to her mouth as tears spilled down her face once more. Alice reached over to stroke her arm, comforting her.

"And then one day, I was on the train home from work, when David's father suddenly appeared and sat next to me. He smiled but his eyes were full of loathing. He told me he knew all about us, and that if I didn't end it immediately, he would tell my father exactly what I'd been up to. He really scared me, so I agreed to his demands." Roz twisted a tissue tightly with shaking hands, then reached forward for her glass. Ellie passed it to her, smiling awkwardly. She took a deep gulp of drink and continued,

"I didn't tell David. I couldn't bear to upset him. But I wasn't going to give him up. Instead, I made sure we were more careful, and convinced him to change our rendezvous locations. I thought it had worked and it did for a while, but David's father wouldn't let go. He found out where I worked and paid me a visit, just to remind me what would happen if I saw David again. I thought about telling David: I thought that we could fight him together, come clean and finally break free. But then it all came to a head," she paused again, staring at the floor as she relived the pain she had buried many years ago. For a moment, it looked like she wasn't going to continue with her story.

Celia put her arm about her shoulders, rhythmically patting the top of her arm.

"It's okay Roz, you don't have to say any more," she soothed.
Roz looked at her with such pained eyes, and shook her head.

"It's not okay though, is it? He destroyed us!" she declared. She took another sip of her drink and dried her eyes before speaking again.

"He sought me out at the train station one day and told me he knew I was still 'carrying on' with David. Of course, I tried to deny it but he just thrust some photos in my hand, and practically spat at me in fury. He'd had us followed, and the proof was right there, in my hand, and he was determined to ruin not just me, but David, and Daddy too. I felt completely cornered. And then I found out I was pregnant."

She faltered as Alice and Ellie gasped simultaneously, flabbergasted. Roz caught Alice's questioning face, her own, filled with absolute heartbreak. Celia took over, saying,

"That's when Roz confided in me about her affair: when she found out she was pregnant. We sat up all night talking, and finally she decided she would tell David about his father's threats, and about the baby. Together they would work it out. But," she paused, looking to Roz for permission to go on with the story. Roz nodded weakly, avoiding eye contact with any of them.

"By the next day, she had changed her mind and said she needed time to think out her next move, what to do for the best. So, she went away," Celia sighed deeply.

Alice stretched her hands out, bewildered.

"But what happened next?" she wanted to know, looking at Celia for an answer.

"I got a letter from Roz two weeks later, telling me that she had lost the baby. She was heartbroken. She had left without telling David, and now she had lost their love child, and she felt she could never return for fear of his father carrying out his threats." Celia struggled not to cry as she recalled that painful missive.

"She said it would be best all round if she didn't come home for a while, if she let David forget about her. And so, she went travelling and then settled in Stratford-upon-Avon. She never came back home," she finished, with a heavy heart.

Stunned into silence, nobody moved. It was a few minutes before Roz spoke.

"I'm so sorry, Celia. You know you are my best friend, not just my sister, and I have been so lucky to have you in my life, but ..." she took a deep breath, composing herself to utter the harrowing words,

"I lied. I lied to you. And I can't forget it, I can't forgive myself. And David is dead now, there's nothing I can do to change that." She spoke quickly, through her tears, visibly trembling. Ellie sat back in her seat, staring at the floor.

"Oh no, oh no," she murmured, shaking her head. Alice gasped, guessing at what Roz was implying.

"What?" Celia looked from one to the other, not understanding.

"I loved David with all my heart, with all my being. And I knew he loved me too. But I couldn't ruin his life. I couldn't ruin Daddy's," her words affirming her own actions.

Celia stared, confused.

"Roz? I don't understand." She looked at Alice questioningly.

Roz continued, her voice quiet and shaky.

"I did go travelling, you're right. I went to France, like I'd always wanted to, but I felt so far away from him. So, I came back and went to Cornwall. To Newlyn. It was like a magnet to my artist's soul, and the community was amazing, they were fantastic to me. They really welcomed me with open arms and took care of me. Then ... then ... oh God, forgive me ..." she struggled with her inner turmoil, trying to find the words.

"I didn't have a miscarriage. I had a beautiful baby: my little, darling girl. I held her in my arms, kissed her and drank in her wonderful, baby smell. I called her my little Cee-Cee, I named her after you ... and then she was gone. I didn't see her again. I had already signed the papers." She was shaking uncontrollably as she turned to Celia,

"I never got to see her grow up or show her to my David. I gave away the most precious thing in the world, and I have never stopped regretting it. Not for a minute."

Celia was holding her hands against her cheeks in absolute horror, her mouth open, eyes wide as she listened to her sister. Ellie gaped, dumbstruck. It suddenly all made sense to Alice; she didn't doubt for one second that the amount of concern, love and support that Roz had ploughed into her when she herself fell pregnant, stemmed from genuine love and affection for her, but she could see now that it was also because Roz knew exactly what she was going through. She knew exactly what kind of support she needed. Alice's stomach ached for her and felt keenly the insurmountable grief she had been carrying around for all these years.

Celia finally broke the silence.

"Oh Roz, what did you do? Daddy would've looked after you, he would!" she cried, sounding like a child. Roz reciprocated her tone,

"No, he wouldn't. How could he? I would have caused such a scandal! Think of his position, think of what people would've said. An unmarried mother with a child from a married man. The local doctor, and the vicar's daughter! Surely you can see, I had no choice Celia, no choice."

Her words silenced the room once more. Nobody knew what to say. What *could* they possibly say after a bombshell like that?

Ellie, for want of something to do, stood up and refilled their glasses, grimacing at the near empty bottle. She went in to the kitchen and returned with a bag of crisps and some biscuits, studiously trying to decipher the ingredients written in French.

"Something to soak up the alcohol," she offered, putting them on the table.

Despairing at their mute response, Roz excused herself and headed for the bathroom, sniffing repeatedly. Ellie stared in question at Alice.

"Did you know any of this, Mum?" she whispered. Alice shook her head, still reeling from shock.

"No, I didn't, not a clue," she replied. They both turned to Celia, who was deep in thought. Alice put her hand gently on her mother's shoulder.

"Are you okay, Mum?"
Celia gave a helpless shrug

"What do we do now?" She felt inadequate, lost for words, and completely caught off guard by Roz's confession.

"How can we possibly make this right?"

"Let her talk," Ellie suggested, "she clearly needed to open up about it," she added, "and I'm guessing there's more to come. We need to just listen, and let her do the talking. We need to show her that we care, that we want to hear what she has to say."

"When did you suddenly become so wise and grown up?" Alice smiled maternally. Ellie gave a little laugh, then sat back down as Roz returned to the room.

She eyed them all expectantly, not quite sure what to do next. Sensing her angst, Alice decided to step in and lead the conversation.

"So, how old were you when you started your affair with David?" she asked gently.

"Eighteen," Roz admitted quietly, giving her a long, knowing look.

Ellie sat up in her seat, abruptly putting her drink on the table.

"Oh my God, am I the only one who hasn't had illicit sex by the age of eighteen?" she retorted.

"Yes!" came the unanimous reply.

Alice swung round to her mother, shocked.

"Mum?" she asked. Celia studied her entwined hands in her lap a little flustered, then said defensively,

"Well dear, I know I'm supposed to be the sensible one, the prim and proper vicar's daughter, but I am human, you know. We all have urges," she stated. "Your dad was four years older than me, don't forget; I was only seventeen when we got together. He was very handsome and *very* persuasive," she divulged, raising her eyebrows suggestively, showing a rarely seen side to her character, fuelled by the alcohol.

"Mum!" Alice cringed, "too much information," she joked in mock horror. Celia widened her eyes indignantly.

"What, so it's alright for you to talk about Elliot but not for me to talk about my Reggie?" she challenged. "He was absolutely heavenly and so in love with me. I thought I was the luckiest girl in the world. And of course, we didn't get married for another four years, so we had plenty of the 'illicit sex', I can tell you!" she said triumphantly.
Alice stuck her fingers in her ears,

"La la la, I can't hear you!" she half sang, giving her mother a mortified look.
Roz chuckled quietly.

"I never knew that," she said, shaking her head.

"Of course not! Why would you? It's not the makings of a great story, is it? I married my beau afterwards," Celia swiftly replied, then holding a hand out to Alice stuttered,

"Oh, I didn't mean it like that, dear! What I meant was, he was there, he was available."
Then realising her second faux pas, stretched out to pat Roz's knee.

"Oh, I didn't mean it like that either!"
She looked awkwardly at the three faces staring at her.

"Oh dear, shall I shut up now?" she asked limply.

"Yes!" they all replied in unison.

Unwittingly, Celia had successfully eased the tension. She took Roz's hand, giving her a weak smile. Seizing the opportunity, Alice asked,

"Do you want to talk about it, Roz?"

Roz nodded, looking at each of them in turn, appreciating their willingness to support her.

"Yes, I think I do. But not now. I'm … I'm too worn out. It's been another hell of a day, hasn't it," she nodded pointedly at Alice, referring to her earlier break-down.

Alice agreed. She felt completely drained once again, emotionally wrung out. Too many ghosts were crowding her mind: ghosts of war heroes, of her father, her grandmother, and most prominently, the ghost of her first love. Elliot.

Chapter Four

Alice woke early the next morning, and glancing across at Ellie's sleeping frame sprawled across the adjacent bed in her customary star-shape fashion, she quietly got up and crept out to the kitchen. Roz was already there, sitting at the table and deep in thought. Smiling up at Alice, she indicated to the fresh pot of tea on the side and pushed her own cup forward in request of a refill. Placing the steaming cups in front of them, Alice sat opposite Roz, taking in her tired, desperately sad expression.

"I'm not going to ask any more questions, Auntie Roz, I just want to repeat Ellie's sentiment of the other night. You truly are an amazing woman; such a strong, loving person and I have been so grateful for everything you have ever done for me. And I'm sorry if I don't tell you that often enough," she said earnestly. Roz nodded, appreciating her sincere words.

They sat in silence, contemplating the past forty-eight hours. Alice's phone beeped, indicating a message alert. It was from Elliot.

'How are you? How is your trip?'

Alice smiled involuntarily, debating her response. She had butterflies in her stomach, just knowing that he was thinking about her.

'Emotional. Ellie knows – she is overjoyed xx A.'

She pressed 'send' before she had a chance to delete the kisses or the intimate signature of just her initial. Within seconds, he responded,

'So am I! Words seem inadequate to describe how I am feeling right now xx E.'

Alice hugged her phone in her hands, her mind filling with all kinds of thoughts, most of which had been shelved for a long time. Roz looked at her speculatively. Feeling a sudden pang of guilt, Alice shrugged lightly, and casually slid her phone back into her bag on the chair next to her.

"Toast?" she offered, wanting to get the day started.

Ellie thoughtfully licked honey from her fingers and brushed crumbs from the table back onto her plate.

"I don't want to carry on with our trip now. It seems quite shallow, going shopping in Amsterdam, with everything that's happened," she confessed, "I feel really drained and so emotional. I honestly don't think I could cope with doing the Arnhem or Anne Frank museums right now either."

"Okay, that's fine, I think we're all a little shell shocked – pardon the pun," Alice replied. "How do you want to work things then?" she asked.

Ellie deliberated for a moment.

"I think we need to start doing some digging around. We need to find Cee-Cee," she stated. Celia looked alarmed,

"Oh, I don't think that's a good idea really," she said in a hushed tone.

"I do!" Roz announced, hope flickering in her eyes. "Yes, I think Ellie's right. I have always wanted to, but not known how to. How to start looking, how to cope," she explained, drawing in a long breath through her nose and breathing out again slowly. Alice nodded in agreement.

Ellie did a tiny fist pump, hissing, "yes", under her breath.

"Okay then," she nodded to her elders, "I think we should go to Cornwall".

"No," Roz shook her head nervously.

"Yes," the others encouraged unanimously.

"Okay," Roz agreed, starting to laugh and cry at the same time.

"And we definitely need more tissues!" Ellie exclaimed as she slid the last of the tissues across the table to Roz.

The next hour and a half was spent packing up their cases and planning a new route. They intended to retrace their steps back to Calais, abandoning their visit to Normandy completely, then once back in England, motor on down to Cornwall. Knowing accommodation would be scarce now that schools had broken up for the summer, Alice spent best part of an hour securing somewhere suitable in the vicinity of Newlyn. Satisfied, she closed her laptop and helped load the luggage into the car once again.

"You need to contact Andrew, dear, and make sure he gave the keys to Auntie May. He went back to Winchester last night and I completely forgot to phone him, what with everything going on here," Celia said.

"By 'going on', you mean the huge, life changing revelation, I take it?" Alice wondered ironically. Celia pulled a frown and nodded,

"But don't tell him any of that, will you?" she added anxiously. Alice gave a snort of indignation.

"Why would I tell him something like that?" she raised her hands questioningly. Roz came into the kitchen just then and joined in,

"Oh, I don't know Alice, it's not like you would ever blurt out a secret that's been kept for eighteen years now, would you?" she challenged humorously. Alice stared at them both defensively, then dropped her hands and laughed,

"Okay, you have a point. But I won't tell Andrew. Promise."

She leant forward and kissed Roz on the cheek before fetching her phone from her bag.

Ellie sidled up to Alice and gave her a squeeze hug. She was wearing a floral ditsy print, sleeveless skater dress, and Alice noted the necklace from Elliot hanging proudly around her neck. She had opted to have her hair up in bunches, making her look younger than she was. It had been her favourite hair style as a child and she would swish her pigtails round with her hands, imitating helicopter blades. Alice smiled at her, returning the hug.

"Ah, my little Heli-Ellie", she chuckled affectionately. Ellie swished her hair, giggling.

"Mum," she started, then hesitated for a second,

"Have you spoken to Elliot at all?" she wondered, hopefully. Alice nodded.

"Yes, I have. I told him you know about him," she informed her gently. Ellie raised her eyebrows,

"What did he say?"

"He is really happy, Ellie. He wants to get to know you," she watched Ellie's reaction. Ellie nodded, her face creasing with happiness.

"Okay. Mum, I know he hurt you and if I were you, I don't think I would ever forgive him but," she paused, searching for the right words,

"But it's different for me. I don't want to do anything that would upset you though," she looked at her mother anxiously, then continued in a lighter tone,

"Having said that, judging by the way he was watching you - my God, he couldn't take his eyes off you - I think he really, really regrets what he did!" she enthused.

Alice let out a little laugh and closed her eyes for a moment, not wanting Ellie to see the extent of her true feelings. She had also been thinking about that; the way he had watched her and held her hand, the way he had spoken to her and been so … so like the Elliot she used to know. It confused her.

By the time they stopped for a coffee break at a roadside café just outside Calais, Roz had had a change of heart.

"I am so sorry girls but I can't do this right now," she explained, "I'm not ready to go to Cornwall. It has been such an emotional rollercoaster these past three days - is it only three days?" she asked Celia, "it feels so much longer," she said, "I just want to go home and rest, think, and plan this properly. Is that okay?"

Everybody agreed, making supportive noises. Alice had also been having doubts about the whole 'rush off to Cornwall' idea too; she wondered what it could possibly achieve, other than to rake up painful memories for Roz of a time when she was at her lowest and most vulnerable. This was her chance to repay the debt of gratitude to her aunt. She had determined to do everything she possibly could to trace Cee-Cee. She knew though, that to take such an important step was going to take a huge amount of resolve, understanding and strength. And Alice, like Roz, was also feeling completely drained of any strength right now.

Returning to the car, just before Alice put the key in the ignition, Ellie turned to her and quietly asked if she thought Elliot would want to see her when they got back home. Remembering his words when she last saw him, Alice explained that he probably wouldn't still be in Brockenhurst.

"I got the impression he was only there for the weekend," she said, her heart sinking at Ellie's deflated expression. Without a second thought, she quickly sent him a text.

'Morning, we have cut our trip short and are heading home. Are you still in Brockenhurst?'
It was only a moment before he replied,

'I'm on my way to a meeting. Is everything ok?'
Alice stared at the question – where to begin, she thought. Typing swiftly, she responded,

'We're fine. Ellie is keen to see you but don't worry. We can sort something soon?"
She leant forward on the driver's wheel, staring at the phone screen, waiting for a response.

Nothing.

Acutely aware that Ellie was watching her expectantly, she silently cursed Elliot. She felt trapped; she was being put in a position of begging favours from the person who had completely torn her world apart before, and she was dreading that he would do the same again, to Ellie.

Just then, her phone rang. It was Elliot.

"Hello Alice, are you okay?" he asked. His voice sounded so close, so warm and her heart fluttered with just hearing him say her name.

"Morning, yes thank you; we decided to change our plans slightly, that's all. Mum's not feeling great, unfortunately," she lied, shrugging and mouthing, 'sorry', to Celia as she did so.

"Sorry to hear that. Listen, can I speak to Ellie, I mean, would she mind speaking to me?" his voice had gone up a notch and Alice could hear a vulnerability in his voice that she had heard before. She had a sudden flash back to the first time he professed his love for her, not quite sure of her response, fear of rejection etched in his face. She had wiped that fear away in the most natural way possible, letting him know just how much she loved him too.

"Alice?" he prompted, bringing her back to reality. She cleared her throat,

"Of course: here she is," she replied quickly.

Ellie took the phone from Alice and stepped out of the car, leaning against the bonnet with her back to the windscreen. Although Alice couldn't see her face she could tell by the animated way her body moved as she talked, that it was a good phone call.

Roz tapped Alice on the shoulder,

"I'm worried," she said gently.

"Don't' be," she gave Roz an optimistic smile, "I think they'll be fine. He really seems intent on getting to know her," she said.

"I meant, I'm worried about you," Roz stated flatly. Alice shook her head, eyes widening.

"No, no, I'm fine, absolutely," she said, "he broke my heart a long, long time ago but I was young. And scared. He was my whole life but now I have Ellie. I have you and I have Mum. So much has changed since then. So much," she affirmed. "I got over it. Over him," she nodded; a little longer than necessary. Roz patted her shoulder again, also nodding but she looked unconvinced.

Ellie jumped back into the car, eyes sparkling with excitement.

"Guess what?" she announced, then without waiting for an answer, gushed,

"Well, he was on his way to a meeting but pulled over on the motorway and phoned them to cancel it! And now he's heading back to Brockenhurst, to take me out this afternoon, for a late lunch," she told them, jigging in her seat like a little child. Glancing at her watch she asked,

"What time will we get home, Mum?"

Alice indicated to the traffic ahead, that they were just about to re-join, as her answer. She was feeling a little irritated by Ellie's joy; jealous even.

Ellie shot her a look.

"Are you cross with me?" she asked abruptly.

Alice turned the key in the ignition and manoeuvred out of the parking space. Not taking her eyes off the road, she shook her head,

"Of course not," she tried to sound breezy.

"Maybe you shouldn't ask him anything about the past, dear," Celia suggested tactfully. Ellie turned in her seat to look at her grandmother.

"I won't. I mean, it's tempting to go in there and read him the riot act but," she looked apologetically at Alice, "but I just need to get to know him first," she said. "He is my dad, after all."

The car fell silent. The realisation of what this simple statement meant for their future, was slowly sinking in.

As they neared Brockenhurst a few hours later, Ellie announced she needed to text Elliot to let him know they were nearly home. Alice nodded,

"His number's on my phone," she said helpfully but Ellie shook her head, pulling her own phone from her pocket.

"It's okay Mum, I've got it on my phone now," she sounded a little possessive about it. Alice shot her a surprised look. Ellie paused her texting.

"Mum, are you okay with this? Really?" she demanded to know, her voice was edgy rather than concerned. Alice tightened her grip of the steering wheel, trying not to respond abruptly. She let out a heavy sigh.

"Yes, I'm okay with it Ellie, and I know how excited you are but please," she kept her voice level, "just understand that in the past few days the man I loved with all my heart, has walked back into my life without any warning. I have told him, and you, a secret I've been carrying for eighteen years that will now change things forever. On top of that, Auntie Roz has unburdened her secret of forty-six years," her voice started to rise, "and that has so many connotations, I don't even know where to start. Cee-Cee is my cousin; she is also your father's cousin. Your father wants to get to know you but we now have another secret to keep from him. This is all such a mess! So please, don't keep asking if I am okay with it all. Just give me a chance to deal with it, in my own way. I feel like I've been transported to some alternate reality and backed into a corner by the people I love. And..." She stopped suddenly as her voice broke with emotion, and stared fixedly at the road ahead.

Ellie leant over and gently squeezed her knee, her face full of concern.

"I'm sorry, Mum. We've reacted differently to all of this. I'm so excited, that I didn't stop to think about what I said," she smiled apologetically. Alice glanced at her, shaking her head.

"No, *I'm* sorry Ellie. It's just all a bit much," she affirmed, "but I *do* want you to get to know him. I do," she nodded. Ellie's face brightened.

"So, when you said, just now, about being backed into a corner by the people you love – does that include my dad?" she probed.

Alice gave a shaky laugh, not quite sure how to answer. Her own Freudian slip had taken her by surprise and she definitely needed head space to sort it all out before she uttered another word. Ellie's casual use of the words, 'my dad', had thrown her somewhat too.

Ellie's phone chimed and she raised her shoulders in exuberance as she read her text, grinning at the screen.

"He's going to pick me up from Grandma's, as soon as we get there," she told them happily. Celia leant forward and patted her affectionately on her shoulder. Alice caught Roz's eye in the rear-view mirror; a look of despair flashed across her aunt's face before she turned away to stare out of the window. It was evident that Alice wasn't the only one with plenty to think about.

Elliot was already there when they arrived, leaning against his car - a sleek, silver Lexus - that was parked in the wide driveway. He raised his hand in acknowledgement, smiling encouragingly at Ellie. She jumped out of the car, then stood for a second, awkwardly unsure as she looked at him. He walked over to her and putting a hand on her shoulder, welcomed her back.

"I know you've just spent hours in the car but do you fancy a drive out to Burley for lunch?" he invited kindly. Her face erupted in a childlike grin and she enthusiastically nodded her acceptance.

"I'll just help Grandma unpack the bags and then I'm ready," she told him.

Alice got out of the driver's seat and slowly stretched her aching back and shoulders, and looking up, saw Elliot watching her. An appreciative smile tugged at the corner of his mouth and he ever so slightly raised an eyebrow, not taking his eyes off her. She suddenly felt hot and flustered, and extremely underdressed in her comfy shorts and vest top. They had been fine for driving in the summer heat but didn't exactly scream of cool sophistication. Elliot, she noted, was wearing yet another immaculately tailored suit, the midnight-blue colour of the cloth enhancing the already intensely blue colour of his eyes. Eyes she didn't seem able to look away from.

"Good journey?" he asked as he crossed the gravel drive towards her side of the car. She grimaced,

"Not bad. The traffic was slow coming into Hampshire though, I lost count of all the caravans," she said lightly, still not able to break eye contact.

"Listen, Alice," he lowered his tone, "thank you for telling Ellie about me." His voice was deep and sincere. She gave an acknowledging nod.

"Well, she had more or less guessed anyway. The minute she saw you she thought you were her father," she told him. Elliot smiled with surprise, a smile that quickly turned to one of pride as Alice briefly relayed Ellie's reaction to finding out about him.

"Are you okay with this?" he asked gently. Alice nodded, trying not to well up, as he unwittingly echoed Ellie's question from earlier.

He frowned,

"You don't look very sure," he noted, a troubled look crossing his face.

She gave a half-hearted smile and cleared her throat,

"I am fine with it Elliot; she needs to get to know you. It's only fair that she does. And it's only fair for you too," she added quietly.

The look of warmth in his eyes was throwing her off guard; all she wanted him to do was put his arms around her and hold her until her exhausted mind drifted off to sleep. As if he had read her thoughts, he said softly,

"You look like you could do with going to bed."

Alice looked startled. His steady gaze was unfaltering, his eyes scanning her face. They darkened as he realised how she had misconstrued his suggestion, and he gave the merest hint of a knowing smile. Leaning towards her, he breathed,

"I meant, it's been a long drive and you must be exhausted."

She closed her eyes for a second, mortified that her thoughts had betrayed her. She nodded and forced a quick smile,

"Yes, I know that's what you meant," she said airily. "I am pretty shattered," she admitted, turning away from him as Ellie half skipped back across the driveway, beaming at them both.

"Ready!" she announced. Elliot gestured grandly to his car, and holding the door open, offered his hand to help her in. As he shut her door, he turned to look at Alice once more, insecurity reflecting in his eyes as he realised the huge step he was embarking on. She resisted the urge to rush over and reassure him, instead she gave an encouraging smile and mouthed,

"You'll be fine."

Gratitude flooded his face and the smile he gave her, made her heart skip a beat. He mouthed back,

"Thank you."

She watched them leave, returning Ellie's joyous wave until they were out of sight. Her hand dropped back by her side; she felt completely sapped of all energy and the urge to cry was, once again, overwhelming. A stab of envy ripped through her chest at the thought of Ellie spending time with Elliot; not because she was worried that Elliot would take her place in Ellie's life, but more that she wished it was *her* spending the day with him.

'Pull yourself together, Alice', she reprimanded herself, retrieving her handbag from the front seat and heading for the house.

Celia and Roz were in the kitchen, a pot of tea already brewing on the side. Alice made her excuses and headed for her room, partly to rest her head and partly to avoid any further Elliot-related conversation. As she left the kitchen, Celia let her know that she would be going to the cemetery shortly.

"I need to tell Reggie that we did the trip," she said. Roz nodded.

"I'll come with you," she replied, "I think it's time I did."

Alice hesitated, not sure what Roz had meant but her head was pounding and she didn't even have the strength to speak, so she left them to it and within minutes of lying down, was fast asleep.

The cemetery, attached to the ancient church of St Nicholas, was on the other side of the village from their house and St Saviour's church where Celia and Roz's father had been vicar. The sisters linked arms as they crossed the footpath alongside the ford, known as 'The Watersplash', that separated the road by St Saviour's with the main street. Ponies and donkeys gathered under the shade of the trees, dipping their feet in the water. A young foal strayed from the pack and wandered up the road, causing the cars to slow down and then stop altogether as it came to a standstill in the middle of the road, idly debating where to roam next. Roz clapped her hands loudly as they walked past it, in a bid to encourage it to move on but the noise fell on deaf ears. She shrugged apologetically to the driver, receiving a resigned smile in return. It was generally an accepted rule that equines, and wandering cattle, had right of way in Brockenhurst.

Stopping off to buy some flowers, the sisters carried on up the street which was now teaming with tourists.

Reaching the top of the street by the train station, they continued over the level crossing and, leaving the traffic behind them, carried on along the winding, leafy lane leading to the old church and cemetery.

Reaching the wooden gate to the cemetery, Celia asked Roz if she wanted to go on up to the church first but Roz shook her head with determination. As they passed through the gates, the traffic seemed to dim to a distant, yet steady, drone. Light aircraft followed the flightpath above their heads, and the numerous trees rustled in the warm summer breeze.

The cemetery was on three levels, the newer cemetery being on the lowest level by the entrance. A flat open stretch of land, flanked by fields and farmland on one side, and tall oak and pine trees on the other. Benches were positioned at regular intervals under the shade of the immense trees, offering a place for contemplation and solitude. Beyond the row of trees, the bank rose to the next level, where the Commonwealth war graves could be found in an immaculately kept patch; the final resting place of nearly a hundred New Zealand soldiers who were wounded in France during World War One and died from their wounds in the Brockenhurst hospital. Rising again, a path led through overgrown ground up to the ancient church at the top of the lane, which was surrounded by equally ancient graves.

Roz hesitated once she had closed the gate behind them, staring with trepidation at the collection of tombstones spread out before her. A central aisle of vivid green, and burnt auburn, smaller, newly planted trees, afforded little shade from the scorching sun: a stark contrast to the rest of the wooded area. The air was filled with the smell of warm grass and soothing pine, combined with the perfume from several graveside bouquets.

Celia gently took Roz's arm and guided her towards the far end of the cemetery, by-passing the pristine granite grave of her husband. Pausing under one of the many solid oak trees, she sat on the bench, indicating for Roz to follow suit. She pointed to the nearest grave: a black, upright headstone with a serpentine top. It was well-tended, with two granite vases sitting in the base, both of which were filled with dried-out flowers.

"There's David," she barely whispered, watching Roz's reaction.

Roz caught her breath and struggled to swallow, her body trembling with shock. She pinched her lips with her fingers to stop herself from crying out in anguish.

"This is too hard," she whimpered, staring unseeingly at the headstone. Celia gave her hand a comforting squeeze,

"I'll just be over there, with Reggie. Okay?" she encouraged, getting up and walking back the way they had come.

Roz sat transfixed, trying to regulate her breathing and calm her thumping pulse. She focused her mind on the rumble of a tractor in the nearby field, and the more intrusive sound of grasshoppers chirping in the long grass at the foot of the oak trees behind her. But she couldn't tear her eyes away from David's name, engraved into the black granite, and embellished with gold enamel paint. The finality screamed silently at her.

She stopped fighting and let the tears flow, reliving the moment when Celia had phoned her to say David had died. Sixteen years had passed but the pain was just as fresh because she had never dealt with it, never allowed herself to believe it. The initial impact had cleaved her chest in two; she had fallen to the floor, clutching the phone, unable to breathe, not wanting to hear the words her sister had uttered. She curled up in her bed shortly after and wept for two days, feigning 'flu, and rejecting Alice's attempts to fuss over her. Helplessly trapped, she had no privacy to grieve and no strength to face it, so she buried it deep within her, refusing to let the devastation resurface.

Standing up, she stepped tentatively towards the headstone, noticing a faded tag on one of the dried-out bouquets in the vase. It read,

'Happy Birthday David,

Missing you with each passing year.

Always in our hearts,

John, Sheila and family xxxx'

Roz smiled forlornly, recalling how close David and his brother, John, had been. She reached out her hand and carefully traced around the letters of his name on the headstone, as if caressing the outline of his face. She kissed her hand and pressed it against the cold granite.

"I thought I had no right to come here, no right to grieve. And by not doing so, I haven't had to admit that you're gone. I've kept you alive, inside me, like a secret treasure that nobody knew about," she confided inaudibly.

Kneeling, she took another look at the inscription, able to focus now that the initial shock had worn off. The craftsmanship was beautifully executed, the simple black and gold, immortalising his memory in a fitting tribute,

> Dr David Elliot Barraclough,
> 28th April 1936 – 14th November 1999
> Treasured memories of a much-loved son
> of Patrick and Jean,
> Beloved brother of John and Sheila,
> Adored uncle of James, Daniel and Elliot,
> Devoted husband of Patricia.
> 'To live in hearts we leave behind
> is not to die'

As Roz read the quote by his favourite poet, Thomas Campbell, a strangled sob escaped her lips. She could hear his voice, soft and deep, whispering those very words to her, as he had done each time they had to part, leaving the sanctity of their love nest and returning to the stark reality of a life of lies.

"For time makes all but true love old," she choked her reply, resting her head where she had placed the kiss. Waves of pain and regret engulfed her, the realisation of what she had done hitting her with such a force, once again.

"I'm so sorry, David," she sobbed, "I left you to live a life without me. I left our daughter to live a life without either one of us. And I left you to spend an eternity lying here, without even visiting you. I have been such a coward and ruined both our lives in the process."

She sat leaning against the solid granite, feeling instantly closer to him.

"I always thought I'd see you again, one day. Time passed and yet time stood still in my heart. Romantic nonsense I know, but I just wish you had walked back into my life, and picked up where we left off," she sniffed, not even having the strength to get up and retrieve a tissue from her bag that was on the bench.

"But if we had, I would've had to face up to what I had done. To confess how I had given away our daughter. I don't think you would have forgiven me - how could anybody - and I couldn't have coped with that. I can't even forgive myself," she admitted heavily.

Her tears subsided as she sat silently for a long while, drawing strength from the proximity of David's spirit.

"I didn't fight. I should have fought for us," she declared. "Would you have stood by me? Against your father, against the world?" she voiced her questions, realising how futile they were now. Emotionally spent, she closed her eyes and allowed herself the luxury of drifting back in time, to a period in her life that was filled with the most intoxicating warmth and love from the only person she had ever allowed to capture, and keep, her heart and soul.

Celia shook Roz's shoulder gently, returning her back to the present. Accepting the outstretched hand, she stood up rather ungainly, her knees stiff from the awkward position she had been sitting in on the grass. Sitting back on the bench, Celia pulled out a flask of tea and some biscuits. Roz smiled quizzically at her. Celia held a cup up,

"Don't knock it; I bet you could do with a cup of tea right now!" she said, taking in her sister's tearstained, tired eyes. Roz nodded,

"Bless you Celia, you're always prepared," she laughed affectionately.

They sipped their tea, silently looking out across the cemetery; the assorted, coloured headstones interspersed with plants, looked graceful in the afternoon sunshine.

"I sometimes wonder if I missed out on life," Celia mused.

"How do you mean?" Roz asked curiously, idly watching a plane pass overhead. Celia shrugged,

"Well, you had this lust for life, this 'get up and go' kind of spirit and you always knew you wanted to be an artist. Just like Alice always wanted to be a teacher, as Reggie had done too. And Andrew wanted to be a lawyer. I never had that ambition, that drive. I just wanted to stay at home and raise a family," she acknowledged. Roz smiled,

"What's wrong with that? You've done a great job," she enthused. Celia grimaced,

"But it's not very exciting, is it! I didn't go off to University and experience that freedom, or travel abroad and see a different kind of life. I just stuck to the straight and narrow, I stayed where I was comfortable," she admitted. Roz turned to look at her, not quite sure what to say.

Celia continued,

"Do you remember that girl, Sally Bates? She was the first one to wear a mini skirt, and those shiny white boots, remember?" she prompted. Roz gave a little laugh at the recollection,

"Yes, I remember her! Oh my goodness, all that make-up and parading up the High Street. She certainly shocked the locals!"

They both laughed.

"Well, I used to envy her. I never had the courage to be different like that. She had all the boys drooling over her, and all the girls idolised her. She was so popular; did I miss out, somehow, by not being more like her?" Celia looked earnestly at her sister, then smiled sheepishly at Roz's horrified face.

"I can't imagine anything worse than you being like Slapper Sally!" she exclaimed, "Whatever happened to her anyway?"

Celia shrugged her shoulders, shaking her head in reply.

"The way I see it is, you got the best deal out of all of us," Roz said thoughtfully, "look at me, look at Alice," she prompted. "Try not to look at Slapper Sally," she added with a derisive chuckle. "You had that precious thing that eluded us – happiness in love. Not a brief affair that ended in years of heartache. You got the real deal with Reggie," She squeezed Celia's arm affectionately, "that lasted a lifetime."

Celia nodded, looking over towards Reggie's grave, knowing her sister was right. She was suddenly feeling unfaithful to his memory for even thinking the thoughts she had just voiced.

"I did love him, you know, so very much," her voice cracked with grief. "He was such a kind, giving man, and did everything for us. He wasn't really religious when I met him but he joined the church because it was part of me.

He was more of a romantic thinker, a bit impulsive and passionate. He was forever quoting poetry to me and reading his endless books," she reflected. "Alice is so like him," she added warmly.

"I remember him as a young boy," Roz nodded, "always on his bike with his little group of friends. They used to get caught scrumping apples up by old Mr Beardsley's place, didn't they?" she chuckled. "What made you choose him then, how did you know he was the one for you?"

"You'll laugh if I tell you", Celia responded reluctantly. Intrigued, Roz shook her head and light-heartedly insisted on an answer.

"Well, it was the summer he finished University and came back home. I was helping out with refreshments for the cricket, with Mummy, and he was on the team. I hadn't seen him really for three years and he had grown up so much. No longer that scrawny, cheeky lad but taller and more muscular, and *very* good looking with his dark, puppy dog eyes and brown, wavy hair," she declared, "It took me quite by surprise, really. I hadn't looked at him like that before" she admitted. Roz smiled affectionately at her sister, enjoying this new side to her that was emerging beyond her usual, old-fashioned reserve.

"Anyway, he was bowling and I was watching, mesmerised by his…" she paused, looking embarrassed, lowering her voice to a whisper.

"The way he was bowling was just so sexy, everything was rippling," she confided, blushing slightly. Roz widened her eyes, making a point of not laughing at Celia's confession.

"He bowled and it hit the stumps and everybody cheered. He let out this victorious 'yes' and jumped up, punching the air, and as he did so, he caught my eye. He didn't break eye contact with me and this grin spread across his face, in a way that said he knew he'd not just won the match but won me too", her eyes sparkled at the memory. "Well, I just melted in to a puddle, right there and then, really," she confessed.

Roz laughed out loud, spontaneously hugging Celia.

"Oh my goodness, only you would find cricket sexy!" she exclaimed.

They sat in mutual silence for a while, mulling over their conversation and recalling teenage memories.

"How about you? What attracted you to David?" Celia's question broke the silence.

"Pure lust!" Roz professed swiftly.

"Roz!" Celia laughingly scolded. Roz smirked, then shook her head,

"I'm only joking, obviously, it was more than that," she looked thoughtful for a moment,

"He had such sad eyes: they conveyed a real depth of unhappiness. That's what struck me about him first, I think. He was so handsome, I mean *incredibly* handsome, he looked like a film star. He had immaculate, black hair, was clean shaven and with the most intensely grey-blue eyes. And always so smartly dressed. But he had no confidence, he wasn't self-assured, he almost apologised for existing. He should have oozed confidence with his looks," she recounted, visualising the face that she had so passionately loved.

"And I'm not joking about the lust bit, he was very sexy, but I think it started out more as a sort of maternal thing; I instinctively wanted to mother him, care for him, take away that self-doubt and sadness." She fell silent, lost in memories and regret.

"Wow, Freud would have a field day with this," Roz attempted to laugh through her tears, "it's verging on the Oedipus complex!"

"Can I ask you something? Did you ever feel guilty about having sex before marriage?" Celia asked tentatively, gauging Roz's reaction.

"Absolutely! I felt more sinful about that than I did about the fact that David was married to somebody else. I absolutely dreaded Daddy finding out, I don't think I could have recovered from that," she confided. "How about you, how did you feel about it?"

"Well that's the strange thing - I didn't feel guilty at all. I have no idea why. I mean, I was the sensible one, wasn't I? Obviously, I didn't tell anybody what we were up to, but I think I always knew that I would marry Reggie and somehow that made it alright," she said, aware that her answer would maybe not be the one Roz wanted to hear. She was right.

"I wish I'd known about you and Reggie, what your relationship was like. Maybe I wouldn't have cared so much then. I would have had an ally," she reflected, sighing deeply. "What if we didn't care about what others thought, or if we didn't think as deeply about things. Would life have been better, or different, do you think?" She stared at Celia, desperation clutching at her chest as she considered the possibilities of what could have been.

"Hindsight is a killer, isn't it!" she muttered in despair, her eyes drawn back to David's gravestone.

Celia took hold of her hand and held it firmly. They had both found love on such an intense level, which had sent their lives off in completely different directions from each other but right now, they were sharing the same sense of loss and grief. The knowledge that nothing could ever bring that love back, was hard to bear.

Roz leant her head on Celia's shoulder, staring fixedly on the gravestone that symbolised the life she had loved and lost: a realisation of her own mortality gnawing away at her stomach.

"Do you think we'll find her?" Celia interrupted her thoughts.

"I'm scared to," Roz confessed, "but also scared not to."

She sat up again and turned to look at Celia,

"I've been so stupid with life, Celia. I need to stop running away. I know I've been here on a kind of extended leave from Stratford since Reggie died, but I need to move on now," she determined. Celia eyed her expectantly, as she continued,

"You asked me if I wanted to move in with you. Well, I think it's time I retired, give up the shop and come back home. I'd love to live with you," she nodded, welling up once more. Celia hugged her and held her tightly,

"Oh Roz, this is going to be wonderful, thank you!"

They laughed together, reaching for tissues from their bags.

"But we're not going to do *this* every day," Roz interjected, nodding at the graves. "Yes, we'll visit them but we're going to live a little too. I don't think our 'boys' would mind," she smiled. "I'm going to take you travelling," she announced.

"Isn't that running away again?" Celia asked quietly. Roz shook her head,

"No. It's going on an adventure. And then we come home again," she paused, thinking about what Celia had said.

"But before we do, we need to find my daughter," she resolved.

The sound of the front door closing as Celia and Roz returned home, awoke Alice. She joined them in the kitchen, grimacing as she rubbed her shoulder to ease the pain there.

"I think I must have pulled a muscle or something, my neck and shoulder ache so much. And my head is still thumping," she complained, reaching for some painkillers from the kitchen cupboard. She watched her mother and aunt, noticing something different about them in the way they were interacting with each other.

"Perhaps a walk would help," Celia suggested, pouring a glass of water for her to take her tablets with. Alice smiled her thanks, pulling a child-like face as she swallowed them.

"I haven't heard anything from Ellie: have you?" she asked them both expectantly. They shook their heads.

"But that's a good sign dear, it means it's all going well," Celia tried to soothe her, noting her anxious expression. "It's all out in the open now, there's nothing for you to hide anymore, so try not to worry," she added.

Alice shot a look at Roz, not convinced by her mother's statement. There were still secrets to keep, shocking ones, and feelings resurfacing, that she wasn't sure how to deal with. And she was seeing a different side to her aunt that was raising unwanted questions in her mind, making her feel uneasy.

"You're right, I need some air," she said abruptly, "I won't be long."

The earlier heat had subsided and grey clouds were beginning to form across the sky, in the typically unpredictable style of British weather. Alice set off at a brisk pace, wanting to put distance between herself and the house. Within minutes she was outside St Saviours church, the welcoming familiarity of the grey, stone building beckoning her in.

Designed and built at the turn of the 20th century, the early Edwardian, gothic style church had been a second home to Alice and her brother when they were growing up. They had spent many happy hours playing in the church, in between services, under the watchful eye of their indulging grandfather. 'Hide and seek' had been their favourite game, crawling in and out of the wooden pews. Or fabricating adventurous stories together, based on the figures featured in the beautiful, stained glass window above the altar. The wooden pews had in more recent times been replaced with purple upholstered chairs, improving the comfort for the parishioners but the window, designed in the Decorated Period of old, remained as a permeant reminder of blissful, childhood days.

Alice pushed open the solid, wooden church door that stood slightly ajar. She smiled at the old memory of holding sheets of paper against it to do brightly coloured rubbings of the huge, ornate iron hinges that sprawled decoratively across the wood. A sense of belonging washed over her as she stepped across the threshold, and pushing the door shut behind her, she basked in the tranquil silence that enveloped her frayed senses. She took in a deep, restorative breath, enjoying the cool, dusty smell that permeated the building. Holding her hand out, she ran her fingers along the edges of the chairs as she walked down the aisle, the spongy cushion yielding a little to her light touch. Out of habit she headed for a seat on the front row, to the right of the altar.

Closing her eyes, she tried to clear her head but thoughts kept pushing their way back in, invading her mind. The fact that Roz had had such an intense connection with Elliot's family, bothered her a great deal. After the initial shock of her confession, Alice had since been feeling hurt that, despite everything they had been through together, Roz had never confided in her. They were inextricably linked though the men they had loved and had children with; their lies had run a parallel course and come to light simultaneously.

Alice was trying with all her might to quash the nagging question that kept resurfacing – what if? What if she had sought Elliot out after she found out she was expecting their baby; would he have come back to her? Would life have been different? And now that he was back in her life, she was scared of her feelings for him. Feelings she had vehemently kept in check for so long. She felt emotionally compromised.

She stared at the altar, hardly breathing, as if listening intently for something. She pinched at the padded seat to distract herself from crying as an anguished sigh escaped her lips.

"Oh Dad, what do I do? I know you're here for me," she put a hand to her chest, "but I could really do with you and Grandpa *here* right now," she whispered to the altar. Absently twiddling small bobbles of cloth on the seat, she continued,

"I don't know who to turn to. Auntie Roz, it turns out, has this longstanding feud with the Barraclough name. Mum is … Mum basically, and Ellie is like a giddy, Disney princess with her new-found Knight. I'm scared of mucking it all up," she admitted, "I need to be strong and let her build a relationship with Elliot but …" she paused, looking up to the panelled wood and carved stone ceiling, then turned pleading eyes back to the altar,

"But I need to know how to move on from this: how to cope. How to let him into our lives for Ellie's sake, without it destroying me. Again."

She stood up and walked slowly to the altar and knelt on the shallow, wide steps; the need to be closer to her father seemed to be soothed the closer she got to this spot. She sat back on her heels, as she had done so many times as a child, and stroked the cool, stone step.

"You two taught me how to be strong and I thought I was doing okay, you know, I was fine. But all it took was one look from him, and I'm back to square one," she hit the ground with the flat of her hand, in frustration.

"I don't think it ever went away, the love I had for him. It never left me. And now I have to deal with that pain all over again but this time, it's different. I have Ellie watching me, armed with a thousand questions that I just don't know the answers to."

She looked across to the lectern, standing on the left-hand side, hearing her father's steady voice in her head. Then back to the altar, visualising her grandfather there.

"Help me Dad. Grandpa. I'm lost. Give me a sign, anything! Tell me what to do," she wept silently, resting her eyes on the crucifix above the altar.

The door opened behind her and turning, she saw Elliot in the doorway, his outline framed by the dappled, early evening light, making him look bizarrely like a spiritual apparition. Turning back to the altar, she asked incredulously,

"That's it? That's your sign?"

She stood up and wiping her face quickly with her hand, turned to Elliot as he walked towards her. She smiled awkwardly, acutely aware that her face was blotchy and puffy from crying.

"What are you doing here?" she asked, a little bewildered. He shrugged slightly,

"I dropped Ellie off, and you weren't there so I naturally gravitated towards the church," he told her, "I knew you'd be here."

His face full of concern, he silently pulled her towards him and hugged her. She melted instantly, and instinctively rested her head against his chest, trembling.

"Ellie told me what happened," he said softly, his voice deep and sincere. She stepped back, breaking away from the security of his hold. Unable to look at him, she asked,

"What did she say?"

"She told me about Arnhem, about how you broke down," he explained, quietly. Relief swept over her and she silently chastised herself, for even doubting for a second, that Ellie would have said anything more personal or revealing. She sank back down onto one of the seats, prompting Elliot to sit next to her.

"Did you have a good time with her?" she asked tentatively. It felt such an alien thing to ask. Elliot smiled broadly, nodding.

"I'm not allowed to tell you, apparently! Ellie wants to, later," he told her. "She is such a wonderful girl – I know I've already said it," he nodded, "but I can't stop thinking it."

He watched Alice for a moment.

"Do you want to talk about it? Your trip?" he encouraged. She looked down at his hand, resting on the seat next to her, resisting the urge to touch it. Nodding, she then relayed the whole scene of the cemeteries, and how she and her mother had sensed her father there, with them. And the absolute bolt of pain she experienced when she saw the photos being put on her unknown grandfather's grave.

"Just seeing Dad's laughing face, holding Ellie. It suddenly hit me that he's not coming back. And so much time has passed that will never be regained…" she stopped abruptly, needing to check her words before she said too much. She was aching to be in Elliot's arms again; his embrace earlier had made her feel safe and comforted. She was very aware that he was watching her closely.

"Dad was my rock, always there for me. Unjudging and so loving. He absolutely adored Ellie," she laughed fondly. Elliot smiled,

"She clearly adored him too, Alice," he said. "I loved the way she spoke about him today, with such genuine affection. And her nickname for him – Gramps," he chuckled.

"Everybody adored Ellie!" Alice exclaimed, "But especially Dad ... and my grandpa. My goodness, Grandpa worshipped the ground she crawled on. She could do no wrong!" she laughed, her eyes lighting up with happy memories.

"Your grandpa got to meet her?" he wondered curiously, "How did he react to ..." he struggled to find the words without sounding uncouth but Alice knew what he meant.

"He never mentioned it to me. He just showed me unconditional love, and constantly made me feel wanted and valued," she nodded, sniffing back tears again. "He christened her - here - and he couldn't have been more proud to do so."

Elliot breathed deeply, looking away.

"He christened me too," he acknowledged.

"Me too!" Alice replied, then laughingly pointed out that he had, in all fairness, probably christened most of the village.

Elliot cast an eye around the familiar building, evoking childhood memories.

"I had a lot of respect for your grandpa. I used to sing in his choir here, you know," he told her.

"I know, I used to watch you," Alice replied, without thinking.

He looked stunned, then grinned as she turned bright red.

"Well, well, Alice Greene – are you blushing?" he teased. She smiled sheepishly and glanced sideways at him. She liked the fact that he was teasing her, flirting a little with her, and she wanted to respond. Touching his hand lightly, she said,

"If you must know, I used to sneak in to help my mum with the flower displays just so that I could watch *you* doing choir practice," she admitted, laughing at his look of surprise.

He took hold of her hand; she caught her breath quickly.

"I joined the choir for one reason, and that was to catch a glimpse of *you* when you were doing the flowers," he stared at her in disbelief.

"Why did we never tell each other this?" he asked, himself more than her. She felt a warmth in her stomach, she so desperately wanted to reach out to him. Leaning in to his arm, she added,

"Did you ever notice me spectating at all of Andrew's cricket matches, and football matches, that *you* also played in? Even in the rain, did you see me standing on the side-lines, like some soggy fawn?" she wondered. Elliot nodded.

"Well, I'm not a fan of sport and I'm not that devoted to Andrew, however much I love him," she looked at him coyly. Elliot stared at her, stunned, his mind racing. She smirked slightly,

"Well, well, Elliot Barraclough – are you lost for words?" she returned the teasing. This felt dangerous and she loved it!

She gently leant her head on his shoulder for a moment and sighed contentedly. Elliot stared straight ahead, not moving.

"Can I see you again? Next weekend?" he asked quietly. Alice moved slightly to rest her chin on his shoulder, answering,

"Oh, sorry but Ellie's away next weekend. She's going to be gallivanting to and fro quite a bit over the summer, I'm afraid," her voice was soft and regretful.

"I know, she told me. It's you I want to see."

He turned his head so that their noses were almost touching. Alice gulped, as she returned his longing gaze.

"Please, Alice," he urged, "I need to see you."

Suddenly scared by his insistence, Alice looked away and he stood up abruptly. She took his hand and pulled herself up, shakily touching his face.

"What are we doing, Elliot?" her voice was barely audible, "I'm scared we'll end up hurting each other again."

He caught her hand and held it to his mouth as he spoke,

"I can't let you slip away again. Please. Just spend some time with me?" he pleaded urgently.

Moving her hand from his, she slid her arms about his waist and rested her head on his chest again, wanting to sink into his body. Her head was spinning with longing, with the need to be close to him, and recklessness was taking over, pushing aside the creeping fear of more heartbreak. Ellie's words flashed through her mind, 'I think he really, really regrets what he did'.

Alice could feel his quickened heartbeat, and sensed his vulnerability once more. She looked up at him,

"Okay, come to Stratford next weekend. I'll show you the sights," she said brightly, trying to ease the tension.

Elliot put his mouth against her hair,

"You're the only sight I want to see," he whispered, then cupping her face with his hands he looked deep into her eyes. He moved closer; Alice licked her lips nervously, knowing he was about to kiss her. He looked troubled for a fleeting moment, then gently rested his nose against hers, closing his eyes. He spoke against her mouth,

"I'm willing to take that risk of getting hurt again. I have to be with you, Alice."

His mouth briefly touched hers before he muffled a groan, and turning away, lowered his head. He slowly let go of her, running his hand down her arm and with a final squeeze of her hand, he walked away.

Alice stared after him. Her legs felt like they were about to buckle beneath her and a weight spread across her chest. She couldn't will her body to move, to follow him. Instead, she silently watched him leave the building, then sat back down, clutching the edge of the seat. Hot tears spilled down her face as she tried to steady her erratic pulse and control her breathing. Clasping her hands together, she went over his words again in her head, re-living his touch and the way he had looked straight into her very soul, as if he wanted to climb inside to find her.

Dragging her mind back to reality, Alice pulled her phone from her bag and clicked onto Facebook. She typed into the search bar the name she had typed so often over the years, in moments of anguish and a torturous need to know the truth. Mary O'Shea, her old flatmate. The person who had destroyed her heart, her sanity, and her life.

Alice stared at the profile picture, hardly able to breathe. The picture had changed occasionally over time but it still carried the same theme: Elliot and Mary, looking blissfully content, laughing at life.

Flicking off the page, Alice stared once again at the all-knowing crucifix, silently glinting above the altar. It was pretty clear, she determined, that Elliot wanted an affair with her. The irony wasn't lost on her, and she knew she should walk away, forget the past four days, before it was too late. But she didn't want to. She was tired of being afraid. Afraid to live. To love. To need.

Her message alert beeped. She knew who it was from, even before she saw his name on her screen. The message leapt out at her,

'You are my drug xxx E.'

Alice held her phone to her mouth and lightly kissed it, a wanton smile spreading across her face.

Chapter Five

Alice debated sneaking up to her room undetected as she let herself back into the house, but she could hear Ellie's excited chatter emanating from the kitchen and knew she would have to show her face.

"There you are!" Ellie exclaimed, jumping up to greet her. She stopped in her tracks,

"Are you okay, Mum? You look dreadful! What's happened?" she questioned, her face full of concern. Alice managed a watery smile, not quite meeting Ellie's eyes, rubbing her troublesome shoulder. Celia chimed in,

"Your poor mother has pulled a muscle in her shoulder and it's given her such a headache," she explained, coming over to put a consoling arm around Alice and ushering her towards a chair.

"How about a cup of tea before we eat?" she asked sympathetically. There was something in the look she gave Alice that said she knew there was more to it and was trying to divert any more questions from Ellie.

Alice nodded gratefully, and shooting Ellie a look, saw how deflated she seemed. Feeling guilty, she stretched her hand out to Ellie's, smiling expectantly,

"So, how was your day with him?" she asked, patting the adjacent chair. Ellie's face lit up again as she sat next to her and relayed a blow by blow account of her day.

"He has such an awesome job; he works for the York Archaeological Trust as a Project Manager. He travels round quite a bit, visiting places and meeting people, as well as doing research and paperwork stuff. It sounds great, doesn't it?" she said, with a sense of pride.

Alice blinked.

"In York?" she asked in surprise. Ellie nodded,

"Yes, he still lives in York. And he doesn't have any children. Except me that is!" she laughed abruptly.

"How do you know that? Did you ask him?" Alice looked shocked.

"Of course I asked him. I mean, I need to know if I have any siblings knocking about, don't I?" she answered tersely, then softened instantly as she added,

"And guess what? He wants to come with us for my registration day at Uni! How great is that! You can both be there to move me in," she grinned excitedly.

Alice listened to Ellie wax lyrical about her new-found dad for a while longer, then making her excuses and blaming her headache, she escaped to the sanctuary of her room. Or at least, she thought she had, but Celia was hot on her heels, quietly closing the bedroom door behind her.

"Did you see Elliot?" she asked conspiringly, then added, "I told him you had gone for a walk, I hoped he would find you," she smiled gently. Alice nodded,

"Yes, I saw him. We had a talk", she admitted, making a huge effort not to think about him for fear of her true feelings reflecting in her eyes.

"I'm glad you two are working it out. For Ellie, if nothing else."

It was a very leading statement and Celia waited for Alice's response. Alice sank down on the bed eyeing her mother, a little confused as to where this conversation was heading but at the same time, she was desperately needing to talk about it.

"He's married though, Mum," she said heavily. Celia sat down next to her.

"Has he told you that? Has he talked about it?" she asked. Alice shook her head. Celia sighed, deliberating over what she was about to say. She covered Alice's hand with her own and squeezed it in a deeply maternal gesture.

"Don't be so bitter and closed about things, Alice. It's time to let go of that resentment. Allow yourself to move on in life. And work things out between you." She paused for a moment, lowering her tone,

"I'm glad he knows about Ellie, I always felt it was wrong to keep it a secret from him," she confessed.

Alice stared at her, completely taken aback. "Why didn't you say anything? And why are you saying this now?" she beseeched. Celia looked away for a moment, perturbed.

"Roz felt, at the time, that it was for the best," she divulged, "but Roz is very headstrong and determined in life and I have come to realise that her strength, as I thought it was, has in fact, blinded her to things."

Celia thought she would feel disloyal talking like this but it was actually a relief to voice her thoughts so honestly. She continued,

"If the truth be told, I have always been a bit jealous of your relationship with her - not that I felt replaced as a mother - just that I have missed out on that kind of closeness with you." She smiled nervously at Alice's astonished face.

"Oh, Mum!" Alice threw her arms about her mother's neck.

"I had no idea that's how you felt," she uttered, full of dismay. "Why have you never told me any of this?" she sniffed. Celia shrugged, not sure herself. There had never been a right time to confront the issues in her head, to air her innermost thoughts. And she was worried about upsetting the applecart; it was easier to just go along with Roz's scheme of things.

They sat in reflective silence for a minute, then Celia spoke again, her tone careful and measured.

"I do wonder if Roz's judgment of everything that went on with you, was clouded by her own mistakes. She should have let us tell Elliot, rather than shut him out like that. Even if he had done you wrong by carrying on with somebody else, he still deserved to know." She looked intently at her daughter, fighting back tears of regret. Alice suddenly looked vulnerable and so childlike and it hit home once again how time had flown by. It didn't seem that long ago that she was, in fact, a little girl needing a comforting hug from her mother.

Alice watched her mother's thought process flit across her face and knew she wanted to say more but was holding back.

"Mum?" she prompted.
Celia stared at her for a moment, hesitantly. She shook her head.

"Nothing, dear. It's just … I think he genuinely loved you. I really do. Just bear that in mind," Celia emphasized, kissing her cheek before standing up to leave the room.

"Get some sleep, you look shattered. I think we all are," she remarked.

Alice fell back against her pillows, listening to her mother's footsteps going back down the stairs. She stared at the ceiling, trying to take everything in. In just four days, her steadfast, comfortable world had been turned upside down and inside out. That chance meeting with Elliot had set off a chain reaction of such breath-taking magnitude, and now nothing would ever be the same again.

Her phone beeped. It was Elliot again.

'Next weekend? xxx E.'

She closed her eyes, reliving the moment when he had wanted to kiss her; she could still feel the heat from his breath against her mouth. Try as she might, she couldn't deny the effect he was having on her. That same, giddy teenage yearning she'd had for him hadn't subsided. That excited hunger for a first love affair was reigniting; memories of their heady relationship filled her jumbled mind, and fuelled a flickering heat in her stomach.

And yet, she knew it was wrong. Ellie was just coming to terms with finding out who her father was; if Alice had an affair with him and Ellie found out, it could devastate her. Elliot was married. He had destroyed her once before – why would this be any different? In fact, there was the potential to be hurt on a much deeper level now.

She got up from her bed and paced the room, tapping her phone against her chin in an effort to focus her thoughts. Stopping by her dresser, she sat down on the padded stool and stared at her reflection in the oval mirror. She touched her cheek where Elliot's hand had been just an hour previously, recalling the potent mixture of desire and uncertainty in his eyes. Her mind flitted to her conversation with her mother, still confused by its content. There was so much doubt brewing in her mind now, so many 'what if's. And the one screaming certainty: life does not have a pause or re-wind button, it just keeps moving forward. You either jump on-board or you miss the ride.

Alice read the text again, knowing the hidden meaning behind the question.

"You're standing at the crossroad, girl," she told herself, "this is it – make or break time."

Her heart started to flutter at the thought of what she was about to do. She quickly texted her reply and pressed 'send',

'Yes. Definitely xxx A.'

Ellie woke Alice up the next morning, gently shaking her and proffering a cup of tea.

"Feeling any better?" she asked quietly. Alice nodded.

"Yes, thanks. I'm sorry about last night, I really didn't feel well," she admitted, smiling her appreciation of the hot tea. Ellie sat cross legged on the bed, running a hand through her curly hair to move her long fringe away from her face.

"I didn't say anything last night but Dad asked quite a few questions about you. Not in a prying way," she added quickly, "but he seemed ever so impressed with what you have achieved in life. He was really chuffed about your job, he said you'd always wanted to be an English teacher, like Gramps. And he told me," she looked a little shy at what she was about to divulge, "that you were always quoting poetry to him and writing out sonnets that you stuck on his kitchen wall, insisting he should memorise them! Is that true?" she laughed. Alice laughed too, the memory replaying in her mind.

"Oh my goodness, I had forgotten that!" she exclaimed, suddenly aware of how many happy, incidental memories she had pushed to the back of her mind. She eyed Ellie curiously,

"What else did he tell you?" she asked. Ellie shrugged,

"Nothing much really; he was very aware, I think, of not bombarding me. He really made an effort to get to know me, asking lots of questions, like, my plans for the future, and where we lived. What my childhood had been like. Stuff like that really," she nodded happily, smoothing down the duvet cover as she spoke. She lowered her voice to a whisper,

"I felt really guilty last night, talking about him. I was just so conscious of Auntie Roz and what she must be going through," Ellie confided, watching her mother's reaction. Alice widened her eyes in agreement.

"Yes. It's been a bit full-on, hasn't it," she agreed. "Listen Ellie, I know we've avoided the subject over the years and maybe I was wrong to, I don't know, but," she paused, reaching for Ellie's hand,

"I am really happy for you that you are getting to know your father. It's a lot for me to get my head round but I think we'll cope," she said. "However, we do need to be careful with Roz. I think she is about to undertake a very painful journey," she acknowledged.

Ellie crawled across to the top of the bed and slid under the duvet to snuggle in with Alice.

"I do love you, Mum. And I know it's hard for you, all this, but I do hope you and my dad can build some kind of relationship. Put the past behind you. I think you two would get on now," she grinned.

Alice could feel herself starting to blush, and judging by the way Ellie was looking at her, she had noted it too.

"He didn't mention his wife at all," Ellie added pointedly, "although that would've been a bit weird, I suppose," she said.

Alice cleared her throat and moving slightly, said,

"Right Ellie-kins, time to start the day. And it's going to be a long one I suspect."

As they left the room, Alice's phone beeped. She grabbed it from the side and dropped it into her dressing gown pocket. Ellie appeared not to notice but as they walked down the stairs, she asked casually,

"Was that a text from my dad?"

Alice started, feeling intensely guilty. She made a point of not looking at her phone.

"Why would it be?" she wanted to know, her voice a little strangulated. Ellie looked surprised at her tone.

"I just thought he might've texted you to say what a great day he'd had with me!" she smiled brightly yet her intuitive eyes were watching Alice keenly.

"He texted *me* to say that," Ellie continued, "And to say he got back to York safely."

Alice drew in a shaky breath. That answered the question of whether he was still in Brockenhurst. She relaxed a little knowing this; his proximity made it difficult for her to think clearly, and disturbed her in a way that she hadn't experienced for many years.

Alice slipped out through the kitchen door into the garden, automatically heading for the tranquillity of the old swing seat. She read the text from Elliot,

'Morning you. Am I dreaming? Is this really happening? xxx E.'

She smiled reflectively as another buried memory resurfaced. She could hear his sleepy greeting of old like it was only yesterday, remembering how he would wake her in the mornings by stroking her face and murmuring, 'morning you'. He had always looked at her as if he couldn't quite believe his luck that she was lying next to him. Equally, she couldn't quite believe her luck that he was looking at her like that.

She stared out across the garden, troubled by her thoughts. These pushed-aside memories that were popping back up at an alarming rate were making it difficult for her to distinguish between the past and the present. Was she dealing with an Elliot from the past, wanting to recapture their youth? Or an Elliot from the present, wanting to build a new relationship despite their impossible situation? How could it last and how on earth could it ever work? There was only one way to find out, she determined. She texted her reply, echoing his sentiment by using her old response,

'Morning you too xxx A.'

As soon as she had sent it, she typed another text,

'If it is a dream, then I'm dreaming it with you xxx A'.

Taking a deep breath, she put her phone back in her pocket. She needed to shift her focus to Roz and try not to linger on the thought of Elliot, however hard that may be. She was also acutely aware that Ellie was watching her whenever Elliot was mentioned, assessing her reaction. Alice snorted a little laugh. The last thing she and Elliot needed was a match maker – especially one that was their daughter.

"Oh, what a tangled web we weave, when first we practice to deceive!" she recited out loud as she headed back towards the house, where Roz was watching her thoughtfully from the kitchen window.

"Right then," Alice said purposefully as, two hours later, she sat in front of the computer in her father's old study. Ellie, Celia, and Roz sat in a semi-circle around the desk, staring at the screen expectantly.

"I'm not entirely sure how to start a search so let's just go with this," Alice said, clicking on to google and typing in, 'tracing a child I put up for adoption in 1969'.

Eleven links popped up and she opened up new tabs to take a brief look at each of them and in so doing, eliminated four of the non-relevant links. Turning to Roz, she smiled encouragingly.

"Ready?" she asked. Roz nodded, staring fixedly at the screen. Alice opened up the first tab, Missing You.net. After a quick peruse she said,

"Okay, this is like a search page for people, not just adopted ones but anybody that's lost contact. It looks like you type in a name to search for details or you can leave a message. So, we'll hang on to this page and have a proper look later. Next one," she continued, clicking on to the next tab, "is Adoption Register.com," she scanned the page, nodding her head.

"Okay, this has links to addresses, emails and other web sites for both adopted children and parents who put up a child for adoption. So, keep this one open too and we'll have a more detailed look in a minute. Next," she glanced at Roz to give a supportive smile, "is Adoption Stories: 'the pain of giving up a baby'..." Alice paused, reading on silently. Celia and Ellie leant forward to also read.

A tangible tension filled the room as they became more absorbed by the content and not able to stand it, Roz got up abruptly and left the room. The other three barely noticed her leave as Alice scrolled down the page and they continued to read. Coming to the end, Ellie stretched across the desk and clicked on to the next tab, all about mother and baby homes in the 1960s. As she navigated the site, dated black and white photos leapt out at them, young faces burdened with untold secrets yet smiling for the camera. A nurse holding two babies, one in each arm. A sterile row of cots with pale mothers peering anxiously at them.

Ellie turned to Alice and Celia,

"Is this what Roz went through do you think? I thought she gave up her baby at birth but it says here, that by law, babies stayed with their mums for six weeks. Six weeks! And *then* they had to give them up. That's just barbaric!"

Celia looked at Alice, a heavy sadness in her eyes.

"We have to ask her. Don't we? Should we?" she sounded pensive, unsure of their next move. Ellie stood up, peering through the window at the garden beyond. She could see Roz sitting under the shade of the parasol.

"Yes, we need to know. How else can we help her? And all of these secrets have to stop!" she insisted firmly, heading for the door.

The three of them silently joined Roz under the parasol, Celia carrying a tray laden with tea and biscuits, which she carefully placed on the mahogany, slatted table. She sat herself next to Roz and taking her hand, looked in earnest at her.

"Roz, for us to be able to help you find Cee-Cee, we need to know what happened, where you were and how she was adopted. Can you tell us? I mean, are you able to share some of it with us? We're not here to judge you, just to help you," she emphasised. Alice and Ellie nodded their agreement. For a moment, Roz looked annoyed at having her hand forced, and turned away, not knowing what to say. She cleared her throat before speaking, still staring across the garden,

"Talking about it makes it real. I don't want it to be real. I don't want to remember what I did or what I went through," she uttered defensively.

"But Auntie Roz, if we are going to look for her then surely *that* is making it real. And it would help you, to talk about it. To come to terms with it. I know if I were you, it would help me to face it," Ellie encouraged sincerely. Roz turned to her,

"The difference is, Ellie, if you were pregnant now, nobody would bat an eyelid. I bet Mrs Shillingstone in the post office would even start knitting bootees for you! People would greet you in the street and ask how you're doing, how the baby's coming along. They would treat you with kindness, and respect you for carrying a new life.

They would even congratulate your mother on becoming a grandmother. In my day, when it happened to me, that kind of reception was so far removed from my reality. You have no idea!" Her eyes flashed angrily as she spoke. Ellie wasn't deterred.

"Then tell me what it was like. For you. What happened to you?" she insisted.

Roz snorted with exasperation, her shoulders slumped and she rested her head in her hands, elbows propped up on the table. Nobody moved, they waited patiently for her to speak. They were quickly becoming experts at listening to confessions and knew how to encourage and coax out the truth from each other. A mixture of wise words, youthful insistence, and sympathetic ears were what was called for and between them, and they had those in abundance.

"I was already three months pregnant by the time I realised what was happening. I'd had my suspicions but tried to ignore it until one day, I was so very sick at work. My boss was lovely, I remember he ushered me upstairs to their flat above the gallery, and his wife Melanie took one look at me and insisted I lay down to rest. She knew. And then I knew, just by the way she was looking at me. Anyway, she had a friend whose husband was a doctor. He came out to examine me, unofficially, as a favour to her. He was actually very sympathetic and told me my options, as tactfully as he could."

Roz looked up to accept the offered cup of tea from Celia. She absent-mindedly stirred it as she ruminated over her next words.

"I say 'options' but there was really only one feasible one. He mentioned gin and hot baths but couldn't advocate it. He asked if there was any chance that the father would marry me. His face was a picture when I flippantly said, 'I don't think his wife would be impressed'. And so, the only course of action was adoption; he recommended I went to my own family doctor and be assigned to a social worker, who would then arrange everything. So, I went home, told Celia all about it and I honestly thought I would be strong enough to tell David, and we could face it together. But in my determination, I had overlooked his father," she paused to sip at her tea, pointedly avoiding eye contact with any of them.

"He scared me. I knew he had the ability to destroy us all. He was so full of hate and self-importance. I knew I had to get away. So, I took my savings and went to France, travelling round all the arty places, just like I had always planned to. I stayed there for nearly two months, by which time I was really starting to show, so I headed back to England. I went to Newlyn in Cornwall and lodged with an artist there. She was very supportive, asked no questions, you know, a very liberal kind of woman. When the time came, I was booked in to a mother and baby home in St Austell, on the other side of Cornwall and miles away from anybody I knew. And that's when it all became very real, very final."

Nobody spoke as Roz took another drink of tea. It felt like an age before she continued.

"The more pregnant I became, the more connected I felt with the little life growing inside me and I couldn't imagine being parted from her. It filled me with absolute panic and I felt completely trapped. I knew I had burnt my bridges by leaving home, by leaving David, without any warning. I knew I couldn't go back to him. I had deceived him and returning home, in my condition, would be catastrophic for everybody. The shame we were made to feel, the other mothers and I, weighed down on me, crushing my spirit. I spent six weeks, before she was born, in that infernal hell hole, having my soul destroyed. Every Sunday we were marched to church to repent our sins and every Sunday, I was reminded of how I had let Daddy down. We were never allowed in the front pews - I had *always* sat in the front pews at home - we had to sit at the back of the church so that our presence didn't offend the locals. It crucified me, it really did. I thought it couldn't get any worse: the shame, the guilt, the panic of not being in control. And then Cee-Cee was born."

    Roz fell silent once more, memories of the suffocating fear she had endured during labour and giving birth, stopped her from speaking. She had been left all alone in the delivery room until the very last minute, without any pain relief and without any real knowledge of what to expect or what to do. An ache gripped at her heart as she remembered the sound of her baby taking her first gasp of air, filling her lungs before letting out a bleating cry. Roz had instinctively reached her arms out to the nurse holding her precious little bundle, but the nurse turned smartly on her heel, without a word to Roz, and left the room with the crying baby. The other staff also quickly dispersed, leaving her alone again. Dazed, in pain and cruelly bereft, she wept into her pillow. Her silent tears turned to gut-wrenching sobs, thunder crashing in her head as she tried to get to grips with what was happening to her, and her body shook as the unbearable reality sank in.

"If they had taken her away forever, right there and then, I think I would have wanted to die but what actually happened was so much worse, in fact. So much worse," she uttered, biting her lip in an attempt to stop the tears.

"I didn't see her for the first two hours; she was taken straight to the nursery. They made it clear to me that I was allowed to see her for feeds and to bathe her. They taught me how to change her, but anything more than that was not permitted. I wasn't allowed to just wander in and pick her up for a cuddle at whim; contact was restricted to feeding time and that was rigidly timetabled. There was always a nurse there to supervise, watching over us like a disapproving hawk. I was told from the onset that I was to breast feed her, it was best for baby. We all had to. I remember some of the girls were scared to but for me, it was my one chance to feel worthwhile. The first time that I held her close and she latched on, was the most incredible feeling in the world. It hurt so much, the pain tugged at my stomach, it actually took my breath away but it was a strangely wonderful kind of pain. In that moment, I truly felt like her mother, like she was a part of me again, outside of the womb. A part of *me*. Nobody else. She was my baby and she needed me, as much as I needed her. That's when I decided I couldn't give her up, I needed to find a way to keep her with me."

"I dared to voice my thoughts to the social worker when she came to see me in the second week, but she dismissed me completely. 'The best thing for baby is to be in a stable family with a home and two parents to look after her. You need to put this mistake behind you and get on with your life', was all she had to say on the matter. But I wouldn't accept that my baby was a mistake, so I persevered. I put adverts in magazines and applied for live-in jobs, anything I could find, but just got rejections. Nobody wanted to employ me with a baby in tow. It was a hopeless situation and I felt completely powerless."

Roz leant back in her chair and sighed heavily, the recollection of that feeling engulfing her once again.

"The six weeks prior to Cee-Cee's birth seemed to drag on for an eternity but the next six weeks just flew by. I treasured every minute, I just couldn't get enough of her. I would go to bed counting the hours until the morning feed when I would be allowed to hold her again. I stared at her incessantly, memorising every inch of her, not wanting to ever forget any of it. She had David's eyes and thick, black eye lashes, and my nose and mouth. She had a full head of black, curly hair - everybody remarked on it - and such a beautiful, chubby face. Her hands were so tiny but she had such a strong grip when she held my finger, or clung to the hem of my top as I held her to feed from me. And as much as I stared at her, she stared back, burning into my heart. She trusted me, I knew that. She trusted me to always love her and I told her, over and over, that I always would."

"And then the day came. I clung to her, hoping, right up to the last minute, that something miraculous would happen so that I could keep her with me. But nothing did. I cried, I pleaded, I begged ... but they took her anyway. She could sense my distress and started to cry too. I could hear her crying as they walked down the corridor with her. I had been told, under no circumstance was I to leave the room, until somebody said I could. I ran to the window and caught a final glimpse of her. A woman was carrying her, carefully but quickly, towards a black car. There was a tall man walking with her. Then they got into the car and drove away, and she was gone. Gone forever. I wanted to jump out of the window after her but it was shut tight. I wouldn't have had the strength to anyway. My reason for living had gone and I had nothing left, I was completely drained, empty. And after all that, I was told to get my things together; it was time for me to leave the home and get on with my life. And all I could think was, what life?"

Celia was holding Roz's hand, squeezing it comfortingly.

"I'm so sorry Roz, I wish I had known," she muttered regretfully. Roz looked at Ellie, her voice challenging,

"Is that what you wanted to hear, Ellie?"
Ellie nodded, not fazed by her aunt, returning the defiant look.

"Yes, it is. And now you know how much this is going to affect you. I want you to realise that you have to confront the past if you want to chase the present. Because if you don't, you'll go in to this blind and that could be devastating for you," she grimaced sympathetically, "I just want to help you. We all do. But it's not like looking up an old school friend on Facebook. This is life changing," she emphasised. "Trust me, I know!" she laughed pointedly, inclining her head towards Alice. Celia tutted in agreement.

"Yes, we seem to have a habit of dropping bombshells of late, don't we?" she remarked drily.

Roz stood up, quickly gathering the cups together onto the tray and headed for the kitchen with it, muttering her intention of refreshing the pot. Ellie offered to help, following behind her. Alice went to move but Celia put a hand on her arm,

"Leave them to it for a bit, dear. Let them talk. I think Ellie is looking at this from a prospective that we can't possibly understand," she acknowledged gently.

Alice sat back down, frowning.

"Do you think Ellie is angry with me, Mum? I mean, it didn't take much effort to tell her about Elliot after all; do you think she resents me for harbouring my secret for so long? For not involving Elliot in her life sooner?" she asked pensively. Celia shrugged,

"Only time will tell, dear. Let her get used to it all in her own way, that's my advice."

She looked towards the house thoughtfully.

"Roz took a huge step yesterday," she confided, "she went to visit David's grave for the first time ever, so she is very low and vulnerable right now. And of course, today's confession has just added to that. She's been in denial for so long, it's almost impossible to face up to it all, but she needs to find a way to do so. I just hope she does."

Ellie filled the kettle and turned to Roz,

"I'm sorry, Auntie Roz, I don't mean to sound so harsh but if the past few days have taught me anything, it's how many secrets and lies have been kept for far too long, without any thought of who they affect. I have waited *so long* to find out who my father is, wondering what he would be like. I'd fantasise that he'd come and find me, treat me like a princess and be so remorseful that he'd not been there for me. But now I find out that he didn't even know about me – I never knew that. I had always thought that he'd married somebody else and didn't have room for me in his life. I have so many mixed emotions right now: I feel absolutely elated to have finally found out who he is and he is so lovely, everything I dreamt of, and more, really. And then I feel this burning sense of betrayal by you all - I am so angry - how could you have known all this time and not once thought I had the right to know too? I have been old enough to make my own mind up for a while now, you know. I should've been given the chance to decide for myself if I wanted him in my life, despite everything he did to Mum," she declared passionately. "And I feel like I've been cheated of him during my childhood. It's one thing getting to know him now but I really wish he'd been around to see me grow up. I know he regrets it too, missing out on so much and not even knowing about me."

"And then," she sighed, her voice dropping a notch, "and then I'm wracked with guilt for even being angry with Mum, after everything that she has been through because of me. I know she wanted to protect me, and I know that he was an absolute pig, putting it mildly, for what he did to her, but the decisions you three made, before I was even born, have had such an impact on my life, and on my dad's. And that can never be redressed. We can't turn back the clock and do it all again differently." Ellie reached forward and held Roz's arm to emphasize her next point,

"You have to realise that your decisions, and the consequences of those decisions, have affected so many people. I know I was the one blabbing on about finding Cee-Cee but I think I was on a high from my own news about my dad. Now that I've had time to let it sink in, I have to tell you, it's not a clean cut, romantic, happy-ever-after, you know. You may find a wounded soul, you may even find she doesn't actually know that she's adopted or worse, that she does know but doesn't want to know you. Have you considered that? Because you really should," she stressed.

Roz stared at Ellie, stunned by her outburst and honesty.

"When did this happen, Ellie? How did you become so wise and mature, right under my very nose?" she smiled awkwardly, giving her a hug.

"Growing up with you and Mum has made me old before my time, I guess," she teased. "To be honest, I think studying History and Psychology has encouraged me to think about cause and effect on a different level: it's made me realise that the consequences of our actions determine our future. I think the only way forward now, for us as a family, is to own up to the past and admit our mistakes. That way, we'll be stronger to tackle the future. I am here to help you, I just think it's going to be an emotional time, and you need to be prepared for that. That's all I am trying to say," she concluded, stacking fresh cups onto the tray next to the teapot.

Roz laughed,

"Oh, that's all you're trying to say, is it?" she retorted. She tenderly stroked Ellie's hair,

"Thank you, Ellie-kins, I really am grateful," she said softly, "thank you for making me talk and open up about it. It has helped. You were right," she smiled.

"I was, wasn't I!" Ellie agreed triumphantly.

"But don't let that go to your head, young lady!" Roz laughed, as Ellie picked up the tray and swanned out to the garden, head held high in mock pride.

The next hour was more relaxed as the four of them sat under the parasol, discussing the information they had read on the internet about adoption and the reunification of birth mothers and their children. Roz elaborated on her account of life in the mother and baby home, and how she had always been led to believe that she would not be allowed to search for her child. She had not had access to a camera, none of the girls had, so there were no photos of their babies. But she did have something better, to remind her of Cee-Cee.

"I painted her. So many different portraits, from all angles. I secretly sketched her when she was in the nursery, and once I had left the home, I used those sketches, and my memories of her, to paint the portraits. It was strangely cathartic; I was terrified of forgetting her and so I had to record every little detail. It helped to keep her alive, close to me, in my head," she confessed reflectively. Ellie looked curious.

"I've never seen any of them, have I?" she asked. Roz shook her head.

"No. At first, looking at them helped me to stay focused and start to rebuild my life; the thought of maybe getting her back fuelled my drive to make something of myself, to build a home for us. But as time went by, I realised that was a futile aim, a dream that would never be realised. So, I had to box them all away. It became too painful to be reminded of her," she acknowledged with melancholy smile. She regarded Ellie thoughtfully, then said,

"Sometimes the pain of wanting something or someone so desperately, can spur you on because you know there is the possibility that one day, you will get what you want. Your dream may become a reality. But I knew that Cee-Cee had gone and however much I missed her, I knew that she wouldn't be missing me, because she didn't know me. I think that's why," she continued, turning to Celia, "I could never accept or acknowledge that David had gone. The thought that we would be together again one day was the only thing keeping me alive, and the only way I could cope with the loss of Cee-Cee. But now that I have finally allowed myself to admit he's gone, forever, I have this desperate need to find her. I don't think I can rest until I do," she declared.

Chapter Six

Later that evening, as the four of them sat round the kitchen table finishing their meal, they went over their plans for the coming weeks over the summer. Alice was taking Ellie to Andrew's the following day, before returning to Stratford-Upon-Avon for a faculty meeting – the last one before she could really switch off from work for the summer break. Andrew had volunteered to take Ellie and his three children to Camp Bestival at Lulworth Castle, in Dorset, over the weekend and Ellie would be staying there until the following Wednesday. Rachel was only a year older than Ellie and they had always been very close cousins, sharing the same tastes in music and fashion, often going to gigs together. The boys were younger: Scott was aged fifteen and Riley twelve, and although keen campers, they were about to experience their first music festival and all the excitement that went with it.

"I think Andrew is actually more excited than all of them put together!" Alice laughed, relaying the conversation she had had with him about it at Ellie's party.

"I wish you and Auntie Laura were coming too." Ellie feigned a child-like sulk. Alice smiled apologetically,

"Sorry Ellie, you know we both have to work. We'll all be together next week for Andrew's birthday though. You'll just have to look after your uncle by yourselves this weekend," she winked mischievously. Ellie groaned, then gasped at a sudden thought.

"Oh, I know: why don't I ask my dad to come with us? He and Uncle Andrew used to be really good friends, didn't they? They could have a great time catching up!" she gushed, her eyes sparkling at her own idea. She looked expectantly at Alice.

"Oh, I'm sure he's busy this weekend and besides, I doubt he could get a ticket at this late stage," Alice reasoned quickly, trying not to look guilty. Ellie frowned at her.

"How do you know he's busy?" she retorted, frustrated that her impulsive idea was being dismissed and not likely to be a fruitful one.

Alice blinked, trying to think of an answer.

"Well, I don't know but ... tickets, Ellie? That's going to be impossible, you know it is," she countered. Ellie sighed heavily, admitting defeat begrudgingly.

"It was a lovely idea though," Celia interjected kindly, "maybe you could plan something else to do with him, dear. That would give you both something to look forward to," she suggested.

"Good idea, Mum", Alice agreed before deftly changing the subject.

"Roz, have you had any further thoughts on how to proceed with the search? Shall we have a look in the morning before I leave?" she proposed.

Roz sighed thoughtfully, running a finger around the rim of her empty plate. She felt drained. The day had been yet another emotional rollercoaster ride and she felt spent to her very core. She squinted at Alice, uncertainty emanating from her eyes.

"Let's see how things are in the morning, shall we? I think I might need a day or two to mull things over. It's not something to rush or take lightly," she acknowledged, glancing across at Ellie, their earlier conversation playing on her mind.

"But only this afternoon you said you were desperate to find her," Alice insisted, feeling confused by her sudden change of heart.

"I am, Alice. I am. But I'm also scared," she stated bluntly, getting up from the table and stacking the dirty plates together, shaking her head at Celia's offer of help. Sensing Alice was watching her, she looked up abruptly,

"You've all been badgering me today but you just won't give up, will you? Why don't you just drop it, Alice!" she snapped aggressively. Alice immediately backed down,

"Of course. I'm sorry. I didn't mean to push you," she apologised quickly, looking towards Celia and Ellie for support. Ellie was scrolling through her phone, seemingly oblivious to the conversation but Alice could see by her fixed expression that she was just using it as a shield. Celia went over to the sink and picked up a damp cloth to wipe down the table.

"I think we could all do with an early night again. I'm exhausted, aren't you?" she pointedly asked Alice. Taking her lead, Alice nodded. Feeling superfluous as her mother and aunt cleared away, she made her excuses and headed upstairs under the pretext of giving Andrew a quick call to confirm arrangements.

She picked up her phone where she had left it on her bed and saw there was a text from Elliot. It had been sent over an hour ago.

'Text me when you're free xxx E.'

She sat down heavily on her bed, a sudden urge to cry engulfing her as she stared at her phone. It wasn't sadness she was feeling, far from it. She had such butterflies in her stomach that she felt she was in a permanent state of wanting to be sick. With nerves. With excitement. With the knowledge that there was no going back now that Elliot knew about his daughter. The relief she felt, having unburdened the secret she had been carrying for eighteen years, combined with the prospect of a future that would involve Elliot - in whatever capacity - was exhilarating.

She typed a quick reply,

'Sorry, long day. I've only just seen your text. I'm free now xxx A.'

She didn't have to wait long for a response. It wasn't quite what she was expecting and a slight gasp escaped her lips as she read it.

'When you said you used to watch me in choir, did you mean it? xxx E.'

Alice smiled as she remembered his stunned expression the previous evening.

'Yes I did. But I didn't think you noticed me. You were my first crush xxx A.'

She laughed lightly as she sent it, anticipating his reaction.

'Really? Since when? xxx E.'

Her smile getting wider, she typed,

'Since forever xxx A.'

Biting her bottom lip a little, she waited for his reply.

'Why didn't you ever let me know? xxx E.'

Chuckling, she swiftly sent a response,

'I think I did when I followed you to York! xxx A.'

She was enjoying teasing him, hinting at the memory of their first night together. His response was instant,

'You followed me??'

Alice stopped still, realising what she had done. She hadn't meant to tell him that, how she had planned to find him in York; not a chance meeting as he had always thought.

'Alice??'

She stared at her phone, hardly breathing. His text seemed abrupt, was he angry with her? Just then, her phone rang. It was Elliot. Taking a steadying breath, she answered quietly,

"Hello?"

"What does that mean? You followed me?", his voice sounded urgent, confused. Alice breathed out sharply,

"I'm sorry, I didn't mean to … I shouldn't have said that. Just … just ignore it, please," she tried to sound dismissive but he persisted.

"Alice, I think we're past the stage of just ignoring things. I'm not going to ignore anything else. I want to know what you mean by that," he insisted.

Alice was silent, uncertain of what to say. It should have been easy to talk to a faceless phone but she could visualise his face so clearly, and he sounded so close, his deep voice resonating in her ear.

"Alice?" he prompted softly, sensing her reluctance.

She closed her eyes tightly and rubbed her forehead in a bid to focus her thoughts.

"Yes. Yes, I followed you," she sighed as she spoke. It was Elliot's turn to fall silent. She continued,

"When Andrew told me you had been accepted at York, I set my heart on going there. I had this crazy obsession with you," she laughed nervously, "but it all happened so quickly. I didn't expect that. I'd planned to go there, build up my confidence and re-invent myself. Then I was going to find you and impress you. But even before I had a chance to do any of that, we just clicked and … had that amazing first night," her voice wavered slightly. "That was my first kiss, you know, not just my first time," she confessed in a hushed voice. Elliot didn't speak but she knew he was listening intently. She moved from her bed and sat at the dressing table, studying her reflection as she continued,

"And it just carried on being amazing. That's when I realised I didn't actually need to re-invent myself because you didn't know me before that night, and I was obviously what you wanted. Or so I thought." She held her breath, waiting for his reply. She could hear the smile in his voice as he spoke,

"You were. You are," he emphasised. "And for the record, I wasn't in the habit of picking up young girls in pubs and getting them drunk before whisking them back to my place," he added lightly, eliciting a laugh from her.

"I knew who you were Alice, of course I did. And I couldn't believe my luck that night. You were the one I had been waiting for," he said, the warmth and depth of emotion in his voice making the back of her neck tingle.

They both fell silent, taking in the measure of their confessions.

"I mean, I'd been sitting at that bar for best part of a year, waiting! So, it's a good job you came along when you did," he joked in a bid to break the tension. She chuckled then said,

"I didn't tell you because I didn't want you to pity me."

"Pity you?" he sounded puzzled.

"Yes, well, I chased half way across the country and threw myself at you at the first opportunity. It does smack of desperation; don't you think?" she pointed out. Elliot laughed softly.

"Well if you think that's bad, have pity on me; the sleazy Lothario hanging out in bars preying on the Freshers students," he mocked. Alice laughed out loud at the ridiculous imagery.

"Oh, Alice," he sighed heavily, "where did it go wrong?" Alice caught her breath. How should she respond to that? Opting to side step his question, she asked,

"Would it have made a difference? If you had known I'd gone to York because of you, I mean?"

Elliot thought about it for a brief moment.

"It would to me, yes," he told her decisively.

Just then, she heard footsteps across the landing. Recognising them as Ellie's, she whispered down the phone,

"I have to go, sorry. I'll text you later," she said as she hung up.

Ellie opened the door and smiled awkwardly, mumbling,

"Can I have a hug, Mum?"

She had changed into her pyjamas and pulled her hair away from her forehead, scraping it up on the sides into a messy top knot, revealing a shiny, freshly scrubbed face. Alice noted her sad expression.

"Okay?" she asked, standing up and holding her arms out. Ellie hurried over and snuggled in to Alice's embrace.

"Grandma and Auntie Roz are talking outside. I don't think they wanted me to hear anything," she told Alice. "Auntie Roz doesn't seem to be handling it all that well tonight, does she?" she noted. Alice agreed.

"Are you okay? Do you want to talk?" she asked gently. Ellie sniffed and shook her head.

"Not really, I just want a hug. There's so much to take in and my mind is buzzing," she admitted. They sat down on the bed and after a few minutes, Ellie brought her legs up and swung round to rest her head on her mother's lap. Alice stroked her back rhythmically, silently watching her as she drifted off to sleep.

Celia and Roz sat side by side on the patio chairs, each with a soft, woollen throw wrapped around their shoulders to protect them from the late-night chill. The silence was punctuated only by a solitary blackbird practicing his nocturnal repertoire, perched high above in the silver birch tree.

"Can I offer you some advice?" Celia ventured gingerly. Roz snorted.

"I have a feeling you're going to anyway, regardless of what I say," she scoffed, fixing her eyes on her younger sister. Celia gave a brief smile, ignoring the gibe.

"You need to allow yourself time to deal with all of this. You're grieving..."

"You don't say!" Roz interrupted sarcastically.

Celia straightened up in her chair, looking away. She very rarely let anything rile her but this was hitting a nerve and she felt unusually angry with Roz; a feeling she was trying desperately to curb.

"Roz, will you just listen to me for once! You have spent a lifetime telling me what to do, it's about time you let me return the favour," she insisted, her voice raised slightly. Not giving Roz a chance to respond, she continued talking,

"What you have been through this week is huge. You have finally confronted David's death and relived the absolute agony of not just giving birth to, but giving up, your little girl. Don't underestimate the emotional impact of that; it's going to hit you right between the eyes and knock you sideways. The crippling realisation that nothing, absolutely nothing, can ever change what has happened will make you so angry and resentful. But you cannot take it out on us, on the ones trying to support you and help you through this."

She met Roz's challenging expression unflinchingly. Roz didn't hesitate with her response.

"But if you know that I will be experiencing anger and grief, they surely you should all accept that. If you are, as you say, supporting me," she retorted. Celia widened her eyes, stunned at how selfish Roz was sounding.

"We *are* supporting you but it works both ways Roz! You need to understand what Ellie is going through right now too. She's coming to terms with finding out who her father is, and all the emotions that go with it," she urged. Roz nodded,

"I do understand and we had a talk about it, so I am trying to be supportive," she insisted defensively.

"You also need to bear in mind what Alice is going through. She's having to deal with Ellie's reactions and with her own feelings at seeing Elliot again after all this time, and telling him he has a daughter," Celia added.

"But he's still alive. She'll be fine," Roz snapped. Celia faltered,

"Is that what this is all about – you're jealous because, unlike David, Elliot is still alive and there is a chance for them?" she asked in disbelief.

"Don't be ridiculous!" Roz refuted hotly, "and besides, he's married so there isn't much chance is there?" She stared angrily into the descending darkness that engulfed the garden.

Stunned into silence, Celia regarded Roz's profile with a sense of creeping disappointment and anguish.

"But it was you and I that ruined their chances," she voiced quietly. "If he had known about the baby, he would've come back. I know he would. *We* were responsible for that; we deprived them all of each other."

Roz turned back to Celia, agitated by what she had said.

"Well it's in the past now, isn't it. Just leave it, Celia," she insisted firmly. Celia didn't stop there.

"But don't you feel even a little bit guilty about it? Because I certainly do. I can't sleep, thinking about it, regretting it," her voice cracked with emotion. "We didn't think of the bigger picture. It wasn't just about Alice, was it?"

Roz raised questioning eyebrows, resigning herself to the fact that Celia would not stop until she had said everything she needed to.

"I will always be grieving for Reggie, every day of my life. But I know he's gone and I have to live with that. We had a wonderful life together, we were truly blessed and I have all those memories to keep him alive. And in a strange way, it gives me strength knowing that I'm not the only one missing him. He was a father, a grandfather, a brother, a brother-in-law," she indicated towards Roz, "as well as a husband. He wasn't exclusively mine."

"And I can't help feeling a little bit panicked by the knowledge that we deprived, not just Elliot, but his parents, his family. We have had the joy of watching Ellie grow up and all the while, her other grandparents are living just down the road, completely unaware of her existence. If I suddenly found out I had an eighteen-year-old grandchild, I would be devastated," she stared desperately at her sister. "I feel so terribly, terribly responsible for so much heartache that is about to unfold. Can't you see that, Roz?" she implored. "Grieving isn't a process exclusively for when somebody has died; grief is all about the pain of regret, of missed opportunities. Of discovering you have a daughter you knew nothing about, and realising that there is nothing you can do to reclaim that lost time."

She held her hand to her heart to emphasise her point.

"We are all grieving at the moment for different things. All of us. And that is hard to bear, as a mother, as a grandmother, a sister. We need to be united on this Roz, not be tearing strips off each other. Please see that."

Celia sighed heavily at Roz's lack of response and standing up, she headed for the kitchen door. Turning back, she said,

"Don't fight it Roz, you have to work through this. It's time to face up to it: all of it."

As the door closed behind her, Roz leant forward in her chair and clutched her forehead with her cold hands. The pressure seemed to ease the ache that had spread across her temples but the ache in her chest kept growing, and spreading up to her throat and down to the pit of her stomach. She allowed herself to visualise David's face smiling at her, comforted by his presence in her head. She screwed her eyes shut tight in a bid to freeze-frame the image, but his face slowly morphed into Elliot's; the smile fading, and his blue eyes filled with contempt. Opening her eyes wide with a gasp, she pulled the throw around her tightly, rocking in her chair as hot tears scalded her face.

"Oh, Daddy!" she wept, clutching her hands together in prayer, "how can I ever be forgiven?"

Alice slid from the bed quietly as her message alert beeped on the dressing table.

'Everything ok? xxx E.'
She smiled down at Ellie's sleeping figure, sprawled across the bed, in a peaceful slumber. She deftly took a photo with her phone of her sleeping angel and sent it to Elliot. The caption read,

'Whatever else we got wrong, we did get one thing right xxx A'
His reply, as ever, was immediate.

'We certainly did. She's beautiful. Just like her mother. Thank you xxx E.'

Alice pulled the duvet over Ellie and slid into bed next to her. She lay on her side in the semi-darkness, staring at the amber glow from the side light on the bedside table. Going over their conversation again in her head, she deliberated over what he had said. Why did he ask *her* where it went wrong? Was it, in fact, a question aimed at her or was he just voicing his regret at what he had done to their relationship? And what could he have meant when he said, that knowing she had gone to York because of him would have made a difference? How?

She reached across and gently ran her finger through the beaded fringe on the lampshade, watching the tiny dots of moulded glass glint as they moved in the light. Stare as she might, no answers leapt out at her. She closed her eyes but sleep eluded her once more until finally, as the dawn chorus started up, the riot in her head subsided long enough for her to fall into a fitful state of unconsciousness.

Ellie and Celia were sitting at the kitchen table finishing their breakfast when Alice came down the next morning. The sun shone brightly through the large windows and the smell of fresh dew floated through the open French doors.

"Morning Mum!" Ellie grinned, "not like you to sleep in. You even beat me!" she exclaimed as, licking her spoon, she lifted her cereal bowl to her mouth and drained the milk from it.

"What time are we leaving for Uncle Andrew's?" she asked, "I need to have a shower but everything's packed," she said excitedly.

Alice told her they would be heading off at midday, giving her time to stay for lunch at Andrew's and get back to Stratford by late afternoon. Ellie nodded in acknowledgment as she collected her bowl and mug together and put them by the sink.

Celia filled a mug with tea from the pot on the table and proffering it to Alice, regarded her tired face with concern. She waited until Ellie had left the room before speaking.

"Couldn't you sleep, dear?"

Alice shook her head. Celia frowned.

"Try not to take any notice of Roz at the moment, she's got a lot of issues to deal with. Don't let her upset you," she urged.

"Oh no, Mum, that's okay. She hasn't upset me. I completely understand that she's going to be all over the place right now," Alice assured her. "Where is she, anyway?" she wondered.

Celia shook her head dismissively,

"I'm leaving her to it this morning, I don't think we'll see her for a while. So, what's bothering you, why can't you sleep?" she asked, changing the subject.

Alice eyes were fixed on the table, deep in thought. Elliot's comments had prompted so many questions to be raised in her head and she wasn't entirely sure how she felt about it all. She ached to be with him again but the increasing certainty of him wanting to talk about the past, bothered her. She just wanted him now, in the present. Was it so wrong to want a physical relationship, without the emotional baggage? She knew the implications, and how wrong it was and yet, it was so tantalising.

Aware her mother was expecting an answer, she sighed slowly.

"Life," she stated simply, briefly looking at Celia who smiled knowingly. She busied herself making a round of toast, watching Alice closely.

"So, when are you seeing Elliot again?"
Celia's question broke Alice's trance and she looked up, startled.

"Sorry?" she asked, flustered, trying to stem the colour rising in her face.
Celia didn't seem to notice as she continued her train of thought,

"Well I just assumed that he'd want to see Ellie over the summer. No?" she asked.

"Oh yes, of course," Alice nodded, forcing a smile. "We haven't arranged anything yet," she said.

Celia passed a plate of toast to her, frowning slightly.

"Are you alright, dear? You seem distracted," she noted, putting a gentle hand on Alice's shoulder. Alice smiled gratefully.

"Sorry Mum, I'm already focusing on my meeting at work tomorrow. There's so much to plan and right now, I'm finding it difficult to keep a single thought in my head," she laughed lightly, feeling a fraud. She hated lying to her mother but what troubled her more, was how easily she could do it. The lies were just tripping off her tongue. Returning Celia's half smile, she desperately wished she could talk to her about it, especially after their heart to heart the other evening but she knew her mother wouldn't understand what she was up to.

Celia nodded,

"Yes, your father was just like that. Always focusing on work and worrying about the students," she agreed.
"Don't forget to live a little though dear; life is too short," she stated purposefully.

Roz hadn't emerged by the time Alice and Ellie were leaving, so Alice gently knocked on her bedroom door. There was no reply. Quietly opening the door a little way, she could see Roz's figure under the sheets, her chest rising and falling slowly in a deep repose. Deciding not to wake her, they left without saying goodbye.

"Give her a hug from us when she wakes up," Alice told Celia. "We'll see you both next week anyway, for Andrew's birthday," she added.

"Phone me when you get home," Celia reminded her. It was her standard parting phrase to both of her children. Not that they needed reminding, she knew that, but she always felt the need to say it anyway.

Alice's mood lightened as soon as they hit the road and it wasn't long before they arrived at Andrew's house, just outside the centre of Winchester. It was a beautiful, Grade II listed, thatched cottage, sitting on a small plot with mature trees outlining a quintessential cottage garden. When Andrew and Laura initially bought the three-bedroomed property, it had been neglected over the years and to the untrained eye, seemed like a poor choice to invest their money in. It had been an extensive labour of love and the fourteen years of dedicated hard work had paid dividends. The cottage had been sympathetically restored to keep many original features but also to accommodate a modern family. A clever loft conversion had created a fourth bedroom and the old store attached to the house, had become Laura's workshop.

A Fashion and Textile Design student, she and Andrew had met at university in Winchester and planned their wedding to coincide with Andrew completing his master's degree in Law. By then, Laura had established her business as a wedding dress designer, working from the spare room in her parents' house. Also by then, she was four months pregnant with Rachel. Ironically, the month that Rachel was born was the same month that Alice fell pregnant with Ellie.

Laura and Rachel greeted them at the door, closely followed by Andrew. Rachel and Ellie were almost identical, both with the 'Greene' chestnut brown, wavy hair and medium build but unlike Ellie, Rachel's eyes were dark brown. Laura also had dark brown hair, which she was wearing in a chic, French plait, trailing halfway down her back. More petite than her daughter, she was also slowly but surely being dwarfed by her growing boys, who she affectionately referred to as her 'mini Andrews'. Despite her petite demeanour, she was definitely the driving force behind the family and nurtured them all with her unfailing love. She hugged Alice with a genuine warmth, always happy to see her, and welcomed them in.

Alice beckoned Andrew to one side and asked if they could have a quiet chat before lunch. Seeing how nervous she looked, he immediately took her arm, and headed for the kitchen and out into the garden. Pausing half way down the cobbled path, out of earshot of the house, he turned to her.

"You're worrying me, Alice. What's happened? Is Mum okay?"

Alice clutched his hand, mortified, as she realised that she had caused such a panic in him.

"She's absolutely fine, Andrew. Sorry, I didn't think," she apologised. The memory of their father's terminal cancer was still very raw, and neither would ever forget the day that they had been invited home for a weekend, only to be told such devastating news.

Relief washed over his face and his shoulders dropped as he relaxed after he had been bracing himself for bad news.

"Then what's up?" he stroked Alice's back affectionately. She smiled sheepishly, struggling to find the words she needed.

"I have told Ellie who her father is and she's bound to want to talk about it," she started. Andrew looked surprised.

"Crikey. Is she going to meet him?" he asked, then added, "are we?"

Alice closed her eyes for a moment, trying to quell the nervous trembling throughout her body. Opening her eyes, she met Andrew's expectant gaze.

"It's Elliot Barraclough," she declared, echoing the words she had used only four days previously when breaking the same news to Ellie.

Andrew stared at her, dumbstruck, his hand dropping from her waist.

"Elliot?" he repeated, as if he hadn't heard her correctly. A thousand questions raced through his mind as he took in this incredible piece of news.

"You mean Elliot, Dan's brother? My best friend's brother? *He's* Ellie's father?" He was becoming more agitated as he fired questions at her. Alice nodded, uncertain of what else to say as she watched Andrew's face harden angrily.

"Then where the hell has he been all this time? Is that why he was at Ellie's birthday party? Good of him to finally show up. If I had known ..." he stopped abruptly as Alice held her hand to his mouth, his eyes widening with indignation.

"He didn't know. I didn't even tell him I was pregnant," she revealed, her voice level in a bid to calm him. She felt surprisingly, insanely protective of Elliot, and couldn't let Andrew continue with his rant, although she did appreciate his overprotective, brotherly concern.

"I told him about Ellie on her birthday. He had absolutely no idea about her until then," she insisted. Andrew ran a hand through his floppy fringe, exasperated by what he was being told.

"Jesus, Alice! what the hell has been going on?" he demanded to know.

They sat under a rose covered, wooden arbour bench, overlooking Laura's wildflower bed. An elongated teardrop patch, edged with lavender plants, it was stuffed full with an assortment of blooms, and teeming with butterflies, bees, and wasps.

Andrew put his arm around Alice and she leant against his shoulder as she told him how she had found out she was pregnant during her second year at university. She was reluctant to tell him about Mary; partly because she didn't want to remind herself of Mary's existence again, and partly because she knew that Andrew had always had a soft spot for Elliot and she didn't want to taint that. It felt curious how she couldn't bring herself to think of Elliot in anything but a positive light now. However, she also realised that too many lies had already been told and she could sense that Andrew was feeling betrayed by not knowing about Elliot sooner. So, she filled him in, with no holds barred, including the extent of their relationship and her feelings for him.

"I knew you two had a bit of a thing when you went to Uni but I thought nothing came of it. I certainly didn't know it was serious," he told her, still reeling from what she had just divulged.

Alice smiled, apologising.

"Well that was my doing really. I don't know, I just felt … I was always the family's 'little girl' and to admit to an adult relationship was hard for me. It felt very awkward. I didn't want Mum and Dad thinking I was doing stuff like that," she explained. Andrew laughed.

"I hate to break it to you but it's not a new thing. Everybody does it, you know!" he teased. She gave him a sardonic smile.

"Yes, I know that now but at the time, I just wanted to keep it to myself. It was exciting, keeping it secret from the world," she conceded wistfully.

"Like an affair, you mean?" he wondered, unwittingly hitting the mark.

Alice looked away swiftly.

"Yes, I suppose so. Something like that", she nodded as thoughts of Elliot, and the weekend ahead, flashed into her mind. She tried to stem the smile that was aching to spread across her face but try as she might, she couldn't stop a little laugh escaping her lips. Andrew looked quizzical but she just shook her head.

"Just laughing at life, that's all," she dismissed.

They sat in mutual silence for a while, idly watching a pair of butterflies performing their courtship dance, spiralling upwards into the sun-washed sky. It was a while before Andrew spoke again.

"How come I never knew any of this? Mum and Dad knew: Auntie Roz knew. Why didn't they tell me?" he sounded indignant. "When I asked Roz who the father was, she said it was somebody you had met briefly but he left without a trace when he found out."

Alice stared at him, appalled. What must he have thought of her?

"I had no idea," she murmured.

"Maybe it was because of my friendship with Dan? Is that it, do you think? Because Dan would've told Elliot? Is that what Roz was trying to avoid?"

He left the questions hanging in the air unanswered as they stared at each other, trying to make sense of it.

"I was in a bit of a state when Elliot left and Roz kind of took over really," she told him. "At the time, it's probably what I needed. But now I'm not so sure," she ventured."How do you mean?" he probed intently.

Alice felt a pang of concern over breaking a confidence but at the same time, she felt that she was overflowing with the burden of it all and needed to offload. It wasn't as if Andrew was a complete stranger; he had a right to know this and she could see that excluding him yet again could potentially make him feel alienated from the family unit. So, she told him of Roz's affair with David, of the baby and the adoption. She explained how betrayed she had felt, not knowing any of this until now, considering how closely they had lived for the past eighteen years. Andrew nodded knowingly. She went on to describe how Roz had reacted to Elliot appearing on the scene, and how annoyed she had seemed. But as far as Alice was concerned, she could see how desperate he was to build a relationship with Ellie. His immediate reaction at finding out about her had been one of joy, not condemnation. He was thrilled to be her father.

"Ellie, as you can imagine, is over the moon with him. Handsome, successful, caring - he is her dream dad," she laughed. Andrew gave an acknowledging laugh, seeing the possibilities in that.

"And, how are you? With him, I mean?" His questions were certainly direct but Alice found it refreshing.

"It's like I'm back to square one. He's still everything I loved about him in the first place," she freely admitted. "We just click. We get on so well."

As she heard herself admitting it, she realised how true it was. How could it be possible to feel like this, after such a long time apart? They had only seen each other three times in the past week and even then, the meetings had been brief and yet, it felt like he had never been away.

"So, where do you stand now?" he asked.

"He wants to see me. For a weekend," she told him frankly.

"Do it!" he enthused, grinning. Alice laughed at his boyish reaction.

"But he's married, Andrew," she said, hating the sound of those words. His face dropped.

"Ah. Well then, that has to be your call," he acknowledged.

Alice looked at him. She wished she could bring herself to tell him about their plans for the coming weekend but somehow, admitting them would mean admitting she was doing something wrong. She'd have to face up to the consequences. All she wanted to do was live for the moment, and revel in the thought of being with Elliot again.

Andrew nudged her, watching her transparent face.

"But should he need it, I know a good divorce lawyer," he joked with a conspiratorial wink.

Lunch was served on the patio and the conversation was dominated by talk of the upcoming music festival. Riley relayed excitedly to Alice all about the entertainment that was being laid on. He was particularly looking forward to the magic shows, he announced, as he wasn't that interested in the music. Chuckling at his enthusiasm, Laura conveyed her regret at having to miss out, but summer had always been her busiest time, and a grand wedding on Saturday, at the cathedral, was occupying every minute of it.

Andrew looked across at Ellie,

"So, Ellie, I hear you've had some exciting news this week?" he raised his eyebrows expectantly. Ellie shot a look at Alice, who nodded consent.

"Yes, I have! I met my dad for the first time on Monday. Well, that is, I met him on my birthday but I didn't know he was my dad then," she grinned happily. Laura was confused, looking at Andrew and Alice then turned to Ellie, asking who he was.

"Elliot Barraclough! And he is amazing!" she declared proudly. Laura sat back in her chair, stunned.

"Dan's little brother?" she asked Andrew. He nodded.

"Yep, Dan's little brother," he confirmed. "Ellie's father is Rachel's godfather's brother. What a neat little family!" he jokingly laughed, shooting Alice a reassuring look.

"And I'm guessing that Rachel already knew this," he added, turning to her with a questioning expression. Rachel and Ellie exchanged a glance.

"Why do you say that, Dad?" she challenged awkwardly. Andrew looked triumphant, knowing he was right.

"Because otherwise, you would be squealing, 'oh my God', at this by now, as you usually do," he discerned, capturing the essence of the two teenage girls perfectly.

Laura disappeared into the house, returning moments later with two photograph albums, placing them triumphantly on the table. Picking up the top one - a white faux leather, padded album, embossed with the words, 'Andrew and Laura's Wedding', in silver lettering - she leafed through it carefully. The pages were separated by thick, opaque, tissue paper and each page was edged with silver. Laura found the page she was looking for and pushed the album towards Ellie, watching her reaction with a delighted smile.

"Oh my God, is that Mum? And my Dad?" she practically squealed, leaning over the page, with Rachel peering over her shoulder.

"And that's Dan, my godfather!" Rachel exclaimed.

Alice stood up and leant across the table.

"Let me see," she insisted, with a smile of anticipation. Ellie beamed at her and swung the album round for her to see. Alice gasped and instinctively held her hand to her mouth. She instantly welled up and stifled a sob, then shakily laughed through it as she studied the photo closely. A nineteen-year-old Alice, dressed in a stunning, floor length, figure-hugging, halter neck dress of soft lilac silk, and clutching a dainty, cream and lilac bouquet, stared at the camera in mock shock as Elliot, to the left of her, and Dan, to the right, planted a kiss on either side of her face. Both young men were dressed to impress, in charcoal grey, morning suits, teamed with lilac cravats to match the bridesmaids' dresses, and holding grandiose top hats out to the side, in a mid-air salute.

Noticing her reaction, Laura squeezed Alice's arm affectionately.

"Yes, that's your mum, Ellie. She was my Maid of Honour, and Dan was Andrew's Best Man. Your dad was one of the ushers. If you turn the page," she prompted, "there's one of Dan with all four bridesmaids, and then there's one of just your mum and dad," she smiled. Ellie turned to find it and both girls let out a dreamy sigh.

"Oh Mum, you two look amazing," she whispered. It was Ellie's turn to well up. She gently touched their faces, noticing how their smiles radiated for the camera. Elliot had his arm about Alice's waist in a casual manner, looking perfectly at ease. As did she: leaning in to him, still clutching the bouquet but in a more relaxed way. Ellie took a photo of it with her phone.

"I'll scan it and print off a copy for you, Ellie," Laura offered readily. "Have a look through and see which ones you'd like," she encouraged. She passed along the second album, explaining that she had given disposable cameras to some of the guests, for them to take informal photos with, which she had then collated into the 'unofficial' album.

"I think these photos are more fun," she chuckled. "There's a lovely one of your Grandpa, girls, doing some very interesting dance moves!" she laughed.

As the cousins poured over the albums, Laura turned to Alice, checking she was alright about it all. Alice nodded, appreciating her concern. Laura whispered to her,

"So, Elliot Barraclough, eh? Good call, Alice. He's gorgeous!" she gave her a cheeky wink.

"Hey!" Andrew grumbled, listening in from across the table.

"But obviously not as gorgeous as you, my lovely man," she cooed, raising her eyebrows at Alice. Alice watched them both enviously. They had the same kind of relationship that her parents had had; that undeniable love for each other, and a friendship that only came from a deep intimacy. They knew exactly what made each other tick, and complimented each other so well. Her mind flitted back to Elliot. Seeing the photos of the two of them had reminded her of just how perfect they had been together. She couldn't wait to see him now.

"Mum!" Ellie's indignant exclamation jolted her from her reverie. Ellie was pointing at a photo accusingly, Rachel sniggering quietly by her side. In the forefront of the picture was Alice's father, attempting a slightly drunken jive with Celia, surrounded by a small crowd of amused on-lookers. In the background, oblivious to the rest of the room, were Alice and Elliot, locked in each other's arms as they danced in the shadows.

"Is Dad grabbing your bottom?" Ellie challenged in disbelief. Alice laughed out loud.

"Yes, that sounds about right," she nodded, causing even more giggling from Rachel, and a mixture of delight and mortification from Ellie. She stared at her mother, seeing her in a new light and not for the first time that week.

"Well I'm definitely getting a copy of this one," she decided, "and I'll send it to Dad," she grinned.

Alice said her goodbyes a few hours later, heading back to Stratford behind her planned schedule but she had been loath to leave. Even though she saw a great deal of Andrew and his family, she was always sad to say goodbye, and the day had been particularly poignant. She was relieved to have finally shared her thoughts and deepest feelings with him, to unburden hidden secrets and to revisit memories of his wedding. She felt lighter in mood and spirit, and more determined in the choices she was making. Andrew helped her into her car and before shutting the door, asked her to keep him posted on any developments regarding Roz's search for her daughter.

"Well, this is going to make it interesting on Wednesday when I see Mum and Auntie Roz. I wonder if I should casually mention that I know all of their secrets now," he joked derisively.

"Don't be hard on Mum," Alice said, "I get the feeling she didn't have much say on the matter regarding my pregnancy. I doubt it was her idea to keep you in the dark. And I'm sorry you were."

"Have fun at Camp Bestival!" she called to the children, blowing kisses to them.

"See you Wednesday!" Ellie shouted happily, running after the car as it left the drive, and waved until Alice turned the corner and headed north for home.

Finally, back in the comfort of her own home, she was able to sit back and get some order in her head. So much had happened, and she hadn't had a chance to think it all through properly without feeling scrutinised. Seeing the old photos of her and Elliot had really jolted her too. She realised how much she had blocked from her mind over the years but more than anything, it hit her how quickly time had passed. She had somehow jumped from that time of youthful excitement and a carefree spirit, to her current, organised and steadfast existence, in one swift step without even noticing the transition. She wondered how Elliot's life had panned out over the past eighteen years. Not the life she saw glimpses of through Mary's Facebook but life for him, through his eyes. Had time hurtled by for him too? And why was he so desperate to forge a relationship with her now? Was it purely because of Ellie? She couldn't quite believe that although that would have been the easy answer. Had seeing her again reminded him too of a time gone by, one that he regretted giving up? Was he already unhappy with his life, before they had met last weekend? And why had he told Ellie that he lived in York when, as far as Alice was aware, his wife lived in London?

Alice's phoned beeped. She jumped up from the sofa to grab it from the table, an expectant smile on her face.

'Night Mum, love you lots like jelly tots xxxxxx'

Feeling guilty for the pang of disappointment she felt that the text wasn't from Elliot, she typed a quick reply to Ellie. Staring at her phone, she wished she had the courage to text him but he had been the one initiating the conversations; what would she say, without sounding desperate?

"So much for sorting my head out", she scoffed as she tossed the phone onto the sofa and headed for the kitchen. It beeped.

'Hello you. Good day? What have you been up to? xxx E.'

Alice felt ridiculously happy, grinning as she replied,

'Hello you too. Been thinking about you all day xxx A.'

He replied instantly,

'Same. Can't stop thinking about you. Can't stop wanting you xxx E.'

She took a moment: that tingling sensation spreading across the back of her neck as she pictured him saying those words. Her breathing became shallow and she had the urge to cry again. She chewed her lip as she thought of a reply. Her eyes twinkled as she typed,

'Don't ever stop. I'm aching for you. Counting down the hours until you're here xxx A.'

She held her breath, waiting. She didn't have to wait long.

'Damn it, Alice, I won't be able to sleep now! Counting... xxx E.'

She chuckled, satisfied with his reaction.

"Be still, my beating heart", she sighed happily. She determined there and then not to focus any longer on the past, or on wondering what was meant by this or that. Or on what state his marriage was in. She wanted to look forward, not back. She could see a chance for happiness and she intended to grab it with both hands and not let go.

Chapter Seven

Alice was woken up on Friday morning by her phone ringing on the bedside table. She was expecting Ellie to call, so answered with a non-communicative grunt.

"Good morning to you too, sleepyhead," Elliot's low tone greeted her. She rolled over to check her clock; it was just after seven. She cleared her throat,

"Sorry, I was expecting Ellie," she replied, smiling down the phone at him.

"Listen Alice, I'm sorry but I have to cancel this weekend," he started. Her heart sank as she heard the words not quite expected before their affair had even begun. Sitting up, she brushed her hair from her face, waiting for his reason.

"So, are you free today?" he continued.

"Well, yes I can be. Yes," she confirmed quickly. He sighed with relief.

"Good, because I'm on the motorway now," he told her, going on to explain how his colleague had had a family emergency, so Elliot was stepping in to front a weekend conference in York. The first lecture starting that evening. Alice interrupted him,

"But don't you live in York anyway? Why are you coming down here?" she was confused.

"I don't think I could survive the weekend if I can't see you first, even if it is only for a few hours," he said softly, his words making her stomach flip over.

"Know a good place for lunch?" he asked. Thinking quickly, she gave him directions to tap in to his sat nav and he relayed his calculated arrival time.

"Meet me in the car park there. I'll be waiting," she assured him, then asked, "do you still eat cheese and pickle sandwiches?"

"Is there any other kind of sandwich?" he joked. She laughed.

"Okay, see you soon. Safe journey," she added.

Elliot was quiet for a second.

"Thanks, Alice," he murmured.

"Thank me when you get here," she murmured back invitingly. Hanging up, she scrambled out of bed and headed for the bathroom. She caught sight of her reflection in the bedroom mirror; her eighteen-year-old self, smiled back at her.

"Oh, what you do to me, Elliot Barraclough," she sighed longingly.

Three hours later, he pulled up in the leafy car park to find Alice waiting there for him, as she had promised. Without hesitation, she hurried over and put her arms around him possessively. He held her close and rested his head on hers. Neither spoke: their embrace saying everything they felt. Alice was the first to break the silence,

"Are you smelling my hair, Elliot?" she teased. He gave a throaty laugh and a loud sniff. She pulled away to look at him.

"Listen, here's the deal," she started emphatically, "We don't drag up the past, we start again. A new beginning, a new future." She waited for his response. He shook his head,

"I can't dismiss our past, Alice. Ellie is part of that. And we were so good together, you and I," he said. Alice's face was earnest as she explained,

"No, I don't mean that - and I would never want to forget 'us' - what I mean is, let's just focus on the now; not what happened, or what went wrong," she insisted. Elliot nodded,

"Okay, okay," he agreed, going along with it. "You look lovely," he added, casting an appreciative eye over her rose and ivory coloured, floral, summer dress. He gently stroked her suntanned arm.

"So do you," she responded, noting his casual chinos and light blue, open necked, short sleeved shirt. He looked completely different out of a suit, she thought; more relaxed, more like the Elliot she used to know.

"So, Miss Greene, why did you invite me to this particular place?" he asked, looking round at the busy car park. Picking up her canvas tote bag, she took his hand and started walking towards the thatched house that they could glimpse through the trees and shrubbery. A delighted smile spread across her face.

"Well, Mr Barraclough, as this is our first date, I wanted to bring you to my favourite place, 'Anne Hathaway's cottage'. Which in my opinion," she informed him, "is the most romantic place on the planet. Perfect for a picnic," she smiled happily.

As they walked up the path leading to the entrance, they passed a sweetly scented bed of roses and lavender bushes. Alice automatically squeezed some lavender and put her fingers under Elliot's nose to share the smell. He gave a knowing chuckle.

"What?" she wondered.

"That's such an 'Alice' thing to do" he acknowledged.

"Your point is?" she jokingly challenged.

"I love you," he declared. This time there was no vulnerability in his eyes; his sincerity was absolute.
Alice stopped in her tracks, staring at him, speechless.

"Surely you must know that, Alice?" he insisted.

She knew. Every fibre in her body knew how he felt since their intense moment in the church, just days previously. But she hadn't expected him to say it, to be so forthright about it. That wasn't part of her plan. She had wanted to be flirty and enticing, not serious. She tried to joke it off,

"I must say, Mr Barraclough, for a first date, you're pretty forward!"
He took hold of her hand again and pulled her towards him slightly, leaning to whisper in her ear,

"Um, you do actually remember our real first date, don't you?" he breathed, reminding her of her spontaneous passion. She laughed softly.

"Oh, I can see you're a tricky one!" she replied drolly.

Alice showed her pass at the counter and they walked through the entrance building and out into the garden that surrounded the beautiful 15th century house, once the childhood home of William Shakespeare's wife, Anne Hathaway. Elliot gave her another knowing smile.

"What now?" Alice asked, watching his amused face.

"Just the fact that you have a pass for this place. You're so predictable," he teased. She playfully elbowed him, feigning irritation.

"Yes well, I happen to appreciate everything that the Shakespeare Trust does, so obviously, I'm going to support it," she made her voice sound haughty.

"Now pay attention as we walk around – I will be asking questions later," she joked.

"Okay, Miss," Elliot snickered, catching hold of her hand again. They stood and admired the cream, brick and timber building for a while as Alice animatedly talked about its history; the fact that it had been built in 1463 and remained in the Hathaway family until the late 1800s, and had been home to thirteen generations of the same family. Elliot loved the structure of it and how the once small, two roomed farm house had been extended and adapted over the years to the magnificent, solid, twelve roomed thatched cottage that stood before them now. Alice relayed the story of William Shakespeare's will, in which he bequeathed the second-best bed to his wife. Initially seen as a snub by some, it was later thought that the second-best bed was in fact their marital bed, as the best bed was only kept for guests; therefore, the gesture was actually an act of love. Her eyes sparkled as she spoke.

"You're a born romantic, aren't you," Elliot smiled warmly, loving her for it.

"I just love a love story," she sighed, squeezing his hand slightly.

They walked up the few steps to the front door and the guide gave Alice a smile of recognition, exchanging brief pleasantries with her. A distinct smell of damp stone, dust, and old books filled the air; it was a smell Elliot regularly encountered in his line of work and one he was not averse to. He commented on the uneven stone floor beneath their feet as they made their way in to the hall, where a small crowd were gathered to admire the artefacts. Alice pointed to a dark, wooden settle and explained in hushed tones that it was supposedly the bench that Shakespeare would sit on with Anne, when he came courting. Dark wooden beams dominated the whole building and together with the dark stained wooden furniture, made it all seem very enclosed despite its size. They wandered through the rooms, peering in at the kitchen and buttery, trying to identify all the different utensils on display.

At the far end of the building was a steep, spiral staircase leading to the bedrooms above. As they ascended the rickety stairs, the wood, worn with age, creaked under their weight.

"I wonder if Shakespeare ever tried to sneak up these stairs for a clandestine visit to Anne's room," Elliot commented, "Good luck with that!"

Alice giggled, picturing the scene. She paused on the top step and turning to look down at Elliot who was climbing the stairs behind her, and called to him in a hushed mock theatrical voice,

"Romeo, Romeo, wherefore art thou?"

Elliot exaggerated taking tiptoe steps, making loud creaking noises,

"CREEEEEAK, CREEEEEAK – yes, I'm coming Anne!" he replied in an equally theatrical tone. He grinned at Alice's delighted face, as she tried to stifle her laughter.

"Shhh! Behave, Miss!" he scolded as he reached the top step, making her giggle even more. He slid his arm around her waist and quickly kissed her hair. Alice gulped, smiling up at him and reciprocating his gesture, slid her arm around him too. It felt so natural to her as she hooked her thumb through his trouser belt loop, an old habit spontaneously resurfacing.

The floor was more uneven upstairs and looking down, they could see shafts of light coming up from downstairs through the wide cracks and gaps in the floorboards. They stopped to admire one of the ancient four poster beds, and Alice told Elliot about the practicalities behind what is nowadays considered a romantic canopy.

"Because the thatched roofs housed so many creatures, like mice, rats, and birds, the canopy was there to stop droppings, and insects, from falling through the patchy roof onto your face as you slept", she grinned. Elliot grimaced,

"I think I've gone off the idea of a four-poster bed now then!" he said. Alice nudged him with her shoulder lightly,

"That's a shame," she whispered, "Mine's a four-poster."

She could hear how flirtatious she sounded, and Elliot's surprised reaction pleased her. He cleared his throat, his grin broadening as he whispered back,

"Really Miss Greene, for a first date, *you're* pretty forward."
They both laughed softly and simultaneously tightened their hold of each other's waists.

They stood for a while in the bedroom, in mutual silence, imagining a time gone by. Stooping down, they peered out of the tiny, lattice leaded window that looked out across the garden, and on to the meadows and woodland beyond. Alice sighed wistfully,

"I love the thought that she would look out of one of these windows in the morning as the sun came up, and think about her lover."

She spoke quietly, visualising how it would have looked back then.

"Of course, it was all farm land rather than these beautiful gardens but, they must have had a special place to sneakily meet up and snatch a moment of love, away from prying eyes," she continued, "I like to imagine him walking across the fields from his house in Stratford, just to reach her, just to be with her," she concluded, deeply infatuated with the idea of their love story. Elliot followed her gaze across the vast cottage garden that unfolded beneath the window.

"Do you think they actually were lovers, before they got married?" he wondered. Alice gave a short laugh.

"Of course they were! Definitely lovers; he couldn't keep his hands off her!" she enthused, "He was only eighteen when he married her, you know, and she was already three months pregnant. And I like to think that he married her because he loved her, not because he had to. Maybe he didn't even know she was pregnant," she concluded, turning back to Elliot. His eyes held hers with a look she couldn't fathom, making her blush awkwardly. She looked away, realising that she had inadvertently hit a nerve. Pointing back to the gardens through the window, she asked,

"Shall we go outside?"

They held hands with an old familiarity as they wandered leisurely through the garden, the billowing flower beds a riot of colour, shape and size. Tall, black hollyhocks jostled with clumps of ruby red poppies, vibrant pink peonies, and lemon lupins, in amongst an abundance of old cottage garden perennials, all indicative of a 15th century garden. Wigwams of fragrant sweet peas were dotted about, their scent gently wafting in the warm sun. Rosemary and lavender defined the herb border, and old fashioned roses basked at regular intervals. Every now and then, Alice would bend over to smell something, encouraging Elliot to do likewise, pointing out and naming the plants she recognised. Looking up, she saw the proprietor of the garden café waving at her. A middle aged, slightly rotund, cheerful character, he came over and hugged her briefly.

"How are you, my lovely? Enjoying the break?" he beamed affectionately, nodding a friendly greeting to Elliot, "She's my favourite customer," he stated. "Enjoying your visit?" he asked Elliot. After a few minutes of light-hearted chat, he wished them a good summer and went back to wiping down the tables. Alice reclaimed Elliot's hand and carried on their journey through the garden.

Weaving their way around the beds and the steadily growing crowd of visitors, she indicated to a path leading away from the house, towards meadows beyond. Tall grasses and wild flowers were left to their own devices here, spreading in lush swathes as far as the eye could see, with the occasional gnarled tree growing in its midst. Splashes of red, yellow, and blue, mingled together with the verdant green, and butterflies busily flitted from one plant to the other. A couple of mown strips on either side of the meadow sufficed as paths, leading onto further patches of undisturbed meadows and orchards.

The hubbub from the crowd grew dim as they put distance between them, and Alice chose a secluded spot to spread out her tartan blanket. The ground smelt like a mixture of warm hay and honey, the air was filled with nearby birdsong and the hushed tones of bees lazily foraging for nectar. Alice lay back on the blanket, sighing contentedly. She kicked off her sandals and stretched her feet appreciatively, her dusky pink toenails shimmering in the sunlight. Elliot stretched out next to her, propping himself up on one elbow to study her face as she smiled blissfully at the sun. He lightly brushed a strand of hair from her face. She turned her smile to him.

"So, um," Elliot spoke softly, his eyes creasing at the corners as he unsuccessfully tried not to grin,

"What are the rules about kissing on a first date?"

Alice propped herself up to face him, moving closer,

"Well, that depends," she murmured thoughtfully.

"On what?" he wanted to know. She gave a soft laugh,

"On whether you're a good kisser," she teased, her eyes inviting.

"Hmm, and how will you find out?" he whispered, inching towards her.

"Oh good Lord, Elliot! Just kiss me!" she laughed out loud. He didn't need asking twice. As their lips met, she was instantly transported back to a drunken evening in York, the same intense explosion of ecstasy erupting throughout her body, making her heart beat wildly and her stomach spin out of control. Elliot wove his fingers through her hair at the nape of her neck, his other hand pulling her waist against him. Her back arched towards him, her body responding instinctively and betraying how desperately she wanted him. She ran her hands across his back, revelling in the intimate touch that ignited memories of so many nights of passion. Locking her hands together at the base of his spine, she held him in a tight embrace. Just when she thought she would burst into flames right there and then, Elliot gently pulled away and their lips parted. Alice slowly opened her eyes, an ardent smile spreading across her face. Elliot was staring at her, elation flooding his eyes and his smile matching hers.

"Tell me I'm not wrong: you feel it too, don't you?" he insisted huskily. Alice nodded, touching his face. He grabbed her hand and kissed it.

"I've been wanting to do that since Ellie's birthday," he admitted, "but I was scared you'd reject me."

"I tried to," Alice answered truthfully, "and failed," she added wryly, nuzzling her nose into his neck.

"We're meant to be, you know we are," he whispered in her ear, drawing her close again.

"I know, but..." she started. Elliot looked at her,

"But?" he prompted, his eyes narrowing slightly. Alice knew she was falling too quickly, she needed to think about their next move. There was Ellie to consider and there was the small complication of his wife. She stroked his cheek and sighed,

"One step at a time, yes? This is our first date, after all," she tried to joke but uncertainty clouded her face and it didn't go unnoticed. Elliot sat up and pulled her up next to him, putting his arm protectively across her shoulders and kissing her briefly.

"You're right," he nodded, "I'm sorry, I don't want to scare you off but I can't believe that you're back in my life again. I know it's been eighteen years but you make me feel like it was only yesterday," he gave a little laugh, "I feel like a teenager all over again and I don't want to lose that. I don't want to lose you," he stressed, earnestly and honestly. Alice reached over and gently kissed his mouth.

"You're not going to lose me, Elliot. I'm going nowhere," she assured him, "And you've got Ellie. She won't let you go either!" she laughed. He grinned, nodding, remembering their afternoon together and how ecstatic she had been in his company.

"Okay, point taken," he agreed, tenderly tilting her chin up to kiss her mouth once more, groaning as he reluctantly broke away. Indicating her bag, he asked,

"Did you say something about cheese and pickle sandwiches?"

They spent the next hour talking animatedly about anything and everything, from their jobs to their favourite books, the NHS to hedgerow planting, the changes in education to the best way to compost tea bags. They stretched out on the blanket again once they'd shared the picnic, the easy flowing conversation unabated. Their earlier passionate kiss had broken the tension between them and now they were content to lie in each other's arms, getting to know each other once again.

"I never talk to anybody like this," Elliot acknowledged wistfully. Alice murmured her agreement, turning her face to soak up the sun.

"Me neither," she smiled lazily, "It's all teenage music, Facebook, Twitter, and shopping, from Ellie, and from Roz, it's the extortionate price of canvas, and the inability to buy decent paint brushes nowadays," she laughed. "Oh, and the impossible parking in Stratford, of course!" she added.

"Why Stratford, Alice? How come you ended up here?" he was curious to know.

"Auntie Roz was already living here when I ... when I needed somewhere to live, so I moved in with her," she replied. He frowned slightly, thinking about what she had just said. He was about to ask another question but changed his mind and fell silent, gently stroking her hair as she rested her head on his chest. She stretched her arm across his stomach contentedly.

"I'm not sure why Roz ended up here though," she continued, "but I suspect Grandpa's influence had something to do with it. He was a huge Shakespeare fan," she said.

She relayed how he had told her bedtime stories when she was little, of Midsummer Night's Dream, and Romeo and Juliet,

"Although he always made it much friendlier than it actually is," she laughed. Her Grandpa would somehow manage to weave his favourite Shakespeare quotes into his Sunday sermons, and as she grew older, and more aware of the subtleties and innuendoes behind the Bard's work, it made her realise how much of a sense of humour her Grandpa actually had. And how his two passions, Theology and Shakespeare, could at times seem intertwined and at others, worlds apart.

"I loved my Grandpa, he was a man of such depth and such kindness," she acknowledged.

"You were so lucky; my Grandfather was the complete opposite," Elliot recalled, an edge of resentment in his voice. Alice lifted her head to look at him, surprised at his tone.

"How come?" she asked, "Was he mean to you?" Elliot shook his head,

"Not to me, no. He didn't even notice me most of the time and when he did, I was just a nuisance as far as he was concerned," he dismissed, "No, he was particularly harsh to my uncle David. My dad sometimes, but mainly my uncle," he confided. Alice rested her head back on his chest so that he couldn't see what she was thinking. She tried to change the subject.

"What about your mother's parents? What were they like?" she asked. Elliot smiled broadly.

"Oh, they were great, just how grandparents should be," he told her, "but I didn't see much of them when I was growing up. They lived in Yorkshire," he said, then reminisced for a while about his annual trips up to the Yorkshire dales to visit them; holidays filled with love, seemingly endless sunshine - even on rainy days - and learning how to drive his grandfather's farm tractor. They had been a huge factor in his choosing York for his University; even though they had both passed away when he was a young teenager, his love for Yorkshire had been lifelong because of them.

"I'm sorry I never met them," Alice said gently, "they sound like lovely people."

"They were," he nodded, "and they would've loved you. And Ellie," he sounded choked for a moment. "Not sure I can say the same for my dad's father," he continued. It was evident he wanted to talk about it, Alice could see that.

"How do you mean?" she prompted. Elliot was quiet for a while, his face twitching slightly as he dealt with conflicting emotions.

"I think he hated people being happy, basically," he started, "always full of criticism. I don't actually ever remember him smiling."

He paused again, debating his next words,

"David was the oldest son, four years older than my dad, and expected to do well. He went to Med school, married the daughter of a top London surgeon - my grandfather's friend - and had a brilliant career ahead of him in London. But it didn't suit him, he suffered from stress," Elliot paused, picking a bit of fluff from the blanket.

"What happened to him?" Alice asked, mindful of how curious she sounded; she couldn't possibly divulge to him anything about Roz.

"He and Auntie Patricia moved back to Brockenhurst. She hated it but it suited him more. Anyway, to cut a long story short, David had an affair."

Elliot stopped abruptly, and sat up. Alice pulled herself up next to him and gently put her hand on his thigh, leaning her shoulder comfortingly against his.

"What is it, Elliot?" she asked, the concern in her voice mirrored in her expression. She realised that talking about his uncle having an affair, was sailing very close to the wind. Was Elliot beginning to regret what he and Alice were embarking on? His mind was certainly in turmoil, she conceded, as she looked into his troubled eyes. He stroked a finger slowly down her cheek, not taking his eyes off her.

"I went travelling with David for a while, a long time ago now, and we grew incredibly close. I realised then how little I actually knew about him. It made me feel quite guilty, inept almost. I had known this man forever but in reality, had not known him at all," he gave a rue smile, then continued,

"He married too young, too quickly. His marriage to Patricia was a sham but he stuck at it, even though they didn't have any children. It was expected of him. Then he fell in love with a local girl."

Elliot smiled at the memory of his uncle's words,

"He said it was like nothing else on earth mattered, just him and her; the love of his life. She made him complete. They had a long, passionate affair and then one day, totally out of the blue, she disappeared. It destroyed him."

Elliot held Alice's gaze, unwavering. She felt uncomfortable but couldn't look away; a hot flush of colour started to creep up her neck. He broke the hold as his eyes shifted to her mouth. She nervously bit her lip, her action causing him to instinctively reach out and touch it, and very gently kiss it. She closed her eyes, the spin cycle in her stomach starting up again. He cupped the side of her face with his hand,

"Alice," he murmured, his breath dancing against her cheek. She could tell by his inflection that he was about to ask her something. She moved her head to rest her forehead against his.

"What happened to him?" she asked, barely able to control her shaky voice but desperate to divert his questions. Elliot let out a slow, thoughtful breath,

"He died inside, went to pieces. He told his father eventually - although I can't understand why - but instead of support, he got condemnation. He was told he'd had a lucky escape. But something in his father's behaviour made David suspect that he had known about it, so he pushed for more information. Eventually his father, my delightful grandfather," Elliot's voice dripped sarcasm, "told David that he had found out about them and wanted to test her, so he offered her money to leave. Quite a substantial amount apparently. And she took it, proving that she wasn't in it for love after all, and David had been a fool to even think that she was," he said. An involuntary gasp escaped Alice's lips.

"What did David do?" she could barely speak, reliving the emotions of Roz's heart breaking confession and trying desperately to steady her own feelings that were rapidly spiralling out of control. How could David's father have lied like that?

Elliot rubbed the side of his face in contemplation, his slight stubble rasping against his hand.

"He absolutely refused to believe it. He looked for her, everywhere. He even suspected she had been pregnant, maybe that's why she left," he shot Alice a brief glance, "but ... nothing. He used his medical position to search records, as best he could back then, but there was no trace of a baby or her. She had vanished." Elliot dropped his head, his voice also dropping,

"He never got over it, Alice. Never. And harsh as it sounds, when he died, I think that was his release from a life of misery." He reached for her hand and held it with both of his. She blinked back tears,

"How did he die?" she quietly asked.

"A massive stroke. About two years after my dad's," he affirmed. Alice looked startled,

"Your dad had a stroke?" she asked, bewildered, "When?"

Elliot stared at her, with a look of confusion. She couldn't gauge its meaning.

"Are *you* okay though?" the sudden thought of losing Elliot to a stroke filling her with fear, "it's not a genetic thing, is it?" she had to know.

"No, I'm fine," he stuttered his words, and seemed distracted. Alice put her arms around him to comfort him, resting her head on his shoulder. Her mind was racing with everything Elliot had just told her and she was feeling guilty at not divulging Roz's secret to him. She felt he had a right to know; after all, Cee-Cee was his cousin as well as hers. He had clearly been very close to David, not dissimilar to the relationship she had with Roz. She felt trapped by yet another secret, another echo of the past.

"So many things don't add up," Elliot said quietly, turning to Alice for an answer. She looked nervous, anticipating what he was going to say next. Surely, he hadn't worked it out; that Roz was David's lover. How could he? She frantically thought of something to say to detract him from his train of thought. Just then, a large tabby and white cat marched up to them, with his tail held high, and meowing earnestly.

"Hello Bubbles," Alice cooed, offering her hand for the cat to sniff in recognition, and then stroked his large head. He emitted a rumbling purr and threw himself down in front of them, blinking his appreciation at the fuss Alice was bestowing upon him.

"Does everybody know you here?" Elliot exclaimed, "Even the cat?"

Alice chortled,

"Well, I do come here a lot," she admitted, "I bring my students here sometimes, it's a great place to sit and read through the sonnets," she enthused, "and Ellie learnt to walk in this field: she took her first ever steps right over there," she pointed to a spot in the distance.

Elliot fell silent, staring at the field, imagining that important milestone in his daughter's development.

"Can I ask you something, just one question?" he rushed his words, seeing her reluctance, "It's not about us," he added, "but I need a completely truthful answer."

Alice straightened, nodding consent.

"Just one," she said. He hesitated before he spoke,

"If you didn't want me..." he faltered and changed his tack, "If I wasn't part of your life, then why did you call our daughter Ellie? It is so clearly *my* name."

Alice reached over and pulled up a coarse blade of rye grass poking out from under the blanket, and slowly started to dissect it. She knew she had to give an honest answer, she felt she owed him that now. She studied the horizon, contemplating her words before she spoke,

"I was terrified of giving birth, absolutely terrified. Being pregnant was one thing but the nearer it got, the more scared I became; of the actual birth and of what would happen afterwards," she breathed out slowly, her voice almost inaudible as painful memories flooded her mind.

"It was agony. I was in labour for hours and the gas and air made me feel incredibly sick, so I avoided it. I hadn't planned on a natural birth but that's more or less what I got," she snorted slightly. "Roz was there to hold my hand but as the pain ripped through me, all I could see in my mind was you. All I wanted to hear, was *you* reassuring me. I wanted to open my eyes and find you there, not my auntie. I even screamed out your name during the final contraction; I honestly thought I was going to die from it. And then the pain was over and I heard a baby cry, and they placed her on my bare chest. I opened my eyes and … and she looked so much like you. And I knew. I had got my wish, you *were* there, in the shape of our baby. And I couldn't think of any other name but Ellie. It's the first words I uttered to her; my little Ellie."

She stared at her lap, waiting for his response. He didn't move, his head was turned away from her. Alice touched his arm gently,

"Elliot?" she whispered.

He stood up, staring fixedly across the field, eventually turning to look down at her. His face, contorted with anguish and regret, was wet with tears. Unable to speak and unable to take his eyes off her, he slowly absorbed her heart-breaking words.

"Why? Why didn't you tell me?" he pleaded helplessly. Alice jumped up to hold him, sensing the tension in his rigid body, as he battled with his feelings. She was regretting her honesty. It was something she had dealt with eighteen years ago, but for Elliot, this was fresh information. Raw emotion.

"Elliot, please," she implored, "This is exactly what I didn't want to happen. The past is the past. You're here, with me, now. Let me just have this time with you, now. Not rake over the past. I want you, now."

She reiterated the *now*. Her voice shook, begging for a response. Elliot abruptly wrapped his arms around her and cradled her head to his chest, pushing his face into her hair. He held her tightly, not wanting to let go.

"Don't ever leave me again," he whispered fervidly.

She wanted to protest and remind him it was he that had left her, but decided against it.

"I won't," she reassured him, "I'm yours, forever."

A short time later, they were back in the car park by Elliot's car, silently clinging on to each other.

"I wish you didn't have to go," Alice murmured woefully. They hadn't spoken much in the last twenty minutes but Elliot had refused to let go of their embrace, keeping his arms possessively around her as they had left the meadow and made their way back to the exit.

"So do I," he agreed, "and I'm sorry. I shouldn't have pushed you for answers. You asked me not to and I can see why. I've ruined the day somewhat, haven't I?" he acknowledged, regretting his actions. Alice shook her head,

"No, you haven't," she stated emphatically, looking into his troubled eyes. She ran her fingers through his hair and down his neck, tenderly stroking him.

"I was too honest, Elliot. I suppose it's because I've never talked about it and the only person I ever wanted to share those feelings with, is you. There's so much I've wanted to share with you but I'm scared that if we get bogged down with the past now, we'll lose the present. I don't think you really understand what you do to me, how you make me feel. It's all happening so fast, it's a bit scary and confusing but at the same time," she paused, willing herself to be brave enough to say it,

"I don't want this to ever stop. I have loved today. I love you. So, so much," she openly confessed.

Elliot's chest rose with a sharp intake of breath. He struggled to keep his grin in check as he cradled her face in his hands, his pupils dilating with desire, making her insides turn to jelly.

"I love you too, Alice," he whispered, "more than you could possibly imagine."

He let out an elated laugh,

"Is this really happening? Is this us?"

He stared at her, adoring every inch of her. She nodded, laughing with him.

"Yes, it is," they said unanimously as their lips met. They kissed like old lovers at the end of a perfect day, secure in each other's devotion and the knowledge that they would be together again soon.

"See you next Saturday," he said as he got into his car. Alice leant in through the open window for a final kiss.

"Text me when you get back to York," she prompted. "Safe journey", she added, suddenly feeling choked. He nodded and smiled yet his eyes conveyed the regret he felt at having to leave.

Alice watched him drive away before getting into her own car and heading back home. All at once the world felt curiously quiet without him there, but she could still hear his voice in her head and smell his aftershave on her body. She was made aware, as she pulled up at a junction, of the huge grin across her face; the driver in the adjacent car gave her a quizzical look, making her laugh out loud. She had forgotten what it was like to feel so deliriously happy, with not a care in the world, her mind just focused on her man.

"My man", she chuckled to herself, refusing to let any nagging doubts cross her mind.

A few hours later, a text arrived from Elliot. It read,

'Back in York. Thank you for an amazing day. You made me feel alive again xxx E.'

Alice responded swiftly,

'Best first date ever! I felt like a teenager all over again xxx A.'

She smiled dreamily at her phone, then typed another message,

'I've missed you so much xxx A.'

Elliot responded promptly,

'I love you Alice. Always have, always will xxx E.'

She stared at the words, 'always have', knowing he was being truthful. Whatever happened back in York eighteen years ago, hadn't changed the fact that he loved her. She needed to give him a chance to explain it all.

"But not yet," she told herself, "just enjoy the moment. Ask questions later."

She typed a response,

'I love you too Elliot. Forever xxx A.'

Much later that night, as she was drifting off to sleep, her book still in her hand, the phone rang loudly by her side.

"Hello you," Elliot murmured, bringing a sleepy smile to her face.

"Hello you too," she replied, stretching like a contented cat. "How did it go this evening?"

"It went okay, thanks, all things considered. I'm shattered now though," he said. "I just needed to hear your voice before I go to sleep," he told her.

"You should be here then," she teased with a little laugh.

"Hey, that's not fair!" he grumbled, "I will be, next weekend. Trust me, nothing is going to stop me," he promised, with a voice full of amorous intention.

"Good," she said softly. They spoke for a little while longer, before she drifted off into the deepest sleep she'd had in a very long time, her mind and soul feeling complete once more.

Chapter Eight

Finding herself unexpectedly free for the weekend, Alice determined to use her time constructively, although she had to admit, it was rather tempting to just sit in her sun-baked garden and daydream about Elliot. She was cursing herself that she hadn't had the nous to take some photos of the two of them the day before, but they had both agreed to turn their phones off, eliminating any distractions during their picnic and consequently, she had forgotten all about it.

'Never mind,' she thought, 'all I have to do is close my eyes and there he is.'
She laughed lightly, feeling incredibly smug.

Alice adored the cottage that, thanks to Roz and her father, she now owned outright. Roz had bought it in the mid-Seventies and had insisted Alice lived with her rent-free. So, when she started earning, she contributed towards the other bills and saved the rest of her income. When Reggie died, he left a substantial amount of money to both of his children. It had come as quite a shock to them to discover how much they were inheriting; it had never crossed their minds that he would be ploughing so much of his income into savings for them. Having inherited his own home from his mother, he consequently had never had to worry about a mortgage and had determined that his children would never have to struggle. He had also invested a great deal of money, and time, into both local and national charities; the one closest to his heart being the War Widows' Association. Although his own mother had been in an incredibly fortunate circumstance financially, thanks to her father's successful business, he had never forgotten the plight of the many others of her generation who struggled to survive after the war, and well into their twilight years.

Alice had used her inheritance and savings to buy the cottage from Roz, who in turn would still regard it as her home. Roz's studio was attached to the cottage and she ran an art gallery and art supply shop in the centre of Stratford, employing two members of staff, both of whom were budding artists. Roz felt she was repaying a debt of gratitude for the chances she had been given when she first started out. She had arrived in Stratford as a penniless, promising artist, embarking on a new life and carrying a heart-rending secret, and much like in Newlyn, was taken in by a successful artist and art gallery owner. Older than her, in years and wisdom, he had taught her everything he knew about business and getting established. He had also tried to help heal her broken heart but could never replace David, so, after several refused proposals, he had to contend with being nothing more than her lover. As middle age caught up with him though, he sought elsewhere for the comforts and security he felt only a wife could bring, and Roz was alone once more.

Setting her mind on researching the websites that they had looked at earlier in the week, in more depth, Alice abandoned the sun lounger and headed back indoors, making a mental note to mow the lawn later. Theirs was not a particularly large garden; it hugged the white-washed cottage in an L-shape, the main bulk of it running alongside the road, blocked from view by a six-foot brick wall. There was a well-established silver birch dominating half the space: its overeager, sprawling branches reaching down to sweep the lawn on one side of the wall and the pavement on the other, requiring regular pruning.

The cottage sat on the road running through the village of Wilmcote, just outside the centre of Stratford-Upon-Avon, and famed for being the home of Mary Arden, William Shakespeare's mother. Alice's cottage was a solid build, with original interior beams. It had been renovated over the years, joining two small, gabled cottages into one, to create a three bedroomed, three reception roomed home. The lounge was the largest room, stretching from one side of the house to the other. The windows overlooked both the road at the front and the garden at the back, affording a great deal of natural light, which bounced off the biscuit coloured walls, giving the room a warm glow in the evening sun. Two large, wine coloured, squishy sofas occupied the majority of the floor space, alongside a matching armchair, and a deep-red and beige tartan, Sherlock, wingback chair. A low, rectangular coffee table offered somewhere not just for mugs, but for a selection of neatly stacked magazines, and remote controls for the television. Floor to ceiling bookcases ran along the length of one wall, with books piled up in some sort of order on the burgeoning shelves. Despite the air of chaos, they were obviously cherished possessions.

The kitchen, accessed from either the hall or through an archway leading from the lounge, overlooked both the side garden by the road, and the back garden. Aside from her bedroom, this was Alice's favourite room and she had certainly put her personal stamp on it. Again, the room benefitted from plenty of natural light and the pale green walls accentuated the view from the windows, seemingly bringing the garden in to the kitchen. Soft ivory coloured Shaker style units contrasted with antique stained, wooden work surfaces, to give a traditional cottage feel with a modern twist. A large, solid, antique pine farmhouse table was positioned by the back window, along with six wooden chairs, painted in soft ivory and finished off with lemon coloured seat cushions. An original window seat had been restored to its former glory and upholstered in the same yellow fabric, with floral scatter cushions in pastel colours. This was Alice's favoured spot to sit and read on a sunny afternoon. A large, photo canvas print hung on the wall, depicting a three-year-old Ellie, blowing a dandelion clock. Alice had caught the profile shot at exactly the right moment, capturing the infantile effort used to purse her lips and blow, combined with the delighted surprise on her face as the seeds exploded into the air. Her dark brown hair hung down gently in angelic ringlets - a sharp contrast to the fresh green of the grass in the background - and her sapphire eyes flashed in the sunlight. It had been Alice's favourite photo of Ellie at that age, and so her parents had had it transferred on to canvas as a present for her twenty-fifth birthday.

 A door leading off from the lounge opened to a small study for Alice. Carrying on the colour scheme from the lounge, it housed a large, wooden desk and chair, with another bookcase but this one dedicated entirely to work-related books. An inviting, comfy armchair in the corner had a checked throw casually draped across it and had been the spot where Alice had fallen asleep on many occasions after an evening of marking. One piece of advice her father had given her from the onset of her career was, never take marking or school books up to the bedroom, otherwise the sanctuary in which to relax and de-stress, would quickly become a workplace to dread. He had been right and she always made a point of switching off from work before going up to bed.

The third reception room, almost as large as the lounge, led on from the study and had been converted into a studio for Roz. There was also a separate entrance to it from the side of the house, utilising the original front door of the former cottage. The bare, white-washed walls - once filled with brightly coloured canvasses - lacked any character, and the wooden floor which had been splattered with paint over the years and not cleaned up, gave it a cliché artist's studio look. An old kitchen table and several shelves, housed paints and paraphernalia, and an equally old, battered sofa, sat in the corner with a large, yellow throw covering it. The smell of paint and linseed oil permeated the room and the neighbouring study, but it was not a smell any of them objected to, and one they hardly noticed anymore.

Alice sat at her desk, turned on her computer and started searching the internet, revisiting the sites she had already briefly looked at. She could completely understand why Roz had found it so overwhelming; the sites were either austere in appearance with stark instructions on how to proceed with requests for information, or filled with nostalgic photos of an era long passed, coupled with personal testimonials of a deeply traumatic nature. Alice stared thoughtfully at the Gov.Uk adoption records page and reaching for her phone, called Celia.

"Has she had a look at the internet at all or spoken about it to you," Alice asked. Celia confirmed what she had been suspecting,

"No dear, she hasn't. She's in quite a bad place at the moment. She's barely eaten since you left," she divulged. "I'm not quite sure how to motivate her to be honest," she added, in a tone of quiet desperation.

Alice listened with concern, scrolling through the internet page as she did so.

"Listen Mum, it says here on the Gov.uk site, that anybody that was put up for adoption before 1975 and is wanting to access their birth details, will need to attend a counselling session first. I was thinking, wouldn't that be a good idea for Roz too. Don't you think she would benefit from some sort of counselling right now? I mean she's grieving for David and her baby; grief that's been bottled up for far too long. What do you think?"

"I've been thinking the same thing, yes. I was wondering whether to contact Eileen, my counsellor with the bereavement support group. I know it's through the cancer trust but she might be able to suggest another group that Roz could attend that would be more appropriate for her," Celia said.

Alice agreed,

"That's a good idea, although I would recommend a 1:1 counselling session. I can't see Roz doing group therapy somehow!"

They agreed that Celia would make some enquiries and they would broach the subject with Roz when they all met up later in the week, for Andrew's birthday. In the meantime, Celia suggested that they leave any further research for the time being, for fear of Roz feeling pressured or that the whole process was being hijacked.

Frustrated by not being able to be of more use, Alice continued to scroll through information and made a few notes so that, come Wednesday, if Roz felt like talking, she would have some information and advice to offer her. That done, she tidied the house from top to bottom in preparation for the following weekend. It didn't need much of a tidy and so, after lunch, she was back on the sun lounger in the garden and thinking about Elliot. It was going to be a long week, she conceded.

Alice packed an overnight bag and set off for Winchester, just after midday on Andrew's birthday; the idea being that they would all be there by the time he got home from work. It was just a small gathering: immediate family and some of his work colleagues. Laura always put on a decent spread and Alice was looking forward to it. She was also desperate to see Ellie and to give her a hug. It had been a very quiet week without her, especially as Alice's weekend hadn't gone to plan. She and Elliot had texted each other though, continuously, throughout the week and she was in extremely high spirits as the weekend approached once again.

Just before she left the house, she texted him to say she was heading for Andrew's and would text when she got there. He replied,

'Safe journey. Love you. See you in 70 hours xxx E.'

Alice chuckled. He had started a countdown earlier in the week and she had been receiving regular texts from him, informing her of how many hours were left until the weekend.

It proved to be an uneventful journey and Alice arrived two hours later, to be greeted by a bubbly, sunburnt Ellie. She jigged up and down as Alice pulled up in the drive and flung her arms around her, squealing excitedly.

"Oh, Mum, I've missed you! Grandma and Auntie Roz are here already and I've got loads of photos to show you all. It was amazing, absolutely amazing!" she gushed, then stopped and stared at her mother.

"What?" Alice asked, bemused.

"You look different. Like, younger. What have you done?" she demanded to know.

"Done?" Alice repeated, starting to blush.

"Yes, is it your hair? Make-up? What's different?" she continued with her questioning. Alice laughed lightly, trying to cover up her feelings of guilt.

"I've done nothing. That's probably it – I've had a week of doing nothing," she smiled genially, putting her arm around Ellie and heading for the house where Laura was waiting on the doorstep to greet her. She received similar comments from Laura and Celia but Roz just regarded her silently, returning the proffered hug with warmth and a whispered apology.

"You've got nothing to be sorry about, Roz," Alice whispered back.

"I keep telling you, dear," Celia said to Alice, "teaching is such a stressful job. See how well you look after just a week's break. You look radiant, dear," she said, her face creasing into an affectionate smile.

They sat in the garden for afternoon tea, listening to Ellie and Rachel's tales from their camping trip, with Scott and Riley occasionally chipping in too but they soon grew restless, and slunk off back into the house to recommence their abandoned games. Ellie jumped up, suddenly remembering the gifts she had bought, and with Rachel in tow, went upstairs to fetch them. Laura took the opportunity to refill the teapot, accepting Celia's offer of help.

Roz turned to Alice,

"How is he?" she asked steadily. Alice looked startled. "Who?"

"Elliot," she stated. "I know what you're up to, Alice. I think you're a fool," she said gently, remembering the heartache she had witnessed Alice go through all those years ago.

"I don't know what you mean," Alice faltered, hating herself for lying. Roz sighed and leant forward.

"You forget; I've been there, done that and got the war wounds to prove it. I may be from a different generation; we didn't have phones and texts but the look … the look is always the same. It's timeless. That Mona Lisa smile you have, when you know something that nobody else does. Except for another mistress, who's had that same smile on her face before. I know what you're up to," she nodded. She didn't look disappointed or even disapproving, just concerned. Alice drew in a steadying breath, not sure what to say.

"He's married, Alice," Roz emphasised. Alice licked her lips uncertainly before she answered.

"I'm not so sure, you know. He lives in York, she's in London," she started. Roz shook her head, interrupting her.

"Has he explained that to you? How he and his wife live separately?" she prompted.

"No," Alice confirmed meekly.

"Well then, he's married. This needs to stop before everybody gets hurt. Think of Ellie," she chided gently. Alice quickly grew defiant, frustrated by being grilled. Of course she had thought about Ellie.

"I know all that, but he was mine first and we belong together. I know we do," she declared passionately. "I've spent my whole life giving. Now it's my turn to start taking back. I've seen how you and David missed out on a great love – I'm not going to do that. I feel alive for the first time in over eighteen years and it feels so good!"

She sat back in her seat realising that her impassioned outburst had more or less confirmed what Roz was accusing her of. She sighed, the challenging look on her face fading as she regarded Roz's expression. She looked tired and deeply sad. Alice deliberated for a moment, then said in a hushed voice,

"Elliot told me about his uncle's affair," she started, putting a hand out to stop Roz's retort, "he doesn't know it was you. I have said nothing to him. He was the one who started the conversation about it," she continued.

"But, why?" Roz asked in distress. She was feeling so vulnerable.

"That's not the point. The point is, David told Elliot that you were the love of his life, and nothing else mattered. He never gave up on you, Roz. And I know, despite everything, I know that Elliot has never given up on me. I know that. I can't miss this chance. Even if it means breaking up a marriage or…"

"Being a mistress," Roz finished her train of thought. Alice nodded.

"Yes. Even that. I don't expect you to condone it but please, try and understand it," she urged, lowering her tone even more as Laura and Celia approached with fresh tea.

In spite of her conversation with Roz, Alice's high spirits weren't dampened and she thoroughly enjoyed the evening. She didn't get much of a chance to talk alone with Andrew but he sent a couple of knowing winks her way. She wasn't sure whether he too had guessed the reason for her good mood, or whether it related back to the conversation they had shared the previous week regarding Roz and Celia. Either way, watching her brother become merrier as the evening progressed, she doubted whether he knew himself why he was winking at her. He certainly liked his drink, she mused affectionately.

Laura appeared by her side, holding a large, board-backed envelope. She sat down next to Alice and handed it to her, saying,

"I've given Ellie a few photos that she has asked for and I thought you might like this one."

She watched her expectantly as Alice opened the envelope and pulled out the 10 x 8" photo, letting out a surprised gasp. It was the one of her and Elliot, from Andrew and Laura's wedding album. She turned to Laura, her eyes questioning. Laura smiled knowingly.

"Andrew told you, then?" Alice acknowledged. Laura took hold of her hand, a grin breaking out across her face.

"He did, yes. You know him, he can't keep anything from me. Sorry," she apologised awkwardly but still grinning. Alice laughed.

"I would never expect him to keep anything from you anyway. You're his best friend, it's what you do," she said, her eyes drawn back to the photo resting on her lap.

"So?" Laura asked, encouraging an answer. Alice couldn't tear her eyes away from the youthful Elliot, captured for all eternity, with a smile that told the world he was in love.

"I'm hooked, well and truly. And facing such a moral dilemma," she muttered. Laura grimaced.

"Look, I can't tell you what to do. Obviously, as a married woman, I can't condone an affair but you two have such a history - you have Ellie - and it sounds like he's completely hooked too. Maybe finding you again, and discovering about Ellie, will be the thing that ends his marriage, before you even embark on an affair," she reasoned. Alice shot her a look. Laura drew in a sharp breath.

"Have you ... are you?" she asked, her mouth dropping open in shocked surprise. Alice couldn't help but smile and started to laugh.

"Alice Greene, I am surprised at you!" Laura feigned scolding her, then put her arm around her and whispered covertly,

"Now, tell me all about it!"

They both erupted with laughter, their mirth drawing the attention of Celia who came over to join them.

"Having fun, dears?" she asked, sitting down and sighing as she took the weight off her feet.

"Yes, we were just watching Andrew getting drunk," Alice told her glibly. Celia tutted, as only a mother would.

"Well, he'll regret it in the morning when he has to get up for work," she remonstrated. "Mind you, your father was just the same when he was younger. Drinking all night, then up with the lark and off to work," she confessed.

"Not as a teacher, I hope!" Alice declared, her eyes widening at the thought.

"No, before then. He had a job as a farm hand when he first left university, to make ends meet before he started doing his teacher training. I know his mother would have seen him right but he wanted to prove he could look after himself. I think he was trying to impress me too, and his prospective father-in-law," she told them, smiling at the memory. Turning to Alice she said,

"I nearly forgot to tell you: Roz and I are meeting up with an old friend of mine tomorrow. She lives here in Winchester, so I thought I'd take the chance," she looked pointedly at Alice, "Do you remember Eileen?"

"Oh, yes. Oh, that'll be lovely. Good," Alice nodded approvingly. Laura looked at Celia, recognising the name.

"Wasn't Eileen your counsellor with the Wessex cancer trust?" she asked, remembering how Andrew would accompany Celia for her bereavement sessions, based at their Winchester branch.

"Yes, that's right, dear. We keep in touch and she thought it would be lovely to meet up before we travel back home again," she smiled a little stiltedly. Alice concluded that her mother wasn't great at telling white lies but judging by Laura's expression, she had put two and two together anyway. If she knew about what was going on with Elliot, then Alice felt sure that Andrew would have told her all about Roz and her baby too.

"I think that's a lovely idea," Laura said, "and it'll be great to see her on a personal level rather than as a counsellor. Don't you agree, Alice?" she added smoothly.

Yes, she knows, Alice thought, trying not to laugh again at the absurdity of all the cloak and dagger business. One day, they might all venture to tell the truth and not have any more hidden secrets, she thought. Just then, her phoned beeped in her bag by her side, as a message arrived from Elliot.

Maybe not just yet, she concluded, with that secret smile on her face.

As Alice and Ellie were leaving the next morning, Andrew snatched a moment with Alice.

"I'm off to Brockenhurst on Saturday, for an evening out with Dan. A late birthday drink," he told her. "Has Elliot said anything to his family yet, about Ellie?"

"Not that I know of, no," Alice confirmed. "I think there's probably lots to consider before he breaks that kind of news," she said, intimating his wife and how she would take it. Alice had tried not to dwell on it but the question had arisen in her mind on more than one occasion. Andrew nodded.

"Right, I won't mention anything then," he said. "And erm... Laura told me!"
He leant forward and gave her a bear hug and kissed her cheek.

"It's your business, please don't think I'm interfering, but if you ever need to talk it through, just call me. Anytime," he said, with genuine sincerity, "I'm here for you."

"Thanks, Andrew, she murmured, appreciating once again, how caring her brother was, and always had been.

Thursday evening and Friday morning were spent getting Ellie packed up for her weekend camping trip with her friends. They were staying at a farm in Hunscote, just under ten miles away from Wilmcote, and had chosen it due to its 'back to basics' approach to camping. The teens were looking forward to a weekend of singing round the camp fire and cooking sausages on sticks. A far cry from their usual sleep overs, which consisted of films, ready meals, and microwave popcorn.

"Brad's bringing his guitar and I've got my ukulele", Ellie grinned, brandishing her purple ukulele triumphantly.

The five friends all lived in Wilmcote and had been through primary and secondary school together but when September approached, they would be going their separate ways to their various universities. Brad was also going to Birmingham University, and like Ellie, would be living in Halls there. Ellie's closest friend, Natasha – Tasha - was heading for Lancaster: Kyle and Amy were going to Manchester and Cardiff and so, they had decided, as a fond farewell to their carefree childhood, they would spend a month of adventures together. This was to be their first adventure; their second one being a trip to Wales, to climb Snowdon.

Alice helped Ellie carry all her equipment over the road to Tasha's house and load it into her car. Amy was already there with boxes of food, and everybody's sleeping bags and pillows. Brad and Kyle were taking Brad's car with tents and cooking utensils. They were an organised group. Alice noted a box filled with beer and spirits. It made her feel a little uneasy but more than anything, it was another reminder that these children were now adults, and about to embark on life's adventures. She gave Ellie a big hug and asked her to keep in touch.

"Phone me when you get there and send me a text each evening to let me know you're alright," she said.

"Will do, Mum. Don't worry, we'll be okay. It's a well manned site, the farm house is right there if we need any help," she explained, again illustrating her sensible nature.

"See you Monday afternoon," she shouted cheerily as she climbed into the car.

Alice waved them off and stopped for a chat with Mandy, Tasha's mum. They had known each other since the girls were little and being close neighbours, had spent many hours in each other's company while their children played together. As she crossed the road back to her own cottage, she felt thankful that Ellie had chosen Birmingham University rather than going further afield, like Tasha was. It meant she could see her, every day if she chose to, and still encourage her independence. She suddenly realised how difficult it must have been for Celia, when she left to go to York. As far as Alice was concerned, it was a huge adventure and one that started well from the onset but for Celia, it must have been hard to adapt to life as a childless mum effectively, with both children gone when still in their teens. She made a mental note to phone Celia and find out how their visit to Eileen had panned out.

'But first, I need to paint my toenails ready for tomorrow,' she determined, as the butterflies kicked in and the minutes ticked by.

Chapter Nine

Alice was up and showered by the time Elliot phoned her at seven to say he was on his way.

"So, I stick on the A46 to Wilmcote?" he wanted to know, "I don't go through the centre of Stratford?"

"No, avoid Stratford altogether," she advised him, "Saturday traffic is hellish. Stick to the A46 and then straight into Wilmcote. We're on Church Road, it's easy to find, just drive through the village and turn left at the 'Mary Arden Inn'," she confirmed.

She stripped her bed and re-made it with the freshly laundered, new bedding that she had bought in the week. The stonewashed, light grey fabric, dotted with dainty bouquets of pale and dusky pink flowers, matched her room décor perfectly. The walls of her gabled bedroom were painted in a soft pink and the room was dominated by an impressive, solid oak, four poster bed. It had been a fantastic find in an antique bazaar some years previously; painted with a hideous red gloss and in need of a little repair. Together with Roz, they had painstakingly restored it, stripping away the old paint and treating it with a lime wash to give it a bleached, white-wash appearance. Their hard work and perseverance paid off; the result was a stunningly beautiful and ornate, period piece of furniture. Alice was loath to obscure the carved, fluted pedestal pillars that made up the framework of the bed, and quickly scuppered her original plan of a traditional canopy and drapes in a heavy chintz fabric. Instead she opted for an antique white, tulle swag canopy, with delicate strings of pink and ivory rose bud fairy lights loosely wrapped around the pillars.

The bed fit comfortably under the high gable and the ceiling sloped down on either side but still afforded room for a double wardrobe on one side of the bed, and a bedside table and rocking chair on the other. The bed faced the door and on the opposite side of the room, there was a wide chest of drawers and a small dressing table, which doubled up as somewhere to store her laptop and a few books. All the wooden furniture, except the rocking chair, had been sanded down and treated with the same lime wash as the bed, to give the room a uniformed look. It also gave it the illusion of being more spacious than it actually was. The rocking chair had been a gift from her grandpa on the birth of Ellie, and Alice had kept it in its original, antique stained, oak state. It had once been his chair, and she had such fond memories of sitting on his lap as a toddler, being rocked as he read her stories. Or made them up, as he often did. It was a wide, robust piece of craftsmanship that had been made locally in the New Forest, which added greatly to its sentimental value.

As she smoothed down the dusky pink chenille throw, stretched out across the lower half of the bed, Alice stood back and surveyed the room with a critical eye. She wanted everything to be perfect. Staring thoughtfully at the bed, she went over to the wardrobe and pulled out a shoebox, stored towards the back of it. Inside, nestled in a pink velour sleepsuit - Ellie's first baby outfit - was a dark grey, plush elephant. About twenty-five centimetres tall and with moveable joints, it had a long trunk, small black eyes and pale grey, velvet suede inner ears, paw pads, and tail. The tail was frayed and the ears were slightly balding, as was the trunk. It had clearly been well loved over the years. Lifting it out, Alice carefully positioned it to sit on one of the pillows at the top of the bed. It looked out of place on the pristine bedding but she smiled knowingly and nodded, happy with the overall appearance of the room.

Sitting at her dressing table, she took time over her make-up; the therapeutic routine helped to calm her nerves and excitement. Carefully stepping into her dress, she moved to the full-sized mirror by her bedroom door, scrutinising every detail. She was wearing a simple, burnt orange, strappy sundress in a soft, cheesecloth fabric that flattered her curves and highlighted her tanned skin. Putting tiny, silver heart studs in her ears, she reached for the necklace on her dressing table and carefully clasped it around her neck. Two silver hearts intertwined, hung on a delicate silver chain; freshly polished with a soft cloth, it glinted in the mirror. Alice touched the necklace gently, smiling at her reflection. Happy with the overall effect, she slipped on some brown, strappy flat sandals and headed downstairs.

Alice stopped herself from running through the lounge when she heard the doorbell. She checked her appearance in the hall mirror before opening the front door, a radiant smile on her face. Elliot was leaning against the wooden pillar of the storm porch, his smile matching hers, looking casual in light grey chinos and a navy, open-necked shirt. From behind his back he produced a large, romantic bouquet of pink roses, purple Peruvian lilies, and lemon freesias, offset with frothy gypsophila. Stepping forward, she accepted the flowers and buried her nose in them briefly before silently grabbing hold of his shirt and pulling him towards her to kiss him passionately on the lips. Walking backwards, she pulled him into the house, their lips still locked. Elliot kicked the door shut behind him and gently pushed her up against the hall wall, cradling her face in his hands as their kiss deepened. She released his shirt and wrapped her arms around him, a little encumbered by the bouquet she was holding. Eventually breaking away, she murmured against his mouth,

"Hello you."
He laughed, surprised and delighted by her greeting.

"Wow, you certainly give a warm welcome," he grinned, running a hand through his hair.

"Not to everyone," she replied coyly. "Just those I want to impress," she added with an impish grin. He laughed and pulled her towards him again.

"Consider me impressed," he murmured, kissing her again before burying his face in her hair, sighing with contentment.

"Let me go and put these flowers in water," Alice said, breaking the silence. She was reluctant to leave their embrace but at the same time was keen to show him round. Taking his hand, she led him through to the kitchen, breathing in the scent from the bouquet.

"These are beautiful, Elliot, thank you," she enthused, studying the blooms in more detail. "I love the smell of freesias, especially the yellow ones," she added, as she filled a vase with water. Looking up, she noticed Elliot staring at the print of Ellie on the wall, the haunted look in his eyes almost reducing her to tears. Leaving the flowers, she crossed the kitchen to stand next to him and gently took his hand.

"She's beautiful," he murmured, gulping hard. Alice nodded.

"Yes, she is. She was three when I took that," she told him quietly. Elliot turned to her, searching her face with pained eyes.

"I'm sorry," he shook his head, "for some reason I hadn't really thought of her as anything other than the Ellie I know now. Seeing her as a toddler is just..." he didn't finish his sentence.

"Making you realise what you've missed," Alice spoke for him. He looked away for a moment and sighed.

"Yes," he said definitely. "But this weekend is about you and me. I'm sorry," he said squeezing her hand. She rested her other hand on his chest.

"Listen," she started tentatively, "I thought, if it's alright with you, I'd like to show you round the village. Where Ellie went to school and where she has her weekend job, that kind of thing. I want you to know about her childhood, I want to share it with you," she smiled encouragingly as his expression lightened and he nodded his approval.

"Then we can come back here and get cosy," she said, lowering her voice and stroking his chest tantalisingly with her fingertips. He brushed the hair back from her face, looking into her eyes with a heart-stopping warmth.

"I'd love that, Alice," he agreed. "Especially the 'getting cosy' part," he breathed, raising an eyebrow suggestively. She laughed lightly and went back to quickly arrange the flowers in the vase. Elliot peered out through the kitchen window, admiring the garden. He pointed towards the tree.

"Is that Ellie's swing?" he asked. Alice grinned,

"Yes, it is. Come and have a look," she invited, pushing the door open and stepping out into the garden. Elliot followed close behind, slowing down to take stock of the planting.

"I can see where you got your inspiration from," he smiled, indicating towards the mass of foxgloves and hollyhocks, erupting from behind well-established rose bushes smothered in pink and yellow blooms.

"Anne Hathaway's garden, by any chance?" he teased. She gave a doleful smile.

"I thought I was being original at first," she explained, "but if you look in anybody's garden round here, you'll see they all have the same planting scheme. Anyway," she continued, "this is Ellie's swing. She had a kid's swing for ages but grew out of it well and truly, so I found somewhere that makes adult swings and I could get it personalised. Look," she said, pointing at the wooden seat. It was decorated with carved flowers and butterflies all around the edges, and in the middle, was Ellie's name, carved in Disney font.

"That's brilliant," Elliot enthused, inspecting the handiwork. "Does she have a middle name?"

"Yes, same as mine. Grace."
He nodded, then frowned,

"Grace?" he questioned. "Ellie Grace Greene?" He laughed out loud, apologising for his mirth, seeing the confusion on her face.

"So basically, you called our daughter EGG," he mocked affectionately. She scowled and playfully hit his arm. It had never even crossed her mind until now.

"I blame you," she accused with mock wrath.

"How is it my fault?" he laughed, holding his hands out defensively. Quick as a flash, Alice replied,

"She should've been a Barraclough," then realising what she had said, she turned away nervously. Elliot took her arm and quietly pulled her towards him. She leant against him, her words tumbling out,

"I'm so sorry, I don't know why I said that. It was stupid, I'm sorry." Her head was bent, nervously anticipating his response. He lifted her chin so that her eyes met his, and he held them in a steady gaze. About to say something, he suddenly caught sight of her necklace and froze. He stared at it, a stunned expression on his face, then reached out to touch it before looking intently at Alice. She swallowed, unable to look away.

"Yes, she should," he said, "but it's just a name after all. She *is* a Barraclough and she *is* a Greene. But most importantly she's *our* child, made from *our* love." His eyes narrowed slightly as he watched for her reaction.

"Tell me differently if I'm wrong," he almost challenged softly. Alice breathed out slowly, trying to control the trembling overtaking her body. She shook her head,

"You're not wrong, Elliot," she said, her voice barely a whisper. "I knew from the onset that she was made from love. She was meant to be." She blinked away tears as she smiled and nodded to affirm her statement. Elliot's face softened instantly, and he wrapped his arms around her, pulling her tightly towards him.

"I have never stopped loving you, not for a single minute. Don't ever think I did," he told her, his voice full of sincerity. He sounded urgent almost, desperate for her to believe him. She moved her head away from his chest and reached up to kiss him tenderly as her answer. They stood in the warm, midday sun, holding each other so closely that they could feel each other's heartbeat.

"This business of not dragging up the past and just focusing on the present, is hard, isn't it?" he said, reading her mind uncannily accurately. She nodded, melting a little further into his embrace. He made her feel so safe, so secure. She didn't want anything to ruin it but she knew she was treading on rocky ground just by talking about Ellie. It must be an emotional minefield for him, she acknowledged, but one they had to work through. Together.

"Let's revisit the past first then," she said. "Let me show you where Ellie grew up and you can ask anything you want about her. I want to share her life with you, I told you that. I thought we could take a quick walk through the village and have a cup of tea at 'Mary Arden's Farm'," she suggested, in a positive tone, determined to get their day back on track. He nodded but resisted when Alice went to move away.

"We're okay, aren't we?" he asked. She looked at him in earnest.

"Yes, of course we are," she said, "I just need to realise that the concept of being a father is all very new for you. I should have more tact," she acknowledged with a little laugh. He watched her for a moment, a slow smile emerging as he spoke

"I think we should start the day again," he said, his eyes twinkling mischievously. Alice raised her eyebrows, questioning his suggestion.

"How do you mean?" she asked. He grinned,

"Well, you could start by giving me one of your very warm welcomes again," he murmured as he lowered his mouth to hers. Laughingly, she obliged, leaving him in little doubt as to whether they were 'okay'.

Several minutes later, they finally moved from their embrace and headed back through the house, arms still wrapped around each other in contented bliss.

"Right," Alice started, shutting the front door behind them, and walking up the short garden path to the gate that led on to the road. She stretched her hand out in front of her, indicating the road.

"This is Church Road. Opposite, is Tasha's house. She's been Ellie's best friend since they were four. To the left a little way, is Ellie's old primary school and to the right, is where she works at 'Mary Arden's farm'," she informed him. "Well, I say 'works' but actually, she's just left there because she wanted to be free over her last summer at home. She started a weekend job there when she was fifteen, so it's been a big part of her life," she added, experiencing a pang of regret. Voicing it suddenly made it all very real. Taking Elliot's hand, she said,

"Let's start with the school."

They walked a short distance along the narrow pavement in mutual silence as Elliot admired the surroundings. The quaint cottages, each one individual, were built with either a mixture of timber frame and old brick, traditional white-washed cob and thatch, or in the classic black and white Tudor style which the area was famed for. In amongst them were some sympathetic, modern builds that added to, rather than detracted from, the character of the village. As Alice had already pointed out, the residential gardens were full to bursting with an assortment of flowers and fruit trees, haphazard in appearance but clearly well tendered.

"I see you're not far from a church," Elliot commented, as they passed St Andrew's church, noting the short distance they had walked from the house. It was an old Gothic revival style building, dating back to the early 1840's, and surrounded by an imposing graveyard.

"Not intentionally though," she said.

"Do you still go to church?" he wondered. She shook her head.

"No. Not here anyway. I used to go, when I went home to visit, but not since Dad died," she told him.

"Did his death affect your faith then?" he asked, intrigued. She thought for a moment.

"Not really. It's strange but I always associated church with Grandpa and Dad, not God; I went because they were there and it was like a family thing to do, and now that they're both gone, I don't feel that need. I didn't ever connect the church with faith. Faith is in your head and your heart, not in a building, surely?" she ventured. Elliot nodded slowly,

"Yes, I can understand that," he agreed.

"Let's be honest, if God is responsible for all this," she gestured around her, "then surely we should be worshipping him out in the fields or ... or somewhere like

Anne Hathaway's garden. Not in a dusty, old church," she proclaimed then added in a hushed voice, "sorry, Dad!"

Elliot laughed,

"You're right. And I'm sure your dad would agree with you," he said softly, putting his arm around her shoulder and drawing her towards him. They had stopped outside the school, next to the churchyard. A small collection of sprawling buildings and a playground, with parking for a handful of cars, made up the village school. Alice pointed out the changes since Ellie had gone there; the old temporary classrooms had been replaced with a new build and the playground had been revamped. They stood leaning against the wooden, five-bar gate, looking at the roof on the new build.

"It's hard to see from here," Alice explained enthusiastically, "but it's a green roof, covered in sedum plants. I think it's a great idea and so easy to do. All schools should have them!" she declared. Elliot was impressed. Anything that improved the environment was a bonus in his eyes. The playground was surrounded by trees and although on the edge of the road, there was hardly a sound to be heard except the plentiful birdsong. He looked across the playground with its patch of artificial turf and painted hopscotch grid.

"It's very small. How many children does it cater for?" he asked. Alice told him about eighty children.

"She was very happy here, and being such small classes, has made friends for life. They all went on to secondary school together," she told him. "Stratford-upon-Avon High, which converted to an Academy four years ago, just as Ellie was choosing her options. She stayed on for the sixth form there too and again, loved it," she said. Elliot nodded, taking it all in.

"She's a very sociable girl," Alice added, "I think she'll get on fine at Uni, both academically and socially," she said with a proud smile.

"She's certainly got a vivacious nature," Elliot agreed. "She's just great, Alice. And everything that you have done for her - your lifestyle and your nurturing - is exactly how I would have imagined it for our children," he said, expressing his innermost thoughts. Alice looked startled.

"How you would have imagined for our children?" she prompted. He let out an awkward laugh.

"Yes, well, I used to daydream once upon a time," he admitted ruefully. Not sure what to say, and surprised at his frankness, she leant over and kissed his cheek.

"Let me take you for tea and cake," she suggested.

They turned round and walked back the way they had come, reaching Alice's cottage within a matter of minutes. Carrying on towards the Green, Alice pointed out various things of interest: where Ellie caught the bus to secondary school, the house she used to baby-sit at, where her friend Brad lived, and the village store where she would spend her sweets money from Roz.

"She was a very indulged child," Alice acknowledged with a wry smile, "but Dad always said, what's the point in having children if you're not going to spoil them," she laughed.

They had stopped on the corner of the Green, under a mature lime tree with branches reaching out in all directions, to admire the large, old, brick building and its array of barns and outhouses, on the other side of the road.

"This is Mary Arden's farmhouse. Originally, they thought that the other building over there," she pointed further along the road to the right, "was her house and so the Trust bought it and renovated it. Then when they realised that they had got it wrong, and that the other house was owned by her neighbour, Adam Palmer, they put the two together to make up the farm," she explained.

"Yes, I drove past this on the way in. They are impressive buildings," Elliot said with enthusiasm. "Do they have pigs here?" he asked, cocking his head to listen to sounds he recognised from childhood days at his grandparents' farm. Alice nodded,

"Yes, they do. Gorgeous, Tamworth pigs. The pig sty is just behind this building. And there are goats, sheep, and cattle too. Come on, I'll show you," she smiled broadly, carrying on along the road.

They stopped again after a few minutes, to admire the house that was initially thought to be Mary Arden's. Much more striking than the red brick building on the corner, and twice the size, its 16th century timber frame and white rendered walls, had stood the test of time and had been restored to reflect its former glory of a wealthy farmer's home. The crooked, exterior walls and roof added to its charm, as did the many leaded, mullioned windows. The familiar planting scheme of roses, lavender, rosemary and other herbs, hugged the narrow space between the house and stone wall that ran alongside the pavement.

"Did you know," Elliot told Alice, "that the amount of timber used in house construction was an indication of wealth in Elizabethan days; so, judging by the number of vertical beams used here, they were fairly well off. It would be the equivalent of parking a Porsche on the drive just to impress the neighbours," he joked. She listened to him appreciatively, saying,

"I love being able to share this with you. Everybody round here takes it for granted. But you really see it for its architectural and historical merit, and I…"

"See it for its romantic worth," he finished her sentence. "I know. That's why we work so well together," he smiled, squeezing her hand. He pointed to the field opposite the farmhouse, following the skyline leading back the way they had come.

"Does your house back on to this field?" he wondered, trying to get his bearings.

"Nearly, yes. The cottages behind mine do. The field's known as the Orchards and belongs to the farm. You can't see my house from here but you can see the field from my house, if that makes sense," she laughed at her awkward explanation.

"You make perfect sense," he murmured, pulling her close to kiss her. She responded willingly, not caring about passers-by, or the fact that they were standing in full view of the farm.

"Did I mention that I love you?" he whispered, gazing deep into her eyes, oblivious to everything except her beauty.

"You did, but you can mention it again if you like," she gave him an alluring smile.

"I love you, Alice Greene," he breathed, against her warm mouth.

"I love you too, Elliot Barraclough," she sighed in reply, snatching another kiss before they moved on.

They headed for the farm entrance, framed by picturesque, arching willow trees, and showing her pass at the reception desk, she led him through to their first port of call: the café. Every member of staff acknowledged her with either a smile, a wave or a cheery, 'hello', from across the room. Elliot looked amused.

"Of course. Everybody knows you here too, don't they? I don't even know why I'm surprised by that," he remarked, as he carried their tray out into the courtyard, looking for an empty table to sit at.

"Well, it is a small village. Everybody knows what you're doing before you've even done it," she laughed, pointing to a spot in the sunshine that was free. They sat down opposite each other, their feet touching under the table.

"You know that Ellie will find out about me being here then, don't you?" he said. Alice nodded.

"I was going to tell her anyway," she said, "I think she has kind of guessed that there's something going on between us, so I thought I'd tell her after the weekend that you've been to visit," she told him, gauging his reaction.

"Good," he agreed. "But not the extent of my visit?" he teased, raising his eyebrow.

"I don't know what you mean!" She ran her foot up and down his calf under the table, pulling a suggestive face. He laughed, revelling in the way she was making him feel wanted.

"So, what are your plans for your summer break? Apart from entertaining me, that is," he asked with a grin. "Do you ever go away on holiday?" he wondered. Alice sat back in her chair, sipping at the hot tea and cradling the cup in her hand.

"Sometimes. Ellie and I went to Italy a couple of years ago. That was such an incredible experience. We've been to Berlin and Paris, and when she was much younger, we took her to Disneyland Paris," she told him.

"We?" he asked.

"Mum and Dad, Roz, Andrew, Laura and their three children. It was at Christmas time and I have to say, the adverts on telly don't do it enough justice. It was truly magical," she enthused, "although, hard work with four, over-excited, young children in tow!" she added. Elliot smiled at the image.

"I'll bet," he said.

"But usually," Alice continued to answer his initial question, "during the school breaks, we tend to go back to Brockenhurst. Ellie gets to spend time with her cousins there. Well, my cousin's children, really. They're all the same sort of age. And of course, Andrew's not far from Brockenhurst, in Winchester, so Ellie spends an inordinate amount of time there with them. Rachel is her twin, basically," she said. "And it does mean I get to relax a bit and let everybody else enjoy her company", she laughed, "and Laura and I have always been really close, especially as we had the girls at more or less the same time," she added. He studied her with a look of pride.

"I've met a few single mums and I can safely say, none of them have done half as good a job as you, Alice. You should be so proud of yourself. And I'm sorry if that sounds patronising, it's not meant to be," he stressed. Alice smiled happily,

"It's not patronising at all. But don't forget, I've had huge support from Roz right from the onset. I'm not so sure I could've achieved as much without that," she admitted readily. Elliot looked thoughtful. He felt jealous knowing that somebody else had helped raise his daughter. He knew it was an irrational jealousy but he couldn't help feeling resentful nevertheless.

"Did Roz not get married or have children?" he asked. Alice let out a derisive laugh.

"Well, if you'd asked me that two weeks ago, I would've said 'no'," she declared spontaneously, "but as it turns out, I would've been wrong," she widened her eyes for emphasis.

"What do you mean?" he asked, curious by her admission. She leant forward, putting her elbows on the table and resting her head on her hands. She looked at him conspiratorially, knowing she was breaking a confidence yet again.

"When I told Ellie about you, it prompted Roz to confess about her past too. She had an affair, a long time ago, when she was a teenager. He was married. And she fell pregnant," she held Elliot's eye contact, wondering how much to tell him. She decided to edit the story. For now, anyway.

"So, she ran away from home. She didn't tell anybody about the baby. Until two weeks ago. It's been heart-breaking, discovering what she went through. The way they treated unmarried mothers was horrendous, Elliot. Absolutely awful," she shuddered as she spoke.

"Can you tell me about it?" he asked tactfully, sensing this was a family secret she probably shouldn't be divulging.

Alice told him about the mother and baby homes: the humiliation and the absolute, concrete resolution of adoption, often against the mother's own wishes. She told him how Roz had fought to keep her baby but failed: how she had described the devastating moment of having to give her away to complete strangers, and was then expected to carry on with her life as normal.

"What about the father?" Elliot asked.

"She never saw him again," she said nervously. He frowned.

"But surely, he would have helped her to keep the baby? What kind of a man would let a woman go through that?" he sounded angry. Alice paused before answering.

"The kind that didn't know she was pregnant in the first place," she uttered.

Elliot sat back in his chair, looking away. He rubbed his forehead, agitated by what he had heard. Turning back to Alice, he looked at her with desperation.

"Is this a family thing? Keeping the fathers out of the picture?" he demanded to know. Alice stared at him, shocked by his tone but also, realising how it must have sounded to him.

"Please Elliot, this isn't about us. What happened to Roz is completely different," she insisted. "I know how it sounds," she continued, "but you can't compare the two.

That's not fair," she said. Elliot sighed deeply, acknowledging what she had said.

"Alright, I'm sorry. It's just a sensitive subject. Please, carry on," he inclined his head, waiting for her to continue. She took hold of his hand across the table.

"No, I'm sorry. I know this is a lot for you to take in, all in one go, but it's been a hell of a fortnight for me too. Meeting you again and telling Ellie about you, and then finding out about Roz's baby," she paused, calming her voice before she continued,

"We're trying to trace her. Roz is desperate to find her. And to be honest, it's all a bit of a mess," she grimaced.

What about the father?" he asked, "will he be told too?"

"He died," she said flatly. Elliot blinked.

"Jesus!" he muttered, under his breath.

"The man that Roz had an affair with, was dominated by his father. His father found out about the affair and threatened to destroy them. Not only the two of them but my grandpa too. She was the vicar's daughter, after all," she explained, hoping he would understand.

"But that makes no sense. How old was he? Why couldn't he stand up to his father? I would have!" he exclaimed.

"But this was 1968, Elliot. Things were different then. I didn't realise how much, until recently. And anyway, Roz didn't tell him about his father's threats. He only intimidated her, not his son. He knew that she loved him and would do anything to protect him, and his reputation," she said firmly.

"1968? So, what did this man do for a living? You said, 'reputation'. That implies he had an important position, doesn't it," he probed. Alice licked her lips nervously.

"I'm not sure. She didn't say really," she lied.

Elliot's eyes narrowed. He knew she wasn't being truthful but decided not to push it any further. Something was nagging at the back of his mind, troubling him.

"Did she love him? When she left?" he asked. Surprised by his question, she nodded.

"Yes, she did. That's what is so heart-breaking. She never got over him, never stopped loving him, but she felt she couldn't go back to him because of what she'd done. She had given away their baby. If I were him, I'm not sure I could have forgiven that. Could you?"

The question slipped out before she had time to think it through. She closed her eyes, silently cursing herself. When she opened them again, she found that Elliot was watching her intently.

"I've forgiven you. I think even if you'd had Ellie adopted, under those circumstances, I would have forgiven you. Because I love you," he replied. "It's the fact that some poor guy fathered a child and never found out about it, that bothers me. I find that really hard to swallow, Alice. And yes, you're right, this is all very close to home."

He was struggling with what he was being told, trying desperately to distinguish between the past and the present.

"When you were pregnant, did you ever consider adoption?" he asked abruptly. Horrified, Alice shook her head vehemently.

"Absolutely not! I mean, I can completely identify with that fear of going through pregnancy and not knowing what the future would hold. That feeling of being alone. But then, as the little life grows inside you, you realise you're not alone after all," she paused, thinking about how she had felt at the time.

"But having said that, a huge part of you is missing. It takes two to make a baby and the puzzle just isn't complete," she told him. "I would never have given Ellie up, not for any reason. She was all I had left of you," she dared to confess.

Elliot looked taken aback by what she had said. They sat in silence for a moment, both thinking about what had just been divulged. Elliot broke the silence,

"How have you started looking for her? Have you even got a name?" he asked tactfully, changing his tone and the direction of the conversation. Alice told him briefly about the information she had found and Roz's reluctance to pursue it.

"She's scared of rejection. And scared of failing to find her, I think. I really want to help but I'm not sure how I can get the ball rolling. Ellie was all ready to go charging off to Cornwall, expecting to find her instantly!" she smiled, remembering her determination.

"Cornwall? Why Cornwall?" Elliot asked

"That's where Roz went when she ran away. She gave birth there, so we should be able to find records fairly easily," she said. Elliot scratched his head, something he always did when unsure.

"That's weird," he muttered.

"What is?" Alice looked confused.

"When David went looking for Linda, the first place he went to was Cornwall. Isn't that strange?" he voiced, shrugging his shoulders, questioning the coincidence.

Alice held her breath. She could feel she was about to blush and focused very hard on not doing so.

"Yes, that is strange. Roz went there on a whim, she said. It's an arty kind of place. Why did David go to Cornwall?" she dared to ask.

"Because they used to go there all the time, for weekends away. He told me they had a love nest there. They hired some rooms; I think it was an artist's studio flat or something. Their secret rendezvous. He hoped she had gone there."

He looked at Alice, noticing the change of expression on her face as the penny dropped.

"She *wanted* to be found, that's why she went there!" she murmured under her breath, realisation hitting her. Elliot leant towards her,

"What did you say?" he asked, trying to catch her words. She stared unseeingly at him for a moment, going over it in her mind, then snapped out of her stunned trance.

"Nothing, it's nothing really," she dismissed, her mind still racing. Roz had still not told them everything, she realised that now.

"Maybe one day you'll trust me enough to tell me everything," he said with a dejected voice.

Alice stifled a gasp, seeing the hurt in his eyes. Instinctively, she reached her hand out to touch his face.

"I trust you now, Elliot. Implicitly." Her eyes conveyed total honesty. "There's just so much to tell you that I wouldn't know where to start," she said, "we have a lifetime of catching up to do."

They sat in silence again, distractedly watching the blacksmith at work in his shed opposite the café.

"So, this is where Ellie worked?" Elliot asked, once again trying to change the conversation.

"Yes. Ellie worked with the animals, mucking out the horses and pigs, and Brad worked here in the café. But they both handed in their notice last month," she told him.

"Are they an item, Ellie and Brad?" he wondered, looking pleased at the prospect.

"No. Although he did once ask her to marry him," she replied lightly. Elliot sat up straight.

"Really?"

"Yes, but they were only six at the time," she laughed, enjoying his momentarily stunned expression.

"Ah well, he probably still loves her then. Falling in love at the age of six is a pivotal moment in a boy's life. Trust me, I know," he grinned with affected sincerity. Alice laughed,

"You did not fall in love with me when you were six! I was only five then," she exclaimed, shaking her head at his ridiculous declaration. He shrugged, still smiling but his eyes were deadly serious.

"Actually, I did. What can I say? You stole my heart when you were only five. I never recovered," he told her simply, raising an eyebrow as if daring her to challenge him. Alice stared at him, lost for words. He was certainly keeping her on her toes; one minute flirty and teasing, and the next, heart-stoppingly honest.

He leant across the table to take her hand, kissed it and wrapped it with both of his, staring at the union he had made with a look of torment.

"Elliot, are you okay?" she asked quietly, "you seem really troubled."

Not taking his eyes from their hands, he inclined his head slightly, mulling over her choice of words.

"Troubled. Confused. Scared, even. I'm trying to find my way home to you but ... I've been so lost," he uttered, his pitch so low that she could barely hear him. She watched him, hardly able to breathe, concerned by the look in his eye and uncertain as to how she should respond. Sensing there was more to come, she said nothing. He looked at her, his expression guarded.

"Are you sure this is what you want, Alice? I don't just mean this weekend. I know we will be incredible together, and I can't tell you how much I have dreamt about this, but I won't be able to stop there. I'll want more."

He watched her reaction, sensing her rising panic at being put on the spot but he needed to be absolutely clear. She nodded, cupping her other hand around his.

"I'll want more, too," she replied avidly. "I told you last week: I don't want this to end. Ever," she insisted, her eyes willing him to believe her. He stared at her for what seemed like an eternity, his eyes softening as he acknowledged her sincerity. His focus shifted to her necklace, the entwined hearts capturing his attention like a magnet.

"You kept it," he said, his tone expressing his earlier surprise at seeing her wearing it. Alice nodded.

"Your nineteenth birthday seems like only yesterday," he remarked with a half-smile. She resisted a flippant age-related reply. Instead she returned his smile, aware of what turbulence his mind was in as it grappled with the reality of everything.

"Do you remember what I said when I gave it to you?" he ventured. She nodded again.

"Yes."

"Tell me," he insisted softly.

"You said, 'as long as you wear this, you'll always know that our hearts belong together'." She uttered words long since memorised. Her voice cracked a little with emotion.

"That's right. I meant it," he said, pleased that she had remembered.

"I know you did," she breathed, looking away.

"Look at me, Alice," he pleaded, letting go of their hands to gently lift her chin up as she looked at him.

"They still do. Belong together," he emphasized, his tone insistent.

"I know," she nodded, "I know." She was regretting that there was a table between them: she so desperately wanted to hold him and quash the doubt and uncertainty she had seen in his eyes.

"That's why I wore it today," she told him, "because I *know* our hearts belong together. *We* belong together," she declared, "and whatever it is that you think is standing in our way, I'm not going to let it. Nothing is going to stop me from loving you or from being with you. Today, tomorrow, next week. Next year," she laughed a little, determined to change the mood. "I'm in for the long-haul, Elliot. If you are," she stated unequivocally. She was relieved to see a smile venturing in his eyes as he listened to her.

"Then we need to talk," he stated, the smile fading. "I know you said about a fresh start and all that, but I honestly don't think I can. And you keep reminding me of the past," he stressed, indicating her necklace. "There are things we need to talk about before this goes any further. I need to know..." he paused, unsure of his phrasing, "I need to be totally honest with you and..."

"You need me to be totally honest, too?" she helped finish his sentence.

He nodded, squinting at her, uncertain of her reaction.

"Look, I know you've planned out our day but I can't do this, Alice. There are things I need to say, to tell you, before I can enjoy any of this," he gestured to their surroundings. Alice nodded uneasily.

'This is it,' she thought. The moment she had been dreading, when he would confess about his wife. 'Please,' she silently begged, 'tell me your marriage is a sham. Tell me it's already over.'

She stood up, holding out her hand to him.

"Come on then, let's go home and talk," she smiled, the smile not quite reaching her eyes. Nerves were gnawing at her stomach and her legs felt like jelly but she was determined not to show it. They headed for the exit, the tension between them unmistakable, both preoccupied by their thoughts.

Neither of them spoke as they walked along the road, although Elliot had a firm hold of her hand. He stopped when, moments later, they reached the Green.

"How about I go and get something for lunch from that little shop. The one I thought was somebody's house at first," he suggested, "and you go back and put the oven on."

Alice nodded her agreement. She sensed he needed a moment to himself.

"Lovely. I'll see you in a minute. You know the way back, don't you?" she teased genially. Her cottage was within sight from the Green, as was the shop. Elliot grinned,

"I think I'll manage, he said, kissing her mouth briefly before crossing the road to the village store.

Seconds later, her phone beeped in her handbag. Pulling it out she saw a message from Elliot.

'I'm so sorry. I'm a bit of an intense idiot! Not quite the romantic weekend you had planned. I just need time to come to terms with everything and think things through but I'm completely blinded by love. And your beauty. Forgive me? xxx E.'

She looked behind her and saw him standing on the opposite pavement, within shouting distance. His head was bent over his phone. She quickly sent a reply.

'Nothing to forgive. I understand it's all a bit much to come to terms with. I am just SO glad we found each other again. Now hurry home so I can show you how much I love you xxx A.'

Elliot looked up, smiled at her and nodded, then carried on to the store.

Chapter Ten

Alice put the oven on and boiled the kettle. Did they want more tea, she wondered, hovering by the tea pot, debating whether to brew some or not.

"This is ridiculous, pull yourself together, girl!" she admonished herself out loud. She paced the kitchen floor then hurried over to the lounge window to see if she could spot him yet. No sign. She was anxious to get their conversation out of the way.

She knew he was married: it wasn't going to be a great shock, so why was she so het up about it? She shouldn't have told him about Roz and her affair. What was she thinking? His mood really changed at that point, she thought. Obviously, it had hit a nerve with him, made him realise what he was doing. And no doubt reminded him of his uncle's heartache over an affair.

"Head meets brick wall," she cursed in frustration, slapping her head with the palm of her hand. She craned her neck to look up the road through the window but still, no sign of Elliot. Suddenly remembering his text, she went back into the kitchen and re-read the words on her phone.

'I just need time.' 'Forgive me.'

Her heart started to pound as she ran to the front door. He's left, she thought in a panic as she wrenched the door open and ran onto the pavement. Elliot's silver car was still there, parked alongside the wall. Instantly feeling a fool, she hurried back into the house and leant against the closed door behind her. She made an effort to steady her breathing and her nerves: she needed her wits about her to cope with the conversation they would be having. If he ever returned from the shop, she thought, growing agitated.

Fifteen minutes later, there was a knock at the door. Alice opened it to find Elliot standing there with two shopping bags and a potted plant in his hands. He bowed deeply,

"Your lunch, m'lady," he announced with a flourish, handing her the bags. She laughed, all her negative feelings instantly vanishing, as she accepted the bags and bobbed a curtsy.

"You were gone a while. I thought you'd got lost," she chided, keeping her voice light but Elliot could see the worried look in her eyes.

"Sorry," he said, putting his arms around her and kissing her tenderly, before murmuring, "sorry," again. He smiled mischievously,

"I was having a chat with the shopkeeper," he explained.

"Oh?" she prompted, relieved at his changed mood.

"Yes, I introduced myself as Ellie's father, and told him that it's taken me over eighteen years to get back with you and that we're about to have the most fantastic sex, that will undoubtedly last the whole weekend," he grinned, raising his eyebrows up and down. Alice stared at him, not quite sure whether he was joking or not.

"You didn't?" she whispered, the colour draining from her face. He laughed unabashed, and taking the bags from her, headed for the kitchen with Alice following behind. He put the bags and the plant onto the work surface, and turned back to her, grinning at her expression.

"Wait. No, sorry. That's what I was *thinking*. What I actually said was, 'what a great village shop you have, thank you very much', and, 'have a nice day'," he chuckled. Alice tried not to laugh, turning away from him.

"You're incorrigible," she scolded.

"I try my best!" he teased, slipping his arms around her waist from behind and kissing her neck. She leant back into him, enjoying the moment.

"Have a look in the bag," he said, his breath on her neck sending shivers down her spine.

"I even found a Bakewell tart. It used to be your favourite," he said, pleased with his find.

"It still is," she told him, looking in the first bag, laughing in surprise as she pulled out a cheese pizza, the Bakewell tart, a bottle of white wine, and a box of Maltesers. Elliot rested his head on her shoulder, surveying the spread as she unpacked.

"It used to be our Saturday feast, remember?" he asked. She nodded.

"Of course I remember," she replied quietly. Looking in the other bag she found a pack of croissants, two Danish pastries and a pot of raspberry jam. She laughed knowingly, nodding slowly, as memories flashed back in her head.

"Sunday breakfast," he reminded her, kissing her neck again. She closed her eyes. She knew what he was doing; he was wanting to ignite memories of their happiest times together. Weekends had always been special for them. Saturdays would be their 'busy' day, when they would either explore the city of York and its plethora of museums, or go to the cinema, or venture further afield into the countryside for a hike and a picnic. Sundays were reserved for lie-ins and lazy afternoons, rarely getting dressed in anything more than their pyjamas, happiest when in their own company and shutting out the rest of the world.

Alice opened her eyes, smiling at the memories. She picked up the pastries to smell them, a satisfied sigh escaping her lips.

"You do know that all of this is actually very bad for you though," she commented. Elliot snorted,

"So is starving. Live dangerously, Alice," he encouraged. She turned in his arms to face him, putting her arms around his neck and rubbing her nose lightly against his.

"I intend to," she spoke against his mouth, before kissing him longingly.

"Now who's incorrigible," he said, with a low laugh. She pressed herself against him provocatively.

"Me," she murmured huskily. Elliot groaned in response, tightening his hold of her.

"I knew from the minute I saw you, on Ellie's birthday, that I should stay away. Run for my life. But I couldn't. You possess me, Alice," he confessed, his voice thick with desire. She moved her head to look at him, a slow smile spreading across her face.

"You can't run; I won't let you. I intend to spend a life time loving you. I'm never letting go of you, Elliot," she told him adamantly. The absolute extent of the love she felt, was mirrored in her eyes, as she gazed deep into his. She could see the relief in his eyes, mixed with the longing he felt for her. He swallowed the lump in his throat before he spoke,

"I love you so much, Alice. This is where I belong, here with you. You are my home and I never want to leave." His voice wavered, betraying the depth of his vulnerability, and moved Alice to tears. Once again, she was taken aback by the intensity of his words and once again, she was at a loss as to what to say next. She needed to move things along, to get the 'talk' out of the way and thereby enable them to start their weekend together in earnest. Brushing her tears away and not taking her eyes off him, she said,

"Don't leave then. Stay here forever." She smiled as he laughed at the simplicity of her statement. Seizing the opportunity to change the conversation, she moved from his arms and took his hand.

"Listen, how about before we eat lunch and have that talk, I show you round the rest of the house," she suggested hopefully. He agreed,

"Yes, please," he said. "Shall I stick the pizza in the oven first?" he asked. Alice shook her head.

"No, we might be a while. You haven't seen upstairs yet," she replied innocently. Elliot raised an eyebrow, chuckling.

"Now you're thinking about all the fantastic sex, aren't you?" he teased, making her blush. She playfully slapped his thigh,

"Promises, promises," she teased back. Elliot's mouth dropped open indignantly, returning the playful slap.

"Cheeky! I always deliver," he almost growled. Alice looked him straight in the eye,

"I know you do. I remember that bit clearly," she winked, giggling at his shocked face.

"Alice Greene, you saucy minx!" he exclaimed with a stunned laugh, pulling her towards him. She rested her hands on his chest, looking up at him, biting her lip.

"Right, Elliot. Tour first, lunch and talk, and then …" she left the unfinished sentence hanging in the air. He tilted his head,

"And then?" he prompted, stroking her back.

"Well, you're the one with all the big talk. You decide," she practically purred. Elliot drew a sharp intake of breath between his teeth, amorous thoughts written all over his face.

"You really are determined to have your wicked way with me, aren't you?" he conceded, playing the game.

"Of course," she laughed, and taking his hand, led him into the lounge through the kitchen archway.

"The lounge," she announced grandly. Elliot cast an approving eye across the room, then looked back through to the kitchen.

"So, I'm guessing that you are responsible for the décor," he noted, recognising her style of old. "It's like walking through a Laura Ashley catalogue," he joked affectionately.

"You're not far wrong," she admitted. "I'm a bit predictable I suppose but I've always loved this look; not quite shabby chic, not quite classic. A happy in-between," she mused, straightening up a cushion.

Elliot had a quick peruse of the book shelves, nodding his appreciation. He picked up a framed black and white photo, and turned to Alice, questioning it. Her face instantly softened, coming over to join him.

"That's my grandpa, when he was a toddler," she told him, beaming at the photo. "I just love how fed up he looks, having to sit on that sheepskin rug, dressed in that ridiculous sailor suit and hat," she laughed. "Every time I look at it, I can actually hear him complaining," she added fondly.

Elliot watched her. Every fibre in his body wanted to reach out to her and hold her close. Sensing it, she turned to him and lightly touched his arm.

"Alright?" she encouraged, the look in his eyes making her melt a little. He nodded.

"Yes. It's just … seeing you here, in your home … it's wonderful. I love everything about it. I love the way your personality is entrenched in every aspect of it: the garden, the furniture, the colours, the books. The photos. It all has your stamp on it and I can feel the amount of love you've poured into it," he spoke with such a passion and yet, she could detect a deep sadness too. A sense of regret.

"I just want to be a part of it," he added wistfully. Alice was quick to respond. Leaning against him, she said,

"You already are. You have always been here, in a way, as part of Ellie."

He smiled at her attempts to appease him and she could see he didn't believe her. She patted his chest.

"Don't you recognise it?" she asked, smiling at his quizzical expression.

"Recognise it? How?" He was baffled. She took hold of his hand, weaving their fingers together, and gently stroked the palm of his hand with her thumb, fully aware of the effect that her touch was having on him.

"We always dreamt of a home like this. Remember how we used to plan?" she reminded him, coaxing him to follow her train of thought, jogging his memory back to rainy days spent window shopping in York.

"That's why I haven't changed my style, because I knew that this is what you wanted too. Call me a fool but I always dreamt that you would come back to me one day. And I wanted to have a home waiting for you. Our dream home," she declared softly, a satisfied smile lighting up her face as she watched his reaction to what she had said. His expression turned from confusion to elation but that was then quickly followed by something else: was it hesitance she could see?

He didn't speak for a while, he just stared at her, willing himself to believe her. As if knowing he needed convincing, she laughed a little and said brightly,

"It's true! You have always been here with me, in one way or another. And now, here you are. For real," she declared triumphantly, her eyes sparkling. Elliot finally found his words,

"*Is* all this true? You wanted me to come back to you? Don't say it if you don't mean it, Alice," he implored, his deep timbre weighted with desperation, studying her face as she responded. Her bright smile changed to one of encouragement, her eyes wide and honest.

"I don't know what else to say to you, Elliot. Of course it's all true," she reiterated. "I didn't actually think you would come back but yes, it's what I have always dreamt of and yes, I want you here. With me. You said it yourself: you've come home," she urged. "And I'm welcoming you with open arms," she smiled irresistibly with outstretched arms, persuading him to let go of his doubts, and give in to her. He gathered her in his arms, holding on to her as if his life depended on it, burying his face in her hair. She could feel his chest heaving and seconds later, felt wet tears seeping through to her scalp. Struggling not to cry herself, Alice felt an incredibly strong urge to wrap him up and protect him from the pain and torment he was going through. She wanted to shut out the rest of the world, and ignore the demands of reality. She seemed to gain strength from his weakness, and determined not to ever let him go, she decided there and then that she would do whatever it took to be with him. Be it marriage breaker or mistress, it didn't matter, as long as they were together.

Once she was sure that his tears had subsided, she manoeuvred her head from under his to reach up and kiss him, stroking his face and subtly wiping away any signs of his distress. She whispered in his ear,

"Welcome home, Elliot. I've missed you so, so much."

Taking his hand, she led him through to the hall and up the stairs.

"If you think you love the lounge, just wait until you see the bedroom," she murmured enticingly. He smiled, still feeling a little raw but enjoying her flirting.

The stairs creaked under their feet despite the thick carpet. Elliot let out an amused laugh.

"Does everything creak in Stratford?" he asked.

"Of course! That's part of the charm," she replied, "don't knock it," she added, in mock defence.

"I wouldn't dream of it," he declared jokingly.

They reached the landing, which again, was light and airy thanks to the large window that overlooked the garden. Four doors led off into the bedrooms and bathroom, and on the walls hung a couple of Roz's paintings. Elliot stopped to study them. One subject was instantly recognisable.

"That's St Saviour's church, isn't it?" he remarked, not really needing confirmation of the church that they had both grown up knowing so well.

"And where's this?" he asked, indicating to a seascape, with multi-coloured boats gently bobbing in a harbour.

"Cornwall," Alice replied. "It's funny, it never occurred to me to ask why, or when, she had painted Cornwall before. I'm guessing that is actually Newlyn," she added thoughtfully.

"Newlyn?" Elliot questioned sharply, "Why do you say Newlyn?"

Alice looked surprised,

"Well, I told you earlier: Roz went to Newlyn when she fell pregnant," she reminded him. Elliot shook his head adamantly,

"No, you said Cornwall. You didn't mention Newlyn," he said. "That's where David and Linda used to go," he told her, staring at the painting. "I went there with him once. I recognise it now. It *is* Newlyn," he stated. Alice quickly opened the first door, opposite the stairs.

"This is Ellie's room," she announced, drawing his attention away from the painting and the questions formulating in his head. Elliot stepped into the room, smiling indulgently at the décor.

"And she decorated it?"

Alice nodded, chuckling quietly. Two walls were painted in a faded orange and the other two, in a deep purple. Her bed, a white cast iron frame with an ornate, scrolled headboard, was covered with a heavy, patchwork quilt. The colours ranged from purple, burgundy, yellow, and pale blue and each block was decorated with shimmering sequins. Strings of voile butterflies hung from the ceiling and the curtain rail had brightly coloured, cloth bunting draped across it; a contrast to the heavy, purple, velvet curtains that were swept back with beaded ties. All kinds of paraphernalia were dotted everywhere throughout the room and the pale, wooden bookcase was stuffed with books, magazines, and pots of make-up. Photos were stuck up on the wall to frame a small dressing table and mirror. Smiling faces laughed at Elliot, as he scoured them to see if he could recognise anybody.

"Is that Rachel, here with Ellie?" he asked, pointing at two young girls, giggling for the camera. Alice nodded,

"Yes, they must have been about nine and ten then," she told him. "And this is Tasha and Amy, and this one," she tapped the most recent photo to be added to the collection, "this is Brad and Ellie, at their prom last month."

Elliot was instantly struck by Ellie's beauty. She looked incredibly sophisticated in a stunning, midnight-blue, floor-length dress. The fitted bodice was encrusted with diamanté, and the softly flowing skirt was dotted with more of the same. Ellie's curls had been swept up into a messy bun, with braids woven through on the sides, offset with dainty forget-me-nots scattered throughout. She was linking arms with a tall, handsome, young man, dressed in a silver-grey suit, and a blue tie to match her dress. His hair was almost the same dark shade as hers and his eyes, a hazel brown.

"They're a good-looking couple," he noted, "Ellie looks beautiful in that dress," he said, his voice full of paternal admiration.

"Yes, she does. Laura made it for her so it was exactly as she wanted it to be," she said. "It's handy having a dress maker in the family," she added flippantly.

As Elliot was leaving the room, he glanced round again and noticed a small, framed photo on Ellie's bedside table, propped up under her lamp. He let out a surprised laugh and went over to pick it up.

The frame was handmade, with padded, red cloth hearts stuck onto a wooden base. The picture was of him.

"Where did she get this?" he asked, taken aback.

"She took a photo of you when you two went for lunch, and printed it off," she smiled at his pleased face.

"You should feel very honoured," she continued, "you have replaced Dylan O'Brien. That frame was made for his photo," she confided. Elliot looked bewildered.

"Who's Dylan O'Brien?"

"'Teen Wolf'. 'The Maze Runner'. No?" she prompted. Elliot shook his head. Alice laughed,

"Oh dear, Daddy, you do have a lot to learn about teenage girls," she grinned, patting his thigh affectionately and taking his hand, led him back out onto the landing.

Next to Ellie's room was Roz's, and opposite, the bathroom. Alice's room was at the end of the short corridor. Briefly showing him the bathroom, with its traditional, double ended roll top bath, and ultra-modern shower cubicle, complete with mood lighting, she ventured into Roz's room.

"It's a bit cluttered in here, I'm afraid. When Dad was ill, Roz went back to Brockenhurst to help, and she hasn't really been back here since. She moved all her stuff out of her studio downstairs, to free up space so that her friend could use it, but he's only here occasionally. I'm not sure what I'm going to do with the studio now that she's not coming back," she shrugged.

"What about a game's room?" Elliot suggested. She shook her head.

"Not really my thing. And before you say it, neither is a gym," she added, sensing his next suggestion. She eyed the stacks of paintings, propped up against the sandy coloured walls and strewn across the bed. She wondered whether the paintings of Cee-Cee would be amongst any of them. Maybe she would have a look later, she thought.

Turning round to leave, Elliot caught sight of a canvas that leapt out at him. He stopped, rooted to the spot.

"What's the matter?" Alice asked with concern. She followed his line of sight to a painting that had always been tucked away in Roz's room, rather than in her studio. It was a profile portrait of a man sitting at an open window, with the sea and a rugged patch of beach in the distance. He had a book in one hand and a cigarette in the other. A bottle of whiskey and a short, stout glass, were balanced on the low windowsill.

"Who's that?" Elliot breathed.

"I'm not sure. It's an old painting, it's always been here." Alice said. "I used to think it looked like you, but older," she confessed. Looking at it again, it suddenly dawned on her exactly who it was and she could tell by his expression, that Elliot knew too.

"I don't understand this," he sounded agitated, turning to Alice for an explanation. She looked helplessly at him.

"What do you mean?" she asked, trying desperately to think of a diversion. Elliot persisted.

"That's David! It absolutely is him," he stressed, pointing at the painting. Alice feigned surprise.

"Really? Are you sure?" she asked, trying to keep her pitch from rising. Elliot was emphatic.

"Absolutely," he said, taking another close look at it. "Everything about it: his face, the way he's holding that cigarette, the whiskey. And it's in Cornwall. Look!" he jabbed a finger at the blue splashes of paint visible through the window.

"Maybe they met there by chance? At the artist's studio you mentioned?" Alice suggested. "I'll ask Roz, when I phone her on Monday," she said in an effort to placate him.

Elliot continued to stare at the painting.

"It is definitely him."

He stood in silence for a while, lost in thought. An idea came to mind and he looked at Alice.

"Hang on though, if Roz knew David, then maybe she also knew Linda. She might even know what happened to Linda," he said, his voice speeding up as his mind raced ahead. "I sort of made a vow to myself that I would find her one day. Even though David's gone, I want to know what happened to her, for my own piece of mind."

"Alright, I'll speak to Roz," Alice nodded, taking his hand again to leave the room that was filled with untold echoes of the past. Her heart sank. What was she doing? How on earth could she carry on with this pretence?

"I'm sorry, Elliot. I can't go on lying … I need to tell you something and it can't wait," she said, aware of how strained her voice sounded. She indicated towards the bed and moved some paintings to one side, making room for them to sit on the edge of it. She took a deep breath before speaking, not quite meeting his eyes.

"You wanted honesty. I think before you tell me what you need to say, you have to hear this first," she said decisively. Elliot watched her face with apprehension, his own unease plainly visible.

"What have you been lying about?" he asked in a level tone, masking any emotion. Alice immediately picked up on it, realising what he was reading into it.

"This isn't anything about us. I'm not lying about us, Elliot," she insisted swiftly. Her response perplexed him. Taking her hand, he asked,

"What then?"

She smiled awkwardly,

"Sorry, this all sounds very dramatic, I know. It's just that I'm not sure how to tell you," she paused, "so, here goes. That painting of David - and I didn't know it was David until you said so - is here because Linda painted it," she said clumsily.

"What?" Elliot let go of her hand and stood up. Alice stood up too and put her hand on his arm, frantically thinking of how to tactfully break the news to him.

"Oh, this is stupid!" she blurted out, frustrated by her own ineptitude, "I didn't know this until after Ellie's birthday, I swear I didn't. Your uncle had an affair with my aunt, and she ran away when she fell pregnant with his child. And their baby was put up for adoption," she said, waiting for his reaction. He just stared at her, shaking his head.

"No. David had an affair with Linda Moore, not with your aunt Roz," he told her. Alice gave him a benevolent smile.

"Roz *is* Linda", she explained. "Her name is Rosalind Moore. Remember how I told you my grandpa was obsessed with Shakespeare? Well, his favourite play was, 'As you Like it', so naturally he named his first child after the main character, Rosalind. My aunt was always known as Linda in the village and at school, but my mum had always called her Roz. When she left home and moved here, she changed her name from Linda to Roz. I've only ever known her as Roz," she said. Elliot stared at her, speechless.

"If my mum had been a boy, he would've been named Orlando. But as she was a girl, she was named after the other main character, Celia. Rosalind's cousin," she finished. She waited expectantly for Elliot to say something. He sat back down on the bed, staring wildly at the floor as it all sank in.

"Who's Orlando?" he asked. Alice gave a little laugh, sitting back down next to him.

"He was the one that fell in love with Rosalind in the play. It's not important, sorry, I'm confusing you. The fact is, Roz - Linda - loved David with all her heart, and ran away to protect his reputation. And somewhere out there, is their daughter," she pointed out.

Elliot scratched his head, trying to make sense of everything Alice had told him.

"So, last week when I was talking about David and his affair - you already knew? And you just let me carry on. Why? Why didn't you say anything then?" he sounded frustrated.

"I wanted to hear his side of it. And I wasn't sure then what to say to you because it was new information for me too, and Roz had told me in confidence. Plus, it was our first date. My mind was elsewhere," she tried to make light of it. He frowned.

"And to be honest," she continued, "I was a little disturbed by the fact that my aunt had had such a passionate affair with somebody who was identical to you. The way she described him, and talked about their relationship, was … well, a bit too close to home."

"Yes, well, when you put it like that…" Elliot nodded. Alice pulled an apologetic face.

"I know it's a lot to take in, believe me I know, but can we just forget about them for a while? Can we talk about it later? And focus on us instead. Like you said, this weekend is about us", she prompted, coaxing him round to her way of thinking.

He took her hand again and studied it, tracing the faint veins with his finger. She could see his furrowed brow relaxing but he was clearly still troubled by what he had just learnt. He lifted his eyes to hers with a look so compelling, she was completely transfixed. Beyond the confusion and uncertainty, she could see the hunger in his eyes and a craving for the comfort he knew she could give him. He brushed her hair back from her face and stroked her cheek with his thumb, not taking his eyes off her.

"Is that it now? No more lies or surprises?" he wanted to know, his voice soft and low. She shook her head.

"No, that's it," she assured him gently. "I'm done. Although, there is one thing you should know," she confessed, resting her hand provocatively on his thigh and trying, unsuccessfully, not to smile. His mouth twitched in response, his eyes creasing as his own smile spread.

"Oh? What's that then?" he wondered, running his fingers lightly across her chin as she replied,

"We've nearly finished our tour of the house and I'm starving," she whispered, stroking his thigh.

"Really?" he murmured, "Do you want pizza or cake?" He ran his fingers through her hair at the nape of her neck and pulled her towards his mouth.

"I definitely want cake," she breathed, sinking into his kiss. Fuelled by the fire burning deep within her and the need for him to possess her, she impulsively laid back on the bed, pulling him down with her. Her head caught the corner of a box canvas, causing her to wince in pain. Elliot immediately stopped, and sat her up to check her head, ensuring she wasn't hurt. She thought her clumsiness would have killed the moment but judging by the look he was giving her, that was far from the truth. He cradled her face and kissed her tenderly.

"Can we take this somewhere else?" he suggested in a hoarse whisper, "I feel like I'm being watched in here by all these paintings," he said, indicating to the many images splashed across large boards.

"Yes please," she agreed, sliding off the bed and reaching up to kiss him as he stood up.

As they left the room, Elliot glanced across at the portrait of his uncle, sorrow clouding his face for a fleeting moment. Noticing it, Alice paused outside her bedroom door and stroked his arm.

"Are you okay?" she asked. He nodded,

"Yes, just very confused. This is all a bit surreal," he confessed. Alice agreed; she could identify with that completely. But determined not to spoil the moment she said,

"I don't mean to be flippant, Elliot, but you need to ignore what's just happened. For a little while anyway, because this is the part of the house tour where you're supposed to be blown away by the beauty of my bedroom," she emphasised dramatically, then added, "our bedroom."

"Okay, okay. Blow me away," he laughed, holding his arms out in resignation. "But it better be worth it," he challenged, raising an eyebrow. She raised hers back at him,

"Oh, it'll definitely be worth it," she murmured, her voice dropping an octave. "Just try and remember the point we were at before I hit my head on that stupid canvas," she added.

"I'm there already," he grinned ardently, stroking the small of her back.

Alice pushed the bedroom door open with a flourish. Elliot leant against the door frame for a moment, surveying the room. He gave a low whistle,

"Wow, Alice, this *is* beautiful," he conceded. He crossed the room to the bed and ran his fingers along the wooden cross beam, identifying it as oak.

"When you said a four poster, I half expected a dark, heavy, Shakespearian thing but I should've guessed it would be something far more romantic," he said. He walked over to the window on the far side of the room to inspect the view. It overlooked the back garden, and the few houses behind hers.

"Is that the field behind those houses?" he asked, pointing to a patch of green that he could spy. Alice joined him at the window.

"Yes," she said, "that's the Orchards. Opposite 'Mary Arden's farm'," she reminded him. He scanned the room again, and spotting some photos on her chest of drawers, went to inspect them. He picked up a group photo of Alice, Andrew, and their parents, taken when Alice was around seven. Smiling, he commented on how he could remember her and Andrew at that age.

"Doesn't Andrew look like your dad when he was younger!" he exclaimed. "I'd never really noticed it before," he added. Picking up the next framed photo, his expression softened even more. He touched the glass with his finger, as if caressing the chubby, baby cheeks that stared back at him.

"How old was Ellie here?" he asked quietly.

"About four weeks," she replied, watching his response with a tightness in her chest. She had been feeling intensely guilty talking about Ellie as a baby ever since his emotional reaction the previous week to her recount of Ellie's birth. It was a strange mix of emotions she was experiencing: regret, guilt, and protectiveness. She had noticed how increasingly protective of Elliot she was becoming. It was almost as if she wanted to mother him, which was a peculiar reaction because the last thing on her mind was anything maternal. But she did want to wipe away all his doubt, and the haunted look she had seen in his eyes on more than one occasion. She knew instinctively that he had been unhappy for a long time and she desperately wanted to rectify that; she wanted to be the one to make him light up again, the way he used to.

Aware that she was watching him, Elliot turned and fixed his eyes on her.

"I still find it incredible that we made such a beautiful child together. She's perfect," he reflected, carefully replacing the photo on the chest of drawers. He held out his hand to her and she hurried into his arms. He looked pleased at her willingness. He slowly ran his hands down her back and up to stroke her neck, weaving his fingers through her hair as he kissed her throat.

"Now, where were we before that canvas interrupted us?" he barely whispered, kissing her with such a breathtaking passion that her legs buckled beneath her. She wrapped her arms around his neck, and legs around his waist, as he lifted her up and carried her over to the bed. Laying her carefully across it, he stood back for a moment to look at her. She had her arms stretched loosely above her head, her tousled hair partially covering her slightly flushed face, and her eyes were burning with desire as she looked at him expectantly. Her dress was rucked up on one side by her thigh and she made no attempt to straighten it out.

"What?" she murmured, her smile telling him she already knew what he was thinking. She patted the bed invitingly but he seemed captivated by the vision of her.

"That's the smile that has haunted me for eighteen years," he said hoarsely and for a fleeting second, his eyes clouded over. He hesitated over his next move.

She half sat herself up, stifling a sigh of frustration.

"I'm not a ghost, Elliot. I'm real. This is real," she coaxed, reaching for his arm and wilfully pulling him onto the bed next to her. As she did so, the grey elephant she had earlier placed on the pillows, rolled forwards and landed in front of him. He stared at it for a second before recognition hit him.

"Elli-phant!" he snorted in surprise. Picking it up he looked at Alice.

"You kept this too?" He sounded confused.

Alice nodded, wishing he hadn't seen it, although initially she had wanted him to. Like the necklace, it was a silent reminder of their love but they had been reconnecting just fine without any more reminders. She could see by his expression that he was armed with more questions.

"Why?" he asked, "Why would you keep the two things that meant the most to you? I don't understand," he uttered. He studied the elephant, noting it's worn ears and feet.

Alice sat in silence, once again unsure what to say next. She had planned everything out in her head: little romantic hints to tantalise him, but she hadn't accounted for the emotional rollercoaster that he seemed to be travelling on. He had given the elephant to her to celebrate their first month together, telling her that his name was 'Elli the elephant' and he was there to remind her that Elliot loved her.

"Because an elephant never forgets … and neither does an Elliot," he had said evocatively, referring to their month of unabated passion. When she had left York on that fateful day, sixteen months later, she had been wearing her necklace, and had automatically put the elephant in her hastily packed bag. She had never wanted to part with them, despite everything.

"He seems to be a bit worse for wear," Elliot remarked, finally breaking the silence.

"Blame your daughter for that," Alice said, trying to make a joke of it. She put a hand on his knee, saying,

"I gave it to Ellie as her first toy. It stayed in her cot always and then when she moved into her first bed, she kept it on her pillow every night. In fact, she's always had it with her until recently. We noticed it was becoming a little fragile, so we packed it away for safe keeping," she explained gently. "So, like I said, you've always been here with us in one way or another," she added. "And I kept the tag too."

She got up from the bed and opened her wardrobe, pulling out the box with Ellie's first sleepsuit in. Underneath it there was a blue ribbon, with a handwritten tag attached. She handed it to Elliot.

"See?" she smiled, willing him to smile back. He recognised his own hand and the words he had penned so long ago.

'Never forget that I love you forever xxx E.'

He looked up at Alice, about to speak, when he registered what else she was holding up for him to see. A tiny, pink velour sleepsuit, with little, grey elephants dotted all over it. He took it from her, feeling the soft material between his fingers and imagining the cherubic baby from the photo wearing it, and how she would have felt to hold. He hung his head, swallowing the tight lump in his throat that threatened to choke him. Alice sat back down next to him, so closely that their thighs were pressing together. She leant against him and rested her hand once again on his leg. He covered her hand with his, putting pressure on it as he sat in silent thought.

"Why are you punishing me like this?" he croaked, staring at her hand. Alice started, shocked by his words.

"I'm not meaning to. Is that what you think? Elliot, I'm just trying to be honest with you. You said that's what you wanted," she insisted, hurt by his accusation. His stillness disturbed her. Had she pushed him too far? Was he right? Was she, subconsciously, wanting to punish him?

He sighed heavily, resigning himself to face the realities he was being forced to.

"What are you doing to me, Alice? Two weeks ago, I was jogging along nicely through life. And now everything is upside down," he said, growing agitated. "You and I have a teenage child. My uncle and your aunt had an affair. Somewhere, I have a cousin. *We* have a cousin! This isn't the kind of honesty I had in mind."

"I know it's a shock about David and Roz, but I couldn't carry on a lie like that," she exclaimed defensively.

"Oh really, you couldn't carry on a lie?" he retorted hotly. "And what about if I hadn't bumped into you?

Would you have ever told me about Ellie?" he demanded. "Don't talk to me about not carrying on a lie."

Alice stared at him, horrified at how quickly the situation had escalated. She clearly *had* pushed him too far. Needing to reign it in, she instantly showed contrition.

"You're right. I'm sorry, Elliot. What I meant was, I can't carry on lying to you *now*. You need to know everything. That is, I need you to know everything," she apologised, squeezing his leg, encouraging him to look at her. He could see she was being sincere and started to calm down. Alice was thoughtful for a moment.

"As it turns out, I'm actually pretty good at lying. I never thought I'd admit it but it does seem to come easily to me," she acknowledged with a self-deprecating humour. Elliot looked at her, wondering at her frankness.

"And what about now? Today? Has all this been a lie?" he challenged, in a level voice.

"No! absolutely not," she was categorical. "I have always…" she paused.

"What? What have you always?" he insisted on knowing, his eyes narrowing.
Alice drew in a decisive breath, determined to be truthful.

"I tried to hate you," she told him, watching his guarded expression. "I tried to stop loving you, God knows I did but I couldn't. I have always loved you. And having Ellie reinforced that love," she said as simply as she could. He still seemed unconvinced.

"And now? Do you love me now?", he asked, "or is this just lust? Because you're pretty good at that too," he commented steadily. Alice tried not to smile at his observation, nervously chewing her lip. She shot him a coy look and scrunched up her nose.

"A bit of both?" she ventured. He raised an eyebrow, not quite smiling but she could see he was amused by it.

"Yes, I absolutely love you but it has been a long time, Elliot, and you are incredibly fit, you know," she laughed, trying to win him over.

"Fit?" he echoed, with a hint of derision. Alice laughed at the look on his face.

"I work with teenagers, what can I say? It means you're hot, sexy, hunky, very good-looking," she teased, reeling off the raunchy compliments.

"I know what it means, I just didn't expect to hear you saying it," he half laughed, watching how her eyes twinkled when she smiled at him. Her coquettish mood reminded him so much of how she was at eighteen: full of excitement and with an infectious lust for life. It's what he had loved about her. He smiled and raised his eyebrow,

"So, I'm fit, am I? Fair enough, I can live with that," he joked, nudging her playfully with his shoulder. Alice laughed, relieved that the tension had dispersed.

"Are we okay? You can understand why I've told you all of this now, can't you?" she asked. "I thought you had a right to know and once you'd seen that painting, I couldn't just lie to you because I wanted to ... focus on other things," she finished her sentence in a hushed tone.

Elliot looked at her, gently pushing her fringe away from her face and tracing the outline of her cheek with his fingers. He touched her mouth, wanting to kiss it but his mind was too jumbled with images of his uncle, making him feel restless and uneasy. He snorted in frustration at Alice's words.

"Well, I have to be honest, it's the 'other things' that I've been trying to focus on too but you keep throwing a spanner in the works with all your revelations," he said. "I'm still stunned by it all. And you never knew?" he reiterated. "Living for all these years with your aunt and she didn't tell you anything about it?"

He believed her and yet, it seemed unreal to him that Roz could harbour such a colossal secret, for so long, from Alice. It smacked of deceit and left a nasty aftertaste. And he couldn't forgive her for the heart-breaking pain she had inflicted on his uncle. Intuitively reading his thoughts, Alice said,

"I had absolutely no idea about it and to be honest, when I found out, I felt betrayed by her. I've shared my life so closely with her for eighteen years; she watched me go through pregnancy and birth, and yet she told me nothing about her baby, or David," she stressed, still not able to get beyond the hurt of Roz's deception. Her mind flitted back to the past as she deliberated over Roz's relationship with her.

"I can see now why she doted on me as a child. And Ellie. We were the closest she would ever get to having a daughter of her own," she mused. Elliot was listening intently to her, growing increasingly incensed by the thought that Roz had raised his daughter, and given up her own without ever telling David about her. Alice continued talking,

"I used to catch her sitting by Ellie's cot, in here, watching over her as she slept. She would have tears in her eyes and I always thought it was because she was feeling sad about what'd happened to me. And she let me think that. She actively encouraged it, in fact. But now I know that it was more than that. It went so much deeper," she frowned thinking about it. So many things were starting to make sense to her now. Elliot interrupted her train of thought.

"What do you mean, 'what happened to you'?" he asked, his voice edgy.

Alice shot him a nervous look and quickly looked away again. He shifted position so that he could face her.

"Alice? What did happen to you?" he demanded. She floundered; she didn't understand the point of his question. A defensive tut escaped her lips before she spoke.

"Mary," she muttered, "that's what happened."

She refused to look at him but could feel him tensing up.

"Mary?" he questioned in a flat, cold voice. Alice nodded, hardly daring to breathe. She knew that the moment of truth had finally arrived; her whole body started to tremble uncontrollably. Elliot didn't speak. She was aware that he was staring at her and glancing at his hands, she saw him clench his fists. How dare he be angry, she suddenly thought. The silence became unbearable. She willed herself to look at him, and was surprised at his expression. He looked worried, scared: not angry, as she had thought, and she instinctively reached out to touch his face.

"It's okay, Elliot. I know about Mary," she nodded, trying to smile. "It's okay."

He stared at her with a stillness that was unnerving, and his expression unfathomable.

"You know?" he acknowledged, wanting confirmation from her. She nodded. Elliot took a deep breath.

"What do you know?" he asked, his voice dropping a notch. Alice clutched her hands together in a bid to control the trembling. She licked her lips, suddenly desperate for something to drink.

"I know that you and I lasted barely eighteen months. You and Mary have lasted eighteen years, and yet, I think you still love me," she uttered in a strangled voice.

"I do still love you, Alice," he said gruffly, "I don't think I told you enough how much I loved you."

Hot tears spilled down her face and she clenched her teeth together to stop herself from crying.

"Yes, you did," she nodded, "that's why it hurt so much," she sniffed.

"What did?" he prompted, carefully wiping her tears away with his hand. She wanted to lean into it and have him hold her to stem the trembling. She didn't want to have this conversation.

"Alice, what did?" he asked again.

"When you and Mary ... when you went off with Mary," she choked, unable to stop the tears now.

Elliot reached across to the bedside table and snatched up the box of tissues there, passing them to her. He watched her wipe her eyes and shakily blow her nose, waiting for her to finish before he spoke.

"Is that why you left? Because of..."

"Mary, yes," she nodded, finishing his sentence for him.

"Right," he nodded slowly. He moved closer to her and put a hand on either side of her face, carefully brushing away the strands of hair that had been stuck to her cheeks by her tears. Concerned eyes met hers, willing her to hold eye contact. She sniffed, offering him a watery smile.

"Alice," he started, "I need you to tell me something." He looked at her expectantly as she nodded. He breathed deeply,

"Who the hell is Mary?"

Chapter Eleven

Alice blinked. She stared at him in disbelief, a surge of anger coursing through her. She jerked her face away from his hands.

"That's not fair, Elliot. I'm trying to accept it but if you're not going to play ball, then how can we possibly continue with this?"

Elliot raised his hands defensively,

"I have no idea what you are talking about, Alice. What the hell is going on?" he demanded, standing up and backing away from her. Alice jumped up from the bed, squaring up to him.

"So, what ... are you denying about Mary?" her voice became shrill. She was so furious that she could hardly focus on his face. She jutted her chin forward, waiting for his answer. He rubbed his forehead, looking away. Alice persisted.

"Do you deny it?"

Elliot turned back to her, his eyes narrowing.

"I'm not even sure what I'm supposed to be denying but, yes. I deny it," he said forcefully, challenging her enraged glare. She was momentarily stunned by his refusal to stop the charade and then remembered her trump card. She marched over to her dressing table and grabbed the laptop, opening it up as she sat back down on the bed. Elliot remained standing, silently watching her. She found the Facebook page she was looking for and triumphantly swung the laptop round towards him.

"I know you don't use Facebook but I do. And so does your wife," she gestured to the screen, to prove her point.

"My what? My *wife*?" Elliot knelt on the floor by the bed to look at the screen, dumbfounded. His eyes stared frantically at the page, pointing at the cover picture of himself and Mary in disbelief. He swore under his breath, looking at Alice.

"What is this? I don't … I don't understand. That's a photo of me but … who's she?" He squinted at the laptop, then realising it was a touchscreen, enlarged the image with his finger and thumb, frowning as he did so. It was a dated photo and not of the best quality, depicting a young Elliot and Mary riding on a merry-go-round. Elliot was laughing and waving at the camera and Mary, seated on a brightly coloured horse by his side, was smiling up at him. Her face was only partially visible.

Alice watched Elliot with a growing sense of disquiet. Something about his insistence was ringing alarm bells in her head. How could he be so convincingly denying Mary's existence? His head snapped up and he stared at her, open mouthed.

"That's your flat mate, scary Mary!" he exclaimed, tapping at the screen. The shock on his face was irrefutable. Alice found it hard to breathe all of a sudden and she felt light headed. She gripped onto the bedcover beneath her to steady herself, trying to regulate her breathing. Her heart was pounding, reverberating in her ears and clutching at her throat.

"Why would you think she's my wife? And what are these photos doing on here?" he demanded, his face taut with mounting rage and confusion. He felt trapped by his inability to understand what was unfolding. Alice pointed a shaky finger to the box of text on the left-hand side of the page. Elliot read it,

'Lives in London, United Kingdom. Married to Elliot Barraclough'.

He jumped up and paced across the room, swearing violently. Turning back to Alice, he shouted,

"And you believe it? Because Facebook tells you to?" His eyes flashed angrily. He took a step towards her, running his hand agitatedly through his hair as realisation dawned.

"Is this why you left? You think I married *her*?" his voice was menacing and barely audible. Alice couldn't speak, she couldn't even move her head to nod. She just stared at him, wide eyed with fear.

"Is it?" he bellowed. She flinched.

"Yes," she nodded, trembling uncontrollably now. He took another step towards her, his mind racing ahead as something started to compute in his brain.

"No hang on, you're lying. Again," he pointed an accusing finger at her. Alice noted that his hand was shaking too.

"Facebook wasn't even around then. So," he strode over to the bed and pulled her up to face him; his grip on her arms wasn't forceful but she could feel he was barely in control of his emotions. He stared intently at her, suddenly faltering; he could see the fear in her eyes. He relaxed the grip on her arms and stepped back.

"I want the truth, Alice. I'm sick to death of your lies," he pleaded gruffly. "Why did you leave?"

Alice lowered her head, numb with shock. She couldn't believe the possibility that she had been under a misapprehension for all these years: that his marriage to Mary had been a fallacy. And yet, he was very convincing as the wounded party in the scenario. She warily side stepped past him to her chest of drawers and pulling open the bottom one, ferreted around under a pile of clothes. Opening a black document wallet, she retrieved the note from Mary which had been ripped up and stuck back together again. She handed it to Elliot. He read it aloud,

'Alice, I don't know how else to tell you this – Elliot and I are having an affair.
It's been going on for a while now.
As soon as he finishes Uni, we will be leaving York together.
You can't even see what has been going on under your own nose!
I suggest you leave us now, before it gets too ugly.'

"Oh Jesus!" he breathed, slumping down onto the bed, pressing the palms of his hands against his eye sockets. Alice hovered anxiously before gingerly sitting next to him, keeping a little distance between them. He looked up, his whole demeanour crushed, and excruciating sadness emanating from his eyes.

"What have you done, Alice?" he rasped. "You believed this?" He could see in her eyes that she did. He held it up to her, aware of its condition.

"And you even laminated it!"

She tried to speak but her throat was unbearably dry. The need to lie down was overwhelming as painful memories flooded back. This made no sense to her at all.

"Are you saying it's not true?" she barely whispered.

"It's not true," he stated. Alice let out a sob,

"But ... it must be true! Don't do this to me, please. I can't take this all over again," she wept. He grabbed her shoulders, forcing her to look at him.

"Did you love me when you left?" he demanded with a sense of urgency. She nodded.

"Yes, of course I did."

He swore under his breath again. Picking up the laptop, he positioned it on his knee so that they could both see it. Scrolling through Mary's Facebook page, he scoured her various posts, looking for something to prove its falsehood to Alice.

"How many time have you looked at this over the years? Do you do it to torment yourself or what?" he asked. He was becoming angry again but she was beginning to realise that it was anger aimed at something beyond their control. He paused his scrolling,

"What does this say? Go on, read it," he commanded, nodding to the screen.

"It's a check-in for the Haymarket theatre," she said, not sure where this was leading. Elliot nodded,

"That's right. And that's my name there, with hers. Yes?"

"Yes," she agreed. Elliot took a breath, lowering his voice,

"Now tell me the date. What's the date on this, Alice?"

She peered at the screen and gasped, her eyes widening. She looked at Elliot, speechless.

"July 24th 2015," he told her, bristling. "Where was I on July 24th?"

"With me," she breathed, "in Brockenhurst, at Ellie's party."

Her eyes flew up to his face, mortified as the truth was sinking in. She could see the same thought process going through his head; the realisation that their lives had been destroyed by a lie. He looked back at the screen.

"This whole thing is a pack of lies. All these check-ins with me, these dates, these photos: they're all a lie. And I recognise this photo now. Can you see me smiling at the camera? Don't you recognise that smile, Alice? That smile was only ever meant for you. *You* were taking that photograph," he claimed, knowing she could now see the truth.

"She was sectioned; did you know that?" he asked.

"What?" Alice exclaimed, shaking her head.

"Scary Mary. She went completely mad. That's not the politically correct term for it, I know, but that's what she did." There was no compassion in his voice, just disdain.

"How could you think I would leave you for her? How could you think I would leave you at all?" he asked, failing to understand her rationale.

Feeling completely drained, she slid her hand across the bed to reach for his. He took hold of it and squeezed it tightly, looking at her with such anguish.

"Then where did you go?" she implored quietly.

"Go?" he shrugged, not understanding.

"I found that note stuck to the fridge door. I waited for you to come home and tell me it wasn't true, but you didn't. You weren't at yours either. I stayed up all night, waiting. Both you and Mary had disappeared, so I thought it must be true. So, where were you?" She watched him as he rubbed his forehead in despair.

"Right," he breathed, "now it's making sense." He moved closer to her on the bed, holding her hand with both of his. She was arrested by the sincerity in his eyes, pleading her to listen.

"I don't know about Mary but I was in Brockenhurst," he started. Alice drew breath to interrupt but he stopped her,

"Please, just listen. This is crucial," he stressed. "I was called out of my lecture that morning. The Uni had a phone call from David. My dad had had a massive stroke and wasn't expected to survive, so I had to get home as fast as I could. I didn't even stop to write you a note, I just ran to your place and told Mary what'd happened. She said she'd let you know. I asked her to tell you to come home too if you could, because I needed you with me. I was scared, Alice," he paused, rubbing her hand to help focus his thoughts.

"You didn't turn up but I just assumed you couldn't get there for whatever reason. I tried to phone your digs but whenever I did, Mary said you were out. I was a bit distracted to be honest, so I wasn't worried. I knew you'd be there waiting for me. I stayed with Dad for three weeks until he was out of the woods. Obviously, it took a lot longer to recover but the worst was over, and so I went back to York." He looked at Alice. They both knew what happened next but Elliot continued recounting anyway.

"You were gone. I couldn't believe it. Mary was very cagey. She said you'd left because you didn't love me anymore. She said you'd been trying to find a way to tell me for some time, so when I had to rush off, you grabbed the chance to leave. I didn't believe her. She looked wild. She had trashed the flat, your stuff was tipped up everywhere. She said that you had done it yourself before you left." He sighed, then added, "well, that explains how she got all your photos, I suppose." He looked at her stunned face, giving her a resigned smile.

"You didn't see it, did you? She'd always had a thing about me; that's why I preferred it when you came over to mine. She made me feel uneasy. She was always touching me when she talked to me and would walk into the kitchen half undressed when she knew I was there. It creeped me out; she was so edgy with it. Then, that night, she made a massive play for me. I mean, full on: she pulled out all the stops but I wasn't interested at all. That annoyed her. It was so obvious what she was up to and I knew then that she was lying about you but there was still the issue of, where had you gone? Why had you gone? So, I got on the next train back to Brockenhurst and went to your house. I was still stupidly convinced that there was a simple explanation but then your mum … well, that's when the nightmare started really," he nodded, tensing up again. Alice wanted to interject but he shook his head.

"You need to know this, Alice. You need to know what you did," he insisted, frowning at her puppy dog eyes. It was almost too painful to look at her as he re-lived his darkest times.

"Your mother was initially quite reticent but once she realised that I wasn't going to leave the doorstep without an answer, she told me that you had gone to France," he recalled. Unable to stop herself, Alice interjected.

"France? Why?"

"I don't know, Alice. She's your mother; you tell me," he snapped. She lowered her head, her mind reeling at the thought of her mother instigating such a deceit.

"What did you do?" she asked.

"I went to France," he stated. "I thought I would find you. I thought my heart would seek you out. I honestly thought it would be that simple. But once I got there I realised my mistake. So, I phoned David and told him what'd happened. He was brilliant. He dropped everything: he organised a locum and was in France within hours. He didn't once tell me that what I was doing was ridiculous or futile, in fact, quite the opposite. We spent two weeks driving round France. If I hadn't been so broken hearted, it would've been a great road trip. That's when he told me all about Linda. It was like one big therapy session; I watched him re-live his pain as he helped me work through mine. Losing you destroyed me." He looked away, his focus falling on the photo of Ellie.

"We eventually came back to England and went to Cornwall for a few days, to Newlyn, and then back up to York. I told David I'd be fine and so he went back home. But losing you killed me, I never got over it. If Mary had said that you'd gone off with someone else, I could've coped with that. I think. The thought that you had stopped loving me and our relationship had been a big pretence was crucifying. I needed to find you. But you just vanished and you clearly didn't want to be found. So, I had to admit it; you had stopped loving me."

He glanced at her, uncertain of telling her any more. Unable to bear the look in his eye any longer, she reached up and gently stroked his face.

"I'm so sorry," she choked. Not wanting to respond to her apology, he carried on talking.

"You know that night you arrived in York? You told me last week that that was your first time. It was mine too. So you see, I had nothing to compare you with; I had no experience of women and I managed to convince myself that obviously I wasn't good enough. I thought about talking to Dan about you, I thought he might find out through Andrew where you were, but that would've meant admitting I'd got it so wrong and that you'd left me. At twenty-one, that's not easy to do. So, I turned to drink."

Alice gasped in dismay.

"I tried to drown myself with it. I thought it would help me to forget, but it just made the pain of losing you even sharper. I tried to rebuild my battered ego by bedding half of York but to be honest, I couldn't tell you how well I did because I was too drunk to take notes. I failed my third year which obviously blew my chances of doing a Masters, so I drank a little bit more. I was admitted to hospital after a particularly heavy night and that's when David came to my rescue. Again. He helped me dry out, got me back on the straight and narrow and back on track to re-do my third year. He saw me graduate two years after you left, and then a few months later, he died. I couldn't cope with that so I hit the bottle again. The two people I had loved the most in the whole world, the two people I had trusted with my life, had both left me. I didn't recover well."

He stood up abruptly and crossed over to the window, staring out at the trees and field beyond. Alice remained where she was, completely struck dumb. She knew that any words of apology she offered would be totally inadequate. How could 'sorry' fix any of this. How was it possible that somebody's malicious lie could have caused such devastation that had spanned eighteen years? How could she have let that happen?

"How could you have doubted my love, Alice? I have loved you my whole life: you were my world," Elliot said hoarsely, not turning from the window. It never failed to amaze her how they always seemed to read each other's thoughts.

"Yes, but that's new information, I didn't know that then. I didn't think you even knew who I was, more than just Andrew's awkward little sister," she said defensively. "I doubted myself; I was the one who did the chasing - well, more throwing myself at you - and it hit me that maybe I had been so wrapped up in it, that I didn't see the full picture. Maybe I didn't ever give you a chance to back away," she implored.

She stared at him, willing him to turn round but he continued to look out of the window. He sighed, listening to her but didn't offer a response. Alice could see the tension in his shoulders and rigid back, knowing he was troubled by the memories he had just confronted.

"Why did *you* believe her? How could you have doubted *my* love, Elliot? It works both ways," she ventured, starting to feel aggrieved that this was all being pinned on her.

"I couldn't believe my luck getting with you in the first place," he said quietly. "You were everything I had ever wanted and it hit me that maybe you didn't feel the same. You were so beautiful and so full of life. Maybe I was holding you back."

Alice snorted in frustration.

"My God, do you know nothing, Elliot? I wasn't full of life; I was painfully insecure and frumpy. *You* gave me life. *You* made me beautiful. And without you, I am incomplete. I couldn't bear the thought of you loving somebody else," she cried hotly. "You should've found me," she snapped, putting the blame at his door. He turned from the window, his face darkening with rage.

"I searched everywhere for you! I went across Europe, for Christ's sake, searching for you. I refused to believe it; I refused to give up on you. But you," he sneered, his eyes glinted dangerously, "you just gave up at the drop of a hat. Did you look for me? No! Did you question it? No!" He strode across to the bed,

"How could you even think, after everything that we had together, how could you think that this," he snatched up the laminated letter, "was true?" He threw it towards her. "You and your family closed ranks because I'm a Barraclough, and you deprived me of my daughter. Just like you all did with David," he snarled. Alice jumped up,

"That's not fair! I didn't know about David. Or Roz. I didn't know any of it," she argued back angrily. "I thought you had left me. I was scared. How could I tell you that I was pregnant, knowing that you had gone off with Mary? I was scared that you'd stay with me out of pity. Or duty. But not out of love. And I couldn't bear the thought of that. So, I panicked and left York," she shouted, shaking with indignant rage.

Elliot became very still. He opened his mouth to speak but hesitated. His eyes narrowed. He held up a finger to stop her from saying anything else. He took a step closer, intimidating her with his proximity.

"You knew you were pregnant … in York? Before you left? You told me you found out in Stratford," he said, his voice dangerously still. Alice held her breath. She could feel the colour flooding her face as yet another lie was uncovered.

"How long had you known?" he asked.

She couldn't speak. She felt completely cornered and everything was unravelling, too fast for her to be able to stop it.

"How long, Alice?" he demanded, raising his voice.

"A few days," she mumbled. She balked at the look of contempt in his eyes. She hadn't meant to deceive him; it hadn't been intentional. She tried to explain herself.

"I was over the moon when I did the test and I thought you would be too, but you were so bogged down with your dissertation, so I decided to wait until the weekend to tell you. I'd planned a special meal on that Friday and I was going to tell you then. It was going to be a surprise," she said meekly. Elliot snorted,

"Yes, well it was a surprise. When I found out eighteen years later," he sneered. His tone incited her anger again.

"I thought you had left with Mary. I thought you had married her," she retorted indignantly.

"Because Facebook told you?" he goaded.

He became still again and Alice swallowed nervously. She knew what was coming as she watched his face register what she had just said.

"Wait a minute … you thought I married her." He pointed a finger accusingly at her.

"So … you think I'm still married to her. Right?"

"But you're not," she emphasised.

"I know that. But you didn't," he spoke slowly. "You think that this is an affair. That I'm married and want an affair. You think, that just one sniff of you, and I'll throw away a marriage of eighteen years to get you into bed." His icy stare shamed her to the very core and yet she couldn't look away. Her lip began to quiver, struggling not to cry with humiliation.

"What do you take me for? Some low life scum who has no morals whatsoever? Well, thanks for that!" he hissed. "The fact that you thought that of me, is bad enough. The fact that you went along with it, is so much worse. What kind of person are you?" he rasped.

Alice stumbled backwards and sat abruptly on the bed, her legs shaking like jelly. She hugged her arms in an effort to stop them from trembling. Elliot didn't let up.

"I know David's affair with Linda – or Roz, as it turns out – was all very romantic but I could never condone it. It was wrong. He should've had the gumption to stand up to his father, divorce his wife and face the consequences. If that's what it took to be with the woman he truly loved, then that's what he should've done. I was bought up to believe marriage is for life. And so were you, actually.

What are you playing at, Alice?" he asked, his tone changing from anger to desperation.

Alice breathed deeply. She felt completely spent. Even brushing the fringe from her face felt like a huge effort. She knew he was expecting an answer and she knew how this was going to end. She had nothing to lose now.

"The thought of living without you is killing me. I'm at the stage where I would rather be your mistress than not be with you at all," she said, knowing how sordid it sounded.

"Really?" his voice dripped sarcasm, "You've managed fine without me for eighteen years. You've never made any effort to seek me out, even though my family live just down the road from yours. So how come you suddenly can't live without me, Alice?"

She stared at her feet, not even bothering to answer. She just wanted it to be over. He watched her, his jaw twitching with frustration.

"How many affairs have you had, actually? How many real marriages have you destroyed because you 'can't live without them'?", he mocked her voice, watching the tears slowly fall from her exhausted eyes. He frowned. She didn't lift her head, her voice a strained whisper.

"I haven't done that. There's never been anybody else."

"Right", he scorned, "In eighteen years? Nobody?" he snorted. Alice shook her head.

"So, you're saying that you've lived like a nun these past eighteen years. I doubt that very much, Alice. I've seen you in action, don't forget. I know what you're like," he taunted.

"Stop it, please," she cried. "I know you hate me, I know I have completely messed up and yes, it is killing me. But there has never been anybody else. I made a vow to Ellie, to myself, that I would never let anybody in to hurt me, ever again. I had Ellie and that was enough. I have only ever loved you. I have only ever slept with you. I have only ever trusted you. I didn't want anybody else," she stressed. The absolute desolation she felt was etched in her face as she lifted her head to plead with him. Elliot looked away.

"I can't believe a word you say, Alice. How can I ever trust you after this? Last week, I went back to York thinking that I knew you so well. It turns out, I don't know you at all," he muttered, defeated.

"If you're prepared to have an affair with me, thinking I'm married ... how can I possibly trust you? How do I know that you won't do that with somebody else, five years from now?" he implored. "Alice?" he urged. She didn't respond, not even to acknowledge that she had heard him. He walked towards the door.

"I have to leave," he stated. Alice finally looked up, her face blotchy and swollen from crying.

"Don't leave me again, Elliot," she begged. He stopped and turned on his heel, facing her angrily,

"I didn't leave you the first time. But for the record, this is what it would've felt like," he snapped.

He slammed the door behind him. She heard him hurry down the stairs and heard the front door also slam shut. She heard him rev up his engine and roar off down the road.

"Please be careful," she prayed, her whole body shaking uncontrollably.

Elliot pulled up abruptly just past 'Mary Arden's farm'. He tapped in a destination to his sat nav. His phone rang: Alice's name flashed up on the screen. He rejected the call without hesitation. Holding his phone, he clicked onto his messages and scrolled through to access the messages from Ellie sent the previous weekend. He stared at the photo she had sent of herself, Rachel, and Andrew, waving at the camera. The caption read, 'Uncle Andrew says Hi Dad!'

She looked so much like her mother as a teenager yet she had his uncle's eyes. His eyes. Ellie was his daughter, not just hers, and they had been deprived of each other by a web of deceit and lies.

He scrolled onto her next message: the photo of him and Alice at Andrew's wedding. Ellie had typed, 'my beautiful parents xxx'. Elliot let out a sob, his chest aching as he stared through his tears at the face he loved.

"Damn you, Alice. Damn you to hell," he cursed. He turned off his phone and tossed it onto the back seat, started up the engine again and drove off at speed down the country road, glancing at his sat nav directions to York.

Chapter Twelve

Alice leant against the kitchen work surface, staring at her phone. She had tried to phone Elliot but it kept going to voicemail. She wasn't even sure what she would say if he had picked up anyway.

'I'm sorry I didn't trust you', 'I'm sorry I lied', 'I'm sorry I thought you were an adulterer', 'I'm sorry I hid your daughter from you for eighteen years'. She could see why he had left.

She went back upstairs to her room and picked up the laptop where it had been discarded on her bed. She forced herself to look at Mary's Facebook page. Elliot laughed back at her. How could she not have seen this for what it was? Why had she been so ready to believe Mary's lies in the first place? Had she really been that distrustful of Elliot, she questioned. They had been so happy together, they were such a strong unit and so in tune with each other; why had she thrown it all away, just like that? Elliot was right: he had searched for her for weeks, months even, whereas she had given him precisely twenty-four hours before writing him off and leaving town. Yes, she was pregnant and yes, she was in shock after Mary's note, but was that really enough of an excuse to not even fight for him or give him a chance to defend himself?

Steeling herself, she clicked on Mary's photos, as she had done many times before but this time, she was seeing them through new eyes. As Elliot had predicted, she recognised some of them now as ones she had taken. None of them were recent. Why had that never occurred to her before? Was it because she simply hadn't considered the fact that Elliot would have aged? She was so used to seeing his face, in her mind's eye, as it was eighteen years ago, that it hadn't seemed odd to her.

She shut her laptop and tried to phone Elliot again, to no avail. She just wanted to hear his voice one more time, even if it was an angry one or a scathing one. She knew she deserved his condemnation but she also knew that he would be hurting too. Her mind flitted to thoughts of him drinking himself into oblivion over her disappearance. She got palpitations just thinking about what he must have gone through: the confusion, the pain, the loss he must have felt. She had gone through exactly the same feelings at exactly the same time, over losing him. The difference being, she had a baby growing inside her. She had her mother and Roz to support her. He had no-one.

She sighed at the thought of her mother; how could she not have told Alice that he had come looking for her? She suddenly remembered the strange conversation that she'd had with her that evening after she had been with Elliot in the church. She knew that Celia had been trying to tell her something then, more than she was letting on. What was it she had said? Alice tried to cast her mind back. It was only two weeks ago, and yet, so much had happened and so many things had been talked about, that she could hardly remember it all. She stared into space, racking her brains.

"That's it!" she exclaimed, as her mother's words suddenly flashed to the forefront: 'I think he genuinely loved you. I really do'. Alice thought about it; why hadn't she reacted more at the time when Celia had said that.

The reason why it struck her as such an odd thing to say was that nobody really saw them as a couple, so how would she have known that he genuinely loved her? He must have been in a very determined state when he arrived in Brockenhurst that night looking for her, Alice concluded.

She remembered Celia saying that she thought Roz had been wrong about things, and Alice couldn't help but totally agree with her now, with hindsight. Roz had obviously chosen to go to Newlyn in the hope that David would go there looking for her. Finding her pregnant may well have forced his hand, and Alice didn't doubt that he would have stood by her and faced the consequences. Why didn't Roz then, think the same about Elliot and Alice? Why didn't she push to find him? Why was she so adamant to keep him out of the picture? Alice couldn't help but feel that she had been railroaded into the whole, single mother route, by her aunt.

She looked at her phone. It had been over two hours since he had left. Where was he now? She tried phoning again: still the voicemail. Almost immediately, her message alert beeped. Her heart started to pound. She instinctively didn't want to read it and hesitated, her finger hovering above the button.

'Hi Mum, having loads of fun here. We survived the night! Hope you're not too lonely without me! Love you lots like jelly tots xxxxxx'

Her heart plummeted. She hadn't even got as far as considering what Ellie's reaction to all of this would be. How could she tell her daughter that she had been deprived of a father because of a vindictive lie that had spiralled into an unstoppable, catalogue of deceit. How could she reveal the extent of Elliot's suffering and pain solely due to her impulsive, misguided and selfish actions. How could she confess to what had taken place between them in the past two weeks; how Alice had been prepared to have an affair with a 'married' man with little regard for the consequences, and how, once again, she had lost him because of her lies. How could Ellie forgive any of this?

Unable to control the trembling that had returned to consume her body, she headed for the bathroom. The smell of Elliot's aftershave on her skin was tormenting her, taunting her. Mocking her. Stepping into the shower, fully clothed, she let the hot water pound her body, in an effort to obliterate her pain and humiliation. She knew there was no way back now. Too much damage had been done. Elliot had seen her for what she was: a weak willed, thoughtless liar, severely lacking in morals. The thought of one day finding him again had carried her through life but even that was gone now. He had found her, and rejected her. And she couldn't fault him on that. The finality hit her with a sickening force. She slumped back against the cubicle wall and slowly slid down to curl up in the fetal position, weeping uncontrollably, the relentless torrent of water offering no mercy.

Eventually her weeping subsided and, feeling completely broken, she peeled off her clothes to wash away the last remnants of Elliot's lingering smell from her body. Wrapped in fluffy towels, she lay on the edge of her bed and giving in to exhaustion, fell asleep.

She woke up with a start a few hours later, gasping for breath. She dreamt she had been drowning in a lake, and as she sank to the bottom, unable to fight against death, she could see Elliot's lifeless body already there.

"Oh God, oh God!" she panted, sitting bolt upright. She grabbed her phone from the side to check it. No messages. No calls. It was ten to seven in the evening; she couldn't believe how long she had slept for. But now her head was pounding and she felt faint with hunger and yet, had no desire to eat. She needed tea. Dropping the towels, she slipped on her bathrobe and headed downstairs to the kitchen.

The half-unpacked shopping bags were still on the side, along with the potted plant. She hadn't really paid much attention to it earlier but now she took time to look at it. It was a fuchsia: a compact shrub with lilac and white flowers. She read the label, noting its name, 'Love's Reward'.

"You've got to be kidding me!" she muttered. Turning on the television in the lounge, she perched on the edge of the sofa, staring unseeingly at it. She couldn't relax, her stomach was in knots and she had a growing sense of unease: a restlessness she couldn't curtail.

She went over everything that had happened in the last two weeks, trying to determine how she could have handled things differently. She could see now how tormented Elliot had been when they were in the church together; not because he was married and wanted her as a mistress but because he was still in love with her and feared her rejection. It was also dawning on her that they would have to see each other again; she couldn't imagine that he would stop his relationship with Ellie because of this. He had already shown himself to be a doting father and even though it was early days, Alice knew that nothing would stop him from being exactly that. He was determined to do right by their daughter. She was also beginning to realise her own glaring fault in her make up: she would either have lies tripping off her tongue with alarming ease, or be divulging secrets of some magnitude without any qualms. Why could she never just stop herself? She sighed deeply and leant back against the cushions, deep in thought and self-analysis.

She must have fallen asleep again because a loud, urgent knock at the door woke her up with a start. It was dark outside now, and a glance at the clock told her it was just after ten at night. Looking through the window, she could see the outline of a car with a light shining on its roof. The urgent knock was repeated. Alice hurried into the hall and opened the door.

"I'm sorry, Alice. I'm an idiot. I'm so sorry," Elliot uttered, his voice raw with emotion. He was carrying a hold-all and had a large cut on his temple. Alice stared at him in disbelief. She noticed, behind him, that a taxi was pulling away from the curb.

"What happened to your head?" she asked, panicked. Elliot touched his temple gingerly. He was deathly pale.

"A tree jumped out at me," he shrugged, "but …"

"Are you okay?" she interrupted, "do you need to go to hospital?" She clung on to the edge of the front door, her legs feeling particularly unsteady. Elliot shook his head.

"I've already been, please don't send me back there. Listen, can we forget about my head," he said, his eyes pleading with her, "It's fine. My car's a write-off but that's fine too. My life is falling apart again and that's not fine.

I'm sorry, I really am," he beseeched, tentatively holding his hand out to her.

She took his hand, beckoning him in and shut the door behind him. Taking his hold-all from him and dropping it on the hall floor, she led him into the lounge. She sat next to him on the sofa. He had a firm grip of her hand, not wanting to let her go. The shock of seeing him hurt, completely eradicated their earlier argument from her mind. She gave him her full attention. She gently touched his face, turning it so that she could see his wound. Three rows of butterfly sutures held it neatly together: the skin a livid red, with a tinge of purple spreading further down by his eye.

"What happened to your car? I don't understand," she asked, stroking his arm. Elliot sighed heavily.

"I went back home to York. I was so angry. I shouted at everything in my flat, from the television to the coffee maker, then got in my car again and headed back here. I stopped off at 'Anne Hathaway's cottage', which was shut, but I got out of the car anyway and shouted at the trees in the car park. I kicked a few stones about and generally ranted at the undergrowth. Then I got lost trying to get back here; I must have taken a back road or something and before I knew it, this ruddy great tree was in front of me and I drove straight into it," he explained, feeling foolish. Alice's hand flew up to her mouth as she gasped in shock.

"I'm okay. The air bag worked surprisingly well so that's good to know for future reference," he commented flippantly. Alice pointed to his wound.

"But your head?" she wondered. Elliot gave a light, derisive laugh.

"Oh that. Well, the front of the car crumpled with the impact, so my door was stuck. I had to really kick it to get it to open and as I was climbing out, it slammed back shut onto my head. But it's a superficial wound. I had to inform the police obviously and then get checked out at the hospital. It's okay, really," he assured her.

They stared at each other, neither one knowing what to say next. Alice finally found her voice.

"Why did you come back?" she whispered, hardly daring to hope for the answer she wanted to hear. He squeezed her hand tightly, determination in his face as he looked at her.

"Because I love you. I'm empty without you, Alice," he declared. "My life had no meaning until you walked back into it, and I don't ever want to feel like that again." He watched for her reaction as he laid himself on the line. She gave a strained smile but he could see it didn't quite reach her eyes. It was words she wanted to hear but she was emotionally spent and wary of saying the wrong thing in response. Elliot frowned, sensing there was a lot of damage to repair.

"I'm such an idiot for leaving earlier and I'm angry with myself for doing it. I'm sorry," he apologised. "I was just so full of rage and so confused. And so scared of rejection that I went into defence mode," he admitted.

Alice looked away, not wanting to be reminded of it. She was starting to shake again. Seeing him on her doorstep, injured, had shocked her and momentarily blanked everything else but here she was again, being confronted with it. He gently brushed her hair back and cradled her face with his hands, trying to get eye contact.

"Alice, look at me, please," he said softly. She reluctantly did as he asked, the unmistakable love in his eyes throwing her off guard. She stifled a sob. He faltered.

"I was just focusing on the fact that I had missed out on so much but then it dawned on me: you missed out too. We missed out on each other," he said, trying to explain his actions. "All I wanted to do today was find out whether you'd left because you didn't love me anymore. I needed to know. But when I found out that you thought I'd gone off with somebody else, married somebody else, it threw me. I realised that I didn't let you know the extent of my love for you, how I really felt about you. I'm angry with myself because I let you slip away," he said, full of remorse.

Alice could see he was struggling to find the words he needed to get his point across. In turn, he could see the extent of the pain he had caused earlier, in her swollen, tearstained face and the mistrust in her eyes; it was eating him up inside. He continued to cradle her face, gently stroking her cheeks with his thumbs.

"I can understand why you left: you were pregnant, and scared. I can understand why you didn't tell me. If I squint in my mind, I can even understand why your family chose to shut me out. I just wish you had trusted me more. Given me more of a chance. I think I deserved that. But I can't change the past, I can only change the future," he paused, willing her to believe him. He swallowed nervously.

"I should've told you sooner but when you're young, you think you have all the time in the world," his words sounded garbled to Alice.

"Told me?" she prompted.

"How I felt about you. I put it off, saving it for later. Stupid, I know," he tried to laugh.

"I don't understand what you're saying, Elliot," she said quietly, sensing a change in his mood. He took his hands from her face and nervously rubbed his chin, staring intently at her. He stood up and pulled a box from his trouser pocket before getting down on one knee in front of her. Her eyes widened and she clutched her trembling hands together on her lap, watching him as he opened the box. She couldn't help but let out a loud gasp of surprise at the familiar, antique, diamond ring nestled on a burgundy, velvet pad. She stared open mouthed at Elliot. He smiled, taken aback and pleased by her reaction. He leant towards her, offering the box to her.

"Alice Grace Greene, I have loved you since I was far too young to even know what love is. I have never stopped loving you and now that I've found you, I never want to let you go. I want to grow old with you. I want to spend my life loving you. I want to care for you, protect you and never make you sad, ever again. Will you marry me?" he asked, his voice cracking a little.

He visibly held his breath, waiting for her response. She reached out and touched the ring lightly with her index finger, wondering how this was even happening. It was an exquisite, platinum, filigree ring featuring an Old European cut diamond, with delicately, shaped shoulders. The diamond was held in place with four claw-shaped prongs and the shoulders were decorated with milgrain edging, in which three smaller, similarly cut diamonds were encrusted on each side. The ring was of an Art Deco design and Alice had fallen in love with it immediately, a long time ago.

She wove her fingers together as if in prayer and held them to her mouth, nervously looking at Elliot's expectant face.

"How did you find that ring?" she whispered. He laughed, knowing she had recognised it.

"I've had this a long time. You dropped enough hints about it, every time we passed that jewellers shop in the Shambles," he smiled, "and so I borrowed the money from David and bought it. He didn't hesitate or say we were too young, he practically forced the money into my hand," he told her, "and I had planned to propose on your twenty-first birthday. I was saving it," he added. Sensing her hesitation, he continued persuasively,

"If I had known how you felt about me, how you had followed me to York, I would've had the courage to propose sooner, but I didn't want to scare you off. I knew you loved me but we were young; I didn't want to be too intense," he willed her to believe him, trying to gauge her thoughts.

"And then everything changed. Seeing my dad near death made me realise how fragile life is, and how much I wanted to spend all of it with you. I was filled with panic at the prospect of you not knowing just how much I loved you, and so, the day I came back to York, I was going to propose there and then. I had the ring with me." His voice had dropped to an almost inaudible depth and she could feel his desperation as he relived it. She ached just thinking about what he must have gone through that day.

"You kept the ring," she mumbled in disbelief, stating the obvious. Elliot nodded.

"If I couldn't give it to you, I didn't want anybody else to have it. I couldn't sell it on or even give it away; it was meant just for you," he whispered. He lifted her chin to look at him.

"Alice?" he breathed, frowning at the distressed look in her eyes. She was rejecting him, he knew it. Fear gripped at his throat, and he dropped his head, snapping the box lid shut.

"I'm sorry," she barely whispered, tears silently trickling down her face.

"You can't just come back and do this, as if nothing happened today. You took my heart and soul, and crushed it. You made me feel like a whore. I'm not a whore; I have only ever loved one person and even though I thought you had chosen somebody else over me, I still loved you. I would do anything to be with you again. Anything. That's not being a whore, that's being in love with my soul mate, my love of a lifetime." She was shaking so badly that she could hardly speak coherently.

"You are the only one that has ever made me feel like that. I only want to do those things with you, nobody else, and you used to love that about us. But today you sullied it with what you said, and you made my love for you sound dirty. You made me feel dirty," she choked, unable to stem the torrent of tears.

Elliot stood up and paced across the room, agitatedly running his hand through his hair, then swiftly came back and sat next to her, taking her hand.

"Don't you think I know that? That's what I have been shouting at myself about all day. I said the vilest things to you, I know I did. As I was saying them, I knew they weren't true. I know it's only been me for you. I know you. I'm disappointed in myself because I can't say the same. I'm the whore, not you," he implored desperately. "I was just so angry at everything. Everything. And I needed to shout and rant. And hit my head!" he let out a nervous, ironic laugh.

Alice watched him warily. He stood up again, aware that he was intimidating her. Rising panic was making it hard for him to breathe and he wasn't sure what to do next. He looked at the door, then back at her. He could see, just by the way her shoulders dropped, that she was expecting him to leave again. That knowledge spurred him on. He made a huge effort to not raise his voice but his determination came through despite the lack of volume.

"If you think I'm going to walk away, you're sorely mistaken. I'm going to stay here and prove to you that we belong together. Whatever it takes," he told her. "I know I said some hurtful things but you hurt me too, you know. To find out that you gave up on me without question … that kills me, Alice. So, we've both been hurt today but we need to get beyond this. Not let anything else stop us or rule our decisions."

Alice was staring intently at him, a glimmer of hope flickered across her face. She could see how genuinely sorry he was. He seized the opportunity and sat by her side once again.

"I was so desperate to get back to you," he said quietly, persuasively. "I should've been here by seven if it weren't for that stupid tree. I was only ten minutes away down the road, and then I got carted off to Warwick hospital and sat for ages in A & E. And all the while I just kept thinking, I need to get back to you. I need you to know that I'm sorry and that I love you. And I trust you with my life. Your name is etched on my heart, Alice. It always has been," he said in a strangled voice, waiting for some kind of sign from her. She blinked, not able to look away but still not wanting to speak. He persisted.

"Look at David and Roz. They missed their chance and there was no need really. Lack of communication and trust killed it. I can tell you for a fact, had he known about the baby, he would've given up everything for her. Even twenty years down the line, he would've still done it. I'm not going to let us miss our chance again." He gently lifted her chin up with his hand and looked at her, pouring everything he felt for her in that one look. He could see how her face softened as her eyes read his. Her breathing became shallow and she bit her lip, visibly sinking into his gaze. He sensed he was winning her over.

"I know you love me too," he urged softly, desperately wanting to kiss her. "What can I do to convince you? Tell me," he begged. Alice started to smile shyly.

"Show me the ring again," she whispered.

"What?" He fumbled nervously for the box that had fallen to the floor, hope coursing through him like a flame.

"I didn't hear what you said earlier; my heart was pounding too loudly," she breathed, her eyes sparkling with anticipation.

"No, that was my heart you could hear," he murmured, then deftly got down on one knee. He could see the answer in her eyes before he had even asked, making it almost impossible not to grin as he asked the most important question in the world.

"Alice Grace Greene," he paused to steady his breathing and stop himself from laughing out loud. She was also trying to control her beaming grin, holding a hand to her mouth, watching him excitedly. He breathed out, determined to do it properly,

"Alice, I love you. I love every little inch of you. I love your smile, your laugh, the way you bite your lip when you want me. I love how you light up my heart just by walking in to the room. I love your passion for things that are important to you. I love the fact that you have given me a beautiful daughter. I love how you love me and I want you to go on loving me for eternity, the way I love you. So … will you marry me?" He had barely finished speaking before she answered.

"Yes, please," she said happily, with tears in her eyes. Elliot exhaled sharply, grinning.

"Thank God for that! And there's no going back, okay? I won't let you change your mind," he jokingly warned her, taking the ring from its box and putting his hand out for hers. She shrugged,

"I wouldn't want to anyway," she practically sang, her eyes dancing as he slipped the ring onto her finger. She held her hand out, moving it to watch the diamonds sparkle as they caught the light emanating from the standard lamp.

Elliot stood up and pulled her to her feet, enveloping her in his arms and squeezing her so tightly that she could hardly breath.

"I am so sorry, Alice, I really am. I thought I'd blown it," he breathed, his mouth pressed against her hair. She squeezed him back.

"Not a chance," she declared, moving her head back to smile at him. She swayed and lost her balance, overcome with faintness. Elliot steadied her, concerned.

"Are you okay? Have you eaten anything?" he asked. She shook her head.

"Let's get some food inside you," he determined, moving to sit her back down, but she clung to him.

"I think I need to lie down," she mumbled, staring at the floor. Elliot gently lifted her head with his hand, studying her face. She started to smile. He raised an amused eyebrow: he recognised that smile. Suddenly aware of what she was dressed in, he took a step back and cocked his head, theatrically.

"Are you wearing anything under that robe, Miss Greene?" he teased, a seductive edge to his voice.

"Yes," she replied defensively, "my necklace." She scrunched her nose, trying not to giggle at his reaction. He touched the necklace with his finger, noting how it glinted in the light.

"Right," he nodded thoughtfully. Alice could see how he struggled not to smirk, playing along with her. He took a decisive breath,

"I think you're right: you definitely need to lie down." He scooped her up in his arms and headed with brisk strides for the stairs. Alice erupted into girlish giggles,

"You mean…" she intimated.

"Yes. Forget the pizza: Fantastic sex is back on the menu," he declared with authority. She wrapped her arms around his neck and leant her head against his shoulder as he effortlessly climbed the stairs with her in his arms.

"About time too, Mr Barraclough," she sighed.

Chapter Thirteen

"Honey, I'm home!" Ellie called in a sing-song voice as she burst through the bedroom door the next morning. She gasped and let out a shocked squeal. Alice pulled the duvet over her head sharply. Elliot sat bolt upright, bleary-eyed and bare-chested, startled by the rude awakening. Ellie stared at him.

"Da-ad?" she exclaimed, "what's going on?" Her voice was high-pitched. Alice pulled the duvet away from her face, wide eyed.

"I wasn't expecting you home today," she faltered, knowing there was no point in trying to deny the situation.

"Well, clearly!" Ellie retorted, then looking round the bedroom she took in the discarded, crumpled robe, and Elliot's hastily removed clothes strewn across the floor. There was a plate with the remains of pizza crust on, along with a half empty bottle of wine and two wine glasses, on the bedside table.

"Have I just stepped back in time or something?" She sounded sarcastic, shaking her head at the surreal spectacle.

"Ellie ..." Elliot started but she put a hand up to stop him.

"No, you don't need to explain. I'm sure you both know what you're doing."
She looked pointedly at her mother, disappointment apparent in her eyes. Heading back through the door, she said,

"I'll go and put the kettle on, and you two," she held a hand to shield her eyes from her father's thick, black carpet of chest hair, "put some clothes on, please."

Elliot sank back against the pillows then propping himself up, turned to Alice.

"Well, that's solved the question of how to tell Ellie," he gave a derisive laugh, "but what was that look all about? I thought she would be pleased," he frowned. Alice groaned, pulling an apologetic face.

"She thinks you're married."

"What?" he uttered in disbelief. Alice rolled over, stroking his chest as if to soften the blow.

"Everybody thinks you're married. I'm sorry," she added meekly.

"Jesus, Alice," he hissed in exasperation, then kissing her briefly he hurriedly got dressed.

"I'd better go down and explain our behaviour to our daughter," he said, "and you..." he stared at her for a moment, the reality of it all hitting him. He grinned, his heart soaring.

"You just stay there. I'll be back," he winked. He stopped at the door and turned back to her with a quizzical look.

"Can I hear geese?"
Alice nodded, laughing at his confused face.

"Yes. They're at the farm," she told him. "I'm surprised the cockerel didn't wake us up. It's the village alarm clock."

"That would've been handy," he commented dryly, then grinned at her before hurrying downstairs.

It wasn't long before Ellie's footsteps could be heard running up the stairs. Alice darted across the room to grab her robe and hastily tied the belt before Ellie burst through the door yet again. She squealed excitedly, clapping her hands and then throwing her arms around her mother, not able to contain her delight.

"Oh my God, Mum! This is awesome!" she shrieked, waved her hands by her face as if fanning away the tears of joy.

"I just can't believe it!" she laughed. Grabbing Alice's hand, she pulled her over to the window to admire the ring in the sunlight. The ring shone brilliantly, mesmerising Ellie as Alice moved her finger to show how it caught the light.

"It's so beautiful," Ellie breathed. She hugged Alice again, resting her head on her shoulder. Alice stroked her hair.

"Are you okay with this?" she asked gently. Ellie nodded.

"Absolutely. I'm just so happy for you. For us. I knew you'd always loved him, before I'd even met him. And that night on my birthday ... I could see a mile off how in love with you he was. You both lit up the room, and that says it all really. It's like a fairy tale," she gushed.

Elliot appeared, carrying two steaming mugs of tea. He smiled indulgently at the pair of them with their arms wrapped around each other.

"I've put your hot chocolate in the bathroom, Ellie," he told her.

"Thanks, Dad. I'm jumping straight into a hot bath," she said, moving towards the door.

"Why are you home early? What happened?" Alice asked, suddenly remembering that she had arrived home a day earlier than expected. Ellie pulled a face.

"Kyle got food poisoning or something. He's been throwing up all night so we had to abandon it. I reckon it was the sausages: not good on the second night. He was the only one who ate them and we're all fine," she said.

"He should be a vegetarian, like you, then," Elliot laughed lightly, "perhaps you should convert him." Ellie nodded earnestly,

"I wish I could, Dad!" she said passionately.

Alice watched their interaction, loving how quickly they had slipped into their role of father and child. They seemed so connected and it made her feel complete.

"Listen, Ellie," she started, "I'm guessing that you know how wrong I got it about everything," she ventured. Elliot rested the mugs on the bedside table and put his arm around Ellie as they both listened to what Alice had to say.

"I am so sorry. I listened to the wrong people and made the wrong decisions. I deprived you both of each other and nothing I say or do can change that. I just want you both to know that I am more sorry than you could possibly imagine," she said impassionedly.

Ellie held her hand out for Alice to come and join in their embrace and she did so willingly. Ellie kissed them both in turn, looking from one to the other.

"It's okay, Mum. There's no point in harping on about it because you're right: it can't be changed. What's done is done. But you two are going to get married, make me legitimate and live happily ever after. That's all the apology I need," she said earnestly. She leant her head against Elliot.

"I just want a dad to love me, the way Gramps loved you. And now I've got that. I've had a great childhood and the future is going to be even better," she started to get choked. Elliot rested his chin on her head, looking at Alice with a mixture of pride and determination.

"And now," she said, ducking out from their embrace, "I'm going to leave you two alone and have a bath," she grinned, shutting the door behind her.

Elliot pulled Alice close, a deeply contented sigh escaping his lips.

"Pinch me," he whispered.

"Why?" she laughed.

"I need to know I'm not dreaming," he said. She kissed him instead and nestled in to his chest.

"You're not dreaming."

"Did you sleep okay?" he murmured, taking her hand and sitting on the bed, reaching for their tea.

"*Did* we sleep? I don't remember that bit," she teased. He passed a mug to her, leaning close.

"As long as you remember everything else, that's all that matters," he teased back, running a finger down her arm. They heard Ellie in the hallway outside the bathroom door, on her phone.

"Oh my God, Rach, you'll never guess what! I just got home to find my mum in bed … with my dad!"

"Ellie!" they both shouted, in unison. Alice stared in horror at Elliot. He just laughed.

"And that's how we tell your family," he said, patting her leg decisively.

An hour later, the three of them were sitting in the kitchen, eating breakfast together. Ellie was on her phone, scrolling through Facebook and Twitter; Alice was leaning against Elliot and he held her hand with both of his. He couldn't take his eyes off her and was being incredibly attentive. Ellie glanced up at them every now and then, smiling.

"I'm not going to let you out of my sight for a single second," he said possessively to Alice, "Wherever you go, I'll be with you."

She chuckled, feeling smug about his devotion.

"I may need to use the bathroom at some point," she laughed quietly. He shook his head like a petulant child.

"No, not one second. Although you can go to the loo on your own," he conceded, "that's fine, but you'll need me with you in the shower," he gave a throaty chuckle.

"Oh my God, I can hear you both, you know!" Ellie exclaimed in mock disgust. She pushed her chair back from the table and put her plate by the sink.

"Right, I'm off to Tasha's. I'll leave you two love birds to do your love bird stuff but please, not in the shower. We all have to use it." She pulled a disgusted face which Elliot reciprocated, making her laugh.

"Actually, before you go: can you be back by six please? We're all going out for dinner," Elliot told her.

"Oh! Don't you want it to be just the two of you?" She looked surprised. He shook his head firmly.

"Look Ellie, I'm not just some guy dating your mum: you're my daughter. You two are my family and that's all I've ever wanted. So, it's not really up for negotiation. I want you both to come out for dinner with me tonight," he told her. "If that's okay," he added, "I don't want to be the heavy-handed dad or anything," he smiled, getting up to give her a hug. She looked incredibly happy.

"I'll be home by six, Dad," she said.

"Good. And another thing: can you spare some time away from your friends at all? I know you had lots planned but I thought we could go on holiday, if you'd like?" he raised his eyebrows expectantly. Ellie grinned,

"Yes, that sounds great! Where?" she asked, getting excited.

"Your choice. Think about it and let me know," he nodded. "Anywhere you like. Caribbean, Mediterranean, you choose." He kissed her head. Ellie skipped to the front door, like a jubilant child.

"See you at six, Mum and Dad!" she shouted happily before slamming the door shut.

Elliot turned to Alice, seeing the absolute look of love she was giving him.

"That was so incredibly kind," she said.

"You reckon? Am I impressing you yet?" he asked.

"Yet?" she laughed out loud, "I don't think you could impress me much more," she said softly.

"Really?" He raised an eyebrow suggestively, "Shower?"

Alice giggled, nodding, and grabbing his hand, ran upstairs.

After a late, lazy lunch, they stretched out on one of the squishy sofas, in each other's arms, talking. There was an air of complete honesty between them now: no secrets left to skirt round and no hidden agendas. The sun shone through the lounge window, warming them, adding to their feeling of contentment.

"What made you stop the drinking and change your direction in life?" Alice asked. Elliot thought about it for a moment.

"It was shortly after my twenty-fifth birthday and I was in a bar, in York, as usual. This old guy bought me a few drinks and we got chatting. It wasn't exactly an intellectual conversation; we were both half cut, but it was company. He was quite smart, a typically flash business man, complete with thick, gold chain and gold watch. As the night wore on, I worked out he was only about forty, not late fifties as I'd originally thought, and he turned out to be a real letch. He was leering at all the girls, making lewd comments and trying out these cringe-making, chat-up lines. He cottoned on that, unlike him, I was quite good with the chat and he was egging me on to pick up a couple of girls for him. I invited this pretty, young girl to join us at the bar, and then he tried to grope her. She left, but not before giving me such a look of disgust and loathing. And then he turned to me, laughing, and said, 'you remind me so much of me when I was your age'. And I had this kind of epiphany moment. I just thought, what the hell am I doing with my life? Is this what I've become? And that was it. I stopped the drinking and the feeling sorry for myself. I went back to Uni to do a Masters in Heritage and got a job with the York Archaeological Trust, and I've been there for thirteen years."

They both fell silent. It was a lot for Alice to digest but she knew she had to confront it. This had been his darkest time. She couldn't even begin to comprehend the depths of his despair. Resisting the temptation to apologise again, she just held him a little tighter. He could sense her empathy and smiled gratefully at her.

"And you've never dated anybody in all this time?" he asked her, "not even a partner for the staff 'do' or anything?"

She shook her head.

"No. I just threw myself in to my work and motherhood. I had no interest in anybody else, I didn't trust anybody else, and I certainly wasn't looking for a father figure for Ellie," she told him. He nodded, understanding how she had felt.

"What about you? Was there ever anybody, I mean, apart from ..." she didn't finish the sentence, not quite sure how to word it.

"Honestly, no. Nothing that lasted longer than a night. Sex is one thing but I never wanted anything more. My heart just wasn't in it. I guess I was in mourning for you. If you had died, I might have moved on. I don't know," he shrugged, "but you didn't die, and so I never had any closure. And I couldn't replace you in my heart. I didn't want those sunny days in the park or rainy days curled up on the sofa, with anybody else but you," he said, frowning at what he was divulging. Unable to stop herself, Alice apologised.

"I know you said, no more apologies, but I am so sorry, Elliot," she uttered. She felt her words were completely inadequate considering the enormity of what he had just told her. She moved so that she could look at him. She touched his face, wishing she could wipe away the years of sadness there.

"I just regret that you didn't believe in me enough to know that I would *never* have done anything to hurt you," he chided lightly.

"It's me I didn't believe in," she replied. "I couldn't understand why you chose me; I was always the plain Jane of the village whereas you ... everybody loved you, Elliot. You were the school heart throb," she insisted. He laughed in disbelief at her absurd statement.

"Hardly! And just to point out, you were never 'plain Jane' in my eyes. You were perfection. Everything I ever wanted," he smiled, kissing her tenderly.

"You definitely got the better deal though," he said moments later. "Your life has had meaning, a purpose. On the plus side, I threw myself into work, earnt a packet and saved a fortune. No family to spend it on," he reflected.

"Oh goodness, don't let Ellie know!" she joked, "She'll take you shopping for an eternity! I'm afraid I've always had to cap her spending."

"But I want that, Alice: to spend it on my family." He sat up slightly, his mind racing. He took hold of her left hand and twiddled her diamond ring.

"Let's not waste any time. This engagement ring needs a wedding one to match. Let's get married at Christmas. St Saviour's is always magical at Christmas," he decided. Alice's mouth dropped open. She could see he wasn't joking.

"But that's less than five months away! There's so much to plan!" she exclaimed, feeling the panic setting in already. Not that she had any experience but had seen enough people go through the process to know that five months was not long enough to plan a church wedding.

Elliot shrugged, a smile on his face that said he wouldn't be defeated on this.

"Then let's hire a wedding planner. All you need to do is pick a dress and be there on the day. Simple," he grinned. Alice shook her head, laughing.

"Hire a wedding planner? Have you not met my mother and aunt? If I hired a wedding planner, there would definitely be a lynching!" She patted his chest as if calming an excitable puppy. Elliot shrugged, gesturing with his hands the simplicity of the solution.

"Then let them do it: they would be perfect for it. They would be in their element fussing over you. The money's there. I'll book the church. You pick a dress and let them sort out all the rest," he said simply. Alice smiled, warming to the idea. Elliot sensed her weakening. He pulled her towards him, his mouth against hers.

"Christmas, then?" he breathed.

"Christmas," she agreed, succumbing to his passionate kiss.

"How did it go?" Alice asked, smiling in anticipation at Elliot as he walked into the kitchen, still holding his phone. He inclined his head,

"Well, not too bad, considering. My mother cried quite a bit but generally she's thrilled with everything that I've just bombarded her with. She can't wait to meet you, and Ellie, and welcome you both into the family," he smiled. "I didn't say anything about David and Roz; I thought I'd save that gem for Friday," he added, pulling a face.

"Friday?" Alice repeated, holding up a cup and indicating to the teapot.

"Yes please," he nodded. "Yes, we've been invited to my parents' house on Friday evening, for a family get-together. Just my parents and siblings, nothing too intense," he assured her, putting his arms around her waist from behind and kissing her hair.

"How did *your* phone call go?" he asked, resting his head on her shoulder to watch her pour two cups of tea. She was a little hampered by him but it didn't bother her; she revelled in his need for physical contact.

"Well, as you can imagine, mum was thrilled, not particularly surprised, and in a bit of a flap about planning a wedding at such short notice. She's going to chat to Martin after evensong today, to see what we can arrange, but she reckons he'll do everything he can to fit us in. He's almost like family, after all," she laughed, remembering how nervous he had been when first appointed to replace her grandfather as vicar of the parish. He knew that following in Reverend Moore's footsteps was going to be a tall order, but with Alice's father there to lend a hand, he sailed through the transition.

"And she's insisting on throwing us a big engagement party, inviting both of our families," she said, "on Saturday."

Elliot looked surprised.

"This Saturday?

Alice nodded,

"Yep, this Saturday. And she wouldn't take no for an answer. She said that as our families are local, most of them should be free. And now that we're going down there for Friday anyway, I can't really put her off," she gave him an apologetic smile.

"Why would you want to put it off?" he asked, reaching past her for his tea. She frowned.

"Well, isn't it all a bit sudden? Don't you mind? There'll be lots of explaining to do and questions to answer." She was certainly feeling nervous about it but Elliot seemed unfazed by the prospect. He took a gulp of tea, shaking his head and smiling at her.

"Listen, Alice, the questions aren't going to go away, so the sooner we answer them, the better. I am desperate to show you off as my fiancée and tell the world that Ellie is my daughter. Saturday isn't soon enough, as far as I'm concerned," he stated.

He leant against the work surface, watching her, deliberating his next words. She raised her eyebrows in question, knowing he had something more to say.

"I made another phone call. To my boss," he started. "I was initially going to tell him I wouldn't be in work tomorrow or Tuesday, due to my lack of transport and head injury but we got talking. I told him all about you, and Ellie, and our wedding plans - he's thrilled, by the way - and he suggested I should take a month's special leave, as of tomorrow," he grinned.

"You're kidding?" Alice exclaimed, "A month? I've got you for a whole month?" she laughed ecstatically, hugging him in delight.

"That's not all," he continued, "I've put myself forward for a transfer to our Nottingham branch, and he's going to sort it as a matter of urgency. It means a three-hour round trip from here each day but that's better than staying in York and only seeing you at weekends. Isn't it?" He needn't have asked really: her face was a picture of sheer happiness.

"So, you might never go back to York again? Do you mind leaving that abruptly?" she wondered, trying not to let her own, selfish joy overlook how he might be feeling at having to make such huge changes in his life, they hadn't had a chance to discuss it properly yet. He snorted.

"I wouldn't care less if I never went back there again. I only stayed there because all my memories of you, of us, are there. But now I have the real deal. This is where I want to be, with you. Not chasing ghosts in York," he said, kissing her cheek. She had that sudden urge to cry again as waves of pure contentment washed over her. She sank into his embrace.

"Well, I made another phone call too," she told him, "to Andrew. He is so over-the-top happy for us!" she laughed. "He was still a little hung over from his night out with your brother, mind you," she added. "I asked if he would give me away. He was a bit choked but chuffed to bits. *And* I had a chat with Laura. She's going to make my wedding dress, and the bridesmaids dresses, but we need to get started as soon as," she grinned, her mind buzzing. "Can you believe it: we're actually planning our wedding!"

Ellie arrived home and listened in astonishment as Elliot ran through all that they had planned so far.

"How long was I out for?" she laughed, a little taken aback. "Is this what it's always going to be like with you, Dad? Snap decisions, no hesitation?" she wondered, in awe of his ability to make it all seem so simple.

"Well, if there's one thing I have learnt in the past two weeks, it's don't dawdle once you have set your sights on something. Don't put it off, just go for it," he enthused.

"In that case, can I legally change my name to Barraclough before I start Uni, please?"
She looked hopefully at them both, not sure which one looked closer to tears. She decided it was her dad.

"Of course you can," Alice agreed readily. "I can sort that out tomorrow, get the ball rolling. It should only take a few days to get a deed poll done but even before that, I can notify the admin office at work about it," she said.

"Thanks, Mum. And I've been thinking about the holiday," she smiled awkwardly, "does it have to be the Caribbean or Mediterranean? Only, what I'd really love to do is finish our trip to Amsterdam, to the Anne Frank museum and then, maybe go on to Germany and Poland. I know it doesn't sound very exciting or exotic but it's what interests me."

Elliot regarded her for a moment, marvelling again at her maturity, enthusiasm and thirst for knowledge. Physically, she was so much like her mother yet something about her spirit reminded him of how he was at her age.

"I think that's an excellent idea, Ellie. I would find that incredibly interesting too," he said, putting his arm around her shoulders.

"Alice?" he prompted, wanting her approval too.

"Absolutely," she said purposefully. "We'd only get burnt in the Caribbean anyway."

"Right, I'll book hotels and such in the morning. Shall we pack up and take our things on Friday when we go to

Brockenhurst, and leave from there for Amsterdam on Sunday, or Monday?" he suggested.

"Like I said: snap decisions," Ellie laughed, running upstairs to change quickly for dinner.

Later that night as they lay in each other's arms, Alice watched Elliot drift off to sleep, unable to do the same. She couldn't switch off; her mind was in such a whirl. There was so much to plan and, tempting as it was, the idea of leaving all the decisions to Celia and Roz concerned her. She had long since accepted that the only wedding she was likely to help plan would be Ellie's but now that her own wedding was on the cards, she wanted it to be perfect and to her own specific instruction. She needed to start a list in the morning, ready to give to Celia on Friday.

Her eyes rested on Elliot's sleeping face and she had to resist the urge to touch it. She had an uncontrollable need to be near him, to be touching him, all the time. She couldn't get enough of him and couldn't wait for him to pack up his flat in York, move in with her and start their life together.

"Elliot?" she shook him gently.

"Mmmm?" He stirred a little.

"I need you to wake up," she whispered, shaking him again. He opened one eye a crack and sighed.

"Again, Alice? It's only been five minutes," he mumbled with a sleepy smile, closing his eye again. She chuckled, shaking his arm.

"Not that. I need to talk to you," she insisted. Elliot groaned.

"Mmmm?"

"Let's get your things from York, tomorrow," she said resolutely. He opened his eyes briefly, trying to focus on her through the fog of tiredness.

"What? I can do that any time. Go to sleep," he sighed, drawing her closer to him and nuzzling his chin into her neck. She moved to prop herself up, leaning her elbow on his chest to support her head. She shook his shoulder with her other hand, aware that she was being annoying but that didn't stop her.

"Yes, but I want to get you moved out of there and into here as soon as possible. That way I know you're not going anywhere," she persisted, in a tone that demanded a response.

"I'm not going anywhere," he said.

"I know but it's symbolism," she replied, lightly tapping his nose.

"Symbolism?" He finally opened his eyes, questioning what on earth she was going on about. Happy that she had his attention, she smiled widely, explaining,

"Yes. Putting your clothes into my wardrobe is a symbolic gesture of your commitment to me."
Elliot laughed out loud.

"Is that code for something?"

"No!" she laughed with him as she heard how it sounded.

"Mmmm, right," he yawned and stretched, rolling her over onto the pillows and smiling down at her. She tried to stifle her grin, her eyes sparkling with anticipation.

"I thought you were asleep," she said, running her hands across his shoulders.

"I was, but your need of a symbolic gesture is more important than my sleep," he whispered in her ear, still chuckling at her double entendre.

"Well, if you insist," she giggled, pulling the duvet over them to shut out the world.

Chapter Fourteen

"Okay, that's done," Alice announced as she walked into the study. She stopped in the doorway, taking a moment to absorb the scene that greeted her. Elliot and Ellie were sitting side by side in front of the computer screen, Ellie still dressed in her Tatty Teddy pyjamas, and both hugging a mug of tea in an identical manner. They turned distractedly from the screen to acknowledge her. Elliot's face softened instantly when he looked at her. Ellie raised her eyebrows in question.

"Sorry, what?" she asked, glancing back at the screen and moving the mouse before looking back at Alice.

"I've downloaded the deed poll forms, which are straightforward enough. You just need to fill in a few things and sign it; I'll ask Tasha's mum to fill in the statutory declaration to confirm who you are and then we can send it off. I've spoken to Admin at work and they've made a note on your file of your name change and that the deed poll form is under way," she explained, stretching across to turn the printer on, next to the computer.

"And if you can wait until after the wedding to change the details on your birth certificate, I've downloaded the forms for that too," she added.

"Why do I have to wait?" Ellie sounded impatient, turning to Elliot for his support. He patted her hand, waiting for Alice's explanation. She tapped the edge of the desk nervously.

"Well, because I left out your father's name on your birth certificate and because we are now getting married, we have to re-register your birth and include all the details. Both of our names. It makes you legitimate," she nodded, sensing Ellie's irritation, "but that can only be done once we are actually married."

Elliot stood up and put his arms around Alice.

"That's great news," he said. He turned to Ellie, with an encouraging smile.

"By Christmas we will officially be the Barraclough family but for now, I am more than happy with my Greene girls. It's just a name, Ellie. You're still my daughter."

She frowned in response.

"It's not just a name to me though, Dad. It means so much more than that to me," she argued. Alice gently butted in.

"Ellie, you can still change your name to Barraclough *now* for everything else: your passport, university stuff, bank details. All that can be done with the deed poll. It's just the birth certificate that will have to wait, that's all." She looked at Ellie, willing her to smile.

"I can't wait to be a Barraclough either, you know," she added, leaning her head against Elliot's chest. She sneaked a look at the computer screen to see what they had been studying so intently. She recognised the site: Missing You.net.

'That explains Ellie's mood', she thought. Reading about other people searching for unknown parents or siblings, had obviously struck a nerve and even though Ellie now knew who her father was, she was still coming to terms with it, and still feeling betrayed by her closest family members.

Alice reminded herself yet again that Ellie would need time to deal with these new emotions and the prospect of having a new extended family, let alone a father. A father who, only two weeks previously, turned up on the doorstep and who now, was moving in with them. Although personally she was thrilled at the speed of things, she realised that it was a huge upheaval for Ellie. Alice had known Elliot all her life whereas for Ellie, he was a new entity. His spontaneous holiday plan had come at just the right time, she thought, suspecting that it wasn't just a happy coincidence. The three of them needed to get away from their familiar surroundings and have a chance to bond, away from prying eyes. Reading her mind, Elliot tightened his hold of her and gave her a look that told her he knew exactly what she was thinking.

"Everything will be fine. We just have to be a bit patient," he encouraged them both. "And in the meantime," he said to Alice, "Ellie and I have decided to get cracking with the search for David's daughter." He indicated for Ellie to show Alice the website they had been looking at.

"Yes, I've seen this site already but haven't had a proper look yet," she said, sitting next to Ellie. Ellie briefly leant her head on Alice's shoulder, pulling an apologetic face.

"Sorry, Mum," she mumbled. Alice shook her head.

"Nothing to be sorry about, Ellie. Everything that you're feeling right now is perfectly natural and I'm here to support you. We both are," she said, looking up at Elliot. He smiled and nodded in agreement.

"So, what have you found on here, then?" she asked them both, changing the subject. Ellie manoeuvred the cursor across the screen.

"Right," she started, "we've had a good look at this site. It's a big search engine, basically. Anybody can leave a message on here, giving as much or as little information as they want about who they're looking for. It's not just adopted people; it's relatives or friends who have lost contact, that sort of thing," she explained. "So, you can type in a name here on the left and click 'search'," she said, typing in 'Rosalind Moore' to illustrate how they had commenced the search. Instantly, the result flashed up in red font,

'Sorry, no match was found using your search criteria'. Alice looked at Ellie.

"So, there's no record of her on here?" she wondered. Ellie shook her head.

"No but if you type in just 'Moore' then about twenty results come up. Dad and I have looked through half of them, reading all the messages but nothing relating to Roz, no," she confirmed.

"So, what now? Is this a good site or are we wasting our time?" Alice asked. Elliot replied,

"Well, we are pretty limited really. I had a look at the Gov.uk site and if we want to try and get adoption paperwork or certificates, that has to be down to Roz, not us. This site seems to be a good place to check because I'm working on the theory that if Cee-Cee is looking for her birth mother, then she may well leave a message on here."

Alice stared at the screen, taking in what he had just said.

"So, you think *she* may have been looking for *Roz*? Is that likely?" She looked from one to the other. Ellie glanced at Elliot, a knowing look passing between them. Elliot rubbed the side of his face, choosing his words carefully.

"Well it is a distinct possibility, yes. Ellie has looked at this site before and..." he paused, "if you hadn't told her about me, she'd decided that after her eighteenth birthday she was going to post a message on here, looking for me," he said gently. Alice's head shot round to look at Ellie, wide eyed. Ellie grimaced awkwardly.

"You've been on here before?" Alice asked in a hushed voice, seeing the guilty expression on her face. Ellie nodded.

"Yes, lots of times. I kept hoping that somebody was looking for me and the more I looked at it, the more apparent it became that I wasn't alone in wanting to find a parent. There are thousands of kids doing exactly the same thing. And actually, those 'kids' are mostly adults in their thirties, forties, even fifties, in a last-ditch attempt to find some sort of trace of where they came from." She met Alice's shocked face with unwavering defiance, her courage returning.

"You have no idea what it's like, Mum. To not know who your parent is. To wonder if they're thinking about you at all. To hope that they're looking for you, as much as you are looking for them. So yes, I think she would be looking for Roz. Even if you feel resentment at being abandoned by a parent, curiosity gets the better of you in the end," she said, "and that need to know, just keeps growing with time." She turned her attention back to the computer, sensing what Alice was going to say next as she drew in breath.

"And before you say it, I know you're sorry," she half laughed. "Oh my God, Mum, change the record!" She looked up briefly, squinting. "Look, just let me work through this in my own way, okay? Now, you two get going and leave me to carry on here. There are over twenty-four thousand messages to look through."

She stood up and stretched, picked up her empty mug and headed for the kitchen.

"Brad's coming over in a bit to help. Is there any food in or do I need to shop?" she asked.

"There's stuff in the freezer," Alice replied distractedly, "Have you told Brad about Roz's baby?" she asked in surprise. Ellie sighed heavily.

"Mum, it's Brad. I tell him everything. Please don't expect me to keep secrets from him of all people." She sounded exasperated. "And don't worry, he won't gossip about it," she added edgily. She gave Elliot a hug.

"Safe journey, Dad. See you later," she smiled, then hugging Alice next, she kissed her cheek noisily and laughed.

"Drive carefully, Mum, and look after our wounded soldier,", she nodded at Elliot's forehead, which was looking particularly livid now that the healing process had started.

"And please, try to get your head round the fact that the truth will out, however hard you try to stop it from doing so. I can't bear all this secrecy, you know; it has to end," she insisted. "A new beginning, a clean slate. Okay?"

"Okay," Alice agreed, returning her hug.

Ten minutes later, Alice was at the wheel of her car with Elliot next to her in the passenger seat. Empty boxes were piled on the back seat, with more in the boot, alongside a couple of empty suitcases.

"Ready for this?" he asked, squeezing her hand. She grinned, nodding happily.

"Ready," she said, starting up the engine. "Let's go and say goodbye to York."

Once they were out of the village and heading for the motorway, following signs for 'The North', Elliot pressed 'play' on the cd player. Andy Williams' voice resonated throughout the car, bringing a surprised smile to his face.

"Andy Williams?"

Alice glanced at him, not wanting to take her eyes off the road, a wistful look on her face.

"Yes, it always reminds me of Dad and that helps me focus on driving, for some reason," she acknowledged. "How about you? What do you listen to in the car?"

"Bryan Adams sometimes but mainly Elvis Presley. Funnily enough, I inherited the CDs from David."

They both fell silent for a moment. Elliot drew in a decisive breath,

"I think we need to start our own CD collection," he announced, turning Andy Williams off. "What about Take That? I remember all your CDs and old annuals! Are you still in love with them?" he teased, laughing. She tapped his leg indignantly.

"Don't diss Take That! And of course I still love them. A girl never forgets her first love; you should know that by now," she grinned. "Laura and I took Ellie and Rachel to see them at Wembley when they got back together with Robbie. Guess who was the most excited out of the four of us?" she laughed, doing a double take at Elliot's astonished expression.

"What?" she wondered.

"Which night were you there?" he asked.

"The first night, of course," she said. "Why?"

"I was there too," he said, "with my niece, Natalie. I don't believe it." He stared at her, astounded.

"Seriously?" Alice exclaimed, "that's so weird because…"

"I thought you were there," he interrupted her.

"Yes! Same!", she said, "I just put it down to listening to all those old songs but I really felt that you were there somehow. To coin a phrase: oh my God!" she laughed, shaking her head. "How come you got the job of taking Natalie then?" she asked, trying to visualise him there with a teenage girl, well out of his comfort zone.

"My choice actually. She's my God daughter, not just my niece, so I always make an extra effort to do things with her. And I got the tickets as her birthday present; she was over the moon," he reflected proudly. "I am officially her favourite uncle," he laughed.

"So, Natalie is … James's daughter?" she guessed, correctly.

"Yes. James and Anne have got Samuel, Natalie, and Anthony. Natalie's the same age as Ellie, so that'll be great for them, I think they'll really hit it off. Samuel will be twenty-one later this year and Anthony's fifteen. Then Dan and Charlotte have got Eddie and Chris: they're fourteen and eleven. James and Anne are both accountants so you'll get free financial advice - whether you want it or not - and Dan is the local GP but I'm sure you already knew that", he said. "You'll get to meet them all on Friday". He patted her leg, chuckling at the look of panic on her face. Changing the subject, he asked,

"Who else was it you liked? Spice Girls and... oh, the Fugees," he suddenly remembered. Alice laughed, nodding at the memory.

"There was that one song you kept singing, over and over again ..." he said as she started to sing,

"Strumming my pain with his fingers,"

"One time," Elliot joined in.

"Singing my life with his words,"

"Two time." His affected voice made her giggle as they continued to sing together,

"Killing me softly with his song, killing me softly with his song, telling my whole life with his words, killing me softly with his song."

They both burst out laughing.

"That's definitely one for our list then," he said, watching the look of pure joy on her face, enchanted by the way she radiated happiness. The knowledge that he was responsible for making her feel that way, filled him with such pride, and a fierce protectiveness, that made his chest ache.

"It's like we've never been apart. This feels so right," he said softly. She glanced at him, with a look that told him she felt the same way.

"I know," she agreed. "I know," she reiterated quietly, focusing on the road ahead.

"You'll be fine on Friday," he said, resting his hand on her thigh. She laughed lightly.

"How do you always know what I'm thinking?" she asked in surprise. Elliot shrugged.

"I just do."

Alice let out a troubled sigh.

"But how do I explain Ellie to your family?" she asked, voicing the question that had been weighing heavily on her mind. She was feeling incredibly guilty at her deception now, realising that she had not considered the bigger picture before. She had just focused on her little unit and successfully blocked everybody else from her mind.

"You don't need to explain anything. They'll be delighted to meet her; she will steal their hearts, trust me. As will you," he said persuasively, sensing her vulnerability.

"I'll look after you," he added. "In fact, my mother seems to think that I was to blame for all of this anyway. She remembers you as a young girl, and said you must've been so scared and felt so alone as a single mum. She told me off for not being more attentive." He pulled a 'what can I say' face. Alice was stunned.

"But that's ridiculous! Didn't you tell her what'd happened?" she asked, her voice a notch higher with agitation.

"Listen, that's probably her way of saying, she doesn't hold anything against you. We were just kids in her eyes. And let's face it, we were. You were only nineteen."

He stared at her, the reality of his words suddenly dawning on him. What must she have gone through, facing a teenage pregnancy alone, without him? Thinking he had left her for somebody else. Dwelling on it made him feel sick with panic.

Alice smiled at him.

"We'll face up to it together," she nodded determinedly. "Our daughter keeps telling me I need to be more honest. I'm not going to let them think you abandoned me, Elliot. I'll just have to show them how much we love each other, and what a beautiful child we made together. The rest is up to them. They can think what they like," she declared dramatically. Elliot laughed out loud.

"Alice Greene: not caring what people think of her. Now that's a new one!" he teased affectionately. She shot him a sardonic look.

"Yes, well, enjoy it while it lasts; I'm not sure how long my courage will hold," she mused.

Elliot watched her, making the most of the opportunity to do so. She didn't seem to have aged at all, she still had that youthful excitement, bubbling away under the surface. That spontaneous passion, reserved exclusively for him, made her glow from within. And despite her confident exterior, he could see the childlike vulnerability that had always invoked such a strong need in him to protect her from the world. He didn't think it was possible to love anybody as much as he loved her.

"I know you're staring at me, Elliot!" she laughed, shooting him a glance. He smirked.

"I was just trying to remember that record that was in the charts when you first arrived in York. Now what was it?" he teased, knowing full well which song it was. Alice pulled a menacing frown.

"Don't you dare!" she warned.

The song, by Smokie, had plagued her throughout her childhood. It had been in the charts just months before she was born, and gained popularity once again eighteen years later, when it was re-released, but with an obscene twist to the lyrics. As Elliot had rightly pointed out, it topped the charts in the same month that she started university, and remained there for at least eight weeks. Everyone was playing it; she couldn't escape it.

"I don't know why she's leaving, or where she's gonna go," he sang, grinning defiantly at her,

"I guess she's got her reasons but I just don't want to know,"

"Elliot, please," Alice groaned.

"'Cause for twenty-four years I've been living next door to Alice," he paused for a second, "Alice, who the fu…"

"Elliot!" she squawked in mock anger. "I'll make you walk if you don't stop!"

He guffawed.

"Yep, we're definitely playing that one at our wedding!"

As they approached the outskirts of York, Alice pulled over and Elliot took the wheel.

"I'm fine to drive a short distance," he insisted, "you've not driven in York before and I know the one-way system like the back of my hand."

Despite not being happy about him driving so soon after his head injury, she was quite relieved that she didn't have to tackle the drive through the city centre. It had been a long time since she had been there and she needed a moment to collect her thoughts as they approached the familiar stomping ground of their student days. She had forgotten how sprawling the city was and how many people there were, even more so during the summer time.

"Oh, I remember climbing up that hill on more than one occasion," she exclaimed as they passed one of York's iconic landmarks, Clifford's Tower. The Norman stone structure, built on the top of a steep earth mound, was the largest remains of York Castle, and a popular spot to survey the rest of the city from its height.

Elliot reached for her hand and squeezed it.

"I'm glad you're here with me," he murmured.

"Me too," she replied, staring out at the red, tall buildings that graced Clifford Street: the imposing, old Magistrates court, with its wide steps leading up to the entrance on one side, and the modern buildings opposite, designed to blend in and merge the new with the old. As they turned the corner into Bridge Street and crossed the River Ouse, Alice smiled in delight at the memory it evoked.

"We used to walk along here by the river, didn't we? I love these old street lights on the bridge," she enthused as the traffic slowed, giving her a chance to admire them close up. Cast iron pillars reached up, with two arms branching out and an old-fashioned lantern suspended from each one.

Elliot pointed to the modern, red brick building at the far end of the bridge, on the left-hand side, hugging the edge of the river. It resembled an old warehouse, both in shape and size, and housed several flats.

"That's where I live."

Alice drew in a surprised breath.

"Oh, wow, Elliot! It's beautiful! What an amazing location," she uttered, scanning the immediate surroundings from a new perspective. Elliot pulled into the underground parking and led the way to the lift, carrying the empty boxes. Alice took the suitcases. She suddenly felt oddly nervous about seeing where he had settled down. It was so far removed from the kind of lifestyle she had in Wilmcote. York was vibrant and full of life; Stratford-upon-Avon was certainly quiet by comparison. Wilmcote must seem practically comatose to him, she thought.

They walked in silence along the spotlessly clean corridor on the second floor. The white walls and identical doors gave it a feel of uniformity, which Alice found a touch austere. Unlocking his front door, Elliot gestured for her to enter, and dropping the boxes and cases, took her hand and guided her through the spacious flat. There were two bedrooms leading off from either side of the hall but he by-passed those, and the bathroom, to lead her straight on into the capacious, open-plan lounge and kitchen. She was instantly struck by the spectacular view from the large, sliding doors that led out onto the river-facing balcony.

"Wow!" she exclaimed. Elliot grinned at her reaction and opening the doors, led her out onto the balcony. The floor, which stretched the width of the lounge, was decked with dark stained wood, complimenting the metal balcony railings. A dark grey, rattan sofa, complete with silver cushions offered a comfortable vantage point, and a collection of plants in steel pots, finished off the look. Solar powered lanterns hung from hooks in the red, brick walls and an all-weather bean bag rested in the corner where it had been casually thrown.

Alice leant against the railings, taking in the spectacular, panoramic view; Elliot stood beside her with his arm around her waist. To the left, she could see the creamy white, distinctive towers of York Minster and to the right, the unmistakable, dark, clock tower of the Magistrates court. In-between the two, a great muddle of pale and red brick buildings made up the skyline, their colours reflecting in the calm water of the River Ouse. Ducks and Canadian geese waddled along the water's edge directly below them, snapping at the gentle ripples to catch scraps of bread that somebody had thrown from the bridge. The chatter from the pub opposite mingled in the air with the early lunchtime aromas and the throb of traffic crossing the bridge.

Alice let out a deep-felt sigh. She leant her head on Elliot's shoulder.

"I'd forgotten how beautiful it is," she said quietly. "I bet this looks incredible at night time."

She remembered the haunting beauty of the city at night; the ancient buildings seemed to come alive at dusk as the street lights were lit.

"Mmm, yes it does," he agreed. "It's my favourite time of day. That, and first thing in the morning," he said, trying to decide which appealed more.

"I see York wake up and wind down again from up here," he added, "but it never stops, it never completely sleeps." He turned back towards the balcony door.

"Tea?"

She nodded.

"Yes, please. What shall we start with, packing-wise?" she asked, stepping back into the lounge. She looked at the lay-out of the room.

"It's like Monica's flat in 'Friends'," she observed, "only more masculine."

The kitchen area was on the opposite side of the room from the balcony. A combination of high-gloss, grey cupboards, chrome appliances and black, granite surfaces, dominated the space, and Alice could spy an array of kitchen gadgets, some of which she doubted had seen much action. The walls were painted white and the wooded floor a similar dark stain to that of the balcony floor. The dining area consisted of a small, round, black table and four matching, wooden chairs with grey seat pads. Two large, charcoal coloured sofas were strategically placed in the main space; one was facing the balcony doors and the other, the wall mounted, wide screen television. A low, glass topped coffee table was positioned between them. Along the far wall there was a wide, black desk with tall bookcases flanking either side. A state of the art Apple Mac and printer gleamed expensively on the polished desk, and a selection of books, DVDs, Blu-rays, and CDs were meticulously ordered on the shelves. Alice wandered over to nose through his CD collection. Elliot joined her, carrying two mugs of tea.

"Sorry, I don't have a teapot: I hope teabags are okay?" he grimaced apologetically. She smiled, shaking her head.

"There's no need to apologise. I know I seem fussy when it comes to tea but I'm really not," she laughed, gratefully accepting the mug. A satisfied smile erupted across her face as she spotted a familiar CD.

"I bought this for you!" she declared, pulling out a Bryan Adams CD.

"Remember?" she prompted, opening the case. It was empty. She frowned.

"Of course I remember," Elliot said. "It's in my car," he explained.

"Do you remember *why* I bought it for you though?" she continued, turning the case over, looking for an old inscription. She found it: 'Love you til I die xxx A'. It was a play on the album title, '18 til I die'. Elliot, being a huge fan of Bryan Adams, had raved about the new release at the time. He grinned at the memory.

"Yes, because you thought it was a fitting title," he said softly, stroking her cheek. Her eyes twinkled thinking about it.

"Eighteen was a great age for me," she said, "I never wanted it to end. I think I suited being eighteen," she laughed lightly, sliding the case back into place, then turned her attention to Elliot. He studied her face that hadn't aged one bit.

"I think thirty-eight suits you just as well," he said, bending to gently kiss her.

"Flatterer," she laughed, secretly pleased at his remark.

"Where shall we start with the packing?" she asked again, taking a sip of tea. Elliot sighed, looking round the room, gauging how much stuff he would actually need to take.

"Let's have our tea on the balcony first," he decided.

They sat in the late morning sunshine, pressed closely against each other and hands entwined, watching the world go by below them. Alice could sense that Elliot was distracted by his thoughts.

"Are you sure you want to leave York; won't you miss it? Wilmcote is very quiet, you know. We haven't really talked about this," she broached the subject with care. His decision to leave his job in York and move in with her had been so spontaneous that she was concerned he hadn't considered the full implications.

He leant his head on hers, squinting at the rooftops in contemplation.

"Yes, York is great but it can be a very lonely place. I'm just a drop in the ocean here. In Wilmcote, I'm already best buddies with your local shop keeper," he joked. "Everybody knows you, Alice. I want that. I want to belong, not just exist," he said earnestly.

"Oh, you'll certainly 'belong' in Wilmcote," she laughed knowingly. "Everybody will know every little thing about you, mark my words," she warned playfully.

"That's what I want," he nodded, affirming his resolve. "But I don't know what to do with the flat. Do I sell it, do I rent it out to tenants or do I advertise it as a holiday let? What do you think?"

Alice thought about it for a while, weighing up the odds. There was no doubting it was a great investment: a property of that calibre would only increase in value but there was the personal aspect to consider.

"Look, it's a beautiful flat Elliot but if it makes you unhappy, let's get rid of it. Sell it," she said. She straightened up to look at him, brushing back her hair and fixing determined eyes on him.

"But we are going to come back to York every year, to celebrate our original anniversary in September. Maybe rent somewhere for a week. I know you've been unhappy here on your own but we were incredibly happy here, together. I loved living in York; it was the happiest I've ever been. They were the best days for me. We have some amazing memories here, and the best way to get rid of the bad ones is to re-live the good ones. And make new ones," she smiled encouragingly, running her hand through his hair.

"And if you decide to keep the flat, we should make it our get-away. We could come here for a long weekend. Or for Christmas shopping. York is beautiful at Christmas time; do you remember all the fun we had doing our Christmas shopping here? It's magical."

She watched him mulling over what she had just said. She could completely understand the dilemma he faced, but now that she had taken the brave step of returning to York, she felt desperate to hang on to a piece of it.

"How about our pub?" she asked.

"What do you mean?" he shrugged, confused as to what she was asking.

"Did you go there much after I left? Was it one of your drinking haunts?" she wondered, her questions very direct.

"No. I never went back there. It was too painful. That was our special place," he confirmed quietly, his eyes conveying his honesty. She slid her arms around his neck and pressed her nose against his.

"Good. Right then, that's where we'll start," she insisted. "Let's pack up your clothes and the things you need now, then go there for something to eat, and let me re-live some of that Barraclough magic," she said with a captivating smile. Elliot let out a laugh.

"Is that what we're calling it now! Better than all that 'wardrobe' and 'symbolism' nonsense from last night," he teased. "Why don't you just admit it: you can't get enough of me," he grinned, raising his eyebrows. Alice pushed him away with feigned indignation.

"Ha! Says you, Mr 'I can't keep my hands off you, Alice'," she retorted. Elliot looked unabashed, shrugging his shoulders.

"I can't and I'm not denying it. I love you like crazy. I want you like crazy. Every minute of every day." He leant towards her, his pupils dilating and a smile playing on his lips.

"But at least I have the courage to say it," he said steadily, challenging her to respond. She bit down a smile and tried to look nonchalant. It failed. She burst out laughing; Elliot watched her expectantly, waiting for her to stop. She tried to be poker faced and control her mounting fit of giggles.

"Okay, okay," she cleared her throat, "Elliot, I can't get enough of you," she said, in a barely controlled manner. He grinned.

"See? It wasn't that difficult, was it?"

She stroked his face provocatively, gazing into his eyes for a moment before a mischievous grin took over,

"And I can't wait to get you home and put your clothes in my wardrobe." She laughed hysterically as he grabbed her and, pushing her down on the sofa, tickled her until she squealed for mercy.

"Watch it, or I might have to withhold the Barraclough magic," he threatened, kissing her as she started laughing again.

Elliot was systematically packing armfuls of books into the heavy-duty boxes. He had decided to take everything with him bar the television and kitchen things. The furniture would be remaining too. He glanced over at Alice, packing up the other bookcase. Except she wasn't: she was too busy perusing through his books and DVDs. He shook his head in exasperation.

"Listen Alice, if you're going to look at every little thing before you pack it, we'll be here all day," he admonished. She scowled at him.

"But I love looking at other people's books and things," she said defensively, shooting him a playful look. He sighed.

"You can have the joy of unpacking it for me and then you can look at everything. How about that?" he reasoned. She let out an exaggerated, deep sigh and put the book she was holding into the box in front of her.

"Are we going to have room in Wilmcote for all of my stuff?" Elliot wondered, surprised at how many boxes he had already filled and how much more there was still left to pack. Alice nodded.

"Yes, I've been thinking: why don't we convert Roz's studio into a study for you?" she suggested, grabbing a handful of DVDs.

"Really?" He looked surprised.

"Well yes, that makes perfect sense, doesn't it? We were wondering what to do with the space anyway. So…", she shrugged, indicating the simplicity of the solution.

"And, after the wedding I want to change the house deeds to both our names," she added casually. Elliot stopped in his tracks, putting down the pile of books he was holding. He moved over to her and put his hands on her shoulders, looking intently at her to gauge her thoughts.

"You don't need to do that," he said. "I don't expect it."

"I know but I want to," she smiled shyly. "It's *our* home now," she emphasised. Feeling embarrassed at the intensity of his stare, she turned back to the bookcase.

"Oh, look, 'It's a Wonderful Life'! You've still got it," she exclaimed happily.

"Alice!" Elliot dropped his hands from her shoulders in exasperation.

"Fine. I'll just pack then," she mumbled ungraciously, stifling a snigger as he scooped up half of the shelf's contents and handed the pile to her, nodding pointedly at the box.

It wasn't long before the lounge was all packed up and they moved to the bedrooms. Elliot showed her the guest room, simply furnished with a double bed, fitted wardrobe, chest of drawers, and a chair. The bed had a grey, tufted linen, headboard with china blue duvet covers and pillow cases. The bed frame, chest of drawers and chair were of a black stained wood. Propped up against the chest was an acoustic guitar. The room looked like it was rarely used and had no personal touches about it.

"There's nothing in here I need, apart from the guitar," he commented, picking it up.

"Do you still play?" she asked.

"Not much," he admitted, "but Ellie was so excited when I told her I used to play, so I think she'd appreciate me bringing this along," he smiled.

"Absolutely! A guitar *and* a ukulele; who could wish for more?" she teased.

"Hey! I think we'll make a great team," he retorted, gently pushing her out of the room and shutting the door behind them.

"Yes, and I can do the vocals," she chuckled, pushing the other bedroom door open.

"Now, that's going too far," he retaliated, laughing at her indignant expression.

Elliot's bedroom reflected the décor of the rest of the flat; white walls and a dark wooden floor, with dark furniture. Fitted wardrobes stretched across one side of the room. He pushed the sliding doors open to reveal overstuffed rails of clothes, neatly sorted in order of colour. What he lacked in personal effects, he made up for in clothes, Alice thought, as she glanced around the simplistic room. A black, faux leather bedstead, a large chest of drawers, a small bedside chest of drawers and an armchair with a reading lamp beside it, was the extent of furniture in the room. The bedding was, unsurprisingly, dark grey with contrasting light grey pillow cases. Alice noticed a framed photo on the small chest of drawers: the only personal touch in the entire flat. Intrigued, she crossed the room to get a closer look. Her heart skipped a beat. Picking up the photo, she sat down on the bed, staring in disbelief. It was the second time that she had been faced with an old photograph of the two of them; an echo of the past. They looked so young and so incredibly happy. It had been taken in the first couple of months of their relationship. An old-fashioned 'selfie', it had been snapped with her camera by Elliot, as they sat on a bench at the back of the Minster.

Alice looked up to find Elliot watching her from across the room.

"How long have you had this?" she asked quietly, her eyes drawn back to it.

"Forever. It was the only one I had though. You had all the rest, but this one, you'd stuck on my fridge door with little heart magnets," he said. She laughed lightly at the memory.

"I haven't got any photos of us," she told him, her voice heavy with regret. "And I hadn't seen any until last week at Andrew's. It's so weird seeing us like that," she said wistfully. Putting it back in its place, she asked,

"What do people say when they see it there?"

"People?"

Alice looked uncomfortable.

"Well, you know, when anybody comes in here." Her words sounded clumsy. Elliot shrugged.

"Nobody comes in here. My parents visit twice a year: James and his lot, a little more often but apart from that, nobody". There was an edge to his voice and she guessed he wasn't comfortable with what she had been implying. She looked away. Elliot crossed the room and sat next to her on the bed. He took her hand, studying it, rather than making eye contact with her.

"Look, if I invited a woman back to my flat, she would want to hang around the next day, not leave. And I told you, I never wanted any of that. So, I never have. If I'm invited back to theirs, then I'm in control: I can leave when I want. That's how it works. And in my drinking days, I didn't live here anyway. I rented a dive, loosely termed a 'studio flat', and to be honest, I don't remember much about it." He scratched the back of his head and shot her a sidelong look.

"Can we not talk about this, Alice. It's done with: it's in the past and I don't want to be reminded of it. Please," he insisted quietly. She nodded, swallowing nervously. She hated the thought of him with anybody else, even though she knew it was irrational to think otherwise. However, the knowledge that nobody else had been in his flat and that his dark days had been somewhere else, filled her with relief. The flat suddenly held a new appeal for her.

"I really screwed you up," she acknowledged, squeezing his hand. She struggled not to say 'sorry' yet again.

"Yes, you did." His reply was heartfelt. The ensuing silence seemed to last forever despite it being, in reality, only seconds.

"Don't do it again," he whispered, lightly nudging her shoulder with his. She looked up at him.

"I wouldn't," she replied instantly. "I know what's what. I'm older and wiser now," she said.

"And more beautiful," he interjected, "inside and out." He ran a finger down her cheek. "If that's at all possible," he added.

"So are you," she smiled. She looked across at the photo again, remembering how Mary O'Shea had used all her photos for her Facebook deception.

"What do we do about Mary?" she asked, aware that she was pushing another subject that could potentially blow up in her face but it had to be confronted.

"Do? There's nothing to do. She's obviously not a well person. I wouldn't do anything, Alice, just leave it. Nobody cares what she puts on Facebook. They don't know us, do they? So, what does it matter?" It wasn't a question; it was a statement, and she decided to drop the subject. Besides, Elliot was right: nobody knew them so it made no difference really. She took a deep, decisive breath and turned to him.

"Let's stay here tonight."

He looked puzzled.

"Why?"

"Well, it's taking ages to pack and..."

"And who's fault's that?" he laughed. Unable to think of a retort, she just nodded, knowing he was right.

"I was thinking, we should say 'goodbye' to York the same way that we said 'hello'," she murmured, rubbing her hand across his chest. He gave a low laugh.

"Were you now?" He raised an eyebrow, watching her eyes sparkle as she anticipated his response.

"But weren't we a bit drunk that night?" he reminded her. She scrunched up her nose, inching closer towards him.

"I wasn't really that drunk. Just Dutch courage," she said, smiling at the memory.

"I wasn't either. Just drunk on your beauty," he said, stroking her arm. Alice looked at him for a second, trying not to laugh.

"Smooth line, Elliot," she congratulated him with a chuckle.

"I thought so," he grinned, hearing how cheesy it had sounded. He leant forward to kiss her but paused, as something occurred to him.

"What about Ellie?"

"She's fine, Brad's with her. He'll stay over," she said.

"Really? You're okay with that?" he wondered, not sure that he was, as an unfamiliar emotion coursed through him. Alice looked surprised, taken aback by his tone.

"Yes, it's fine. He's always staying over." Her heart melted a little at his paternal instinct to protect Ellie.

"I'm telling you, Alice, he's biding his time," he said, laughing lightly as she shook her head. He continued,

"Forgive me, but you didn't even know about Roz, so I'm thinking that you're not as observant, or clued in, as you'd like to think you are."

She laughed. He wasn't wrong about Roz but she knew he was wrong about Ellie and Brad. Not wanting to crush his new-found parental enthusiasm, she let it go.

"I think I'm fairly clued-in about you," she countered, biting her lip. "I know exactly what you're thinking right now," she cooed, teasing him. Elliot drew in a sharp breath between his teeth, running a finger down her neck. He smiled wickedly as he leant forward to whisper in her ear,

"So, do you fancy some of that Barraclough magic now?"

"I knew it!" she laughed. "Do you even have to ask?" she smiled, throwing herself backwards on the bed with wanton abandon.

Alice wandered into the lounge, only wearing one of Elliot's t-shirts, that barely covered her thighs. He smiled at her from the kitchen, where he was busy making tea. She stretched and yawned noisily.

"Did I fall asleep?"
Elliot nodded.
"Yes, you did. I was about to bring you some tea. I see you found my clothes," he noted, admiring her bare legs. She smoothed the top down, rubbing the material between her fingers, smiling coyly.

"You don't mind, do you? It's so lovely and soft."
He shook his head. It made him feel good, seeing her in his clothes.

"Of course I don't mind. You always did steal my tops anyway," he laughed, handing her a mug of tea. She leant against him as he kissed her hair and put his arm around her waist, his hand spread possessively across the small of her back.

"I've decided: we should keep the flat. Rent it out as a holiday let and use it as our get-away," he told her. "You were right, it is a great place. You've just breathed life into it and that's all it needed: a bit of Alice."

Alice let out a satisfied sigh. It was exactly what she wanted to hear.

"Listen, it's way past lunch time; shall we go and get something to eat from the pub?" he suggested. "What do you fancy?"

She hesitated, staring out at the city beyond the balcony. Suddenly she was in no rush to leave the intimacy of the flat, or to get dressed again.

"Maybe we should save the pub for later, as we're staying the night," she ventured. Elliot's face creased in a knowing smile.

"I'll order a pizza for lunch," he nodded, reaching for his phone.

"And I'll unpack 'It's a Wonderful Life'," Alice grinned, elated that he could still read her like a book. A look of pure love passed between them.

"Go and grab the duvet. Let's make an afternoon of it," he asserted, sharing her reluctance to move on with the day. He watched her ferreting through the box, in search of the DVD, overwhelmed once again at the intensity of his feelings for her. From the minute she had walked back into his life, everything had seemed to slot into place. His life had meaning, a purpose. He knew he belonged to her, just as she belonged to him.

"Thank you," he said huskily. Alice looked up, frowning a little.

"What for?"

"For being you. For making me complete," he smiled.

"We make each other complete," she said, returning his smile before continuing with her search.

"Got it!" she exclaimed, brandishing the DVD triumphantly. "Now, hurry up with that order – I'm starving!" she emphasized, disappearing into the bedroom and returning moments later, with the duvet wrapped around her and dragging behind her, in regal splendour.

It was after eight by the time they had finally finished packing Elliot's things. The suitcases and boxes were neatly stacked in the hallway, and spare bedroom, ready to be stowed in the car the following morning. Alice cast an eye over the boxes, deciding that some serious reorganisation would be needed once they were back home; they would have to get more bookshelves, and another wardrobe. Or two, she thought, glancing at the bulging suitcases. For the time being, they would have to utilise the space in Roz's unused bedroom. A satisfied smile spread across her face; organisation was something she took pleasure in, and making room to accommodate Elliot's belongings was the best feeling ever. Elliot grabbed his keys and indicated the door.

"Ready?" He caught her smile. "What are you looking so pleased about?" he asked. She shrugged happily.

"Life is pretty perfect right now, that's all," she chirped, brushing past him towards the door.

"It certainly is," he agreed, catching her hand as he followed her out of the flat.

Down on the street, they joined the summer evening's gentle stream of pedestrians and traffic crossing the Ouse Bridge. It was hard to believe that the solid stone, three arched bridge, was a listed building; its beauty was easily overlooked in the bustle of modern life but both Alice and Elliot appreciated its importance in the city's history and indeed, their own history. They had spent many happy walks along the riverside, stopping to feed the ducks that congregated under the bridge, and to watch the boats silently glide through the wide expanse of water.

As they strolled hand in hand through the jumble of streets, working their way across the old city, they reminisced by pointing out favourite shops or places that had been of significance to them. Alice stopped frequently to admire shop windows, and Elliot reminded her why everything took so long when she was around, which of course, encouraged her to stop even more frequently. Not that he minded: he was in no hurry and was lapping up every minute spent with her. He was seeing the city in a completely different light with her by his side. It was as if she were magically lifting a dark veil that had shrouded the city he knew, and flooding it with light and happiness.

They eventually arrived at St Helen's Square and followed the well-trodden path of old, up Stonegate. This, along with The Shambles, had been Alice's favourite place to shop in. The long, narrow, pedestrianised street was home to an assortment of shops: some, nationwide favourites and some, exclusive boutiques. Like with most of York, the higgledy-piggledy collection of buildings defined the city's individual character and celebrated its architectural heritage, by putting the old structures to good use in the modern world. Black and white, timber frame buildings jostled for space alongside red brick, and white rendered ones: each, three or four storeys high and each unique in shape and style. Some with bow windows, some with over-hanging upper floors, and some with ornate, carved wood trim around the windows and door frames. It was easy to visualise how this Medieval street had once looked; it had been one of the major highways through York, connecting the Minster at one end with the heart of the city at the other. Back then, it was already known for its shops although then, you were more likely to find book stores and goldsmiths, rather than 'Weird Fish' and 'Lakeland'. The streets would not have been as meticulously swept clean, and the air would have been filled with the pungent smell of rotting rubbish and household waste - a smell that permeated the whole city - in contrast to the present-day aromas emanating from the plethora of tea shops, and the sweet, floral notes from the abundance of hanging baskets that adorned the shop fronts.

Nearing the top of Stonegate, the pub's welcoming sign stretched high across the street; without it, the entrance would be missed unless you knew it was there. Accessed through a narrow snickelway - one of many that York was famed for – 'Ye Olde Starre Inne' boasted to be the oldest pub in the city, with its licence dating back to 1644: the year that York was under siege by the Roundheads during the English Civil war. The pub was steeped in history and although it had been expanded and renovated over the years, it had managed to maintain its Olde Worlde charm and was a popular haunt with tourists and locals alike. It was for this reason that Alice's knowledgeable student rep had bought them to the historic pub on their first day in York, back in 1995. The same reason that Elliot and his course mates, keen students of York history, favoured the pub. And now, twenty years on, as the pair of them turned down the familiar snickelway with its white washed walls, a rush of memories hit them both. Elliot squeezed Alice's hand and they exchanged a knowing look, smiling as they read each other's thoughts. The trapped smell of stale beer and cigarette smoke, that lingered in the walkway, conjured up such a vivid recollection of her first night in York, igniting butterflies in her stomach and an excitement that crept through her body. It was a smell that, over the years, had always transported her back to that night; it had been such a pivotal moment in her life.

They crossed the inner courtyard, navigating their way round the outdoor seating, to the door that led through to the main bar. They paused in the doorway, peering into the adjoining rooms, smiling at the faces that turned to acknowledge them. Stepping into the large bar room, Elliot gave a little laugh of relief.

"Doesn't seem to have changed that much, does it?" he remarked.

Just for a second, Alice half-expected to see her Elliot of old, sitting at the bar. The completely irrational thought took her by surprise but highlighted just how intensely heightened her emotions were right then. She clung on to his steady grip as they headed for an empty table on the other side of the room, her legs feeling oddly shaky.

"Shall I get drinks in before we decide on what to eat, or do you want to choose now?" Elliot asked, picking up the menu from the table and passing it to Alice. She studied it for a moment.

"Do you know what, I really fancy a burger and cider please," she smiled. "Pizza and burger in one day; I think I'll have to go on a diet after this," she joked.

"You'll do no such thing!" Elliot retorted. "You're perfect just as you are. You can eat what you like."

Alice looked pleased. She hadn't been fishing for a compliment but loved how readily he bestowed them on her.

"In that case, I'll have some of the chocolate fudge cake for dessert, please," she grinned, scrunching up her nose appreciatively at his indulgent smile.

When Elliot went to the bar, Alice took the opportunity to sit back and take a good look at her surroundings. He was right: it hadn't changed much since they were there last, eighteen years previously. The retro, flocked wallpaper screamed of a time gone by, as did the abundant photographs in their heavy, dark wooden or gilded frames, depicting aspects of life in York over the years. The parts not graced by wallpaper were panelled from floor to ceiling, with the same dark wood that was underfoot and around the bar. The furniture was a collection of old, upholstered, spindle back chairs, wooden bar stools, old tables, and faux leather, padded, benched seating that hugged the walls and corners. Opposite the bar was one of the pub's fireplaces, where she and Elliot had huddled in front of a roaring fire, on many a cold, winter's evening. Its stone hearth was empty and lifeless now but she could almost smell the ash and hear the crackle of logs on it, as she reflected on past times.

Looking across at the bar, she saw that Elliot was staring at her as he stood, waiting patiently, to be served. She could tell by his expression that he had been staring at her for some time; watching as she had been recalling deeply buried memories – the effect of which was evident in her eyes. She held his steady gaze, smiling at him. He smiled back and in that moment, she could see that he was just as effected by it as she was. She could see something else too, in his expression: a look of wonder. As if he couldn't quite believe that she was there. As if he wanted to reach out and touch her, just to make sure that she was real.

Returning with their drinks, Elliot sat next to her and raised his glass.

"Here's to us, planning our future together. It's been a long time coming but I'm loving every minute of it," he, said, his voice full of sincerity. Alice clinked her glass against his.

"Me too," she agreed, twiddling her engagement ring and watching the light reflect off it.

"Honeymoon: any thoughts on where?" he wondered. Alice was taken aback, although she didn't know why; she should have realised that he had probably already planned it in his head anyway. His eager face was watching her expectantly and she didn't have the heart to tell him that the honeymoon hadn't even crossed her mind yet; she was still reeling from the shock and panic of getting married in under five months.

"I'm not sure. Anywhere with you will be perfect," she gave him a bright smile. Elliot saw right through it.

"I'm rushing you," he conceded, "sorry." He stared at his beer glass, watching the condensation trickle down the side.

"No, you're not rushing me exactly," Alice insisted, putting her hand on his knee. "It's just that my head is full of dresses and flowers and … and you. Here you are, all of a sudden, back in my life and I can't think further than the next five minutes let alone five months," she gushed, her voice sounding shaky. Elliot looked at her, appreciating her honesty. She smiled.

"It's what you do to me Elliot. I look at you and I just melt. All I can think about, is lying in your arms. How can I possibly plan anything in this state?" She watched the satisfied grin spread across his face as he took on-board what she was saying.

"I love it when you tell it how it is," he said softly, watching her blush. She struggled to think of a smart retort but couldn't. For the exact reason that she had just pointed out.

Elliot drew in a decisive breath, looking round the bustling bar room. Raucous laughter could be heard from the adjoining room and the air was filled with animated chatter.

"You were saying earlier about how you loved York at Christmas time, with the atmosphere, the lights and shopping. And I was thinking - as we're getting married at Christmas - how about we go to Europe, to the Christmas markets? Germany or Austria? I've never been but I think you'd love it." He saw the look of delight on her face at his suggestion.

"Oooh yes, that would be amazing!" Her eyes danced excitedly as she thought about it.

"Austria," she determined, "as we're going to Germany next week. I've never been to Austria. Have you?"

Elliot shook his head.

"Vienna?" he suggested.

"Yes!" she sighed as he, yet again, had read her mind. He pulled out his phone to do a google search just as their food arrived, so quickly put it away again. Thanking the waitress, he looked at Alice, indicating to his plate.

"This veggie burger looks great; I could easily get used to this. What made Ellie choose to be a vegetarian?" he asked.

"Pigs," was the simple reply. Elliot looked confused.

"Her job at the farm was to look after the pigs. And she fell in love with them, instantly. It wasn't a hard decision for her," she acknowledged, remembering the tears and fervent outbursts as the fifteen-year-old Ellie came to terms with the harsh realities of farming and the meat industry.

"Ah, yes, well I can understand that. I went through something similar when I was younger, with the pigs on my grandfather's farm," he nodded. "So, you stopped eating meat altogether, too? And Roz?"

"Yes, we did. It seemed the easier option and to be honest, I do feel better for it. And Roz would do anything for Ellie anyway," she said. "But I don't expect you to change because of us," she told him. Elliot shook his head.

"But I do. I want to. If my daughter has such strong ethics and feels so passionately about it, then I am absolutely going to respect that. Consider me converted," he declared. "Besides, I'm not a great cook, so I'm more or less at your mercy," he added, laughing at his own admission.

They talked non-stop whilst they ate, discussing wedding plans, holiday plans and their honeymoon. Once they'd finished eating, they slouched in their corner seat and Alice leant into the crook of Elliot's arm, perfectly content, as they chatted about family, old friends and life in general. They laughed, hysterically at times, as they recalled school and childhood anecdotes: all the while their past drawing them even closer together.

Elliot returned with another round of drinks, making himself comfortable again. He patted her thigh.

"So, does this count as our fourth date?"

"Well, let's see: 'Anne Hathaway's' was our first date, last week. Then you came to mine on Saturday for our second date, when we had our first fight and then you proposed. Not bad for a second date!" she laughed. "Then you took us out for dinner with our daughter, for our third date, yesterday. So yes, this is, in fact, our fourth date," she agreed. Elliot nodded, raising an eyebrow. He lowered his voice.

"So, what do we class earlier as? An in-between-dates date?"

Alice chuckled softly, her eyes twinkling impishly.

"Or, a warm-up for the end of our fourth date…" She erupted in giggles at Elliot's face.

"Damn it, Alice! You out-do me every time," he chided, pleased with the way she responded to his flirting.

"Well, stop being so corny, and give me a kiss, then," she demanded, beaming at him.

They stayed in their corner of the pub, oblivious to the rest of the room and totally absorbed in each other's company, until last orders were called. Standing up and stretching, she leant against his chest, smiling up at him.

"Thank you, this has been amazing. The perfect date."

He put his arm around her shoulders and whispered in her ear, echoing his words of twenty years ago,

"Fancy coming back to mine for coffee?"

She laughed out loud, shaking her head.

"How did I ever fall for a line like that?"

"I don't know but I'm glad you did. I won't judge you," he grinned, putting his hand up to acknowledge the barman as he bid them a goodnight.

Once outside and back on Stonegate, Alice stopped and looked up and down the street, with glee. The stars were out in the clear, inky sky, making a perfect backdrop for the illuminated, cobbled street. Amber lights softly shone at regular intervals, interspersed with the brighter, shop window lighting. Behind them, the flood-lit Minster glowed like the colour of sun-baked sand: warm and inviting. Alice took Elliot's hand and walked the short distance to the Minster. They stood in silent awe, staring up at its Gothic splendour. The south side had always been Alice's favourite aspect of the building, with its many lancet windows, all pointing upwards to the spectacular, stained-glass, rose window, positioned under the ornately carved gable.

They carried on along the path that ran to the right of the Minster, leading into College Street and the back of the Minster, passing the imposing statue of Emperor Constantine lounging in his seat, with his heavy sword at his side. Elliot stopped under a tree and pulled Alice towards him. She tilted her head quizzically, trying to stifle the smile that was aching to erupt.

"Why have we stopped here?" she asked, feigning ignorance.

"Well if memory serves, this is the spot where you practically pushed me up against this tree, and kissed me. Without any encouragement on my part, I have to say," he teased. Her mouth opened defensively.

"I did not 'push' you! I fell over and you caught me … and then I kissed you," she concurred graciously.

"My mistake," he apologised gallantly. He gently brushed her hair back and cradled her face in his hands, staring at her intently. She rested her hands against his chest, steadying herself.

"You're doing it again," she murmured.

"Doing what?" he barely whispered, stroking her cheek with his thumb. She cleared her throat, drowning in the depths of his blue eyes. She could feel his quickened heartbeat against the flat of her hand.

"Making me melt," she sighed. He raised an eyebrow, a slow smile twitching at the corners of his mouth. He ran his thumb across her lips and down her neck, then stopped still, hardly breathing as he seemed hypnotised by her.

"It's been very surreal tonight, being here with you," he said, reflecting on the past few hours. "It almost felt like I was watching a ghost of you, in the pub. I was terrified that you would suddenly vanish again." He breathed a heavy sigh. "Such a bizarre feeling."

"I know, I felt odd too," she agreed, watching his troubled face, realising just how difficult it had been for him.

"But we're both still here and we've made some new memories today," she prompted, lightly kissing his mouth.

"We certainly have," he smiled. "I just have to pinch myself every now and then to make sure it's all real. And it is."

"Well, it feels very real to me", she said, slowly running a provocative hand down his chest and across his midriff, knowing the effect it was having on him. He cleared his throat, emitting a low laugh as he did so.

"Come on, let's get you home," he said decisively, taking her hand.

"Why, what's the rush? It's a beautiful night," she said, wanting to linger in the city centre. He nodded in agreement.

"It is, and so are you. And what I want to do to you right now, I can't possibly do in public," he confessed.

"Oh, really?" she laughed, leaning in to him and kissing him longingly, running her hands across the back of his thighs, blatantly taunting him.

"You're not fair!" he grumbled.

"Come on then – race you!" she giggled, pulling him along as she started to run back towards Stonegate.

It took them less than ten minutes to walk back to the flat: unlike the half hour it had taken to walk to the pub earlier. Alice voiced her surprise at how quickly they had arrived home.

"I didn't realise it was that close! How come it took us so long to get to the pub in the first place then?"

Elliot shot her an exasperated look, holding his hands out in question.

"I have no idea," he jokingly mocked. "Maybe because you stop every five seconds to look at something?" He chuckled at her indignation and watched her disappear into the bedroom, returning moments later with the duvet and pillows. She headed for the sliding doors.

"I have chosen to ignore your comment but suffice it to say, you'll just have to get used to it, Elliot Barraclough. The two girls in your life, love to shop. And we like to take our time over it," she declared defiantly, suppressing a smile. He conceded defeat with a bow.

"Point taken. Where *are* you going with that duvet?" he asked, baffled.

"Ever done it on the balcony?" she asked straight-faced. Elliot nearly choked as he emitted a startled laugh.

"What?"

"Slept. Have you ever slept on the balcony? What did you think I meant?" she smiled innocently. A little too innocently. He shrugged his shoulders, trying to contain his laughter.

"No, I haven't," he said, opening the balcony doors for her and relieving her of the bedding, which he dropped it onto the rattan sofa. The solar lanterns twinkled invitingly and the scent from the potted jasmine hovered in the warm, night air. Alice leant against the railings, taking in the night time skyline, loving the buzz it gave her. It made her feel alive. She turned to Elliot, standing by her side, flashing him a satisfied smile.

"Good. Let's make another memory then," she suggested. "And you can show me exactly why we had to rush back home." She put her arms around him and snuggled in to his chest, breathing in deeply. He stroked her hair, resting his cheek on her head. She could feel him grinning.

"What I had in mind doesn't involve sleeping," he said quietly. She smiled contentedly, hugging him a little tighter, whispering,

"I know. Who needs sleep anyway."

They set off ahead of the commuter traffic, early the next morning and arrived back in Wilmcote by nine o'clock. Ellie greeted them at the door, in Tigger pyjamas, giving them both a big hug.

"I got your message; the tea's brewing," she said. "No need to ask if you had a good time," she added cheekily, noting their radiant faces. She stepped out, barefooted, onto the pavement and peered into the back of the car at the mass of boxes.

"I'll get Brad to lend a hand emptying this lot," she volunteered, hurrying back to the door on tiptoe, her arms folded across her chest to protect her against the early morning chill. She gave Elliot another hug.

"Welcome home, Dad," she sighed happily. He hugged her back, kissing her head, suddenly feeling very emotional.

"Is Brad still here?" he asked. Ellie nodded.

"Shhh," she put her finger up to her mouth and indicated he follow her into the lounge. She gently nudged the figure that was sprawled ungainly across the sofa, in a deep sleep. Ellie's fuchsia pink, silver-starred, dressing gown was draped over his top half, covering the side of his face: a mop of unruly, dark brown hair poking out from under it. Ellie crouched down beside him, shaking his shoulder.

"Brad," she said quietly, "they're home. Wake up!"

Brad opened his eyes, momentarily disorientated. Seeing Elliot standing there, he quickly stood up, shrugging the dressing gown from his shoulder, and straightened out the baggy shorts and t-shirt that he'd been sleeping in. He stretched out his hand to shake Elliot's.

"Hello," Brad smiled genially, "it's so good to meet you. Ellie has talked about nothing else for the past fortnight." He shot a grin at Ellie, who nodded unabashed.

Elliot could see immediately what his appeal was. He had an open, honest face and eyes that sparkled with a jubilant love of life. He looked older than eighteen, despite the child-like freckles that spread across his nose and cheeks. His stubbly chin indicated that he had been shaving for some time, ahead of most young men of his age. He had such a friendly demeanour about him that Elliot couldn't help but instantly warm to him.

Alice walked in from the kitchen, carrying a tray with four mugs of tea on. She put it down on the coffee table, smiling maternally at Brad.

"Alice!" He held his arms out to give her a hug, surprising Elliot by his open affection.

"Congratulations!" he said earnestly, looking at them both. "Mum is over the moon and says you have to go and see her a.s.a.p. And she can't wait to meet you," he indicated to Elliot. "She is a bit miffed though, that everybody at the farm has already met you, before she has," he said, pulling a face. Elliot looked confused.

"I'm sorry?"

Alice put her hand on Elliot's arm.

"I did warn you; I'm sure everybody knows by now about our engagement," she nodded emphatically. Brad gave a confirming nod of his head too.

"Yes, everybody does. You're the talk of the village," he affirmed. Elliot laughed.

"Wow! No pressure then," he joked, his delight clearly evident on his face.

Ellie sidled up to Brad and held his hand, as they exchanged an excited smile.

"Anyway, we've got some news too," she said, taking a deep breath, her face flushed with joy. Elliot shot Alice an 'I told you so' look, which she chose to ignore.

"What is it?" she prompted. She was in no doubt that Elliot had misconstrued Ellie's announcement but she had to admit, a small part of her wouldn't have been completely surprised.

Ellie did a little jig of excitement before saying, in a high-pitched voice,

"We've found Cee-Cee!"

Chapter Fifteen

Alice and Elliot stared open-mouthed at Ellie as her startling announcement hit home. Alice sat down heavily on the sofa; Elliot followed suit.

"How... I mean, surely not? Already?" Alice floundered. She couldn't believe that Ellie had managed to succeed with their quest, in less than twenty-four hours. Something of this magnitude surely would take much longer? She said as much to Ellie, who perched on the sofa next to her.

"I know; I'm as amazed as you but it's true, Mum. Brad and I have been up all night on this. Let me show you both," she encouraged.

They went into the study and crowded round the monitor as Ellie opened one of the many tabs she had up. It was Missing You.net.

"My hunch was right, Dad," she grinned, "she *had* been looking for Roz. And so had her son," she said.

"Her *son*?" Elliot and Alice reacted in unison. It hadn't even occurred to either of them that Roz may have grandchildren. Ellie pointed to the message box, half-way down the page. It was edged in pink.

'Category: Adoptions.
Seeking: Lin Barraclough
Location: Cornwall
Message: I am searching for my birth grandparents. My mum was born Celia Barraclough on March 23rd 1969, in St Austell, Cornwall. She is 44 today. She was adopted at

6 weeks old. Her mother's name on the birth certificate is Lin Barraclough but the father is not named. We know that Lin was 22 and unmarried. My mum has been trying to find them but with no luck so far. I am hoping to have more success. If anybody knows of Lin or her partner in 1969, please contact me with any information. Thank you.

Posted by: Conrad Charlton on Saturday 23rd March 2013

Ellie looked at her parents who were both silently staring at the screen. She noticed how Elliot took Alice's hand and squeezed it: how tears trickled down Alice's face and how Elliot swallowed several times, trying not to follow suit.

"She was looking for Roz; how do we tell her that?" Alice uttered, visualising how Roz would react to it.

Ellie moved the mouse and clicked onto the next tab.

"I found Cee-Cee's original message too, once I knew which name to type in to the search bar," she told them, pointing to a message box on the now familiarly formatted Missing You.net page.

'Category: Adoptions.
Seeking: Lin Barraclough
Location: Cornwall

Message: I am searching for my birth parents. I know that my mother was Lin Barraclough but not who my father was. I was born forty years ago today, on March 23rd 1969, in St Austell, Cornwall and put up for adoption when I was six weeks old. My birth name was Celia Barraclough. I only found out that I was adopted eight years ago, when my (adoptive) mother died. I desperately want to find my birth parents, to tell them that I have a good life and was raised by loving and caring parents. But I also want to know where I came from and who my birth parents were. Lin Barraclough was 22 when I was born and she was unmarried. I can only guess as to why I was put up for adoption and I hold no grudges, just sadness for the situation. I would dearly love to find them both. If anybody has any information on Lin Barraclough or remembers her in the St Austell area during 1969, please get in touch.

Posted by: Isabelle Charlton on Monday 23rd March 2009'

"2009?" Elliot wondered, looking for confirmation from Ellie that the date was right. She nodded.

"Yes, this is obviously before her son, Conrad, posted a message. I mean, his is two years old and hers is six, so they've been looking for a while," she acknowledged. Her tone was quiet, not the same excited Ellie that greeted them a few minutes earlier. She could sense that they needed time to digest the news.

"And I noticed that both messages were put up on her birthday so it's obviously something they talk about when they're together as a family," she said. "Birthdays do that to you: make you reflect on life," she added, trying to make it sound like a throw-away comment but in so doing, revealing a touching truth about herself. Elliot shot her a smile, his look telling her he understood.

He scratched the back of his head, studying the text again, breathing deeply.

"She used David's name," he noted. "Lin Barraclough. No wonder they haven't found her."

"Unless she was hoping that one day she would be a Barraclough?" Ellie suggested. "You said that she'd obviously gone to Newlyn in the hope that David would look for her there, didn't you, Mum? So maybe she was leaving clues for him, in case he ever put two and two together and looked for a baby."

Alice distractedly tapped her fingers on the desk, wracking her brains as to what to do next.

"We need to let Roz know about this and then help her to contact one of them back. Should it be Conrad, do you think? Rather than Cee-Cee … Isabelle, I mean," she corrected herself, her eyes drawn back to her cousin's name on the screen. It was such a peculiar feeling; seeing it there in print made her somehow, very real, very alive. And very much part of the family. And yet, Alice was feeling apprehensive about taking the next step; how would this affect the rest of her family? Elliot's family? His parents were still reeling from the shock of discovering they had a granddaughter - one they had yet to meet - and here she was, about to unburden even more secrets and introduce even more relatives into the mix, that they had no idea about. How could she best handle this?

"I've already made contact," Ellie piped up, interrupting Alice's thought process. Her mouth dropped open as she stared in surprise at Ellie.

"But … without asking Roz first? This is huge, Ellie!" she said, her voice expressing the unease she felt at the speed that events were developing. Ellie let out an abrupt laugh, shaking her head.

"I'm well aware of what 'huge' is, Mum," she retorted, indicating to Elliot. "I'm going through it myself. Dad is, too." She met Alice's gaze defiantly. "Listen, if we don't act now, we may miss the chance. Roz is too scared of rejection, or of what she may find, so we can help her by paving the way first," she explained passionately. She looked to Elliot for support. "Dad?"

He smiled apologetically at Alice.

"She's right, Alice. We need to step in and help Roz as best we can. If there is a chance to make contact with her daughter, then we should be grabbing it, without any hesitation." He could see that she knew he was right: that's what was scaring her. Putting his arm around her, he said,

"The truth has to come out. There's no way of stopping it now and to be honest, I think our families would rather hear it all in one fell swoop than in a slow, steady trickle. Don't you? Fresh start, clean slate. Our lives are being changed forever and I know that's scary but at the same time, I'm desperate - and excited - to meet those changes head on. We can't hide from this, Alice."

Alice sighed heavily, wiping the errant tears from her face. She gave a sheepish smile.

"You're right, both of you. I'm sorry."

She shook her head, not knowing what else to say. It struck her again how alike they were, father and daughter, both earnest and straight to the point. And in the process, unwittingly making her feel inadequate and highlighting her faults: her fear of telling the truth and facing the consequences.

"So, you replied to him, on here? How long will it take before you get an answer, do you think?" she asked, showing willing, and determined to get Ellie's earlier elation back on track. Ellie shook her head.

"No, I thought about it but I'm not sure how soon he would get the message. So, I used Facebook," she said, reaching forward to click onto another tab. Before she did so, she explained her process.

"I did a search on Facebook and there are a few Conrad Charltons but I only needed to write to one of them. I knew it was him," she said with an assured air. Elliot frowned.

"How?"

Ellie clicked on the tab and it opened on Conrad Charlton's Facebook page. Alice gasped loudly: Elliot stared intently at the familiar face that leapt out at him, his jaw twitching as he battled with a surge of emotions.

"He's the spitting image of you, Elliot," Alice exclaimed in a hushed tone, peering at the screen. He nodded.

"Yes. He's David's grandson, alright. Without a shadow of doubt."

The black-haired, blue-eyed young man that triumphantly saluted the camera with a foam-topped, German style flagon of beer, had all the physical traits of a Barraclough. It was a portrait photo but even so, Elliot knew that he would be tall with an athletic build, as all the Barraclough males were. His expression emanated a self-assuredness that was neither proud nor vain, but confident and secure in life. A confidence that came from nurture and a freedom to grow. It was the same expression that Elliot had had at his age.

"Ellie showed me the photo of you two when you were younger," Brad said, "and the likeness between you and him is staggering!"

"Have a look at this one, then," Ellie said, scrolling through photos on his page. She stepped back and held her hand out, indicating to a picture of a woman in her forties, with shoulder length, black hair. Her grey-blue eyes danced happily as she smiled for the camera, holding a fluffy, fudge coloured kitten up to her face.

"This is Isabelle," Ellie announced.

"And doesn't she look like an older version of Ellie?" Brad prompted.

Alice held her breath and her skin tingled with an explosion of goose bumps, causing her to shiver. She clutched her hands together tightly under her chin, as if in juvenile prayer, mesmerised by the image on the screen. Brad was right: it was like looking at a vision of Ellie from the future. Alice tried to imagine how Roz would react to this photo; the unmistakable likeness between her daughter and her niece was startling. Roz had doted on Ellie from the minute she was born. She must have seen Isabelle in her, Alice thought. She must have been so struck by the likeness between the infants and somehow allowed the two to merge into one. Maybe that's why she was so desperate to keep Ellie close to her and so determined to keep Elliot out of the picture. It was a chance for her to finally be a mother, to live out her maternal fantasy with a child that was undeniably a Barraclough.

She sighed deeply. But at what cost for everybody else? Her mind was in such a turmoil and she hadn't yet had a chance to come to terms with what Roz had done to her own relationship with David and to their child, let alone to Alice's relationship with Elliot. The consequences were stacking up, waiting to be addressed.

Ellie clicked onto another photo: a selfie taken by Conrad, standing cheek to cheek with his mother, both grinning up at the camera which was held aloft and reflecting the sun behind them.

"David would've been over the moon to have had a grandson," Elliot said wistfully. "I wonder how old he is: he would've been born before David died, don't you think? He looks about nineteen but it's hard to tell," he mused, regarding the young man's features.

"He's twenty, actually. And he has two sisters, younger than him; Marnie is seventeen and Lily is fourteen. Conrad's at Uni in London: guess what he's studying?" Ellie gabbled, "Painting. He's an art student!" she declared, not giving anyone a chance to offer a guess. "Can you believe it?"

"How do you know all this?" Elliot asked, surprised by her wealth of information. "Is this all on Facebook?"

"No, he messaged me back," she grinned. "We were on chat for an hour before he went off to work this morning, shortly before you came home."

Alice and Elliot stared at her with baited breath, waiting for her to continue.

"Like I said, I've been up all night on this - we both have - searching on Missing You.net and Facebook and then I sent him a message at five a.m. I really didn't expect to hear back so soon but he replied the minute he woke up this morning, at half past six."

She looked pleased with herself, laughing lightly at her parents' astonished faces. Her face softened, appreciating how she had caught them off guard with her bombardment of information.

"I've found out so much about them. Do you want to see the messages?" she volunteered, clicking onto the speech bubble logo. A stream of messages popped up on the screen, each one becoming longer in length as the two of them had cautiously introduced themselves, and once comfortable to chat, got to know each other in more detail. Elliot eagerly scrolled through them, a buoyant smile stretching across his face as he read, but Alice turned away, slowly rubbing her forehead.

"I need to phone Mum to tell her about this and arrange to see Roz as soon as possible. Maybe at Andrew's? We have to tell her in person, not over the phone," she said. Ellie looked up, her memory jolted by the mention of her grandmother.

"Oh, I forgot! Grandma phoned yesterday. She said she'd been trying to reach you but couldn't get through. The vicar has a free date for you … in December. Saturday the nineteenth," she nodded excitedly. Alice and Elliot stared at each other, wide eyed. Elliot grinned, his grin broadening when he saw the flicker of panic in Alice's eyes.

"You've got nothing to worry about, everything is under control. Okay?" He held her shoulders firmly, encouraging her to respond. She nodded, a choked laugh escaping her lips.

"Wow, oh my goodness, it's really happening, isn't it?" she looked from Elliot to Ellie, her voice sounding breathless. They both laughingly nodded in agreement.

"Yes, and not soon enough!" Ellie retorted indignantly, winking at Elliot.

Alice sat down on the chair and stared absently at the computer screen, her mind racing.

"Right, well then. We need to see Laura as soon as possible for a fitting. I need to talk to Mum about arrangements, flowers and food, that kind of thing," she held a hand up to stop Elliot's interjection. "I know what you're going to say and yes, I will leave them to plan it all but you must see, I need to make sure that what they're planning is, in fact, what I want," she stated. Elliot held his hands up and took a step back, shaking his head.

"Okay, you can give them their orders but then, you *have* to leave them to it, Alice. The whole point of this was so that you wouldn't be worrying about it," he said, "and looking like a scared rabbit in the headlights."

Ellie snorted,

"I don't think you realise what you're asking of Mum; she is the queen of organising. This is like torture for her, Dad," she said, theatrically patting Alice's arm in consolation, pulling a face.

"Oh, ha ha," Alice mocked. "I can take a step back, you know, and I will … just as soon as I have organised their organising," she laughed, reaching for the phone. "So, when shall we see Roz and Mum? Today? Tomorrow?" she looked to Elliot for an answer.

"Tomorrow," he replied decisively. "I wouldn't be happy for you to drive any more today. Besides, I don't know about you, but I'm shattered," he added.

"*You're* shattered?" Ellie tutted loudly, "what about me and Brad? We've had no sleep all night," she emphasised, then, seeing the secretive smile that passed between her parents, she groaned loudly.

"Oh my God, I don't want to know why you're so shattered! It's like living with love-sick teenagers, honestly," she flounced out of the room, dragging Brad with her. "Come on Brad, let's get some breakfast."

Elliot pulled Alice towards him and wrapped his arms around her, sighing with satisfaction.

"Well, Mrs Barraclough-to-be, we have a date. I can't wait to marry you."

"Me neither," Alice murmured. "And I promise not to panic too much," she grimaced, knowing how unconvincing she sounded. Her mind was already racing ahead, calculating how many weeks they had left. She would need to get that list started straight away. Sensing he was already losing her to a whirl of frenzy, Elliot tilted her chin to gently command her attention.

"If it gets too much for you, if you feel overwhelmed or worried about anything, let me know. You must be honest with me, every step of the way. This is it now, Alice. This is us. Our life together has just begun - again - and I don't ever want you to feel alone. We face everything together, okay? Good and bad." Concerned eyes watched the tears trickle down her face and he frowned as he wiped them away with his thumb.

"It's okay, everything will be okay," he whispered. Alice gave him a weak smile. She was aching to cry, her chest and throat hurt from the effort of holding back the torrent that threatened to burst its banks.

"I've been alone for so long, Elliot," she mumbled, "and as it turns out, there was no need for it. I just wish Dad was here to see us together." She wasn't entirely sure why her father had popped into her head so vividly right then; maybe it was Elliot's paternal tone or maybe it was the feeling of being safe once again. Either way, the fact that her childhood dream of marrying Elliot was fast becoming a reality was almost too much to bear.

He held out his little finger for her to lock hers with his, as they used to do whenever they made a promise.

"Together," he smiled.

"Together," she agreed. And then she sank into his arms and wept.

They set off for Winchester by mid-morning the following day, with Alice once again at the wheel, Elliot beside her in the passenger seat and Ellie behind him. They had stowed all of Elliot's boxes in Roz's bedroom for the time being, freeing up the studio for Alice to decorate and transform into a study for him.

"Right, Mum and Roz will be there by midday too. I suggest we tell Roz our news straight away before the wedding talk and dress fittings start. But ... how do we broach it?" Alice voiced her concern, glancing at Ellie through the rear-view mirror.

"Do you want me to tell her? No offence, Mum, but she takes it from me. She tends to be a bit bossy with you when she's feeling vulnerable or caught unawares," Ellie ventured. It was no exaggeration: Ellie could do no wrong in Roz's eyes. Roz doted on them both but had had no qualms about letting Alice feel the sharp edge of her tongue, on more than one occasion. Maybe it was born from a comfortable familiarity, or from having treated her like a daughter for so many years. Their relationship had always been a close one but not necessarily always a smooth one.

Alice nodded her agreement. Elliot chipped in,

"Maybe I should be the one to tell her? After all, this is my family too. Isabelle is my cousin as much as yours," he said. His voice had a distinct edge to it and Alice shot him an uncertain look.

"Really? Don't you think you have too many issues with her to do something like this? We have to be tactful. She is very raw at the moment," Alice responded. Elliot opened his mouth to reply but thought better of it. He shrugged defensively and shook his head, turning to look out of the window. Alice put a consoling hand on his leg at the same time as Ellie put her hand on his shoulder and rubbed it affectionately.

"Dad, I know what you're thinking, I do. Trust me, I went through a moment of absolutely hating her last week but we have to see beyond it. The past is done," she said quietly. "Besides, look at us now. A united family. Don't you think that's going to be intimidating enough for her to face? I know she has done so much damage and I know how wronged you feel on David's behalf, let alone what she did to you and Mum, but there are more people to consider now. Let me do this." She squeezed his shoulder before sitting back in her seat.

Elliot looked at Alice, pulling an apologetic face. She shook her head.

"It's okay. I'm not sure how I'm going to react to either of them today, after everything that I've learnt about what happened behind my back, so God only knows how you're feeling," she said, trying to stay focused on the road and not allowing herself to dwell on the day ahead.

Rachel was waiting to greet them when they pulled into the drive, hugging Ellie as she jumped out of the car, and then threw herself at Alice, squealing with excitement.

"Congratulations! I can't believe it!"

She stood awkwardly for a moment as she looked at Elliot, visibly sizing him up. He smiled and held out his hand.

"Hello, I'm Elliot and I'm guessing you must be Rachel?"

She grinned, taking his hand, nodding.

"Oh my God, you are the spitting image of Uncle Dan!" she exclaimed, leading them towards the front door, chatting animatedly with Ellie.

Elliot took a possessive hold of Alice's hand, pulling her back for a second.

"I may need your help with this. I didn't think I was going to feel this angry but ..." he squinted at her. She nodded, understanding exactly what he meant.

"Together," she whispered. He smiled, keeping a firm grip of her hand as Laura appeared on the doorstep, her arms outstretched in greeting and a huge welcoming smile on her face. Her eyes sparkled as she regarded Elliot and putting her arms around him, hugged him warmly. She raised her eyebrows approvingly at Alice.

"Welcome, Elliot. It's so lovely to see you again, after all these years. And, congratulations, you two!" she said, stepping back to turn her affections to Alice. She took her hand to study the ring.

"Oh, my word, you're right Alice: it *is* beautiful. Absolutely stunning." She flashed a smile at Elliot.

"Andrew's at work but he's going to nip home during his lunch hour to see you. I can't tell you how happy he is about you two," she said, linking arms with him and guiding him through the door. She paused in the hall, regarding them both and lowering her voice.

"Emotions are running high through there," she indicated to the lounge, "so just be warned. I think they're both quite nervous to see you, and your mum has gone into over-drive in a bid to plan the perfect wedding," she grimaced. "And I think she's missing your dad very much right now," she added, gently touching Alice's arm. Alice caught her breath and swallowed the lump that had risen in her throat. She looked to Elliot for support. He reclaimed her hand and squeezed it with both of his, his unwavering gaze calming her nerves,

"Shall we?" he nodded towards the door.

Celia jumped up as soon as they walked into the room and held her hands out to them, rushing forwards.

"There you are, dears!" She hesitated. Alice could see how wired she was; a combination of trepidation and remorse was etched in her face. Her eyes were wide and red-rimmed, betraying earlier tears. Any negative feelings Alice harboured, vanished instantly and she willingly responded to the proffered embrace. She could feel her mother's body trembling with pent up emotion, and knew instinctively how difficult this must be for her. What should be a time of joy, planning her daughter's wedding, was marred by guilt and loss, and Alice hated to think of what she was going through.

"I love you, Mum," she uttered, not trusting herself to remain dry-eyed as she saw Celia well up, nodding a mute response. Still holding onto Alice, she looked at Elliot and reached out a hand for him, her eyes pleading his forgiveness. He took it and silently inclined his head. Letting go of Alice, she hugged him next, clinging on for longer than the normally accepted length of a 'welcome' hug.

"I am so happy for you both. So happy," she sniffed, finally holding him at arm's length and reinforcing her sentiment with a vigorous nodding of her head. He smiled awkwardly. Seeing her again took him right back, making him feel like a teenage boy once more. It felt strange to think that this familiar face from his childhood, someone he rarely spoke to but saw often in the village, would shortly be his mother-in-law.

Glancing past Celia's shoulder, he made eye contact with Roz, and froze. They had never met but he recognised her from the photographs in Alice's lounge. He wasn't even sure if he had seen her at Ellie's party and if he had, he certainly hadn't registered who she was as she had been distinctly absent from Brockenhurst during his youth. In that instant when their eyes met, he wanted to hate her for everything that she had done but he could see the absolute pain and heartbreak in her eyes - as if she had seen a ghost - and in that same instant, he felt a strong sense of his uncle in the room.

Roz got up and swiftly disappeared through the French doors, into the garden. Elliot followed her, hurriedly excusing himself to Celia. A few steps behind her, he called out in a low tone,

"Linda?"

She gasped in shock and swung round, a haunted expression on her face.

"David?" she murmured in a confused state. Elliot swiftly covered the ground between them, holding out his hand to steady her.

"No, I'm Elliot," he said gently.

"Of course you are. You look so alike. You even sound like him," she uttered, taking his hand. He could tell she was aching to reach out and touch his face as she stared at him in wonder, her hand hovering in the air, shaking slightly.

"How old are you, Elliot?" she asked.

"Thirty-nine," he confirmed. She nodded slowly.

"He was thirty-two. But with a few more grey hairs than you," she smiled, waving a finger at his hair. Her smiled faded as she drifted back in time, and she leant heavily on his hand, not seeming to notice him there.

Laura appeared at the door, beckoning to Elliot.

"Andrew's here," she announced, urging him to come inside. She smiled meekly at Roz before turning back into the house. Elliot offered his arm to Roz and they walked back inside at a slow pace. He could tell she needed a few seconds to regain her composure before facing the inquisitive faces that had witnessed her hasty exit moments before.

Andrew was in the lounge with his arm around Alice and grinning widely. He bounded towards Elliot, taking his hand and pumping it enthusiastically.

"Congratulations!" he chortled, his face flushed with emotion. He beckoned Elliot to one side, lowering his voice so that nobody else could hear what he had to say.

"I'm so sorry about everything. If I had known about you and Alice, that you were the father, I would've told you about Ellie. There's no way I would have kept that from you," he insisted. Elliot nodded, patting his arm.

"I know. And thanks. Alice told me how you were … misinformed … about who Ellie's father was," he said, glancing across the room at Roz. Andrew followed his eye-line.

"'Misinformed' is one word for it, yes. I prefer, 'lied to'. It's more truthful," he snorted. Elliot raised his eyebrows in agreement.

"Yes, well, I'm dealing with it all. And so is Ellie."

They stood in mutual silence for a moment, surveying the room. Elliot smiled instinctively when his eyes rested on Alice, watching her talk animatedly with Laura, both glowing with excitement. It was evident that wedding plans were afoot. He turned to Andrew.

"The bottom line is, I never stopped loving Alice. And finding her again … finding Ellie … has been incredible. Too much time has been wasted," he reflected with a passion. Andrew patted his shoulder.

"Too true, my friend. And I for one, promise to make sure that nothing will stop me from walking her down the aisle. Although by the looks of things," he nodded towards his wife and sister, "she'll be running down it to be by your side," he laughed.

Ellie stood up and called for everybody's attention. Andrew grabbed a glass from the sideboard and tapped it.

"Speech, speech," he called theatrically, before sitting down next to Laura, grimacing at his empty glass.

"Okay, good: you're all here now," Ellie started nervously, standing in the middle of the room. She glanced round at each one of them, her focus finally falling on Roz.

"Auntie Roz, I'm sorry to put you on the spot but Mum, Dad, and I are sick of all the lies and deceit, and so I have to tell you, we *all* know about David and about your baby. Uncle Andrew, Auntie Laura, Rachel … all of us. And we don't judge you. We love you". As she spoke, the tremble in her voice subsided and the volume grew in strength as she regained her confidence. Roz stared fixedly at her, not moving a muscle. Celia glanced nervously at Andrew, fearing his condemnation but was rewarded with an encouraging smile and wink. She reciprocated, breathing out slowly. Ellie continued speaking,

"Dad and I started searching for her…" She paused as a collective gasp was emitted and everybody turned to look at Elliot. He perched on the arm of the sofa, next to Alice, feeling unusually uncomfortable by the sudden attention. He smiled at Ellie and nodded for her to continue.

"And … it turns out that she has been searching for *you*, for years. Her name is Isabelle Charlton and she's been searching for Lin Barraclough. She couldn't understand why you were nowhere to be found. She assumed that you didn't want to be found," Ellie's voice wavered as she watched Roz's face crumple.

"You've found her?" Celia asked in a hushed voice. Ellie nodded.

"And how do you know all of this: what she was thinking?" Laura asked the question on everybody's lips. Ellie took a deep breath.

"Because her son told me." She turned to Roz. "Your grandson, Conrad, is dying to meet you. He can't wait. He sounds really lovely. He's been helping her look for you but it was tricky because you lied about your name. Roz, you have to stop lying." Ellie suddenly burst into tears, uncontrollably sobbing. Elliot was by her side in an instant, holding her tightly against his chest and gesturing to Alice for a tissue. Ellie took it, nodding her thanks. He held her patiently until her sobs subsided.

"Can you carry on, Dad?" she sniffed. He scanned the room, feeling every bit as emotional as Ellie but more able to control it. Clearing his throat, he continued on her behalf.

"I can't take any credit for this; I just got the ball rolling. It has been Ellie and Brad that have devoted their time, and given up their sleep, to find Isabelle. I think it's safe to say, we are witnessing the effects of sleep deprivation here," he gave a wry smile and kissed the top of Ellie's head, then addressing Roz, he said,

"There is so much to tell you but I don't think it's fair to overload you with it all now. You need time to take this in. I will tell you though, she is the image of David," he nodded, "as is Conrad. We have photos of them - when you're ready - and a contact email. Conrad's waiting for you to get in touch. He's desperately waiting," he reiterated. He squeezed Ellie, who was still leaning on his chest, her arms wrapped around his waist.

"And, Auntie Roz," Ellie added, "when Isabelle finally tracked down her birth certificate and found out where she was born, she moved the family down to Cornwall. She felt she belonged there."

"Which part of Cornwall?" Andrew asked. Ellie paused.

"Newlyn. Isabelle gave up her job as a midwife, to paint. She's an artist. And the really bizarre thing is, her husband, Tom, is a doctor. He's the local G.P." she told her, smiling at the irony. "Honestly, you can't make this stuff up!"

All eyes turned to Roz, who sat in silence, her eyes fixed on the carpet. Laura spotted the whites of her knuckles as she clenched her fists in an effort to stem her tears.

"Right, come on girls, lend me a hand in the kitchen; I think we need a cup of tea."

"Or something stronger?" Andrew voiced hopefully, waving his glass at her. Laura tutted.

"You've got to get back to work, darling. I'll have a drink waiting for you when you get home later," she winked. He stood up regretfully, following Laura into the kitchen.

Elliot crossed over to Roz and crouched beside her chair, taking her hands in his and uncurling her fists with his thumbs. She looked up at him, seeing an image of the man she had loved and lost, and whimpered. A torrent of hot tears cascaded down her face and great sobs wracked her body. Elliot gently pulled her head to his shoulder and he cradled the side of her face, letting her weep. Celia made a move towards them but Alice held her back. She was astonished by Elliot's actions but knew that he and Roz should be left alone for a while.

"Let's help them in the kitchen, Mum," she said pointedly, heading for the door. Celia followed, glancing back at the touching sight. She hurriedly left the room, knowing she too was about to cave in to tears.

As Roz's sobs slowed, Elliot pulled her to her feet and guided her to the sofa, enabling him to sit next to her. Seeing how sapped of energy she was, he put his arm around her and held her comfortingly, as he would a child. Eventually she found her voice, searching his face as she spoke.

"Have you really found her? It's really her?"
He smiled.

"Yes, it's her. You called her Celia Barraclough, didn't you?"
Roz nodded.

"Yes, I named her after the two people I loved the most in the world," she said, her voice hoarse from crying. "In my defence, we were encouraged to put false names on the birth certificates. I used David's name because I wasn't allowed to include him on the record and that felt so wrong," she told him. "I did love him so very much, you know." She sniffed loudly, trying to clear her nose.

"I know. He loved you too. He talked about you endlessly and with such a passion," Elliot said. He wanted to say more: how it had destroyed David's life to lose her and how he had never been able to get over it, but he could tell that she already knew that.

"Elliot, I need to ask you something," she ventured, not quite able to meet his eyes. He inclined his head.

"Okay. What?"

"The inscription on David's gravestone: where did it come from?"

Elliot straightened up to look at her, thinking back to recall the words.

"To live in hearts we leave behind is not to die," he quoted. She nodded, biting her lip as she welled up again. He sighed heavily at the memory.

"He made me the sole executor of his will and his instructions were very specific regarding that. He said it was a message for Linda. A message from the grave. He said that she would know what it meant. I didn't know then that Linda was..."

"Me," she finished his sentence. Elliot nodded. He regarded her silently. All animosity had vanished and had been replaced with a strong urge to protect her, to ease her pain. This was the woman that his uncle had loved so completely, and he felt a duty of care on his behalf.

"If it's any consolation, he knew you loved him. He went looking for you - he went to Newlyn - but you had disappeared. He said he knew there must've been a real reason for you leaving, not just that you gave up on him. But he couldn't find you. He did try." Elliot fell silent, his words echoing what he also went through, searching for Alice.

"Do you think he would have stood by me? Faced the scandal?" She watched him, squinting as she braced herself for his reply. He thought for a moment, choosing his words carefully.

"I think … I'm learning … there is nothing to be gained by 'what if'. We can't change the past; we can only learn from it and move forward. And the way you move forward is by building a relationship with your daughter. And your grandchildren," he smiled. "But to answer your question: yes, he would have stood by you. I have no doubt about that. I'm sorry," he apologised.

"*I'm* sorry, Elliot," she responded. He nodded.

"I think he understood why you left; it was an impossible situation at the time."

"No, I mean I'm sorry about Ellie. About Alice," she corrected him. He looked at her with a guarded expression, a lump forming in his throat. Roz tentatively rested her hand on his arm.

"When she found out she was pregnant, I should have encouraged her to look for you. I should have looked for you. But I was scared of what your grandfather would do to her. Especially as you had supposedly disappeared with somebody else. I think my own fear took over; I was scared to have any connection with your family. I thought my own secret would be revealed and David would hate me for what I had done. To us and to our daughter. I seem to make a habit of destroying lives and I have been running scared and guilty for the whole of my adult life because of it," she choked on her words, turning away to blow her nose.

Lost for words, Elliot watched her, reflecting on her confession and wondering if they ever would be able to get beyond this. He was determined to find a way. As if reading his mind, she gave him a tentative smile.

"Don't mess it up, like I did. Take your chance and be happy in life. Alice loves you with all her heart and I know that she has never stopped loving you over the years. Not for a second." She took his hand. "Forgive us all. Please?"

She waited for his response, noticing how his hand shook as he rubbed the back of his head. He met her gaze squarely, barely able to control his breathing, nodding.

"Of course," his voice was thick with feeling. He stood up abruptly.

"I'm sorry, can you excuse me for a minute?" he pointed towards the door. Roz nodded.

"She's in the kitchen: it's just through there, down the hall."

Elliot strode into the kitchen, smiling briefly at the expectant faces that turned to him.

"Excuse us," he acknowledged them, taking Alice's hand and swiftly exiting through the back door into the garden. She trotted alongside him, wondering what was going on. Half-way down the path and out of sight of the kitchen door, he turned to her and gripped her shoulders, staring intently at her.

"Tell me you love me," he demanded gruffly, his eyes pleading. Alice smiled, stroking his face.

"I love you, Elliot," she soothed him. "I love you with all my heart."

He hugged her tightly, not wanting to let her go. Alice could feel how his whole body trembled.

"Elliot?" she prompted quietly. He shook his head, unable to speak, breathing into her hair. She tightened her hold of him in response, stroking his back. They remained there for some time until eventually he found the strength to move away and look at her.

"I'm sorry. I know we've talked about this but I *am* sorry for doubting your love, for even one moment. I blamed you for keeping Ellie away from me but I can see now … I can see exactly what happened, how your aunt dominated your life," he paused as Alice opened her mouth to interrupt him.

"Let me finish," he said, "I don't blame her. I can see how her life was destroyed by my grandfather and she, in turn, destroyed us: again, because of my grandfather." He sighed, reflecting on Roz's words once more.

"Just listening to her made me realise how close we came to living the same fate as she has. Never seeing each other again and me never knowing about Ellie. I can't bear that thought. I can't." He was visibly shaking now.

"You're forgetting Ellie," Alice said. "She would've found you. She was pretty determined to exercise her rights to know about you, once she turned eighteen," she assured him. Elliot frowned, unconvinced.

"Marry me tomorrow. Let's just go to a registry office and do it. Anywhere, I don't care where. I just want to marry you now. Right now," he insisted. Alice stared at him, seeing he was deadly serious.

"We can't," she responded tactfully, sensing he knew that anyway. "Too many people want to see us walk down the aisle now that they know about us. Think about your mum. Ellie. Your brothers. They'll all want to share our day, we can't deprive them of it," she coaxed, "however tempting it is. Besides, as far as I'm concerned, we're already married. In here," she patted her chest. He smiled, calming down.

"And I want to wear a pretty dress and be a princess for the day," she laughed. He chuckled.

"Okay, okay. If it makes you happy," he conceded. She nuzzled his neck.

"You make me happy. Being a princess for the day is just an added bonus," she chirped. "And if it's at all possible, I love you even more for what you did today with Roz. That was truly special."

Elliot smiled, pleased at her remark.

"How special?" he asked, playing for attention. She chuckled.

"I'll show you when we get home."

He raised an eyebrow dramatically

"Wow, *that* special, eh?"

They walked back down the path, arm in arm, knowing that the day had been another major hurdle that they had successfully overcome. Now all they had to tackle was meeting with Elliot's family: the engagement party, reunifying Roz and Isabelle, and finally, their wedding day. As they ran through the list, he grew impatient.

"It's not too late to elope, you know. We could be in Gretna Green by this evening and forget about everybody else," he urged half-heartedly. Alice shook her head, pushing the kitchen door open. They were greeted by Ellie and Rachel, brandishing fabric swatches, noisily deliberating over which colours would suit them best for their bridesmaid dresses.

"Sorry, too late!" Alice laughed, kissing his cheek before being whisked away by Laura to be measured for her wedding dress.

Chapter Sixteen

Two days later, they were on the road south again. The car was packed with cases for their holiday and Ellie sat in the passenger seat alongside Elliot at the wheel.

"Are you sure, Dad?" she asked, grinning. He laughed.

"If you ask me that one more time, Ellie, I'm going to think I should have something to worry about."

He had surprised her the day before, when his car had been returned from the garage, by putting L plates on the front and rear of it. He handed her the keys.

"All insured for you. Let's take her for a spin, shall we? And tomorrow, once we're off the motorway and onto the A34, you can drive. If you'd like?"

"If I'd like?" she squealed happily, "I've been itching to do this since my first lesson but Mum's been too scared," she jigged as she spoke.

"Cautious, not scared," Alice corrected her, raising her eyebrows at Elliot. He casually put his arm about Ellie's shoulders, showing a united front.

"She'll be fine, Alice. Just veer away from any trees," he said to Ellie, touching his forehead.

They pulled up in Celia's driveway a few hours later, a little behind schedule but all in one piece. Ellie pressed the horn to announce their arrival and beamed at her grandmother's surprised face.

"Oh, well done, dear!" she encouraged, giving them all hugs and ushering them into the house.

Just one look in the kitchen told Alice that 'Operation Engagement Party' was in full swing; food and drink was stashed on every available patch of work surface and the table was laden with freshly baked goods. Shopping bags stuffed with crisps and other snacks could be found on the floor, conveniently placed as a tripping hazard for any unsuspecting by-passers.

"Goodness, you have been busy," Elliot remarked, taking in the spread.

"Oh this; it's nothing, dear," Celia breezed, waving a dismissive hand at the room. "The main bulk of it will be done tomorrow morning, but I have finished your special sausage rolls, Ellie," she added, offering her a plate piled with pastry parcels.

"Not a scrap of pig in sight," Roz interjected as she entered the room, smiling at their guests. She headed straight for Elliot to hug him first.

"Hello again," she said demurely. Alice noted how much calmer she seemed, more her old self.

"I've had a reply to my email, from Conrad and I'm meeting him on Monday," Roz announced, pulling a face mixed with apprehension and joy.

"That's great!" Elliot enthused. "Where?"

"Southbank. Celia's coming with me," she smiled at her sister, "and we'll take it from there."

"Are you coming with us tonight, Roz?" Alice asked, taking a warm sausage roll from the offered plate and nodding for Elliot to do likewise.

Roz shook her head.

"No. And please tell your mother, Elliot, that I'm grateful for the invite but as I said on the phone to you, Alice, I can't do it. A room filled with David look-alikes ... I don't think I'm ready for that just yet," she said with a wan smile. Elliot put a consoling hand on her arm.

"Are you still okay with what we talked about? Bearing in mind that you'll be seeing them all tomorrow, here," he asked her. She nodded.

"Yes, I think now is a good time. Tell them about Isabelle, about David. And his father: please do reiterate how he determined the course of events. It might help them to understand what happened to you and Alice too, and why Ellie was kept a secret from them."

Her face reflected her consternation at the thought of their reaction to the news that Elliot would be imparting. And she wished she had the courage to be there but at the same time, felt she would be intruding. This was something they'd need to digest in private.

Celia watched her sister with a sinking heart. She was steeling herself for the meeting with Elliot's parents and felt seriously let down by Roz; they should be facing this together. After all, they both made the decisions regarding Alice's fate eighteen years ago, and the consequences had been easy for Roz to live with, all those miles away in Stratford-upon-Avon. It had been less so for Celia, living in such close proximity to the Barraclough family.

"Okay, let's do this," Elliot said, in an upbeat tone, trying to allay the nerves he could feel emanating from the three women standing next to him on his parents drive. They eyed the house with apprehension, from a safe distance, not wanting to move any closer. It was a beautiful house, more so than Alice remembered from teenage years when she would pass by it, hoping for a glimpse of Elliot. An old, converted coach house, it stood proudly on a sweeping, gravel drive, lined with Silver Birch trees. The substantial, red brick building was smothered with creeping ivy and wisteria; large tresses of lilac-blue blooms had been trained to hang from the wooden beamed, storm porch. Fading, long, bean-like seed pods were replacing the spent blooms, adding an early, autumnal structure to the established plant.

Answering Ellie's questions, Elliot told them that the four-bedroomed house had been extended over the years, improving the old kitchen and adding a large conservatory which opened onto the south-facing garden. The triple garage, to the side of the house, had been adapted to house a swimming pool. It had been installed after his father's stroke, as part of the rehabilitation programme.

"It's also very popular with the grandchildren. I think Dad has to fight to use it during the school holidays," he grinned. He took Alice's hand and rang the doorbell. Ellie linked arms with Celia, giving her a smile of encouragement. Her own stomach was doing somersaults but she suspected that Celia was feeling even more nervous than she was.

Sheila opened the door wide, a warm smile on her weathered face, ready to greet them. She was elegantly dressed in a sleeveless, Chanel-style shift dress of soft green linen, with low heeled, comfortable sandals on her feet. A string of pearls hung around her neck. Her short hair, once brown, was greying all over and she made no attempt to hide the fact; opting to embrace the aging process naturally. Of a medium build and height, it was evident that her sons did not get their physique from her genes, although she was unmistakably their mother. Her bright, blue eyes shone with joy when they rested on Elliot but resisting the urge to bestow her attention on him first, she focused on the woman who's hand he was holding so possessively.

"Alice! Welcome to the family," she said full of sincerity as she hugged her, her Yorkshire lilt very noticeable. She looked at Ellie next and her body sank a little as she took in a laboured breath. She beckoned Ellie towards her and hugged her too, before clasping her granddaughter's face with her hands to study her intently, drinking in her image. Her emotions got the better of her and she retrieved a tissue from her pocket.

"Oh my goodness, I promised myself I wouldn't cry," she laughed through her tears, dabbing at her eyes. "I shouldn't make promises I can't keep, should I! That'll teach me," she joked, clutching Ellie's hand with hers.

"You are absolutely beautiful, Ellie, but of course you would be: just look at your mother," she gushed, glancing proudly at Elliot. She turned to Celia and held out a hand; not as a hand shake but as a gesture of friendship.

"Hello Celia, you are most welcome to the family too," she nodded, with a look that spoke volumes. The effort it took her to say it, was immense and yet, she did actually mean it. She could see the uneasiness in Celia's eyes and posture, and it gave her the strength to be the magnanimous one. She kissed Elliot on the cheek and stroked his arm in a deeply maternal gesture; the look they shared saying how moved they had both been by the moment. She then ushered them into the lounge where ten pairs of eyes turned to greet them.

The room was large, with an imposing, mahogany fire surround dominating one wall. A display cabinet, filled with ornaments and photographs, stood alongside it and in the far corner, a baby grand piano had pride of place. Sofas and armchairs filled the remaining floor space, all currently occupied by Elliot's gathered family.

Alice paused in the doorway, suddenly overcome with nerves but before anybody had a chance to say anything, a young girl jumped up from her seat in surprise. She was the same age as Ellie, and looked remarkably like her, in build and facial features, with black hair which hung half way down her back, and startlingly blue eyes that widened as she exclaimed,

"Ellie?"

"Nat? Oh my God, Nat!"

The girls rushed towards each other in noisy greeting, unwittingly commanding everybody's attention as they watched the delighted pair.

"*You* are Uncle Elliot's daughter?" she asked, her mouth dropping open in exaggerated shock. Ellie nodded, beaming.

"Yes! Are we … are we cousins?" she wondered, mimicking the shocked expression. Just then, Elliot's brother, James, stepped forward and offered a hug to Ellie.

"Ellie, how lovely to see you again. I had no idea you were my niece," he smiled, moving over to Elliot, patting him on the back and offering a hug to Alice.

"Hello Alice, I'm James. Lovely to meet you, and congratulations you two!" he grinned, looking from one to the other. Physically, he resembled Dan and Elliot but his whole manner was much more reserved; he was softly spoken, shy almost, and happy to take a back seat in his brothers' company.

Caught completely off guard by Ellie and Natalie, Alice stumbled on her words as she thanked him. Elliot chipped in,

"James, how on earth do you know Ellie?" He watched in confusion as James's wife, Anne, also greeted Ellie with familiarity. Dan sidled up to her next, hugging her and saying,

"My word, Ellie, you have grown since I saw you last."

Elliot turned to Celia, who shook her head, as confused as he was. He noticed how Alice smiled awkwardly at Dan. Sheila came to their aid, taking centre stage and holding her hand up for silence.

"Well, what a surprise this is," she laughed, beckoning her husband to join her. Just shy of six feet tall, John was a couple of inches shorter than his sons but towered over Sheila. His black hair was shot through with white, giving him a distinguished air which was emphasized by his smart suit trousers, pale blue shirt and navy tie. He walked with a stick and despite a pronounced weakness down one side, he still maintained a proud stance. Seventy-five years old and living with the after effects of a severe stroke, he was looking good for his age. His grey-blue eyes had the same warm twinkle as his wife's; they softened even more so when he looked at her.

"It would seem that Ellie isn't a stranger to some of you. Natalie, can you explain, please?" Sheila invited, smiling at her granddaughter. Natalie nodded amiably.

"Of course, Gran. Well, I met Ellie a couple of years ago, at Amber's sixteenth birthday party. Amber, my best friend, is Ellie's cousin," she said.

"Yes, Amber's grandma is my Gramps big sister, Auntie May," Ellie added.

"And so, we've met up quite a bit during holidays and that, you know, whenever Ellie's been down to stay. This is so great!" she hugged Ellie, who was standing beside her.

"And James?" Elliot prompted, "how do you…" he gestured to Ellie. James nodded.

"Ah well, this lovely young lady spent the weekend with us earlier this year, for Natalie's eighteenth birthday. If you recall, she declined a big party," he pulled a mock sad face at Natalie, "and opted to have a sleep-over weekend with friends. Amber and Ellie were both invited, he explained.

Recognition crossed Alice's face as she remembered dropping the girls off at Natalie's house, not realising that she was part of the Barraclough family. She frowned, trying to recall something.

"But … were you at Ellie's eighteenth then, Natalie?" she asked. Elliot shook his head, knowing the answer.

"No, we were in France, on holiday," she said. "Uncle Elliot phoned me, in a bit of a panic, asking what to get for an eighteen-year-old. I didn't know he meant Ellie. What did he get you in the end?" she asked Ellie, who tapped her necklace in reply. Natalie nodded her approval and smiled at Elliot.

The room fell silent as they all digested the fact that Ellie had been walking among them without realising her connection to the family. John cleared his throat and straightened up, having been leaning heavily on his stick.

"Well, I think we all agree: we are absolutely delighted to welcome Ellie, and Alice ... and Celia ... to the family. I am so proud of you, son - we all are - and I couldn't be more thrilled about your engagement. Do you have a date yet for the wedding?" he asked hopefully. Alice glanced at Elliot, seeing how choked he was at his father's words. She answered for him.

"Yes, we do. December the nineteenth."

There was a flurry of approving remarks and John raised his glass in the air.

"To Alice and Elliot, and their wonderful future together. Finally," he declared, winking at Elliot.

Realising that the new arrivals hadn't yet got a glass to toast with, James efficiently guided Alice and Celia to the drinks cabinet, taking their orders. Dan clapped Elliot on the back.

"Good to see you, Elliot. You're looking well," he started, eyeing his younger brother thoughtfully.

"Well, this is certainly a turn up for the books. I didn't see this one coming."

Elliot gave a half-laugh and shrugged his shoulders.

"No, neither did I," he said. "You knew Ellie?"

"Of course. I haven't seen her for some time, mind you but when she was little, I saw her often. Rachel's birthday parties, mainly, you know, when I did the dutiful Godfather bit," he laughed. They both knew he revelled in the role and had a huge soft spot for Rachel.

"I wish you'd told me about you and Alice. I could've put you straight; I've always known where she was and that she'd had a baby," he said, gauging Elliot's reaction. "Andrew was gutted when she fell pregnant. He couldn't believe that some slime ball had done that to her and then just buggered off. He was ready to punch somebody's lights out, for quite some time," he said. Elliot dropped his head, sighing. Dan watched his reaction.

"Does that explain the drinking, then? Because she left you?" he asked quietly. Elliot stared at him, taken aback by what he said. Dan snorted.

"Oh, come on, Elliot. We all knew about your drinking. Mum was worried sick about you, for Christ's sake. Especially after David died; she had relied on him to look after you. I mean, he did it willingly, it was his choice, but he did keep her and Dad up to date with your progress. He didn't divulge what you had been through though. He said, 'when he's ready, he'll tell you'."

"I had no idea," Elliot muttered. "I thought I was going through hell on my own."

Dan put an arm on his back.

"No, you were never alone but none of us knew what had happened or why you suddenly dropped out of life, so we had to sit it out. Be here for you when you were ready to turn to us. I have regretted it, over the years, that I wasn't more proactive with you but by the time I'd decided to step in, you seemed to be back on your feet."

They looked at each other in silence for a few moments, before Dan continued.

"I've always had my hands tied here, with the surgery and looking after Dad, but James engineered regular visits to York just to make sure you were okay. We love you, Elliot. You're our little brother," he nodded, not wanting to sound too sentimental but meaning it nevertheless. He took a deep breath in, choosing his words carefully.

"Listen, if you ever need to talk, you know, about anything ... just say. This kind of thing, this revelation, discovery, call it what you will: it can take its toll. I'm not suggesting you're rushing into anything, really I'm not but just give yourself time to sort it all out in your head, come to terms with it. You've missed out on a huge chunk of life and if anything - and I mean anything - goes awry, you could find yourself taking a huge step back. The ugly thing about addiction is, it resurfaces when you need it most but want it least."

Elliot stared at his feet, absorbing Dan's weighted words.

"I don't have a problem with drink anymore," he defended.

"I know, I know but just be kind to yourself. And as for Alice, this is huge for her too. She's great, I love her to bits. I've seen her grow from an awkward teenager to a fantastic mum and I know, from Andrew, that she has struggled to get to where she is." He gave a little laugh as something occurred to him.

"I often wondered why she didn't have a man in her life. Now I know. You two are perfect together; all I am saying is, you've both been through a traumatic time. Just bear that in mind and look after each other. As I'm sure you will," he clapped his hand on Elliot's back again, to indicate that he had said all that he wanted to. Elliot smiled and nodded, glancing up to seek out Alice. She was deep in conversation with James, Anne, and Dan's wife, Charlotte. Ellie was surrounded by her new cousins: the centre of attention, which, judging by her infectious laughter, pleased her immensely. His father sat on the side of the room, proudly watching his grandchildren. Celia and Sheila were sitting together, in silence, sipping at their drinks.

"December the nineteenth is not that long away. Do you need any help with the organising?" Sheila ventured.

"Oh, yes, that would be lovely. Thank you," Celia replied, trying not to sound too startled by the offer. They slipped back into silence, watching the room. An explosion of teenage laughter brought a smile to both their faces. Sheila sighed deeply.

"This is going to be hard to forgive, Celia. But I'll find a way." She looked at her, her determined features hardening as she voiced her thoughts.

"We are neighbours, we have been for years; our children played together. Andrew and Dan have been best friends since they were four years old. Four years old! I can't believe that you could do this: you of all people!"

Celia chewed her lip, fiddling nervously with her glass.

"I know and I am so sorry. I knew it was wrong. I didn't want to…" she faltered. Elliot appeared by her side, having been listening covertly to their conversation.

"Mum, I don't blame Celia for this and you shouldn't either. If anybody's to blame, it's Grandfather," he said boldly. Sheila looked confused, cross even.

"What on earth are you talking about?"

Elliot scanned the room, making sure that everybody else was distracted as he beckoned his father over.

"Why don't the four of us go and make some tea or something, in the kitchen?" he suggested, raising his eyebrows pointedly at Celia. She nodded her consent. The sooner they got this over with, the better, as far as she was concerned.

Once in the kitchen, Elliot encouraged his parents to sit down and they gathered round the table, facing each other. Sheila and John listened intently as Elliot and Celia took it in turns to relay Roz and Alice's stories in full - not scrimping on details about Roz's affair and pregnancy - and concluded with the discovery of Roz and David's daughter and grandchildren.

John sat for an age with his head in his hands: slowly, rhythmically massaging his temples, staring vacantly at the table. Every now and then, he let out a heartfelt tut as he processed what he had just been told. Sheila stood up and intimated for Celia to do the same, putting her arms out to hug her. They clung to each other, rubbing each other's backs as a sign of solidarity in their grief.

Elliot stood by the window, staring out into the garden. The daylight was fading, the last straggling rays of sunshine lingered longingly on the warm roses in their pristine bed. He felt spent, completely drained. His whirlwind week had finally culminated in the unburdening of discovered secrets with his parents: his family had welcomed his daughter and bride-to-be with open, unjudgmental arms and he had managed to turn around the anger he felt towards Roz, into a more productive feeling, of empathy.

"Do you want tea, Elliot, or something stronger?" his mother asked, interrupting his musing. He remembered Dan's comment.

"Tea, please," he nodded. He sat down next to his father, not knowing what to say. John clutched Elliot's hand that rested on the table, shooting him a sidelong look.

"Thank you. This can't have been easy for you to deal with."

Elliot shrugged, giving a noncommittal smile.

"It's okay, Dad. I just feel incredibly sad for … so many people. Including myself and Alice. Too many people have been hurt by the actions of two, twisted, bitter minds," he confessed plainly, images of Mary O'Shea and his grandfather flashing before him.

Sheila and Celia re-joined them at the table, Celia passing round the mugs once Sheila had poured the tea.

"I'm not wanting to knock your faith, Celia, but this is what I believe religion does to people. Unless you are really strong-willed, it can dictate your life. You let others rule you, make decisions for you because you are scared to admit to what you have done. If Roz had told your parents about her pregnancy and not feared divine retribution … who knows what would have happened," Sheila said. Celia eyed her nervously, not wanting to disagree but not comfortable with what she was saying. Sheila continued,

"I've never been much of a church goer, neither was my father. He would say, 'well it's all very well getting dressed up and trogging off to church, but who's going to milk the cows while we're all over there having a sing-song'," she laughed as she fondly mimicked her father's strong, northern accent.

John stood up slowly, accepting Elliot's offer of support.

"If you'll excuse me ladies, I think I'll just go upstairs and rest my eyes for a moment," he said, inclining his head politely. Elliot held the door open for him, following close behind. Sheila watched them anxiously, knowing how troubled her husband was by the news of his brother's love affair, and his father's scheming that ultimately destroyed David's life. She turned back to Celia, wanting to redress her comments on religion.

"I had every respect for your father and for Reggie," her face softened as she smiled consolingly when mentioning his name. "John and Reggie used to be friends when they were younger: did you know that?"

"Really?" Celia was surprised. "But surely there was an age gap?"

"Not in a village cricket team, no," she chuckled. "and your Reggie was an ace apparently. The youngest bowler on the team."

"I had no idea they were friends," Celia's voice wobbled at the thought of Reggie. It didn't go unnoticed.

"John says your Reggie was a bit of a tearaway, a bit of a rogue but a real charmer," she winked.

"Yes, he was," Celia sighed wistfully. "That's what I loved about him. I think it was a lack of a father figure when he was growing up, that made him how he was," she said.

"Don't talk to me about father figures – especially after what I've just heard!" Sheila declared. They shook their heads in unison and on realising it, laughed together.

"So, how did you meet John then? Did you come here from Yorkshire or did he go there?" she asked, feeling the mood was becoming lighter and they were establishing a camaraderie.

"Ah, now there's a love story. A bit like yours but it was me that was the tearaway," she shared conspiratorially. "He was on a placement at our local surgery in Pateley Bridge. He was the talk of the village when he arrived. Every girl's dream. Tall, dark and handsome, and *not* a farmer! Not that there's anything wrong with farmers but it was so refreshing to meet somebody that smelt of aftershave with a faint base note of antiseptic, rather than the usual wet hay and hen coop smell that most of the young men I knew smelt of. And he was intelligent, well spoken, well dressed … just everything about him had the village holding their breath and swooning at his feet."

"So, did you meet him at the surgery? Were you his patient?" Celia's eyes widened at the thought.

"Good Lord, no! It was rather a convoluted way of meeting but I was pretty determined, I can tell you. He was lodging with my aunt's sister-in-law, Sally. My mother would usually pop round there once a week with Sally's order of eggs. It was an excuse for a cuppa and a gossip with her, and an escape from the farm for half an hour. Anyway, on that particular day, my mother was unwell. Not like her to get sick but she had a nasty bout of 'flu so I jumped at the chance to deliver the eggs, hoping to bump into John. And I was in luck. He was there, sitting at the kitchen table, politely drinking tea with Aunt Sally. His face was a picture when he saw me: I don't think he'd had much experience of talking to girls, especially not a farmer's daughter dressed like Bridget Bardot. That was my idea of 'Sunday best'," she raised her eyebrows mischievously. "I was nineteen then and he was twenty-six. I was the youngest of five, always behaving older than I actually was, and super-confident with it. John was so painfully shy, and I thought he wasn't interested despite all my efforts but as I was leaving Aunt Sally's, he suggested he walk with me back home and check on my mother. And after that day, I found more and more reasons to meet up, 'by chance', until he picked up the courage to ask me out on a proper date. I could see it in his eyes: he was terrified, because he was in love with me! Well, he stayed in Pateley Bridge for another two years after his placement finished. They jumped at the chance to offer him a job at the surgery. And then I came down here with him after we got married." Sheila's smile was captivating as she reminisced, painting such a clear image of their romance.

They sat in comfortable silence, finishing their tea. Sheila fixed her eyes on Celia.

"I was so sorry when I heard about Reggie. I can't imagine what it's like. I mean, we came close when John had his stroke, and a part of him did die that day, but he's still here. I couldn't bear to be without him. I'm sorry. If there's ever anything I can do or, if you ever want company, I'm here," she said in earnest. They held hands across the table, their wedding rings glinting under the kitchen light. A new friendship had just been born.

Elliot took off his watch and laid it on the bedside table, before lying down next to Alice. He propped himself up on his elbow, as they carried on their conversation; the amber glow from the side light throwing gentle shadows across the room.

"That went better than I expected. They're all so lovely, Elliot," Alice enthused, smiling at the thought of their evening together. He grunted his agreement. Brushing a strand of hair from her face, he asked,

"Why didn't you mention that Dan had met Ellie? That he had seen you over the years, and seen her?" He looked hurt, making her blush awkwardly.

"I'm sorry, that was wrong of me but I could see how cut up you were about missing out on Ellie's childhood and I thought, if I told you that Dan knew her, that would just be rubbing salt in the wound," she explained. He frowned.

"You're right, it would." He leant forward and kissed her lightly then cast an eye around the room.

"This is so strange. I'm in your bedroom, in your parents' house," he said.

"Yes. And?"

"It's just, I'm finally living my teenage fantasy," he laughed, arching an eyebrow. Alice stretched under the duvet, twiddling her toes.

"Mmm, me too," she whispered, running her fingers up and down his arm.

Elliot looked at her for a moment, as if trying to read her thoughts.

"Am I rushing you?" he asked. Alice laughed abruptly.

"We have slept together before, you know!"
Elliot laughed,

"No, I mean, with the wedding. Am I rushing you too much?" he urged. She reciprocated his posture, propping herself up on one elbow to face him.

"Are you having second thoughts?" she asked.

"No, it's just something Dan said," he replied, trying not to let his brother's words play on his mind too much. Alice sighed, giving him a reassuring smile.

"Look, yes, it is a rush but I understand. We know we belong together, we always have done but you have this need to put a ring on my finger and claim me as your wife. You have to be the dominant male. I understand," she teased. He rolled her over and pinned her down with his forearms, smiling at her.

"Is that right? You're even more sexy than you were in my teenage fantasy," he growled, teasing her back.

"I'm not sure I want to know," she giggled. He bent to kiss her when there was a brief knock at the door and Ellie burst in, making him roll over and sit up quickly, pulling the duvet across him.

"Night, Mum! Night Dad!" she trilled, crossing over to the bed and leaning on them to hug them.

"Thanks for this evening, I absolutely love my new family," she practically sang with happiness as she skipped back to the door, pulling it shut behind her.

"I have to say, *that* didn't happen in my fantasy," Elliot retorted. There was another knock at the door and Celia pushed it open.

"Goodnight dears, sleep well, see you in the morning," she called in a hushed tone.

"Night Mum," Alice called back.

"Night Celia," Elliot echoed.

The door closed behind her. Elliot slumped down next to Alice, punching his pillow into shape.

"Yep, well that's just killed my fantasy. Dead," he mumbled gruffly.

"And you, the dominant male," Alice giggled, stretching her arm across his chest possessively.

Chapter Seventeen

By the time Alice and Elliot emerged the following morning, the kitchen was out of bounds and breakfast was being served in the garden. Celia ushered them through the lounge French doors, and passed a tray of tea and toast out to them. She and Roz were in their element, and worked perfectly as a team. Celia thrived on flapping and lived by her lists, whereas Roz was more laid back and relied on her memory rather than pieces of paper.

"Don't forget that you're meeting with Martin this morning, at ten," Celia reminded them, sticking her head through the kitchen window to check that they were listening to her.

"Yes, fine, Mum," Alice placated her. Roz stepped out through the kitchen door to speak to them.

"And you've got a few appointments to look at wedding venues after that," she said.

"Yes, I know, Roz," Alice nodded. Celia thrust a piece of paper through the window and waved it at her.

"Here's the list, dear. The Balmer Lawn Hotel is the first one to look at and Careys Manor after that. And then two more. I've allowed time in-between each appointment for you, and written a list of things to ask."

Alice took the paper and passed it to Elliot, giving him a knowing smile. He raised his eyebrows.

"Regretting turning down my elopement idea now?" he whispered. She nodded.

"Where's Ellie?" she called to the kitchen.

"Oh, she was up and out first thing. She's gone out for breakfast with Amber and Natalie. They are so excited to be bridesmaids. It's a shame Rachel couldn't be here until later. Oh well," Celia said, talking at speed as she flitted between tasks.

Elliot looked pleased.

"It did work out rather neatly, asking my niece and your cousin to be bridesmaids, without even realising that they're best friends," he said. Draining his cup, he stood up and held out his hand for hers.

"Shall we? Let's get to the church," he smiled, pulling her up and into his arms. "Do you realise it's less than three weeks since that evening when we very nearly kissed in church?" he murmured, stroking her cheek. Alice looked surprised.

"Three weeks? Is that all? It feels like a life time ago," she said, shaking her head in disbelief.

"It is a life time ago," he agreed. "We are going to have the most fantastic life together, Mrs Barraclough-to-be," he grinned, kissing her hand.

Celia appeared at the kitchen door, brandishing a note book.

"Here you go, dears: your wedding planning notebook. Just jot everything down in there," she nodded officiously, passing it over.

"It's okay, Mum, I already have a notebook," Alice said, dismissing it. Celia passed it to Elliot.

"You make notes then, dear, for me. *This* is the notebook we're using. Otherwise I'll get all confused," she waved a hand in the air, illustrating her scrambled brain.

Elliot accepted the book, nodding his thanks, biting down a smile as he glanced at Alice.

"We're only doing this the once, okay?" he insisted once they were out of earshot of the kitchen. Alice laughed quietly.

"Listen, you suggested a big wedding, you suggested wedding planners. I knew this is what it would be like and I did try to warn you. There's no going back now; they would never forgive us," she said with conviction, trying not to laugh at him.

As it was, they had a perfect day, meeting with Martin at the church: being given the grand tour of beautiful venues that they had only ever seen in passing: wandering hand in hand through the village, and finally, getting ready together for their engagement party.

"Can I look yet?" Elliot asked for the umpteenth time, sitting on the edge of the bed, with his hands over his eyes. He had been ready for a full twenty minutes before Alice and had been told to face the wall when, ten minutes later, Ellie came through to help her with her dress.

"In a minute!" they both exclaimed again, tutting.

Elliot dropped his hands, keeping his eyes shut and rearranged his tie. It was new, as was his shirt, and felt a little unfamiliar. He had been given strict instructions to wear a steel grey suit and Alice had presented him with the newly purchased silver grey shirt and ruby red tie. She and Ellie had spent Thursday shopping in Birmingham and they had been in high spirits over their finds. He was unsure about the colour of the tie – not his usual choice – but could see by the look in her eye, that she had planned it for a reason.

Guests had been arriving whilst they were getting ready and Elliot surmised, by the increased volume in chatter, that there was already a full house.

"Ready!" Ellie called, "but cover your eyes before you turn round."

Elliot did as he was asked, smiling at the shy, giggling noises they were making as they positioned themselves in front of him.

"Ta-da!" they sang in unison. He opened expectant eyes and caught his breath, completely taken aback by the vision in front of him.

"Oh … wow!" he breathed, his eyes lighting up. Ellie clapped her hands and did her customary little jig, pleased with his response. She did a twirl on the spot, showing off her ruby red, silk fringed, flapper dress. Above knee-length, the strappy, V-necked dress shimmied as she moved. She'd had her shoulder-length hair straightened; the lack of curls emphasising the ornate, diamanté headband that she was wearing across her forehead. The intricate, twisted band was finished off with a diamanté feather which was encrusted at its base with tiny pearls. An equally ornate diamanté band was sitting half way up her arm, above her elbow. Around her neck, she wore her silver, crescent moon and ruby stone necklace - her eighteenth birthday present from Elliot - and on her feet, silver, open-toed, high heels.

"Look, I'm as tall as Mum," she grinned.

Elliot stared at Alice, utterly spellbound. She was wearing a silver grey, heavily beaded, 1920's style dress, that hung from her effortlessly, showing off her curves. Sleeveless, it was cut low at the front with a plunging back, revealing her tanned skin down to the base of her spine. The scalloped edged hem sat just above her knee and the voile-like fabric floated as she moved. The Art Deco diamond design of the beadwork emphasised her waist and hips, with hundreds of silver beads shimmering like tiny stars when they caught the light. Her bobbed hair hung loosely around her neck and her natural waves left untouched by Ellie's straighteners. She too wore a diamanté hair band, although hers was less ornate that Ellie's so as not to detract from the dress, and it sat simply in her hair, rather than across her forehead. Around her neck, she wore her intertwined hearts necklace but opted for no other jewellry, wanting her stunning engagement ring to be centre stage. Flapper style, t-strapped, steel coloured, satin shoes with chunky, kitten heels, finished off her outfit. She was a picture of perfection.

Elliot got to his feet slowly, the pride and love he felt vividly etched on his face. Ellie linked arms with him and Alice, and turned towards the large mirror above the dressing table. They stared at their reflection, and Ellie nodded with delight.

"It works: we're completely co-ordinated. Dad, your tie matches my dress - and it's my birthstone colour - and your shirt matches Mum's dress. We are Team Barraclough, not doubt about it!" she declared, with a little cheer. Elliot beamed at his girls.

"Who planned this, then?" he asked.

"Mum, of course. I told you: queen of organisation," Ellie emphasised. "Shall I go down now and announce your arrival? Are you ready?" she asked.

"No," they replied simultaneously.

"We go down together, the three of us," Elliot said in a decisive tone. Alice nodded.

"Absolutely. This is your night too, Ellie," she smiled, kissing her cheek.

Andrew spotted them first as they came down the stairs, Ellie leading the way. He wolf-whistled and started to clap, swiftly being joined by Dan: their raucous behaviour signalling for everybody else to turn and watch the trio's progress, and join in with the applause. Once at the foot of the stairs, Elliot gave an elaborate bow and held his hands out to show off his fiancée and daughter, who both gave a curtsey. Alice blushed but Ellie lapped up the attention, playing to her audience. Relatives crowded forwards, with outstretched arms and hands, in a bid to physically convey their congratulations to the happy couple, and it was a while before they could make their way across the hall to the lounge.

Celia and Roz had surpassed themselves. The lounge had been transformed and was filled with pink, white, and silver, heart-shaped balloons: banners that were stretched across the walls, with the words, 'congratulations on your engagement', emblazoned across them, and strings of silver, filigree heart-shaped fairy lights which were draped across furniture and suspended from the curtain rails. Beautiful bouquets of freshly cut flowers, in shades of pink, red, and cream, were dotted around the room and the air was filled with the scent of old roses, sweet peas, and stock.

A table had been placed in front of the window: on it, a large, heart-shaped, engagement cake alongside a laden, six-tiered cupcake stand. The cake, made up of two hearts joined together, was covered in pale pink icing, with intricate piping work around the edges in a deep red colour. The inscription, in the same colour, read, 'Congratulations on your Engagement', on one heart and on the other, 'Alice & Elliot, together forever'. Cute, edible, sugar hearts on wires were bunched together in the top corners of the cake, their colours matching the balloons that filled the room - pink, white, and silver. A deep red ribbon running around the sides of the cake, added the finishing touch. The tiered cake stand was piled with freshly baked cupcakes, sitting in white, lace effect cases and topped with bold swirls of buttercream, in either pink, deep red or cream. Each one had a scattering of dainty, edible pearls, silver stars or red hearts. The cake topper figurines, hand-crafted from modelling paste by Alice's aunt Lucy, were a remarkable likeness of them. The man, dressed in a navy suit, with black hair and blue eyes, was down on one knee and holding his hand out with a tiny box in it, to a woman. She was wearing a pink, 50's style dress, with dark brown, bobbed hair and equally brown eyes.

Rose petals were scattered across the white, linen tablecloth and the base of the cake stand. To the side of the cake were three photos, in silver frames. One was of Elliot, aged five, beaming with a toothy smile for the camera. There was a similar one of Alice, also aged five, portraying a more shy demeanour, and the third photo, was a copy of the one that Laura had given Alice, taken at her wedding to Andrew. The whole scene was enchanting and brought Alice close to tears as she took it all in. Celia and Roz looked pleased as they silently watched her reaction, each clutching a jug of their signature Pimms cocktail. Elliot appeared at their side and gently took Roz's arm.

"Can I borrow you for a second?" he asked, giving a sympathetic smile as she tensed up, knowing what was about to happen. She handed her jug to Celia, nodding, and clearing her throat. Celia watched them walk towards Sheila and John and for once, she was in no rush to be by her sister's side. It was Roz's turn to face up to things, she thought, depositing the drink on a large, side table stacked with glasses, and busied herself with her guests.

John put his arms out to embrace Roz and Elliot noticed how his eyes conveyed a deep sadness.

"Hello, Roz. Lovely to meet you," he said with a quiet voice, unaware of how he sounded so like his brother. Roz hugged him back, trying to keep a grip on her emotions. Her trembling body betrayed her and didn't go unnoticed. She glanced nervously at Sheila, not sure how to greet her but she needn't have worried: Sheila also offered her a hug and echoed her husband's words in greeting. John drew breath to speak but Sheila beat him to it, her smile fading.

"I should hate you for how you treated our Elliot," she started, with a crack in her voice. John put his hand on her arm but she shook her head, defying him to stop her. He dropped his hand.

"I should but I don't," she continued, her blue eyes considering Roz with a degree of coldness but also, of pity.

"We've heard all about it: how you were threatened by John's father and how you …" she paused, lowering her voice, "how you were driven to such drastic actions. I think you've been punished enough and so, I am prepared to put my feelings aside and focus on the future, for the sake of Elliot and Alice. You'll have to forgive me though, if it takes a while. You have no idea, I think, of the damage you did. To Elliot. And to David," she said.

"Sheila," John interrupted, "that's enough." It was a command and yet, his tone was gentle and full of compassion for his wife's feelings.

Roz blinked. She was unaccustomed to being spoken to so forthrightly: she had clearly met her match. A small part of her was bristling with indignation but she saw sense and didn't rise to it. Instead, she lowered her eyes and nodded meekly. Sheila sighed, almost disappointed at Roz's subservience.

"I wonder," John ventured, "if you wouldn't mind fetching us a drink please, Sheila?" he asked. Knowing she was being dismissed, albeit ever so tactfully, she concurred and turned smartly on her heel. Spying Celia on the other side of the room, she made a beeline for her.

John indicated for Roz to sit next to him and Elliot followed suit. John was clutching a brown, A5 envelope, which he slowly patted on his knee as he deliberated over his choice of words. He smiled kindly at Roz, noting the trepidation and pain hanging heavily in her eyes.

"David told me about you, shortly after you had met. He was a changed man: so happy and full of laughter, full of life. It was evident that something major had occurred and when I quizzed him on it, he took me into his confidence. Naturally, I was shocked at first but any fool could see that his marriage to Patricia was a total farce. He didn't tell me your name or anything about you. He said it was best if I didn't know, and all he was prepared to tell me was that he loved you 'beyond all reason'. Those were his exact words: 'I love her beyond all reason'."

A wistful smile crossed his face as he recalled his brother's confession. Momentarily lost in his own reverie, he didn't notice Roz's distress at his words but Elliot did. He took hold of her hand and squeezed it, in a bid to comfort her. John continued,

"When I returned to Brockenhurst in the summer of '69, with my new bride, he was a shadow of his former self. I have to say, I was shocked by it. He looked broken. Not knowing how to approach him, I turned to my father instead and asked if he knew what had happened to David. He said no, he had no idea. So, I approached David. We went for a drink, or two, and he broke down. He told me that Linda - that was the first time I had heard your name - had left him. Without any explanation. And then, as quickly as he caved in, he regained his composure and said, it was understandable: it was an impossible situation at the time."

"That's what he said to me, too," Elliot interjected. John turned to Roz.

"You have to understand; my father was a bit of a tyrant. Very old school. We lived by his rules and his word was always to be abided by. I was too scared to ever question it and in a way, I didn't really consider how much of a tyrant he was, or how manipulative he could be, until after his death. That's when I discovered an awful truth and it rocked me to the core, if I'm honest," he nodded, his eyes filling with tears which he swiftly wiped away with a handkerchief. Elliot's brow furrowed in confusion as he waited for his father to continue. He had no idea what he was talking about.

"Dad?" he questioned, "what's happened?"

John patted the envelope once more, taking in a deep breath.

"As David had already passed on, it was down to me to be the executor of my father's estate. There wasn't much to do, he was very organised and thorough. But I did discover one box of paperwork that had clearly been left untouched for many years and hidden away at the back of a filing cabinet. In it, a pile of letters - communication - from a private investigator. It appears that he had been employed by my father, at some point. Well, 1968 to be precise." He looked pointedly at Roz; her defeated expression telling him that she knew exactly what he was referring to. He handed her the envelope.

"I think these should belong to you," he said, his tone heavy with remorse at what had been done. Roz's eyes flew up to his in horror. She vehemently shook her head.

"No! I don't want to see his poisonous letters!" she choked, pushing his hand away that was clutching the envelope. John was mortified at her reaction.

"Oh, my dear, I wouldn't dream of giving you anything so awful. Absolutely not," he assured her. He offered her the envelope again.

"Please. Take it," then hesitating, he spoke to Elliot, "is there somewhere more private, perhaps?"

Elliot led the way into the hall and through to the study. He shut the door firmly behind them. Roz sat down at the desk and tentatively accepted the envelope. John gave her an apologetic smile, knowing what was about to come. She was expecting letters of some description but what she found instead was a bunch of black and white photographs, secured together with a wide, elastic band. Instantly recognising them, she dropped them on the desk as if they had burnt her hand, and proceeded to stare at the top photo, unable to touch it. Elliot looked over her shoulder.

"Oh, good grief!" he uttered. "May I?"

He picked up the pile and removing the band, flicked through them. The photos were very stylised; depicting an era long gone, they were candid shots of the two lovers embracing, laughing, smiling at each other in such an intimate way and kissing passionately. The snapshots had predominately been captured by the sea, and Elliot recognised the harbour in the background, as Newlyn. What struck him the most, was the likeness between David and himself. Also, the breath-taking beauty of Roz, as a young woman, and the way in which David looked at her with absolute devotion. She had long, ash-blonde hair with a wispy fringe that partially masked her clear, oval eyes. Her skin was flawless and her wide, generous mouth carried an irresistible smile in every picture. Their love for each other was unmistakable and it made Elliot's chest ache to think what they had both gone through, at the hands of his grandfather. He pulled up a chair next to Roz and placed the pile in front of her, resting his hand over them.

"It's okay, Roz. I know these caused you untold pain years ago, but ironically, my grandfather did you a favour, in a twisted kind of way. These photos are incredible! Nobody gets photos of themselves like this; they tell such a genuine story. There's nothing false or posed about the looks between you two and yes, it's an intrusion but it has captured the essence of you, of your souls, for eternity. You have something to show Isabelle now and trust me, she'll be able to see for herself how in love her parents were." His tone was soft and persuasive, wanting to convince her that it was alright to confront the past. The shock of seeing David was a punishing one but the wonder of what the photos truly revealed was compelling and Elliot knew that, eventually, Roz would draw comfort from them. And maybe some kind of closure.

"When you're ready, there's no rush," John said, resting his hand on her shoulder. Roz turned to look at him, with a thin smile. She felt young and vulnerable once more; just seeing a glimpse of David immortalised in black and white, hastily transported her back to her teenage years. She so desperately wanted to pick up the photos and lose herself in them but was, at the same time, afraid of what she may find. Torment and heartache, or a chance to vividly relive a time in her life that she treasured with all her being? Her eyes lingered on the pile in front of her, weighing up the odds.

"Maybe later," she murmured, nodding at Elliot as he slid them back into the envelope and opening the top drawer, placed it carefully on top of the paperwork in there.

"Thank you, John," she said, voicing her gratitude. "I'm so sorry," she added, not knowing where to start with her explanation of what had occurred all those years ago. John held up his hand.

"Roz: no apologies, not now. Elliot and Celia told us, in great detail, exactly what happened. I know Sheila was curt earlier but she's a mother and Elliot is her baby, her youngest son. Give her time to come to terms with it all, eh?" he said, without a trace of accusation or malice.

"I think she is beyond livid with my father," he continued, "having heard what he did but he's not here to vent on, so she is feeling very frustrated about it." He wasn't making excuses, he could fully understand his wife's feelings; they were not that dissimilar to his own.

"What happened to … David's wife?" she asked, not able to bring herself to say her name out loud.
Elliot snorted, shaking his head.

"Well, David provided for her in his will, financially, but the bulk of his estate was left to me. It was a total shock, to be honest, but I think he was making sure I would be provided for too if I didn't quite make it back on to the straight and narrow," he confessed. "She disappeared straight after his funeral, without even saying goodbye to the family."

They fell silent, each lost in their own thoughts. Elliot broke the silence.

"I'll never forget his face - grandfather's - at David's funeral. He should've been heartbroken at burying his son. It's not something you expect to do: outlive your children. Dad was in a wheelchair, still rehabilitating after his stroke, and my grandfather stood behind him, watching David's coffin being lowered into the ground, with such a vitriolic look on his face. As if his sons had proved him right; they had both failed at life. One by having a life-changing stroke at the age of fifty-seven and the other by dying, long before his time. I have never known such a bitter, cold-hearted man. Sorry, Dad," he apologised quickly, realising the harshness of his words.

"Oh, no need to apologise, Elliot. You are absolutely right. He lied, he manipulated, he cheated on my mother. Many times," he confided. Roz looked horrified and noticing it, John nodded slowly.

"Yes. He was a serial adulterer. And an absolute hypocrite. Of course, I didn't know this at the time but Mother confided in me after David's funeral. She was broken hearted. She said her boys were the only good thing in her life; a life of being trapped in a marriage to someone she hated." He stopped abruptly, not trusting himself to speak any further. Elliot swore under his breath, putting an arm around John's shoulders. He and Roz looked at each other in shock, bowled over as yet another secret was revealed, the connotations of which were immense.

"Come on, you two: let's re-join the party and celebrate the future. Let's forget about him, he doesn't deserve our time. My fiancée and daughter need me - need us - to celebrate with them," Elliot said, heading for the door.

"There you are!" Dan exclaimed, spotting them as they emerged from the study. "We've been looking everywhere for you; it's cake cutting time," he grinned.

Everybody had gathered in the lounge, crowding round the table. Elliot and Alice stood behind it, waiting patiently as Celia and Sheila made sure that all the guests had a drink in their hand. Elliot winked at his mother, acknowledging how she had stepped in to help. He held up a hand for hush.

"Thank you all for coming. The night is young and there is plenty of food and drink, thanks to Celia and Roz. And when I say, 'plenty', I do mean, plenty," he paused as knowing laughter erupted across the room. Celia shook her head with embarrassment, blushing at his teasing.

"Before my beautiful, amazing, adorable fiancée and I cut the cake," he grinned as Alice followed her mother's example by turning a crimson colour, "I would just like to say a few words. I know you have probably all found out, in dribs and drabs, the story behind me and Alice. I have always loved this woman, always. It was always my plan to marry her but fate dealt us a blow and we parted. Until three weeks ago, when Ellie turned eighteen. Ellie," he beckoned her over to his side and held her hand as he continued,

"I cannot express how proud I am to be this wonderful young lady's father. And how proud I am of Alice for raising her, nurturing her and guiding her through life. I missed out but I don't dwell on that; my mind is firmly fixed on the future, on the day I marry this incredible woman," he said, taking Alice's hand and raising it in the air. "And with that in mind, I would like to invite you all to be there, on December the nineteenth," he grinned as a cheer went up, instigated by Dan and Andrew.

"It's going to be a winter wedding but I have to stress, despite that, we have opted *not* to have a 'Frozen' themed one. Sorry girls," he laughed as Ellie, Rachel, Natalie, and Amber groaned their disappointment.

"And before I finish: it's not very conventional, our wedding, so in that vein … I'd like to ask James *and* Dan, to both be my Best Man. I wouldn't want to do this without you two, by my side."

He laughed as James and Dan hugged each other and Dan started whooping. He made his way over to the table, making wind-up actions to Elliot, intimating he wanted to say something too.

"And, here he is - my brother - coming to steal the show," Elliot said, shaking his head in mock despair.

Dan held his glass in the air.

"I just want to say, James and I are so proud of you, Elliot. You are the best kid brother in the world and we know how much you love Alice and how long you have waited for this day to happen. You two are perfect together; you belong together, and I know you will make each other happy for the rest of your lives. So, without further ado, please … raise your glasses to the future Mr and Mrs Elliot Barraclough," he shouted triumphantly.

Everybody chorused,

"Mr and Mrs Elliot Barraclough!"

"Now, cut the damn cake and let's all eat, drink and be merry," he ordered, amid boisterous applause.

The celebrations carried on long into the night and it was twenty to two in the morning by the time Celia shut the door on the last guests. She slumped into her armchair, leaning her head back and letting out an exhausted sigh. Elliot stuck his head round the lounge door.

"There's a fresh pot of tea: would you like a cup?" he asked.

"Yes please, dear," she nodded wearily. "Tell Alice and Laura to leave everything; I'll clear it up in the morning," she said, waving her hand in the general direction of the kitchen.

"Too late, it's almost all done now," he told her, smiling. "What are we going to do with the sleeping beauties over there?" he asked, looking across at the sofa on the far side of the room, where Andrew and Dan were sprawled, in a deep, drunken sleep.

Celia shook her head fondly at the sight of them.

"Just leave them to it, dear. It won't be the first time that they wake up together in the morning, wondering what on earth happened the night before," she laughed. "It's not that often that they get to let their hair down but when they do, they certainly go to town with it. Where are Ellie and Rachel?" she asked, suddenly aware that she hadn't seen them for a while. Elliot raised his eyebrows, giving her a knowing look.

"Laura helped them to bed. They over-did the Disaronno. Just a little," he smiled.

"Oh dear, are they alright?". She looked concerned. Elliot nodded his head.

"Don't worry, they're fine. They'll feel it in the morning, mind you but that's all part of growing up, isn't it; being eighteen and 'allowed' to drink."

Celia regarded him thoughtfully for a moment.

"I don't really know what Andrew and Alice were like at eighteen. They'd both left home so I missed all that," she said, her quiet tone full of regret. "What was she like,

Elliot?" she asked. Surprised by her question, he perched on the arm of her chair.

"She was perfect. Beautiful, funny, clever, and not too wild," he laughed. "We had the best time, being students. I didn't want it to ever end." His voice trailed off, suddenly aware of who he was talking to. Celia patted his knee.

"I wish … I wish I had known about you. About the two of you. If she had told me that she was in a relationship, I could have stopped worrying about her. I worried about her so much; you hear such awful stories about students getting drunk, walking home alone and being attacked," she sighed heavily. "If I had known that she was with you, I could've slept easier. And I could have understood more about what was going on when Roz suddenly announced that she was pregnant. My baby girl: pregnant! And without ever having had a boyfriend - or so I thought - it made no sense to me. No sense at all." She looked up at Elliot, a strained, tired smile on her face. "We did a terrible thing to you, Elliot. I thought you were some sort of Casanova. I did you such an injustice."

They stared at each other in silence. Elliot was aching to agree: to argue his case, but he was tired of doing so. Enough had been said.

"Look, I have been over it a million times in my head in the past week and the bottom line is, we all got it wrong. One way or another," he said. He stood up and headed for the door.

"Time to move on. That's all we can do. Move on and make the most of the future."

He paused in the doorway, concerned by how deflated and frail Celia appeared. He could sense she was missing

Reggie more than anything at that moment. It had been a day of celebration, a day of love, and now that it was over, she had no-one to share the night with. Elliot was acutely aware that he, on the other hand, would walk into the kitchen straight into the willing arms of Alice. They would then fall into bed together, exhausted by the day yet united in love, and drift off in each other's arms. Fate had reversed the tables and he couldn't help but feel a pang of guilt at being so incredibly grateful for it.

"I'll get you that tea," he said, hating how trite he sounded but not knowing what else to say.

Chapter Eighteen

"How are they?" Elliot asked Alice when she came downstairs the following morning. He was sitting at the kitchen table with Andrew and Dan; three mugs of tea, two of which as yet untouched, in front of them. She stopped behind Elliot's chair, wrapped her arms around his neck and kissed his head.

"The girls are fine," she smiled. "In better shape than these two," she teased. Andrew was barely supporting his head with his hand, his elbow resting heavily on the table, and Dan was leaning back in his chair with his eyes closed.

"Hey!" Andrew complained, "we're in fine shape, thank you very much."

Dan grunted his agreement, opening one eye to look at her. She laughed, reaching over and ruffling her brother's hair, knowing how much it annoyed him.

"Will Ellie be fit for travelling today?" Elliot wanted to know, keen to get going on their trip across Europe.

"Yes, she can sleep in the car if she's feeling rough," she said, pouring herself a mug of tea.

"Where's Mum? And Roz?" she wondered.

"Mum's gone to church," Andrew said, "and Roz is in the study."

"Church? After last night?"

She was sometimes surprised by her mother's devotion to the church and reluctance to sway from her routine. Elliot was not so surprised.

"Maybe it's her way of being close to your Dad," he suggested, remembering the lost look on her face in the early hours.

"Maybe," she agreed, knowing he was right. She always felt close to her dad in the church, so it would figure that Celia also found great comfort there. She patted Andrew's shoulder.

"Laura's in the shower and she says, make sure Scott and Riley have some breakfast before they go out to play."

"Ah," he grimaced, pointing at the open kitchen door. "Too late, sorry."

"Andrew!" she scolded. "What are you like?" she sighed with exasperation and sticking her head out of the door, called the boys in. They were kicking a football about, in their bare feet, shouting heatedly at each other as they practiced their tackling skills.

"Dad's getting your breakfast, boys," she called, chuckling at Andrew's dismayed face. Pouring a second mug of tea, she headed for the study and tentatively knocked on the door before opening it.

"Can I come in?" she asked, spying Roz at the desk. She nodded, smiling at her. Alice astutely noticed the sadness lurking in her eyes, and the pile of photographs that had been spread across the desk.

"Tea," she announced, placing the mugs on the desk and pulling up a chair. She glanced at the photographs, not wanting to pry but desperately curious to see them.

"Okay?" she asked. "Elliot told me about them," she nodded towards the pile. "Have you … have you looked at them yet?"

Roz sighed and gave a reflective laugh.

"Yes. I have. And he was right: they are wonderful photos of us. I had forgotten … no, not forgotten exactly, more … not allowed myself to dwell on, how happy we were together."

She gathered them up and handed them to Alice.

"Talk me through them?" Alice prompted. Roz's eyes widened, uncertain of her request.

"Please," she encouraged.

They sat side by side, pouring over the images as Roz relayed events, places, memories evoked; all the while, her smile getting broader. She pulled one photo from the pile and held it up, staring at it intently, her mind leaping back four decades. They were on a rugged stretch of beach, in a cove strewn with angry looking rocks and very little sand. It had a menacing yet beautiful air about it. David was sitting propped up against a large slab of stone, close to the water's edge, that had been smoothed by the relentless tide. He was staring out to sea and Roz was lying with her head resting on his lap, her gaze following his. He had his arm draped across her chest, holding her securely against him. They looked so peaceful, contented; a stark contrast to the ominous clouds looming overhead.

"This was Lamorna Cove; a little patch of Heaven. I had no idea we were followed. There was nobody there!" She shook her head, trying to fathom the depths of cunning that had resulted in that photograph.

"We spent a weekend there, in a little cottage. Away from our usual place. David wanted me to paint him but the weather wasn't on our side. As you can see," she said, pointing to the sky. "So, we spent most of the weekend tucked up in our little, stone retreat," she smiled at the memory. "We didn't mind being stuck indoors. As it turns out, it was a perfect, perfect weekend." A wistful look crossed her face and Alice could see she wanted to say more but held back.

"They all were. Perfect." She put the photo back on the desk and tapped it with her finger.

"I'm going to put most of these in an album but also frame some of them. I'd like to see them every day. We deserve to be remembered, like this," she said, straightening her back with determination. Her eyes shone brightly as she looked at Alice.

"Thank you, Alice. For pushing, for prying, for persisting." She hugged her tightly and kissed her cheek, whispering her thanks again.

"Are you going to be okay tomorrow? I'm sorry that I won't be here for you," Alice said, standing up. Roz shook her head.

"Don't worry about me; I'll be fine. Celia will be there with me. You go and enjoy your time with Elliot and Ellie; before you know it, it'll be Christmas and wedding fever!" she laughed, sniffing away errant tears. She also stood up and they embraced again. Alice could sense Roz's sadness ebbing away and being replaced by a new, positive energy. She felt relieved and happier to go away, leaving her mother and aunt to it, knowing that they were looking forwards and not backwards any longer.

Three hours later, they were ready to set off for Calais. Dan had gone back home and Andrew had gone back to bed, leaving Celia, Roz, Laura and the boys to wave them off and then enjoy a peaceful afternoon together.

"I just want to stop off and see my dad before we hit the road," Elliot said, pulling the car into his parents drive. Ten minutes later, satisfied with his father's lifted mood, they settled back into their seats as Elliot reversed onto the road. Sheila and John waved from the gate until they were out of sight. Elliot smiled triumphantly at Alice and Ellie.

"Right, here we go: our first family holiday," he said. Ellie nodded happily, waving a handful of twenty pound notes in the air.

"And look what my new grandparents just gave me! Two hundred pounds spending money!" she chortled. Alice turned to her, her mouth dropping open in disbelief.

"What?" She turned to Elliot, about to protest but he shook his head.

"Let them enjoy their moment. They are over the moon to have a 'new' grandchild," he said, his tone gentle yet firm.

"I could get used to this!" Ellie's excited voice highlighted Alice's fears, and she tried to convey as much with the urgent look she bestowed on Elliot. He was having none of it, pointedly not looking at her but his smile told her he knew exactly what she was thinking.

"Just let her enjoy it, Alice," he insisted quietly, flicking on the cd player.

"What's this?" Ellie asked, frowning as she failed to recognise it.

"Eighteen til I Die," her parents replied, in unison, spontaneously reaching for each other's hand. Elliot lifted her hand to his lips and taking his eyes from the road for a brief moment, gave her look of indisputable adoration.

"Here we go," he said.

"Here we go," she agreed, her grin matching his. She looked out of the window, watching trees flash past her and disappear as the car picked up speed, leaving the New Forest behind them. And with it, they left behind the years of pain and regret, confusion and doubt. The sun beat down on the road ahead, heralding a new beginning, and she was more than ready for it.

"Ready?" Celia asked, motivating Roz to move from her seat as the train pulled in to Waterloo station.

"Ready as I'll ever be," she replied with a nervous laugh, smoothing down her stone coloured, linen trousers.

"Are you sure I look alright?" she quizzed Celia again. Celia reached across and straightened the neckline of Roz's pale blue and white, polka dot, gypsy-style blouse. The soft, viscose fabric flattered her figure and the colour accentuated her eyes. Eyes that widened with apprehension as she gingerly stepped from the carriage onto the platform.

"Got everything?" Celia prompted, alighting next to her. Roz patted her large handbag, nodding.

"Photos. Glasses. Tissues," she confirmed. They stared at each other, frozen to the spot; no words were necessary to convey their feelings at that moment. Monday morning commuters surged past them, hot-footing off the platform to break from the crowd, only to be swallowed up by a swirl of suits with disposable coffee cups, heading for the next stage of their daily journey. Needing to take control of the situation, Celia took Roz's arm and guided her towards the barriers and one of the many exits from the vast station, asking a guard on the way for directions to the Southbank Centre.

Pushing the door open, Celia paused at the top of the steps leading out onto the pavement, mesmerised by the wall.

"What is it?" Roz asked, concerned, glancing apologetically at the people behind them who were having to slow their descent to avoid bumping into them. Celia pointed to what had captured her attention; her eyes scanned the list of names on the Roll of Honour plaques occupying wall space on either side of the steps.

"Green and Moore: look," she said, squinting, "or is that ... no, it's Moores. Not one of ours then, and the Green is without an 'e'. Oh well," she waved a dismissive hand, catching Roz's exasperated expression.

"Really? Really, Celia?" she chided, shaking her head. "A time and place," she muttered, unsteadily tackling the worn, stone steps. Her legs were threatening to give way as nerves engulfed her. Celia caught up with her, taking her arm yet again.

"Sorry, Roz," she mumbled, silently cursing herself for being so thoughtless. Her mind always flitted when she was anxious: a defence mechanism since childhood, when faced with any type of confrontation.

They hesitated at the crossing, unsure of which way to go. People were rushing in all directions, so it wasn't a simple case of following the crowds. Roz tried to make eye contact with pedestrians, to ask directions, but heads were either bent or focused on a spot in the distance. Cars drove erratically, with horns sounding as angry as the drivers' faces. The air was heavy with the smell of hot tarmac and exhaust fumes, and the frantic sounds of city life. It was almost too much, too overwhelming; she was close to tears, when Celia suddenly exclaimed,

"Look! Southbank." She pointed to a sign, partially obscured by the crowds.

Hurrying along, they soon reached the steps leading up to the Southbank centre and it wasn't until she was nearing the top that Celia realised she was walking alone. Roz was way behind, clutching onto the handrail, her face ashen. Celia quickly back-tracked and put a comforting arm around her sister's shoulders.

"Alright? There's no rush, we're here in plenty of time. Shall we stop somewhere for a minute?" she asked, looking round at the various coffee shops and restaurants. Roz shook her head abruptly.

"Just give me a minute, I'll be fine," she nodded, trying to convince herself more than anything.

They stopped at the top of the steps, by the large, bronze, bust of Nelson Mandela, giving Roz a moment to quell her shaking nerves. Celia looked at her watch, smiling encouragement.

"We've got twenty minutes before we're meeting him. Shall we go and find a seat and catch our breath: give you time to calm down a little? We said to meet him just outside, round the front of the Festival Hall, didn't we?" she asked, making a move once again; this time, more slowly.

The front of the building overlooked the River Thames, and the London Eye loomed up on the left, behind the Golden Jubilee Bridge. The paved area directly outside the Hall was packed with tables, chairs and a sea of parasols.

They picked a spot near the entrance, under the shade of one of the large, grey parasols: a wise choice, as the mid-morning sun was already hotting up. Celia went in search of tea and returned moments later, with tea for two and some cake.

"I chose carrot; I hope that's alright with you? Their fruit cake didn't look that inspiring," she said in a hushed tone, not wishing to offend anybody that happened to be listening.

"You mean, it wasn't as good as yours," Roz smiled, knowing exactly how her sister's mind worked. She was always reluctant to pay for anything that she thought she could have made a better job of herself. Baking cakes was Celia's forte whereas Roz had never found the inclination or time to be that creative in the kitchen. She preferred to create works of art on canvas, not on a cake stand.

They stirred their tea, both staring out across at the Embankment, which was prettily framed by large, London Plane trees in full leaf.

"Roz," Celia's whispered voice was urgent and she indicated with her eyes to a figure behind Roz. A tall, dark-haired, young man approached them: a wide, quizzical smile on his face.

"Roz? Celia?" he asked. They both nodded, recognising Conrad from his Facebook photos. Celia stood up and tentatively offered her hand to shake his. He took it, laughing awkwardly and then moving towards her, held his arms out, saying,

"I think a hug is more in order, don't you?"
Celia reciprocated his laugh and hugged him.

"I'm Celia, your great aunt. And this is Roz," she gestured, willing Roz to her feet, "your grandmother." Her voice wavered for just a second but she maintained her smile, taking a moment to look at him more closely. He bore such a striking resemblance to Elliot and Dan and yet, she could see he had some of Roz's features too: her nose, in particular. And her mouth. Dressed in baggy jeans, a fitted, black t-shirt and worn, black, canvas baseball boots, he was the epitome of a typical student. He wore his black hair short, and gelled up at the front. White, in-ear headphones hung round his neck and a small, grey, backpack was slung across one shoulder.

Roz got unsteadily to her feet, holding on to the table as she tried to compose herself. Noticing what an effort it was for her, Conrad's face softened and he moved in to hug her.

"Hello," he said, his tone gentle. "It's so lovely to meet you."

Their eyes met, mirroring each other's struggle to contain themselves. Roz drew in a shaky breath, smiling at him.

"It's lovely to meet you too, Conrad," she replied, sitting back down, prompting him to sit next to her. Celia remained standing.

"Would you like some tea, dear?" she offered, fetching her purse from her bag.

"Umm, coffee please. Black, one sugar. Thank you," he beamed. Celia doubted there was a single bad bone in his body; his whole demeanour was that of a well-mannered, grounded young man. Yet he had a carefree air about him, which reminded her of Roz at that age: excited by life and its endless possibilities. She noted his paint-stained finger nails, and flecks of paint on his forearms that had been overlooked in the shower.

Conrad looked earnestly at Roz, giving her his full attention.

"Thank you for coming to meet me," he started. "You have no idea what this means …" his voice faltered and he laughed lightly at his words. "Of course you do, I'm sorry. It's just that … Mum has been looking for you for so many years now," he stared at her, searching her face for answers to his unvoiced questions.

"Where do we start?" he asked. Roz reached for her bag.

"I'm not sure, Conrad. I suppose, we could start with me? I know a little about you from Ellie," she said.

"Ah, Ellie!" he interrupted, grinning. "I reckon we'd get on like a house on fire. Have I got any other cousins?" he asked, his eyes lighting up as she nodded.

"Yes, you do. David - your grandfather - had a brother, John. John has three children, and my sister, Celia, has two. Between them, John and Celia have nine grandchildren. Ellie is one of them. Her father is David's nephew, Elliot."

Conrad nodded.

"Yes, she told me. It took a while to get my head round it all. So, her father is my grandfather's nephew, and her mother is my grandmother's niece. Your niece?"
He raised quizzical eyebrows, wanting confirmation that he'd got it right, a cheeky smile playing on his lips. Roz nodded, with a sheepish look.

"Yes. We thought we'd keep it in the family," she joked, warming quickly to his sense of humour and acceptance of the situation. He patted her hand as he laughed. They watched each other for a moment, pausing the conversation as Celia arrived back at the table with his coffee.

"Thanks so much," he smiled, "that's great."
Roz pulled an envelope out of her bag and passed it to Conrad.

"I have some photos for you. For ... for your mother." She licked her lips nervously. "I was given these two days ago, and printed off some copies for you. It's a long story," she said, shaking her head.

"That's okay. I've got all day. If you have?" He sat back in his chair, watching her. Roz blinked, unsure where to start. It had been a secret for so many years and here she was, expected to talk about it to a complete stranger. Except, he wasn't a stranger, she reminded herself. Just one look told her that he was a Barraclough. She opened the envelope that he had left untouched in front of him, and spread the photos out.

"This is David. And me. We were in love, many years ago," she started. Conrad picked up the nearest photo and studied it closely. He could instantly see the family resemblance. He smiled at her.

"And he was older than you? Married?" he asked. Roz sensed he already knew the answer so she just nodded.

"It's not as sordid as it seems," Celia chipped in, feeling the need to defend Roz's honour. Conrad looked surprised.

"Oh no, I didn't mean to imply that at all. Please don't think I did," he said, turning to Roz, "it's just that Mum and I have read so many stories about adopted children, during our search for you, and they were mostly as a result of affairs or similar situations. I'm not judging you, in any way," he said sincerely.

"What about your mother?" Roz asked boldly, "does she judge me?" She tried to keep a steady focus on his face, not wanting to show the turmoil in her head. She needed to know yet dreaded the answer.

Conrad carefully replaced the photo onto the pile and considered her, his telling smile showing his embarrassment at her direct question.

"She doesn't judge you but she has struggled to come to terms with it all, yes. You've got to understand, she didn't know she was adopted until after Nan died. Mum was thirty-two. She was shocked, to put it mildly. She was pregnant with Lily - my little sister - and grieving for Nan. This was fourteen years ago, now. I was only six: I don't really remember much of it, other than my Nan's funeral, but apparently Mum fell out with Granddad for a while. She was so angry with him, for telling her but also, for not telling her sooner. He had wanted to, but Nan was scared of losing her, so they put it off."

He took a sip of his coffee, looking at them both, debating whether to continue with his train of thought. He opted to do just that.

"Mum set about trying to find her birth parents immediately. She managed to get a copy of her birth certificate, with your name on," he nodded at Roz, "and she realised then, that you were unmarried. I don't ever think she felt resentful but she did go through a stage of feeling abandoned. She told me this on her fortieth birthday, so I must've been fourteen then. She had a massive ... crisis, I suppose. A realisation that life was passing her by and she'd been carrying the knowledge of you for eight years, and not done much about it, more than get her birth certificate. You see, Lily was born shortly after Nan died, and Mum became quite depressed; I think it was all too much for her. So, she left it alone. Until she hit forty. We put an ad on the internet - the one Ellie found - but nothing came of it. I know she did try to find out more but she kept hitting brick walls, really. Personally, I think she was scared. She did tell me that she'd always felt like something was missing, like she wasn't complete. She'd put it down to being an only child but once she knew that she was adopted, it all seemed to make sense to her." Conrad paused, noticing how Roz reached for a tissue and discreetly blew her nose and dabbed her eyes.

"Okay?" he asked. Roz nodded.

"Anyway, Mum left it again. Life kind of rushes along, especially when you have a family to look after. But it was eating away at her. I didn't realise until a few years ago, that the reason we always went to Cornwall for our holidays was because she'd found out that's where she was born. We live there now; did Ellie tell you?" he asked.

"Yes, Newlyn; is that right?" Celia asked.

"That's right. She wanted to move to St Austell, her town of birth, but she fell in love with Newlyn and said she felt at home there," he looked at Roz when she gasped.

"What?" he wanted to know.

Roz couldn't speak for a moment. She tapped the table, trying to calm her shaking body. Finally, she found her voice again.

"Newlyn is where David and I used to go. We rented a flat there and went there as often as we could. We always had to hide at home but in Newlyn we could be ourselves," she smiled, indulging in the memory.

"How long were you together?" he asked tactfully.

"Just over four years."

He looked surprised.

"Four *years*? Sorry, I thought … I don't know, I thought it had been a short-term thing. Four years!" He looked at her in a new light and his eyes reflected the sorrow he suddenly felt.

"What happened? Can you tell me about him?" he asked, his tone apologising for prying.

"We fell in love. He was the most wonderful person, so kind and loving. He was a huge Elvis fan: always listening to his records. We used to dance, in our little room, with his portable record player in the corner. He loved reading too but his favourite thing was to watch me paint. He said it relaxed him and he felt closer to me somehow. He'd had a very unhappy life until he met me. We knew it was wrong, but for us, it was right. And Newlyn was our 'home' for four years. He loved the sea; he said he felt like he was free from all constraints when he was in Cornwall, with me." Roz looked at the photos on the table, her smile fading and her eyes looking troubled.

"And then his father found out. He had us followed. He threatened me. Several times. And then I found out I was pregnant, with your mum. So I …" She let out a shaky breath, not able to say the words but knew she had to. She had to be honest. She knew that whatever she told Conrad today, would be relayed to Isabelle, and Roz needed her to know the truth.

"So I left. I left my home and I left David. I was scared. Actually, I was terrified," she nodded. "David never knew. He never knew that I was pregnant or that our baby had been taken away for adoption. She was loved, you know. I loved her with all my heart, you must understand that. Handing her over was the worst thing I have ever had to do. They had to prise her from my arms; I begged them not to take her. I begged them! The panic that clawed through my chest hurt so much, I could hardly breathe. I lost everything. Everything." She started to cry quietly, turning to Celia when she handed her some tissues. She pleaded silently for her to carry on. Celia did so.

"Our father was the parish vicar and David was the village doctor. They would have both been destroyed by David's father. Roz left to save them, save their reputations. She tried to keep her baby but in those days, it was unheard of. She had no choice, Conrad. No choice."

Conrad reached across and rubbed Roz's arm, consoling her.

"I know you loved her," he said. Roz was puzzled. He continued,

"I had a long talk with Granddad, before I put the ad online. He told me that the baby - Mum - was crying when she was handed over to them and wouldn't stop. She cried for weeks, constantly. The doctor said she had colic but Granddad felt, in his heart, that she was missing her mum. He also said, on the day that they took her from the home, he could hear a woman wailing, absolutely broken hearted. It made the hair on the back of his neck, stand on end. It was the most spine-chilling sound, one he's never been able to forget. He felt it was wrong, what they were doing was wrong. All he could do was to love the baby like his own, and try to make her life perfect. He said he felt he owed it to the woman he heard crying that day. That *was* you, wasn't it?"

He didn't need an answer, he could see he was right. Roz buried her face in another tissue, unable to hold back her grief any longer.

"Does your mother know this? What you have just told us?" Celia asked anxiously.

"Yes. Yes, she does," he nodded. "She was going to come with me today but I thought it would be best if I met you both first. Break the ice, you know. I think this is going to be very painful for Mum. I know it is for you too but ..." He left his sentence hovering, unfinished, not knowing what to say next. He looked at Roz with concern as her body shook with each sob. He glanced at Celia, mouthing,

"is she alright?"

Celia frowned: they both knew the answer to that question. They sat silently, waiting for her to calm down and regain a shred of composure.

"I'm sorry, I'm sorry," Conrad muttered, feeling foolish at his keenness to impart what he knew. Roz sniffed repeatedly, wiping her nose with her sodden tissue.

"No, I'm sorry. You have done nothing wrong. It's still very raw, even after all these years," she told him.

"So, where is David now?" he asked cautiously, not wanting to cause further upset. Roz and Celia stared at each other.

"Didn't Ellie tell you?" Celia asked, stunned.

"No. Why?"

He looked from one to the other, his face dropping as he realised the truth.

"He died, sixteen years ago," Roz told him, with a heavy heart. Conrad hung his head.

"I suppose that's not the kind of news you tell over Facebook messenger," he said, "so I don't blame her for that."

They fell silent, neither one knowing what to say next. Celia desperately tried to think of a way to change the conversation.

"So, you're an Art student, here in London?" she prompted.

"Yes, I am. I'm at U.A.L., Camberwell college; It's not far from here, just a tube away. I love it. I did a Foundation diploma in Art and Design and now I'm doing a B.A. in Painting. It's obviously in the genes!" he laughed, lifting the mood.

"Sorry, what is U.A.L.?" Celia asked him.

"University of the Arts London," Roz and Conrad chorused, then smiled at each other, acknowledging their mutual interest.

A message alert sounded on his phone. Apologising, he pulled it from his pocket and looked at the screen. He let out a deflated sigh and pulled a face of frustration at his phone. He then looked behind him, squinting into the distance towards the Golden Jubilee Bridge.

"Is everything alright, dear?" Celia asked, noting his concerned expression. He looked at them both.

"Sorry, something's come up," he mumbled, a furtive look on his face. He stood up abruptly, looking round, searching the crowds.

"Do you need to leave?" Celia asked, in surprise. Conrad shook his head. He lightly touched Roz's shoulder.

"I'm sorry, I … this wasn't planned but …" He rubbed the back of his neck, looking nervous.

"What's the matter?" Roz frowned, an uneasy feeling engulfing her. A shadow fell across the table.

"Mum?"

Chapter Nineteen

Roz swung round, startled by the figure that appeared behind her. A choked gasp escaped her lips and she clutched a hand to her chest, her heart racing out of control. She didn't need a Facebook photo to know who it was; she knew it instinctively. She felt it to the very core of her being, that this was her daughter. A burning, prickly heat coursed through her body, smarting her eyes as they widened in shock.

"It is you, isn't it," Isabelle said. It wasn't a question: it was a statement. Roz nodded, watching her daughter's face crumple with relief, with happiness. Without hesitation, Roz quickly got to her feet and wrapped her arms around her, pulling her close to her chest. Isabelle responded, squeezing her tightly. They stood in each other's arms, tears cascading down their faces, neither one needing to speak. Conrad slowly sat down again, next to Celia, anxiously watching the pair of them as they wept. Their laboured breathing, as they tried to control the sobs that wracked their bodies, was the only sound they made for some time. Celia passed a tissue to Conrad, noticing how he sniffed repeatedly. He shot her a grateful look.

"Mum arrived in London last night. She wanted to be here for me, once my meeting with you two was over," he quietly explained to her. Celia looked at Isabelle, her heart aching at the sight of Roz holding her in such a maternal way. Their connection was deeply touching and so natural, so instinctive. It struck her how vulnerable and child-like

Isabelle seemed: her whole posture screamed of insecurity, begging for reassurance.

"Does she drink tea, or coffee?" Celia asked Conrad in a hushed voice, feeling the need to be useful.

"Tea, please. Do you need a hand?" he offered.

"No, dear, thank you. You stay here with them," she told him, disappearing once again to re-stock the tea tray. By the time she returned, a few minutes later, Roz and Isabelle hadn't moved but there was a comfortable stillness about them as their tears subsided. Eventually, they parted sufficiently enough to take a good look at one another. Isabelle smiled shyly at Roz, who was staring at her intently, taking in every detail of her face.

"I'm sorry, I couldn't wait," she said, turning to Conrad briefly. He shrugged, giving her a knowing smile. Celia could see how protective he was of her: the deep affection between them was heart-warming to observe. She did think, however, that Roz and Isabelle would need some time alone. She indicated for them to sit down as she passed round cups of tea and coffee.

"I picked up a selection of cakes and biscuits," she offered, then moved round to Isabelle, holding her arms out in greeting. She could feel how Isabelle's body shook as they embraced.

"Hello, dear. I'm Celia, your aunt," she smiled, knowing that introductions seemed superfluous but felt the need to carry on with them anyway. Isabelle smiled at her, appreciating the gesture. She blew her nose before taking the seat in between Roz and Conrad.

"I'm sorry if I startled you. I wasn't planning to come today but after Conrad left to meet you, I thought, this is ridiculous; I've been waiting for this day for so many years so, why am I putting it off?" She was softly spoken with a lilt in her voice that Roz recognised.

"Where did you grow up?" she asked, not able to take her eyes off Isabelle's face.

"Kenilworth. It's a town just outside Warwick. Do you know Warwick at all?" she replied, frowning slightly at Roz's reaction.

"Oh, my dear!" Celia exclaimed, looking from one to the other, stunned by the coincidence. Roz took hold of Isabelle's hand, cradling it in hers.

"I've lived in Stratford-upon-Avon since … since you were born. Just fourteen miles away from you," she croaked, trying not to cry again.

"But … not Cornwall, then?" she asked, trying to process the new information. Roz shook her head.

"Mum, listen," Conrad interjected, "I think there is so much for you two to talk about. If it's okay with you all, I suggest Auntie Celia and I," he grinned at his use of the word 'auntie', "take a wander down to the Tate Modern and give you some time alone. Yes?"

"I think that's a wonderful idea," Celia agreed, hurriedly finishing her cup of tea. Conrad stood up, resting his hand on his mother's shoulder for a moment.

"Okay, Mum?" He raised questioning eyebrows. She smiled meekly, nodding.

"Right then: have you ever been to the Tate Modern?" he asked Celia, grandly offering her his arm to link with hers.

"No, I haven't, dear," she enthused, accepting his arm. Their animated chatter slowly faded into the distance as they made their way alongside the Thames, with Conrad pointing out buildings of interest on both sides of the river.

Now that they were alone, Isabelle and Roz regarded each other in silence, their joy evident in their faces despite the hesitance and awkwardness they felt.

"There are so many things I want to ask you but I'm not sure where to start," Isabelle admitted. "I had a long list, all prepared in my head," she laughed lightly, "but that's just vanished!"

Roz picked up the envelope that Celia had hastily stuffed the photos back into when Isabelle had appeared at their table.

"Let me start then, by telling you about your father," she suggested gently. "I have some photographs for you."

They sat side by side, Isabelle completely engrossed by what Roz told her, as the story of her creation unfolded. Roz didn't flinch from detail, however painful or intimate; she needed Isabelle to understand how, and why, events took the course they did. She needed her to know that she was born out of an unequivocal love. This was the moment that she had been longing for, and the one person she had wanted to open her heart to and pour out its contents that had been harboured in secret for too long.

Isabelle stared off into the distance. Dazed, overwhelmed and spent from tears, she searched for adequate words to describe how she was feeling.

"I am so sorry. Sorry for everything that you went through, everything you endured." She squeezed Roz's hand as she spoke. "I feel so guilty now, knowing all of this," she said.

"Guilty? Why?" Roz was confused.

"I've had a good life. I've been loved and cared for: spoilt, really. Cherished, doted on. I knew no pain or heartache, until my mother died … I mean …" A fleeting embarrassment crossed her face.

"I know who you mean," Roz said gently, "and it's okay to talk about them - your parents - they raised you."

Isabelle drew in breath, determined not to cry again until she had finished what she wanted to say. Her quivering bottom lip betrayed her composure.

"Dad told me, the day after we buried her, that I was adopted. I was horrified! As if I hadn't endured enough pain already, he saw fit to pile on more hurt and confusion, when I was at my most vulnerable. I hated him for it. Hated how it made me feel. I was lost without my mother; I felt resentful that she had died when she did. I know it's part of grieving but I did feel so angry with her, for leaving me. I was pregnant with Lily and I needed her." The pain and grievance she had so keenly felt was written in her face, her eyes flashing with anger as she spoke. She grappled for the right words to continue.

"The loss I felt after she died was one thing, but it didn't even come close to the loss I felt when I found out that I was adopted. It confirmed my greatest fear; a recurring thought I'd had when I was growing up. I'd always felt lonely: not alone, just lonely. As if something was missing, a part of me was missing. I remember watching a programme about twins and how they have this fundamental connection; even if they were separated at birth, they could still sense each other. They felt incomplete without the other twin. And so, I asked my parents whether I had been a twin: had my twin died?

Obviously, they said no. I have thought, many times since then, that that would have been a good time to tell me about being adopted. I had, unwittingly, handed them the perfect opportunity to do so." She shook her head, her anger shifting into remorse. She met Roz's steady gaze.

"After I received my birth certificate, I dreaded finding out that I was an 'accident', a 'mistake' but deep down, I just knew that wasn't the case. It's as if I knew somebody was carrying me in their heart." Her voice broke and she paused to regain control. "I knew it was you. There was a kind of glow, an aura, about you. I texted Conrad to say I was here and for him to stand up so I could see where he was. And I saw you, before he'd even got to his feet. I just knew," she choked, unable to hold it in any longer. Roz held her close, stroking her hair, not caring that her own tears were left unchecked.

"What a pair we make!" she joked and they both laughed through their tears. They watched each other for a moment, both experiencing the same rise of euphoria, of relief, of feeling complete.

"Where do we go from here? What do we do next?" Isabelle asked, already planning in her head the logistics of getting their families together.

"Well, if my sister were here, she would most definitely say, 'have a cup of tea, dear. The rest will sort itself out'." They laughed as she fondly mimicked Celia's voice.

"Come back to Brockenhurst with us," Roz said earnestly. "You have a wonderful family there, that are desperate to meet you. David's family; they have been deprived of too much and it's time to rectify that." She waited expectantly for her answer, not wanting to let her go back to Cornwall so soon.

"Yes, okay. I'd love that," she nodded, with an excited, nervous laugh. "And then, perhaps you could come back with me to Newlyn? To meet your granddaughters. And Tom, my husband," she smiled, a vulnerability lurking in her eyes, fearing rejection. It swiftly disappeared when Roz nodded her head emphatically.

"Absolutely," she stated. "You are so much like David," she spontaneously added, her voice barely a whisper, marvelling at the resemblance. Isabelle gave a shy smile.

"That's how it should be, Mum," she responded, loving how it felt so right to be calling her that.

Three hours later, Roz, Isabelle and Celia were on the train back to the New Forest. Conrad had dashed across London to fetch Isabelle's suitcase from his flat in Camberwell, and escorted them back to Waterloo.

"Are you sure you can't come back with us, dear?" Celia repeated her offer. He shook his head with regret.

"Sorry, I can't. I'm working tonight and tomorrow lunch. It's a busy time of year and if I don't turn up for shifts, they'll just employ somebody else. Bar work is not the best job in the world but it suits me; I can fit it in around my Uni work. Plus, I get a discount on drinks," he winked at Celia. She smiled at his mischievous humour. They had spent a fun couple of hours together and she had really taken to him. He had a similar temperament to Dan; charming, over-confident and cheeky with it but with a sensitive side too. He hugged them all warmly and watched them go through the barriers when their train arrived.

"Goodbye ladies!" he shouted loudly and waved with exaggerated gusto, laughing when they turned to give him an embarrassed, polite wave, back. He gave them a cheesy grin and thumbs-up and then disappeared back into the crowd.

Celia checked her phone as soon as they took their seats. She didn't have Sheila's number - mobile or landline - so had to send a text to Dan, informing him of Isabelle's arrival later in the afternoon. Luckily, she had his number on her contacts list, courtesy of Andrew. She could imagine the flurry of excitement it had caused and had received several texts back, relaying dinner arrangements from Sheila and an offer of being met at the station by James. She smiled at her phone, feeling in high spirits. It had been a successful, if surprising, day and she was thrilled for Sheila and John's sake that Isabelle had agreed to meet them so soon. And she was over the moon at the reception Roz had received from both Conrad and Isabelle. It could have been so different; the potential was there for recriminations and lack of understanding or reluctance to build bridges. But as it turned out, they all came to the day with positivity and a desire to move forwards. Everything was coming together nicely.

Sheila and John were on the doorstep ready to greet them when they arrived later in the afternoon. They welcomed Isabelle with open arms, ushering her into their home. Sheila turned to Celia and squeezed her arm in silent thanks.

"This is becoming a bit of a habit; we've seen each other three times in just four days," she joked, making an effort to extend her comment to Roz, knowing she needed to include her and put her personal feelings to one side.

The rest of the family were waiting in the lounge; it really did feel like a re-play of the previous Friday to Celia's mind, only this time it was Isabelle that was facing their curiosity, not her. Isabelle balked for a second as she took in the eager faces smiling at her. It wasn't so much the intensity of their stare but more the fact that she could see such striking resemblances between the teenagers and her own children. Introductions were made and she was put at ease very quickly. John invited her to sit with him on one of the sofas, encouraging Roz to follow suit.

"While we wait for Dan to arrive - he's just finishing up at the surgery - I have something you might like to see, ladies," he smiled, opening a large, photo album. It was filled with photographs of David and John, documenting their childhood from birth to adolescence, mainly in black and white but there were some delights in the form of colour photos too. John chatted animatedly about their youth, describing holidays to the seaside and the many adventures they'd had exploring the coast and, nearer to home, in the surrounding forest. There was a distinct absence of parents throughout the album: a fact that Roz commented on. John gave a wry smile.

"Well, Father didn't come with us on holiday or days out. It was always just us and our mother. She took charge of the camera. As you can probably tell by our smiles, he wasn't really missed."

He apologised to Isabelle, feeling his comments had sounded disrespectful but she shook her head.

"Not at all. I've heard the whole story, so please, don't feel bad," she put his mind at rest. "I have some photos too, of my children, if you'd like to see them," she said, ferreting around in her bag for her phone where her photos were stored. She passed the phone round, describing her children to them all and before long, was deep in conversation with Charlotte and Anne, discussing their children's developments and milestones. Natalie handed the phone back to Isabelle.

"Is Marnie on Facebook?" she asked eagerly. Isabelle nodded.

"Oh yes, she practically lives on Facebook!" she laughed.

"Oh, good. Can I send her a friend request, then?" she asked hopefully.

"She would love that, yes. Absolutely."
Natalie looked pleased.

"I'll do that, then. Tell her to look out for 'Nat Bee'; that's me," she grinned.

"Nat Bee?" Isabelle wondered.

"Yes. At school, there were two Natalie's in our friendship group so I was always known as Nat Bee. It's stuck with me," she explained, distractedly scrolling through Facebook, searching for Marnie.

John turned to Isabelle.

"So, your parents: how do they feel about this, about you meeting us?" he asked tactfully, wanting to ask so many questions but aware of what an emotional day she had already had. Roz watched Isabelle attentively: it was the question she had been afraid to ask.

"Well, Mum died fourteen year ago. She had stomach cancer; it wasn't an easy or dignified death," Isabelle started. "But Dad is still alive. He's eighty-six now and lives next door to us, in Newlyn. We all moved from the Midlands to Cornwall, together," She glanced at Roz, smiling awkwardly. "Dad's happy about it, he really wanted me to find my birth parents," she said. John smiled kindly.

"And what were they like, your parents?" he prompted. Isabelle gave a little laugh.

"Where to start! Well, they're both Irish: Michael Reynolds and Lily Norton. They were forty years old when I was adopted, and I was their only child. Dad was a managing director of a pharmaceutical company and travelled around quite a bit with work, but when he was home, he doted on me. And Mum. We were a normal family, really. Happy, comfortable and I never wanted for anything - Dad made sure of that," she smiled fondly. "They loved each other, I could see that. Dad was devoted to her. They met when they were in their mid-twenties, completely by chance. Dad's old University friend married one of Mum's cousins. Mum said she noticed him because he'd never been to a Catholic wedding before and he looked like a fish out of water. She felt sorry for him and went over to talk to him, during the reception. And that's how they started," she smiled.

"So, you're Catholic?" John asked. Isabelle shook her head.

"No. Dad wasn't, so..." she tailed off. John could see she was feeling uncomfortable and changed the subject just as Sheila and Celia joined them from the kitchen.

"Well, we have a wedding coming up; I'm sure Roz has told you," he said. Isabelle looked at Roz, surprised. Celia intervened.

"I don't think they've had a chance to talk about it yet," she said pointedly. "It's my daughter, Alice..."

"And our son, Elliot," Sheila interrupted, giving Celia a friendly wink.

"Oh, of course: Ellie's parents. Yes, I do know about them, Conrad told me. I didn't realise they were getting married though. When's the wedding?" she asked politely.

"December nineteenth," Sheila and Celia chorused. "And your family are all invited, obviously", Celia added.

"Including you dad," Roz said with consideration, her voice sincere.

"Thank you," Isabelle blinked as the emotions of the day threatening to catch up with her. John patted her hand.

"Do you like roses, Isabelle? I grow old roses, partly for their beauty and gorgeous scent but also for the challenge. They're not the best behaved of plants," he chuckled, standing up.

"Come and have a wander in the garden, my dear", he invited, shooting his wife a knowing look. It was clear that he wanted to enjoy a moment with his niece, by himself. It was also clear that Isabelle was beginning to feel overwhelmed by it all. A moment alone would do them both good, she thought, intimating as much to Celia and Roz. It touched her to see them together and she knew that John would be feeling a sense of responsibility towards his brother's daughter, and at the same time, a chance to feel close to David through her.

"You did the right thing, finding her," she said quietly to Roz. "Thank you."

They looked at each other in silence and Sheila was taken aback by what she could see. She had decided, in her mind, that Roz was a difficult, deceitful and spiky person but now she could see a depth of despair and a deeply buried pain that had been unearthed. It suddenly hit her that her spikiness was simply a front, a shield, to help her cope through life. Surprised at her own spontaneity, Sheila hugged Roz tightly and then rubbed her back, in a soothing manner.

"She's here now. With you, with us. This is the start of a new chapter for you. Put the past to bed, Roz. Enjoy the present." As she said the words, she knew she was telling herself as much, not just Roz. If Elliot and John could forgive Roz, then she needed to do that, too.

There was still a film of morning dew on the benches when Roz and Isabelle arrived at the cemetery early the next day. Roz wiped it away with a tissue, before inviting Isabelle to sit with her. It was a strange turn of events; only three weeks previously, it had been Celia beckoning Roz to take the same seat in front of David's grave.

"Sixty-three is no age to die, is it?" Isabelle commented, reading the inscription. "How old was John when he had a stroke?"

"Fifty-seven," Roz replied, nodding her agreement at Isabelle's shocked face. "I know. Tragic. And both such lovely people, such caring and giving men. It seems so wrong, doesn't it? When you look at all the .."

"Arseholes in the world," Isabelle finished her sentence. Roz laughed.

"Well, yes. Not quite my choice of words, but yes," she said, struck again by the likeness between Isabelle and David. In temperament as well as looks.

Isabelle reached for her hand and they sat in mutual contemplation, enjoying the serenity and the warmth that the rising sun cast down. A large, ginger cat purposefully wove its way through the tombstones, its sights set on the bramble covered hedge at the far side of the cemetery. Isabelle watched its determined progress, focusing her thoughts on its gleaming coat that seemed to glow in the sunshine.

"Why did you put so many things off, do you think? I mean, why didn't you attempt to find David again? He hadn't gone anywhere: he was always here. And if he loved you, surely, he would have forgiven you for what you did? Not that what you did was wrong," she said quickly, "you had no choice and he would have understood that, I think. Don't you?" She turned steady, questioning eyes to Roz, waiting for a response. Commanding an answer. Roz let out a heartfelt sigh.

"I have asked myself the same question, so many times," she replied, thinking her words would be a sufficient answer.

"I'm not asking for my sake; I've had a great life and been so loved. I just feel such sadness for you. You missed out: why? Because you were worried about what people would think? That's crazy! Whatever era you live in, surely being with the one you love is more important than what people will think? Giving up a child ... allowing yourself to be put in that position ... because of not wanting people to think badly of you ... is ..." she stopped abruptly, feeling her rising frustration was hindering her words; her true feelings were bleeding through her calm façade. Changing her tone, she continued.

"You didn't give him a chance to make a choice. To decide: you and me, or his wife. I think you know which one he would have chosen. I know, and I never met him but I can see in John, what he would have been like. David wasn't a child and neither were you, really. He was thirty-two years old and more than capable of taking care of you. Of us. I'm not judging you, I'm just trying to understand," she said, giving Roz a forceful look.

"But it *was* a different era and we had *no* choice. Unmarried mothers were made to feel like outcasts," she replied, her voice pleading for understanding.

"Unmarried mothers have been around for centuries. Okay, granted: in this day and age, nobody cares anymore but - and this is my point - mothers have been having illegitimate babies for centuries, in this country, and they still kept hold of them. Scorn and scandal passes; you can live with it. Giving up the man you love and giving up your child: that doesn't pass. That doesn't go away and that must be unbearable to live with. How do you live with that?" Isabelle was unrelenting. She needed answers and Roz had none to give. None that were acceptable, it would seem.

"When Lily was born, I held her in my arms and looked at her and thought, how could I possibly give this little miracle away? How could I continue with life, knowing that she was living her life away from me? I knew by then, that I was adopted - that I had been given away - and that was a really difficult concept to deal with as a new mum. I couldn't have carried on, I don't think; it must have crucified you." Her tone was heartfelt as she looked at Roz and it was clear that she was grappling with a see-saw of emotions.

"It did," Roz uttered, glancing at David's gravestone.

"Then, why didn't you look for me? Once I had turned eighteen, you could've looked for me. Why didn't you?" she pushed. Roz stared at her, appalled at her directness. It hit a nerve with such a force.

"I didn't think I was allowed to and anyway, what would you have done? If I *had* found you and told you who I was: what would you have done with that information?" she retaliated. Isabelle didn't hesitate over her reply.

"I would have built a relationship with you. You wouldn't have replaced my parents but instead, you would have been in my life *along with* my parents. Knowing of your existence would have answered so many of my questions. I always *knew*, in my heart, that I wasn't Mum and Dad's natural daughter," she said, passionately. "But you didn't give me that choice. My parents didn't give me that choice. It was my right to know and they denied me of it. David was still alive then, when I turned eighteen." She let that statement sink in for a moment, giving Roz something to think about.

"What would *he* have done, do you think?" she continued to push.

Roz stared at David's gravestone, her mind racing with the possibilities.

"What is the point of dragging up the past? It can't be changed," she pleaded, her voice raw with emotion.

"It's not the past for me though. This is all new for me. Finding you and discovering about David - my father - is all new. And it hurts. It really hurts." Isabelle stood up abruptly and turned away from Roz, wiping angry tears from her face. Roz wanted to join her but her legs felt weak, she was drained of strength.

"But yesterday, you said you understood. When I told you about everything, you said you understood," she reiterated, pleading for reason.

Isabelle ran her hand across the top of David's gravestone, not wanting to look anywhere else but there.

"I know, but yesterday was a different day. I was in shock. I was euphoric. Since then, I have met my father's family: my uncle and aunt, my cousins and their children. Your sister - another aunt - and seen photos of my father, my grandparents, great grandparents. I've seen where they all grew up: the church I should have been christened in, the school you and David went to. It's another life. It's like, somebody up there is saying, 'and this is what you could have had but didn't get'." She stared out across the cemetery, battling with her thoughts.

"Mum and Dad had no family. I had no grandparents, no siblings, no cousins. No history. I knew nothing about their childhood other than my father was from County Down, in Northern Ireland and my Mother, from a little village near Dublin, in Southern Ireland. Two opposing religions, one forbidden love. They had to make a choice:

family, or each other. So, they left their families behind and ran away to England, thinking they could make a new family. Except Mum was infertile. Life is so ironic, don't you think?" she snorted.

Roz summoned up the strength to get to her feet and put her arm around Isabelle, struck dumb by her outburst. She could see the child within, crying out in grief. A child that felt lost and bewildered, thrust into a new world, filled with love and endless reminders of what could have been.

"I don't know what to say, Isabelle," Roz sighed, shaking her head and gesturing with her hands at the futility of words. She encouraged her to sit back down, watching her with a heavy heart. She ached for the pain that she had caused and had no words of comfort. They sat in silence once more.

Isabelle noticed Roz glancing at her watch.

"Are you coming back with me to Newlyn today?" she asked quietly.

"Do you still want me to?" Roz replied, expecting to be rebuffed.

"Of course!" Isabelle replied, looking at her with wide eyes. "Don't you see? *You* are the part of me that has always been missing. I'm not going to let that go, just because the truth is uncomfortable. You can't shirk from this one," she reproached. "Look, I'm sorry. It's been an intense two days. Of course I want you to come with me, and I know we can't change the past. I know. I'm just trying to come to terms with it, that's all," she said, sounding more reasonable.

Roz nodded, remembering Conrad's concern over how upsetting Isabelle would find it. Roz cursed herself for underestimating the impact it would have on her; meeting family, learning about her heritage and visiting her father's grave.

"I'm sorry too. I got carried away, wanting to share so many things with you. Of course you need time to digest it all, I understand that," Roz agreed. "One thing I do want to add though: David and John were very similar in temperament. They were both completely downtrodden by their father, David more so, being the eldest. And the strength of spirit that you see in John, has come from his wife, Sheila. She has guided him through life and he has taken on a part of her personality. Dan and Elliot are very much like their mother and James is more gentle, like John and David. Yes, David had his own mind and yes, he did have strong opinions but when it came to his father, he was totally dominated by him. And that got him down, knowing that he was controlled by a man who had very little, if any, love for him."

"Then where do I get my feisty side from? I see it in Conrad, too. When I met Dan yesterday, I thought it must be a Barraclough trait. No?" she questioned. Roz laughed.

"Well, yes, I can see what you mean about Dan. And David had that fun, impetuous side to him too but very few people saw it. However, your feistiness ... well, ask any of my family and they will tell you: you get it from me," she laughed.

Isabelle took the bouquet that was lying on the bench and arranged the flowers into one of the stone vases on

David's grave. She touched the cold marble, visualising his face.

"I'm so sorry I didn't get the chance to know you," she whispered, "but thank you for giving me life. I will always make the most of it, in your honour."

She straightened, seeing Roz wipe tears from her eyes.

"This was never going to be easy, was it?" she said, sitting back down next to Roz and taking her hand. Roz snorted an ironic laugh.

"No change there then!"

They sat for a while longer, hand in hand, each sending silent thoughts to David's spirit.

"Come on, then, Mum," Isabelle determined, "let's get you back to Newlyn. You can meet your grandchildren and then," she paused as a cheeky grin crossed her face, "you can show me where your love nest was." She laughed at Roz's shocked face.

"Don't act all innocent with me; I think I am living proof that you two had a love nest. And used it, frequently." They laughed together and before leaving, each placed a kiss on David's gravestone. Roz felt lighter: a huge burden had been lifted and she felt an exuberance bubbling up from within. She felt alive.

Chapter Twenty

Roz had been right when she said, 'before you know it, it'll be Christmas'. The weeks flew by in a flurry of excitement and life changes. Isabelle, Tom and their children quickly became a part of the family, with frequent visits to Brockenhurst, dividing their time between the two households. This, along with the wedding preparations, drew Roz, Celia, Sheila and John closer, and they became a tight unit, sharing an unlikely but inevitable bond; a friendship that would remain steadfast into their twilight years. Isabelle's father, Michael, often joined them and he too formed an alliance with Roz and John, not wanting to intrude but wanting to share in their lives. Ellie left for University and although Alice saw her often on Campus, her visits home were sporadic as student life dominated her time. Her parents could see how she thrived on it and enjoyed watching her blossom. With the cottage to themselves, Elliot and Alice slipped easily into life together, working throughout the week and keeping the weekends free for each other. Occasionally, they would visit Brockenhurst or Winchester, but their favourite way to spend it still remained from old; an adventure-day on Saturday followed by a lazy day at home, when they would turn off their phones and shut out the world, possessively cherishing their time alone.

Finally, Friday 11th of December arrived: the date was marked with a big red star on their kitchen calendar. It heralded the end of term for Alice and the start of two weeks' annual leave for Elliot. He wasn't due to return to work until December 28th, after their honeymoon and the Christmas weekend. They had planned to travel down to Brockenhurst and spend the week before the wedding with their families. Alice's Hen-do had been the previous weekend; a night out in Stratford with family, and friends from work and the village. Isabelle and her girls had made it too and together with Roz, the Greene and the Barraclough ladies, they had all bunked down in Alice's cottage for the weekend. Elliot had gone back to Brockenhurst for a weekend with his brothers, nephews, Conrad, Tom and Andrew: paintballing and Go-Ape had been on the agenda, along with the obligatory village pub-crawl once the younger boys were in bed. John joined them for this, and he and Elliot inevitably ended up looking after the two reprobates, Dan and Andrew.

The run-up to the wedding was all going according to plan. The organising had been done and only last minute finalising remained; Celia, Roz and Sheila had done a sterling job and Laura had worked like a trouper to have Alice's dress and six bridesmaids' dresses completed on time. Alice's original choice of four attendants had been extended to include Marnie and Lily: again, reinforcing Isabelle's place in the family and uniting the new, young cousins with their peers. And under the guise of 'usher', they had decided to include all the male cousins too. Conrad, along with James's son, Samuel, aged twenty and twenty-one respectively, were indeed the official ushers, supported by Andrew, Dan and James's sons: Scott, Eddie and Anthony, all aged fourteen and fifteen. Riley and Chris, only aged twelve and eleven, were deemed too young (and too eager) but they would nevertheless be wearing matching suits along with the older boys. It was going to be a perfectly co-ordinated and sublimely orchestrated wedding: a fairy-tale dream.

Elliot systematically loaded suitcases into the car as Alice stood in the hall and checked them off against her list.

"Don't forget to make room for the skis; it's forecast to snow in Vienna next week," she said brightly. Elliot stopped in his tracks and stared at her.

"Skis? What skis?" He looked frantically round the hall. Alice started laughing.

"I'm teasing you. Obviously," she grinned. Elliot pulled a face.

"Well, I don't know: you seem to have packed just about everything else for every eventuality. Why not add skis to the list and be done with it?" He ran his hand through his hair as he eyes up the assortment of bags and hold-alls still to pack. He smirked at Alice's indignant face.

"I'm teasing *you*. Obviously," he countered, putting his arms around her and kissing her hair.

"Tell me again why Ellie's not coming with us tonight," he prompted, disappointed that she hadn't returned home from university yet. Alice gave him a patient smile.

"She's coming home tomorrow and is going to spend a few days here first. Tasha's due home tomorrow too, and Amy the following day. They're desperate to catch up. I'm not sure about Kyle but he'll be back in time for the wedding, I know that much," she told him.

"And Brad's coming back with her tomorrow?" he asked. Alice nodded.

"Yes, and he'll be driving her down to Mum's on Wednesday and he'll be staying too. His parents are driving down Saturday morning, with Tasha's, and they've all booked in to an hotel. Mum offered to put them up but I think they felt they'd be imposing. Especially as we've got your family coming down from Yorkshire."

She eyed Elliot, smiling at his wide eyes. As their wedding day drew nearer, he had become more stressed about the preparations whereas Alice had become much more laid back, with a deep feeling of contentment enveloping her. They were both shattered but she didn't seem to notice it; she just buzzed along, on a euphoric high.

"Everything is under control. It's all sorted," she soothed. "We just need to hit the road and enjoy being made a fuss of by our parents for the next week."

And 'a fuss' is exactly what they got. Celia and Roz greeted them with big smiles and even bigger arms when they finally arrived in Brockenhurst later that evening.

"A nice cup of tea, dears, and then we're off to Sheila's for a late dinner," Celia informed them as she passed them brimming cups of tea and a plate of mince pies. Elliot sank back into the sofa, smiling his thanks.

"Mum and Dad's?" he wondered, surprised that he didn't know anything about it.

"Yes, dear. Just a quiet dinner, to welcome you both home. Just us. On Sunday, however, we're all invited to James's for dinner. Did you know about that, dear?" she asked. Elliot frowned, shaking his head.

"Probably but to be honest, my brain is like a sieve at the moment," he admitted.

"I think the journey to work every day is taking its toll," Alice added, pulling a concerned face at her mother. "It's a long trek, to Nottingham and back, on a daily basis," she said.

"Well, you can catch up on some sleep this week then," Roz interjected. "There's only one or two things for you both to do and the rest is up to us. You can both relax and enjoy the break from work," she smiled, patting Alice's arm affectionately.

"What do you need us to do?" Alice asked, watching her mother produce her notebook and pen.

"Well, Alice: you and Ellie have got a trial with the hairdresser on Wednesday afternoon and …"

"A trial?" Elliot interrupted. Celia gave him a tolerant smile, accepting his interruption with good grace.

"Yes, dear. She needs to make sure she knows what to do on the day. So, whatever you decide to do with Ellie's hair, that will be replicated for all the girls. Yes?" she asked Alice, who nodded her reply.

"Is that a thing people do? A trial for your hair?" Elliot couldn't decide whether he was amused or impressed by the notion. A quick glance in Celia's direction told him he should be impressed. She had her 'no nonsense' face on and probably wouldn't appreciate his laughing at it. He skirted round the issue.

"And what do you need me to do?" he asked. Celia checked her book.

"Well, dear, tomorrow you're meeting Andrew in Winchester to pick up the suits," she told him, pausing for him to acknowledge her instruction. He obliged.

"Yes, I spoke to Andrew about it last night," he confirmed.

"Good. So, you need to take a list - which I've printed out for you - and check everything off against it. There are suits for you, Andrew, James, Dan and your father. Then there are seven more suits for the boys. They all went for a final fitting the other day, which was a good job because one of them had grown. Who was it, Roz?" She turned to her sister, trying to remember.

"Dan's little one, Chris," Roz replied. "He's shot up!"

"That's right, Chris. Bless him." Celia gave a maternal smile then turned back to her notebook.

"And that's all you two need to worry about. We've paid a small, extra fee to get the suits a week early but once they're here, there is nothing to dash across the county for. Laura is bringing the dresses over on Sunday, when they come for dinner at James's." She smiled triumphantly, reaching for her tea cup and holding it up to salute Alice and Elliot.

"Cheers, dears," she smiled, sighing with satisfaction.

"Well, I can see where you get your organising skills from," Elliot said quietly to Alice, leaning his head on hers as they sank deeper into the inviting sofa. Celia smiled, appreciating the acknowledgement.

"Well dear, being married to Reggie and helping Daddy with the church admin, did teach me one thing: chaos and harmony do not make good bedfellows," she stressed earnestly. Roz laughed loudly.

"Oh good Lord, Celia! You do say the funniest things," she continued to chuckle. Celia joined in with the laughter, hearing how dated it sounded.

"But you have to admit, it is a valid point," she said, knowingly nodding her head and then glancing at her watch, jumped up from her seat.

"Oh my goodness, look at the time! We'll be late for Sheila and John."

Elliot could barely keep his eyes open as he got ready for bed a couple of hours later, back in Alice's old bedroom. He was fast asleep within minutes and slept through the alarm the next morning, not stirring until Alice gently shook him. She put a mug of tea by the side of his bed and sat on the edge, rhythmically stroking his temples and into his hair. She was concerned at how tired he seemed of late.

"Have you thought any more about looking for a different job, nearer to home?" she asked, voicing a question she had already raised more than once. Elliot pulled himself up and leant against the headboard, moving forwards to allow her to prop a pillow up behind him. He smiled at her concerned face.

"I have, yes. But," he held up a hand as she drew in breath to say something, her face reflecting her anticipation.

"But, it's early days and I didn't want to say anything before the wedding. However, there is an opening - or at least, the possibility of one - with the Shakespeare Trust." He laughed as Alice squealed with excitement.

"You are kidding! You're not kidding, are you? Why didn't you tell me?" she clapped her hands then closed her mouth and struggled to pull a straight face as Elliot sighed, shaking his head at her.

"I can't think about it now, Alice," he said, seriously. "But I promise, I will tell you all about it on our honeymoon. Okay?"

He stroked her face, sensing the thousand questions playing on her lips and the effort it took her not to squeal excitedly yet again. She grinned widely.

"Okay. But can I just say one thing? I knew brainwashing you with Shakespeare would pay off in the end", she practically sang as she snatched up her towel and headed for the bathroom.

"Shall I leave the shower running for you when I've finished?"

Elliot nodded, drinking his tea.

"Yes, please: I'll be there in a minute."

Alice loved everything about Christmas: the build up to it, the decorations, the busy shops and the general high-spirited atmosphere that the season invoked. She loved the village decorations and lights, both in Brockenhurst and Wilmcote, although her favourite ones were in the town centre of Stratford-upon-Avon. Strings of coloured lights outlined the gabled, old shop fronts, and garlands made from hundreds of red and white lights, stretched across the main street at regular intervals, creating a festive archway for shoppers. Her own decorations were always up by the start of December, a tradition she had continued from her childhood. She was particularly excited to hear that snow was forecast for the upcoming week; maybe she would get a white wedding after all.

Absently gazing at the twinkling lights on the Christmas tree in the lounge, she mentally ran through her list of things she would need to unpack ready for next Saturday. Some things would be needed throughout the coming week and then repacked ready to take away with them on their honeymoon.

Oscar, one of Celia's fluffy, well-fed cats, strutted into the room, demanding Alice's attention before attacking an enticingly low-hanging bauble on the tree. He rolled around underneath it, wriggling from side to side, swishing his tail and in so doing, upset the carefully positioned stable scene. Gently shooing him away, Alice repositioned baby Jesus and his crib, smiling at the memory of how she and Andrew would squabble each year as to who's turn it was to put Jesus in the stable.

Celia had kept the same decorations for years, not wanting to part with the happy memories they held, and was thrilled at how her grandchildren enjoyed them just as much as Alice and Andrew had. There was a train-track running in a large circle, following the edge of the tree apron, with a battery-operated Santa train that played carols as it ran on its continuous loop. The stable scene was placed to one side, doubling up as a railway station, in young Alice's mind. The wooden stable had been handcrafted by her Grandpa, and the assorted nativity characters had been collected together from the Christmas church fayres over the years. The donkey had seen better days; teeth marks evident along its back indicated that it had doubled up as a teething toy at one point.

"Right, I'm off now." Elliot's announcement broke Alice from her nostalgic trance and she jumped to her feet with a ready smile.

"Got the list?" she asked. He patted his jacket pocket to confirm, giving her a knowing smile.

"As if I'd forget it."

They both laughed, hugging each other tightly.

"I've just texted Andrew to say I'm on my way. It should only take about half an hour, there's no traffic according to Google maps," he said.

"Safe journey. Phone me when you get there. My phone's on charge in the kitchen but I'll hear it. If not, phone the landline," she said, kissing him. She stood on the doorstep and waved, watching until he was out of sight.

Closing the door behind her, she listened to the silence. Celia and Roz had gone to the church to stash away the Orders of Service that had arrived from the printers; then they were going to check on the floral arrangements with the local florist before dropping in to Sheila's for a cup of tea. It had been a long time since Alice had some alone time, and she wasn't quite sure what to do with it. She decided to unpack her jewellry and make up, ready for the following Saturday; she had a nagging feeling that she'd forgotten something.

She carefully unpacked their clothes for the week and thoroughly searched through all their luggage. Twenty minutes later, her fears were confirmed as she realised she had left her pearl ring at home, in Wilmcote. It had been her eighteenth birthday present from her parents, and she absolutely had to wear it on her wedding day: it was her 'something old'. Cursing her own forgetfulness, she hurried back downstairs to text Ellie and ask her to bring it with her. She stopped in confusion, staring at the work surface where she had left her phone on charge next to the kettle. It wasn't there.

"Hello, Alice."

Alice swung round, gasping in horror at the figure standing in the kitchen doorway. She must have been hiding behind the door when Alice had walked in.

"I love this country tradition of leaving the front door unlocked so that anybody can wander in. You never know who's going to turn up, do you? Well ... surprise!" The woman's thick, Irish voice dripped with menace.

Unable to move, paralysed with fear, Alice stared into the dark, unmistakable eyes of Mary O'Shea. Her pupils were so dilated that they almost completely obscured the blue of her irises and her hair looked different: it was dyed red and cropped, but her face was the same. The face that had haunted Alice for eighteen years.

"I hear you've been messing around with my husband," she said, her eyes boring into Alice's, the menace unrelenting. Alice nervously licked her lips, trying not to show how terrified she was. She didn't doubt Elliot for a single second and despite the twisting knot in her stomach, she felt the need to fight for him rising. She wasn't going to let Mary destroy them again.

"He's not your husband," she dared to utter, bracing herself for Mary's reaction.

Mary moved slowly towards her, her eyes widening, annoyed at Alice's defiance. Her voice was slow and deliberate.

"Is that what he told you? You always were a gullible, little sap. That's what he liked about you. You would believe anything he whispered in your stupid ear," she scorned.

Alice backed away from her, slowly being hemmed in to the far corner of the room. Her eyes frantically scoured the work surfaces for her phone but there was only a tea-towel, nothing else. Her eyes darted back to Mary's face when she heard her laugh.

"Looking for this?" she taunted, holding up Alice's phone. "It made interesting reading, all those dirty texts you've been sending to each other. No point in denying it - it's all here, on your filthy, little phone. I think I'll hang on to this," she said, putting it back in her pocket.

She paced around the kitchen, all the while getting closer to Alice. She stopped by the wide, windowsill and picked up a framed photo of Alice holding a new-born Ellie. The expression on her face filled Alice with panic; Mary was becoming incensed and increasingly agitated. She shot Alice a look of pure loathing, waving the photo frame at her aggressively.

"You got away with stealing my baby girl but I won't let you get away with stealing my husband again," she spat.

"What?" Alice was barely able to speak, terror gripping her as she slowly realised Mary was completely unhinged. Instinctively, she worried for Ellie's safety. Was she okay?

"I know what you did. You snuck into the hospital and stole her," she jabbed her finger at Ellie's face, "while I was sleeping. I told them what you had done but nobody believed me. Nobody," she screamed, spit flying from her lips. As if flicking a switch, she instantly became still again. The stillness alarmed Alice more than the screaming. Mary moved closer, inching her way towards Alice.

"You snuck in and stole my baby. Just like you snuck into my life and stole Elliot. I saw him first. He was mine until you turned his head with your pretty face and your filthy, sluttish body. I know what you did, you filthy whore."

Try as she might, Alice couldn't look away from Mary, she was hypnotised by her black-eyed stare. And terrified about what would happen next. How could she get away from her? Should she try and placate her, humour her?

"Please," Alice started but Mary spoke over her, not interested in anything she had to say.

"I know what you stole from me and I'm going to make you pay," she said, stopping just inches away from Alice. She smelt of stale, cigarette smoke and unwashed clothes. She was so close that Alice could feel her breath on her face as she spoke.

"If I can't have him, nobody can. Especially ... not ... you," she emphasised, poking a hard finger at Alice's chest. Mary grabbed her upper arm and turned her towards the kitchen table, pushing her.

"Sit down," she commanded. Alice sat, momentarily relieved to take the weight off her legs, weak from fear. She watched Mary pacing back and forth, muttering incoherently to herself, over and over again, seemingly forgetting about Alice. Seizing her chance, she made a move to run towards the kitchen door but Mary turned and slammed her fist into her shoulder.

"I said, sit down!" she screamed, glaring at her, clenching and unclenching her fists. Alice sat back down, trying not to cry from the pain in her shoulder. She didn't dare look at Mary but lack of eye contact made her more nervous. She needed to watch her to gauge what she was thinking, what she was planning to do.

Mary crossed to the fridge and pulled off a wedding invitation that was stuck to the door with magnets. She read the wording and held it up to Alice with a sardonic expression.

"So, you're getting married next Saturday?" she goaded. Alice dared to look at her and nod her head.

"Yes," she said, her unwavering voice not betraying her fear.

"No, you're not, you stupid, little whore! That's why I'm here. To stop you. To stop him," she said angrily, pacing back and forth again. Alice decided to try reasoning with her.

"Are we just going to wait for him to come back? He'll be gone for quite some time. Why don't we…"
Mary interrupted her,

"No, he won't. Because *you* sent him a message telling him to turn round and hurry back home because you had taken a fall and can't move your leg," she said, patting Alice's phone in her pocket. She sneered at her.

"What do you think I was doing all this time down here, when you were faffing about upstairs? Well?" she taunted.

As she spoke, they heard a car pull up outside and the car door being hastily slammed shut. Mary darted towards the work surface and snatched up a large, kitchen knife from underneath the tea towel, where she had obviously hidden it. Alice whimpered. Mary turned and held the knife to Alice's throat.

"If you so much as peep, I'll slit your throat," she hissed. "I'll deal with you next."

The front door opened and Alice could hear hurried footsteps in the hall.

"Alice?" Elliot called, with panic in his voice. He took the stairs, two at a time, calling again. Mary pressed the blade against her windpipe, her eyes fixed on the kitchen door, waiting. They could hear him hurrying back down the stairs, towards the kitchen.

"Alice?" He sounded frantic, his voice unbearably close. He pushed the door open and rushed in to the room.

"Look out!" Alice screamed as Mary ran towards him, the blade flashing as she swung it above her shoulder to plunge it into his chest. Emitting a guttural scream, Alice grabbed her from behind, pulling her backwards. Mary lost her balance and missed her mark, sinking the blade deep into his left thigh and pulling it down his leg. With an agonised grunt, Elliot fell to the floor. Mary froze for a second, transfixed by the fountain of blood pumping from his leg; a haunted look flitted across her face before she dropped the knife and ran towards the front door.

Quick as a flash, Alice grabbed the tea towel and knelt down next to Elliot, hesitating for a split second at the sight of the wound. There was a deep, wide gash where a mass of livid, pink and purple skin and muscle bulged out from, and a pulsating flow of dark red blood quickly soaked into his trousers and onto the floor. She wanted to scream, to cry, but automatic pilot kicked into gear and she took control of the situation, remembering everything she had learnt on her basic first aid course. She ripped the slashed material to expose the wound more clearly, quickly folding the towel lengthways a few times and placing it over the wound. With one hand on his groin, where the blood was pumping most profusely, and the other trying to hold the skin together, she pressed the towel down firmly to stem the blood flow. The towel was instantly soaked through, proving ineffective but nevertheless acted as a barrier between the wound and her hands.

"Where's your phone, Elliot? Elliot?" she urged, applying more pressure as she felt the blood squelching through her fingers. Elliot was shaking uncontrollably, staring blindly at her, his breathing becoming laboured and shallow. Alice pushed harder into his groin with one hand and swiftly moved the other one away, needing a free hand to find his phone. It was in the trouser pocket of his right leg, as she thought it would be. She dialled 999, smearing blood across the keypad in the process.

"Ambulance," she stated and was immediately through to an operator.

"My fiancé has been stabbed in the thigh. There is blood pumping out, it's everywhere." She spoke rapidly, starting to shake. She held eye contact with Elliot, concerned at how pale he was and noted black rings that were forming around his eyes. He stared back at her, terrified and unable to move. He groaned as pain ripped through him and he put his hand over hers, squeezing it and pushing down to help her apply the pressure. Alice listened intently to the operator. She asked for both of their names and the address, then said,

"Put me onto speaker phone to free up your hand." Alice did so and put the phone down, reapplying pressure with both hands.

"Can you tell me exactly where the wound is, and how deep?"

"It's up by his groin. The knife went in up there and … his leg is split open … it's about twenty-five centimetres … half way down to his knee," she replied, her voice shaking so much that it was difficult to articulate.

"And is it deep?" she prompted.

"Yes," Alice breathed, clearing her throat.

"How much blood would you say he's lost: more than a cupful?" she continued. Alice closed her eyes for a second, trying not to focus on it.

"Yes, definitely."

"Now, you need to elevate his leg, Alice. High as you can but maintain the pressure at all times." The operator's voice was clear and reassuring yet authoritative.

Alice glanced across at the chairs around the table but knew that to grab one would involve moving and she couldn't do that. So instead she crouched forwards and slid his leg up onto her shoulder, twisting herself round to a sitting position, with her legs splayed on either side of him, enabling her to continue maintaining pressure. She slipped in the blood that had pooled across the floor and she felt her stomach lurch. The pungent, rusty smell hit her nostrils and she vomited so violently that she didn't have time to turn away. Elliot stared at her with wide eyes as she vomited again, onto his stomach.

"I'm sorry," she choked shakily.

"Alice, what's happening?" the operator demanded calmly. Alice tried to wipe her mouth on her shoulder.

"It's okay, I've just been sick that's all," she said, clearing her throat. She was aware of Elliot's hand slipping from under hers and she watched in terror as his head slumped to the side and he lost consciousness.

"Elliot! Elliot! Oh God, hurry up please," she screamed at the phone, "he's dying. He's dying!" she sobbed.

"Is he still breathing, Alice?" she asked. Alice stared at his chest, frantically blinking away the tears that were hindering her sight, frustrated that she couldn't use her hands to wipe her face.

"I don't know, I can't tell," she started to wail. "Elliot! Elliot!"

"Alice, you need to stay focused. They will be with you soon. You need to stay with me now. Is Elliot breathing?" The firm voice snapped her back and she stared at his chest again, willing it to rise and fall but still couldn't be sure if he was breathing.

"The ambulance is nearly with you, Alice. Is the door open?" the operator asked. Alice could hear her conferring with somebody on another line. She started to feel faint and vomited again onto Elliot's lap. He stirred and groaned. She cried out loud with relief.

"Alice, the crew are here. Do not move until they tell you to," the operator instructed her, "you're doing well, Alice," she affirmed.

She was aware of sirens and footsteps, a voice calling out from the hall and then two paramedics appearing by her side: one bent at Elliot's head, talking to him and the other, put a hand on Alice's shoulder, carefully easing Elliot's leg from her.

"Alright, Alice. We'll take it from here. Can you stand up?" He offered to help her. She felt faint and disorientated, not wanting to move. She kept her hands firmly on Elliot's thigh; they were stuck there in amongst the blood and skin. She started to shake violently, trying to listen to what the paramedic was saying. More voices and footsteps: they were joined by two policemen and moments later, a familiar voice. Alice looked up in recognition, pleading for help. Dan stood in the doorway, medical bag in hand, staring in horror at the bloody scene that greeted him.

"Jesus, what the hell happened?" He dropped his bag and pulled her to her feet, holding her against his chest. She instantly caved in, unable to stop the tears, sobbing uncontrollably.

"Andrew phoned to say *you* had been hurt. What happened?" he reiterated. He held her close, watching the paramedics working on Elliot's unresponsive body.

"Pete?" Dan recognised one of them. Pete looked up briefly, acknowledging him.

"Dan! Is this your brother? I thought I recognised the name," he said. "He's lucky: another three millimetres and this would be a different story. The knife just missed the femoral artery. Extensive muscle and tissues damage though: he'll definitely need surgery and a transfusion when we get him to hospital. Sorry, mate," he said gruffly. "Do you know his blood group?"

Dan nodded.

"Of course. He's O rhesus positive." He knew the information would speed things up at the hospital.

The other paramedic was talking loudly to Elliot, trying to illicit a response while inserting a cannula into his arm and setting up a drip. Dan asked one of the officers to pass him a chair and he sat Alice down on it. He could sense that she wouldn't move far from Elliot. She had stopped crying and was staring at Elliot's face, dazed and in shock. One of the officers crouched by her side, offering her a tissue.

"We need to ask you some questions, Alice. Is that alright?" He spoke softly, waiting for her response. She nodded, not taking her eyes off Elliot.

"Can you tell me what happened here today? Do you know who did this to Elliot?" he probed. Alice nodded again, not able to speak. She licked her lips. Her throat was so dry from crying and being sick, it burned. Dan was on his knees by Elliot's head, talking to him and Alice was watching him closely. She could see he had gained a response. Her body crumpled with relief and she started crying again.

"Do you know who did this, Alice?" he repeated. Alice turned to him, a wave of anger coursing through her at the thought of Mary.

"Yes. Mary O'Shea. She tried to kill him," she said, reliving the look on Mary's face as she had lunged for Elliot.

"She was aiming for his heart. She wanted him dead but I ... I managed to stop her. Is he alright, is he breathing?" she suddenly asked the paramedic, distracted by what they were doing. Dan looked up, forcing a smile.

"He's still here, Alice."

"And what happened next: where did Mary go?" the officer continued, anxious to glean some information. Alice stared at the kitchen door. It was a real effort to speak; her mouth felt out of sync with her brain.

"She ran out. I think," she paused as a thought struck her, "or did she run upstairs? I don't know. She was hiding.

She was hiding, waiting for us. She was going to kill us," she blurted, shaking uncontrollably, doubling up and rocking on her seat. Dan looked at the policeman.

"Enough, I think," he said, getting to his feet and coming over to her. One officer had left the room and gone upstairs. The other, nodded at Dan's request and spoke on his radio, giving Mary's name. He looked apologetically at Alice.

"I just need a description of her."

"My height, quite stocky, with short hair. Dyed, bright red," she told him, sniffing through her tears. "And black eyes. No colour, just black," she added, shutting her own eyes to blot out the image of her. She opened them again when Dan put his coat around her and crouching beside her chair, held her tightly, comforting her.

"She's crazy, completely crazy. She's convinced that she's married to him. She thinks Ellie is *her* baby." Alice stared helplessly at Dan, trying to make sense of what had just taken place. It had all happened so quickly, so unexpectedly.

Dan helped her to her feet on the paramedic's command. Elliot was on a stretcher, being wheeled out to the waiting ambulance. The officer spoke quietly to Dan before he guided Alice out and helped her into the ambulance. She turned to him with wide eyes,

"Don't leave me," she begged. Dan shook his head.

"Of course not. I'm coming with you," he assured her, strapping her in and sitting next to her, fixed his own strap. He reached across and put a hand on Elliot's wrist, checking his pulse, just to put his mind at rest. Elliot's eyelids fluttered and he opened them briefly; Alice instinctively reached forward to touch his face but the strap hindered her and all she could do was let it hover in the air in his general direction. She rested it on the rail of his stretcher, needing to be connected with him in some small way.

The blue-lighted journey to Southampton was swift but allowed both Alice and Dan time to recover sufficiently, ready for the busy chaos of the hospital. There was a small medical team awaiting their arrival and Elliot was immediately whisked to Resus. Panic engulfed Alice as she watched him being wheeled away; a sudden weight hit the pit of her stomach and her legs buckled. Dan took her arm and headed for the waiting area nearest to them. They passed a full-length mirror in the corridor and she caught sight of herself for the first time, staring in shock at her own reflection. Her ashen face was heavily splattered with blood, smeared across her brow where she had been pushing her fringe away from her face. Her hair was sticking up in clumps, caked in blood. Her pale blue sweatshirt was also covered in large patches of dark red, and her light grey jeans were completely soaked in the blood that she had been sitting in on the kitchen floor. The material was glued to her legs and she could feel that blood had soaked through her underwear to her skin. Looking at her feet, she saw how she had left faint, red footprints as she walked in her blood-soaked slippers. Her hands were caked in it too. It was fair to say, there was very little of her that wasn't covered in Elliot's blood. Her stomach lurched again and without warning, she vomited on the floor. Dan steered her into a treatment room and leant her against the sink in the corner while he called for help. She felt very off-balance and the world slowly turned black as she slid to the floor.

When she came to, she was lying on a bed in the corner of the room. Muttering apologies, she tried to sit up but was firmly told to stay where she was. Dan was nowhere to be seen. The nurse standing by her bedside, placated her.

"He's just gone to make some calls. The police are here, wanting to talk to you," she said, eyeing her pale face. "I told them to wait for a while."

"Elliot?" Alice asked tentatively. It was the one question screaming in her head but she daren't voice it, scared of the reply. The nurse patted her arm, smiling.

"He's in surgery."

"And?" Alice pushed.

"And when we know more, we'll let you know, but he's responding well," she nodded. "Can I get you a gown or something to change into: make you more comfortable?" she suggested. Alice shook her head. Being 'more comfortable' was the last thing on her mind. The nurse passed her a cup of water, encouraging her to drink, before leaving the room.

The same two police officers that had been at the house, came in to ask further questions. Feeling more capable now, Alice told them everything she knew about Mary: her personality when they were flat-mates, how she had cold-heartedly deceived Alice, her obsession with Elliot and her catalogue of lies about the two of them on Facebook, that had continued for years. She also divulged what Elliot had told her about Mary's behaviour and mental state after Alice had left York, and that at some point, she had been sectioned. Dan had re-entered the room at the start of the interview and sat quietly, listening to it all.

"And how did she know that you would be at your mother's house this weekend?" the policeman asked. It was the question that Alice had also been asking herself.

"Did you tag yourself in anything yesterday or today, on Facebook or any other social media?"

Alice went cold, realising what she had done. She nodded. Her Facebook post for the previous day had been,

'Back in our hometown for the wedding of the century. Love my Elliot so much'. She had added Brockenhurst as their location; not just Brockenhurst but also her custom-made tag of 'Chez Greene', which, through the wonders of technology, would have given a more precise location, pinpointing her parents' home.

"It sounds like she probably knew where you were anyway, even if you hadn't said anything on Facebook. Stalkers are very devious," he said, closing his notebook. "We haven't picked her up yet but her description is out there. In the meantime, we'll position a car outside your house tonight. My colleague is there with your mother at the moment," he told her. Alice couldn't bear to imagine what Celia and Roz must have gone through, coming back to that horrific sight in the kitchen. She felt sick at the thought of it.

Once the policemen had gone, Dan came over to the bed, checking her pulse and pulling her lower lids down to look at her eyes. He frowned.

"You look a bit anaemic. Is that usual?" he asked. Alice shrugged.

"I'm not sure. I'm tired but it has been full-on lately, both at work and at home," she said, raising her eyebrows. "Any news?" she asked hopefully.

"He's out of surgery and in recovery. High as a kite on morphine probably but he's okay. He's okay," he said gently, watching her well up with relief.

"I can't believe I led her right to our door," she murmured, appalled at the consequences of an innocent remark on Facebook.

"Don't beat yourself up about it. The police said it: stalkers find a way, they always do," he tried to comfort her but she wasn't convinced.

"And she has my phone!" she suddenly remembered, picturing Mary looking at all her personal things on it: photos, messages, emails. She became acutely aware of how vulnerable she had made herself; how everybody with a smartphone made themselves vulnerable to abuse.

"Ellie's on her way," Dan said, interrupting her thoughts. "We didn't want her to travel alone so Brad is driving her to Andrew's, and he'll bring her down here. We just need to know she's safe."

It was mid-afternoon by the time they were allowed to see Elliot. He had been transferred onto a ward and put in a side room, affording him some privacy and better security, close to the nurses' station. He was very groggy but managed to give them a smile when they quietly walked into the room. His smile quickly faded when he saw the state of Alice. She apologised, grimacing through her own smile of relief, noting how he had some colour back in his cheeks. They pulled up chairs, not wanting to sit anywhere near his leg. Dan discreetly lifted the sheets to take a look at it, giving him a nod of approval.

"Well that certainly looks better than it did a few hours ago," he pulled a face, trying to make light of it. Elliot took a firm grip of Alice's hand, searching her face for answers. She told him briefly what had taken place, not wanting to burden or tire him with details. Dan snorted, shaking his head.

"Alice, he's got the scars to prove it happened: you don't need to gloss over it. She was coming for you, Elliot. She wanted you dead, and Alice saved your life today. Twice. She stopped that knife from being plunged into your chest and then she stopped you from bleeding out. I reckon she's a keeper," he winked at Alice's embarrassed face. Elliot tightened his grip.

"I know. I intend to keep her forever," he said vehemently, not taking his eyes off her.

They kept their visit short, appreciating his need for sleep and a chance to recover from the anaesthetic. James arrived and promising to come back later with Alice, took them home. He had thoughtfully covered the back seat of his car with a sheet and had a thick blanket to wrap around her. Within seconds, she was fast asleep.

Chapter Twenty-One

Word of the attack quickly spread and the village of Brockenhurst was on high alert and in a state of shock. There was no shortage of offers of help, people wanting to show their concern and care in any way they could. Prayers for both families were said in church, where the shock was felt most keenly, by the parishioners; Alice's parents and grandparents had always played such an important part in their lives as had the Barraclough doctors, and the thought of somebody committing such a ferocious crime against Elliot and Alice, rocked the community.

James had taken Alice straight to his parents' house from the hospital, where Roz, Celia and Ellie were already being settled. It had been decided that they would all stay there for the time being, for security reasons but also to avoid the distress of seeing the blood-stained kitchen. It was quickly ascertained that the floor would need to be replaced and James organised for a local floor fitter to carry out the job immediately. It was one of the perks of being an accountant: always knowing somebody prepared to do a favour.

Despite the huge shock, they were all adamant that the wedding would still go ahead; no-one more so than Elliot. He was discharged on the Wednesday, being sent home with a bag of medication, crutches, a wheelchair and strict instructions to rest his leg as much as possible. There would be a lengthy programme of physio and follow-up appointments at the hospital over the coming months, and he received discreet advice to not be shy about seeking counselling. This recommendation was also extended to Alice. Mary was still nowhere to be found.

The family had gathered together at Sheila and John's to greet Elliot home from hospital. Andrew, Laura and their children had driven down for the evening to be there too. James and Dan went to fetch Elliot and while they awaited his arrival, the rest of the family debated what things would be off-topic for the time being. Obviously, he needed to know that the police had, to date, not been able to locate Mary despite the on-going investigation.

"What I do *not* think he should know, is what they found in her flat," Sheila stressed. A chorus of 'absolutely' reverberated round the room.

"What did they actually find? I've not been told much," Natalie piped up, looking pointedly at her mother. Anne looked away, not wanting to say anything. Charlotte glanced anxiously at Chris and Riley sitting in front of the television screen. Sensing her reluctance to talk in front of them, John stood up and headed for the door.

"Boys, who's up for crisps? Coke?" he enticed, smiling as they eagerly jumped up and followed him into the kitchen.

"Eddie?" Charlotte prompted but he shook his head.

"No thanks. I want to hear what they found too. I am fourteen, Mum. I do know things," he stressed. Andrew tried not to smile, resisting the temptation to ruffle his hair. His and Dan's boys were growing up so fast and it was easy to overlook the fact that they were far more astute than given credit for.

"Alice, is it okay?" Charlotte asked. Alice nodded, smiling her appreciation at Charlotte's concern. Laura rubbed her arm, comforting her. Charlotte sighed deeply, not sure that she actually wanted to voice it but knew it would come out eventually; better that the children heard it from her first.

"As you know, she had been under psychiatric care for many years, on and off. Apparently, she flitted about from place to place but was mainly based in London. She lived in sheltered housing for a while but when the police tracked her current address, she's in a bedsit, in a house with other vulnerable people. Not being looked after as such, but the authorities know where she is. Anyway …"

"Auntie, what did they find?" Natalie interrupted, growing frustrated by her longwinded account.

"Anyway," Charlotte repeated, "she had built a shrine to Elliot. Quite literally, a shrine. An altar, with a crucifix, and candles around framed photographs of him. Not just old ones either; she had up to date photos of him too."

"The police showed me photographs of it," Alice interjected. "It was as if she were mourning somebody who had died. As if Elliot were dead. There was even a small wreath on the altar. It made my blood run cold: really disturbing," she said, giving an involuntary shiver at the thought of it.

Charlotte continued,

"The rest of the room - the entirety of it - was completely covered in photos of Elliot, along with dozens of pictures of babies, cut out from magazines, and pages of text ripped out from books. A poem. And she'd copied it out onto bits of paper and stuck them to the wall," she said, frowning as she spoke.

"What poem?" Rachel asked in unison with Natalie.

"'Remembrance', by Emily Brontë. It's a poem about death and mourning," she told them. "But the most disturbing aspect of it all was, there were recent photos of Elliot and Alice, together - we think she'd got them from Facebook - which had been circled in red, with the words 'death', and 'traitor', and 'whore', scrawled underneath, and Alice's face had been scribbled out."

The room fell silent, each lost in their own thoughts as to what could have driven somebody to such extremes; to harbour an obsession that lasted for so many years.

"We've all got photos of you two on our Facebook, haven't we?" Anne said to Alice. "My cover photo is of all of us at the engagement party. And yours, Ellie, is of the three of you on holiday. It's scary to think, even somebody that we're not 'friends' with, can see them and print them off. I'd never considered it before."

A car horn sounded outside and John stuck his head round the door.

"They're here," he announced.

Alice, Ellie and Sheila went out to greet Elliot while the others waited in the lounge. Sheila paused at the lounge door, looking at everybody.

"No more talk about this now. The wedding is the only thing on our agenda; that's all Elliot wants to focus on," she nodded, smiling at her grandchildren, knowing how upsetting this whole experience had been for them. They needed to put it to the back of their minds, for Elliot's sake, which was easier said than done when Mary was still at large.

Elliot was wheeled into the room and Andrew instigated everybody to stand and give him a round of applause. He smiled sheepishly, visibly moved by the reception. Natalie was the first to throw her arms around his neck.

"Welcome home, Uncle Elliot," she smiled, her smile not quite reaching her eyes. It shook her to see how fragile he seemed, how vulnerable he looked. In her eyes, he had always been her towering hero, unfazed by anything in life. It scared her to think that somebody had wanted to kill him and she was wishing she hadn't pushed her aunt to give her the details.

Dan made sure that the family gathering was kept brief, and together with Alice, he helped Elliot upstairs and onto the bed, then checked on his dressing before leaving them to it.

"Get some rest: I'll be back in the morning. Good to have you home, Elliot," he nodded, giving Alice a hug and a kiss on the cheek.

"Any worries at all, just call me. Doesn't matter what time. Okay?" he said to her quietly. She smiled.

"Thanks, Dan. For everything," she said, feeling so grateful to have such unconditional support.

Alone at last, she helped Elliot to get undressed and into bed and quickly joined him, lying in the crook of his arm, resting her head on his chest and wrapping her arm across his stomach. She let out a deep sigh of relief.

"I've missed you so much," she murmured. He tightened his hold of her.

"I'm sorry about the honeymoon," he said quietly. Alice turned her face to look up at him.

"Don't be! It's all sorted; James got a refund through the insurance and I told you, Isabelle found us a little cottage not far from them. It's a romantic get-away, just outside Marazion. We'll get some food in or go out, whatever you want, and we've got the place to ourselves for the week, knowing that Tom is nearby if you need anything," she said, repeating what she had already told him the previous day.

"But I don't want to go anywhere, while *she's* still on the loose. Do you?" he asked, staring into the semi-darkness. Alice shook her head.

"No," she admitted. "No, I don't."

They lay in silence, Alice aware that Elliot was watching the bedroom door, the tension evident in his body. She hadn't slept much all week for the same reason; the fear of Mary bursting into the room to finish the job. At least Alice had been able to jump out of bed and check the landing but Elliot must feel so hampered by his injuries, she thought.

"Get some sleep. We'll talk about it in the morning," she said, stroking his chest, knowing that his medication would help him to drift off. She lay awake for a long time, listening to his rhythmic breathing, and keeping an eye on the door.

It felt like she had only slept for a matter of minutes before Sheila knocked gently and came in with a breakfast tray for them.

"Morning," she whispered, putting the tray down on the wide, bedside chest of drawers. She studied Alice's face.

"Did you sleep any better, with Elliot here?" she asked, already knowing the answer. Alice grimaced.

"Not really but just having him home is enough. I'll catch up with sleep later," she said, thanking her as she was handed a cup of tea. Sheila sat on the edge of the bed and they chatted in hushed tones for a while until Elliot stirred.

"Let me know when you need a hand to get downstairs. Dan said he'll be over before morning surgery so, any time now," she said, glancing at her watch. She patted Alice's arm and leant over to give Elliot a kiss, before returning back downstairs.

Alice was deep in thought, going over what Charlotte had told the children, when she suddenly noticed Elliot watching her intently.

"What is it?" he asked. She looked uncomfortable and shook her head.

"Alice, that look on your face … I know you," he insisted, "what's going on?"

She hesitated over her words, trying to broach the subject tactfully.

"I think Mary had a baby at some point. She said some things and … I was thinking," she paused, nervously sipping her tea. "In your drinking days, do you think … was there any chance that you slept with Mary? Without realising it?"

Elliot was aghast at her insinuation.

"Absolutely not! I mean, when I say I was drunk, I wasn't that drunk that I didn't know who I was ..." he paused, snorting with frustration. "I was trying to re-build my destroyed ego, Alice. The last person I would've slept with was Mary. She just wasn't my type, in any way, whatsoever." He was incensed that she had even contemplated the notion of it.

"I'm sorry, I'm sorry." She realised how tactless she'd been and berating herself for it, tried to explain.

"She was so adamant that she 'saw you first'. What does she mean?"

Elliot sighed. He didn't want to talk about Mary but she had found a way to ensure that they did. They would never be able to forget her now.

"Well, she did I suppose. She was in my Halls in my first year but she wasn't there for long. She dropped out, for health reasons, after the first term. And then she obviously started again the following year, when you met her," he said tersely.

"Health reasons? What was wrong with her?"

"I have no idea. But at a guess, I'd say mental health issues," he retorted. "I didn't really pay that much attention to her, to be honest. She was very quiet, very intense. We shared the kitchen but apart from that, didn't really connect. I had my 'History boys'," he gave a light laugh at their self-styled title, "and I assume she hung out with the English Literature group but I don't know," he shrugged dismissively. "I was surprised to see her again but didn't really think anything of it until she got weird, when you two became flat mates."

Alice stared at him, wondering why she had never known any of this. Or had Elliot told her, a long time ago, and she had simply forgotten it? Things suddenly started to make sense.

"Is that why she befriended me? To be near you?" she pushed. Elliot shrugged his shoulders.

"I have no idea. Maybe. But I certainly didn't encourage her: even before you and I got together. I wasn't aware of anything, that she fancied me or anything. But she made it pretty obvious when you two shared a flat in your second year. Yes, then I knew. But I thought she would understand that I was off-limits. She was *your* friend, for God's sake!" He tried to stretch his left leg, scratching at the dressing, his frustration intensifying.

"Can we drop this now. I didn't sleep with Mary O'Shea. Absolutely not. Jesus, Alice! Hasn't she done enough damage to last a life-time? Why are you even asking me this?"

He tried to swing his leg round to get out of bed. Alice jumped up to help him but he put his hand up to stop her.

"I'm fine." He turned and glared at her. "That you could even think I would father a child with *her*, is unbelievable. You just keep piling it on, don't you! First, I'm married to her and now, this." He tried to reach for his crutches, swearing in anger. Alice made a move to pass them to him.

"I don't need your help!" he growled fiercely.

Dan walked through the door at that moment, stopping in surprise at the angry exchange. Alice ducked her head and hurried out of the room, grabbing her dressing gown from the back of the door as she left. Minutes later, she stood in the shower and wept as, yet again, Mary driving a wedge between them. She knew it was insensitive of her to ask the questions that she did, but she was trying to understand what had pushed Mary to such extremes. What had happened to the girl that had been her best friend for over a year?

Alice stayed in the bathroom for a long time, not wanting to face anybody, but eventually she emerged and cautiously peered into the bedroom. There was no sign of Elliot; Dan had obviously helped him downstairs. Getting dressed, she ventured down to the kitchen. She knew that Roz and Celia were already out but she hoped that Ellie would still be there, rather than just Sheila. She needed an ally.

"Alice!" Dan called her from the lounge doorway; he had heard her coming down the stairs. She smiled awkwardly. He held out his hand.

"We're in the lounge," he said, his tone indicating that she should join them. Elliot tried to stand up when she entered the room, looking full of remorse. Dan looked pointedly at him, then at Alice, indicating she sit down. She remained standing, not sure what to do. He left the room, briefly rubbing her arm as he walked past her.

"I'm off to work, so I'll see you both later," he said.

"Please, Alice," Elliot implored, getting to his feet, clumsily using the crutches. He hopped over to where she was standing.

"I'm so sorry. I had no idea what was going on in your head. I thought you were just … I don't know … trying to blame me, or something." He spoke quickly, wanting to put things right. "Dan told me about her flat. What the police found. What you had to see," he looked distraught.

"I would have wondered too, if I were you. I would," he nodded. "But I can categorically say, I did not sleep with her, so whatever she is fixating about, is not because of any relationship I had with her," he stressed. "I am as confused as you are about it all." He wobbled on his crutches. Alice supported him and smiled.

"I wasn't blaming you; I was trying to understand, to make sense of it all. I'm sorry too. I should've been more tactful..."

"No, you should have told me the truth," he interrupted. "But I know that it was Mum's idea, to protect me. In future though, my rule still stands: no lies. No hiding things. We tell each other everything, okay."

"Okay," she agreed, helping him to sit back down.

The doorbell rang and seconds later, Sheila beckoned Alice into the hall. The same two police officers that had attended the incident at Celia's house and had been keeping the family updated with the hunt for Mary, were standing in the hall. Sheila ushered them into the kitchen and she and John disappeared into the lounge, firmly closing the kitchen door behind them.

Twenty minutes later, Alice came through to the lounge, having shown the police out. Her eyes were red-rimmed. Celia and Roz had returned in the meantime and the five of them looked at her expectantly.

"They've found Mary," she announced shakily. Sheila burst into tears with relief and Celia followed suit. Elliot stared at her, knowing there was more.

"Where did they find her?" Roz asked. Alice sat down on the edge of the nearest chair, looking at Elliot, holding his eye-contact, willing herself to speak. Her voice trembled.

"Hanging from a tree, in Wilverley woods."

Nobody said a word, stunned into silence by the news.

"The coroner said that she'd been there since Saturday morning. So, she must have gone there straight after …" Alice couldn't bear the look on Elliot's face. She moved to sit next to him and held him tightly.

"Did she hang herself because of me?" he breathed, swallowing repeatedly. Alice shook her head.

"I don't think so, but she did think that she'd killed you. She left a note. For me."

She held up the envelope she'd been clutching and handed it to Roz, asking her to read it. Roz obliged.

'Alice, I'm sorry that I killed Elliot but he was mine first.
I was his girl.
They took him away from me.
And then they took our baby away from me.
And I was left with nothing.
But now I can be with them again.
They're waiting for me in Heaven.
And you can rot in Hell.'

"What does that mean?" Celia asked. Alice shrugged, not understanding it herself.

"Did the police tell you anything more about her? Did she have family?" John asked quietly.

"No. Nothing. Nobody reported her missing and she has no next of kin. She was all alone in the world," Alice said, her heart sinking.

"You sound sorry for her," Sheila accused. "She tried to *kill* Elliot. She destroyed your lives, Alice."

"I know and I hate her for it but part of me can't help feeling sorry for her. Just the thought of her dying, alone, and nobody finding her for days. Nobody caring," Alice stressed. Sheila stood up abruptly, shaking her head.

"I can't agree with you. I am just relieved that it's over. She can't hurt either one of you anymore. She drove my son to drink, to the brink of despair and then, this," she said, pointing at Elliot's elevated leg. "And if you hadn't been there to stop her, he would be dead. And you would have been next. This could have been a double funeral, not a wedding. So, no, I can't feel sorry for her at all."

She turned away, blinking with rage. Roz stood up and offered her a hug, looking pointedly at Alice. Alice looked at the floor, not knowing what to say.

It was a sombre afternoon and evening, after such an intense week of emotions. They all felt drained and ragged. Celia's kitchen floor had been finished and with help, the house had been cleaned. Now that the danger of Mary re-appearing was no longer applicable, she and Roz felt it was time to return home. Ellie had spent the day with Natalie and came back in time to help pack their things up, although she opted to stay at Sheila's for another night, along with Alice. They snatched a moment alone upstairs and Alice told her everything that had occurred earlier in the day. She knew she had upset Sheila but in turn, Mary's death had really upset her.

"Mum, you need to sort this out with Gran. I can see what you're saying but that woman wanted you both dead. I'm glad she's gone. And as far as Gran is concerned, she has found it incredibly difficult to come to terms with her son being stabbed. Imagine if that were me, being stabbed. How would you feel then?" Ellie reasoned.

"But, that's not my point. It's the fact that Mary was a friend. She destroyed me. She destroyed Elliot...", she paused, looking at Ellie as her mind ticked over, realising what she was saying.

"And she deprived me of a father," Ellie added. Alice nodded.

"Yes, so why am I even wasting my time feeling anything for her? I don't understand it myself," she said with frustration.

"Because you care, Mum. But she didn't care. And that's what made her dangerous. She didn't care who she hurt," she stressed. "Gran needs to know that you love her son, more than anything. Put it right," she encouraged as they hugged each other.

"I haven't had a chance to talk to you properly about Uni. We've missed you," Alice said, noticing how Ellie blushed a little.

"I bet you haven't! The house all to yourselves; come on, that must be pretty perfect for you?" she teased. Alice smiled, knowing she was right. About that and about Sheila. She sent up a silent prayer for Mary and then put her out of her mind. For good. She found Sheila in the kitchen and made her peace. Then she joined Elliot in the lounge and curled up next to him on the sofa.

"I love you, Elliot. If I could turn back time and do it all again, I'd like to think I would've had the courage to move in with *you*, and tell the world how much I love you. And how there was nothing wrong with it."

Elliot raised an eyebrow.

"I wouldn't have missed that for the world!" he laughed. He looked at his watch, calculating. "In thirty-six hours precisely, you will be my wife." His heart beat faster just thinking about it and yet, he couldn't resist teasing her.

"We've both got regrets, Alice, but one thing I will never regret, is … seducing you on your first night in York," he grinned, laughing at her expression. "Seriously, I will never regret not giving up on my first love. My only love. And as for all the rest, we have an eternity to make up for lost time. Starting with our honeymoon … in Cornwall," he said, pulling a defeated face. "It doesn't have the same ring to it as Vienna, does it?"

"I don't mind what it sounds like. Besides, good things happen in Cornwall, so I'm told," she grinned, relieved that the nightmare was over and she could allow herself to be excited about their wedding again.

Chapter Twenty-Two

Their wedding day dawned with blue skies and sunshine; bitterly cold but with no sign of the forecast snow. Alice was up and showered by half past five, checking the itinerary that had been stuck on the bathroom door. There was another copy on the fridge door in the kitchen. In capital letters, at the very bottom of the minute-by-minute list, were the words, 'GET ALICE TO CHURCH FOR 11 A.M.!!!!' Alice could feel Celia's stress in every single one of those exclamation marks.

Sitting on her bed, with a towel wrapped round her, she picked up her phone and called Elliot. He had tried to reason with her the night before, not wanting her to leave him and spend her last night in her own childhood bedroom, but she had insisted; everything had to go according to plan and tradition had to be upheld.

"Morning you," she murmured when he answered his phone. He grunted sleepily.

"Morning you too," he spoke through a yawn as he stretched.

"Anybody up?" she asked brightly.

"Yes, of course. James has already been in twice to wake me and Dan is waiting to do his valet duties in the bathroom", he said. "Mum's getting her stuff together to come round to yours. Dad's not up yet though."

"Well, I'm not sure if my mum's even been to bed but she bought me tea at five and Roz is buzzing about downstairs. Ellie and Rachel are up and I think chaos is about to ensue, according to the timetable," she chuckled. She heard Elliot rustling something.

"Okay, have you got it in your hand?" he asked.

"Yes. Have you?" she replied.

"Yes. After three: one, two, three …"

Alice held her phone under her chin as she carefully opened a beautifully wrapped, small, oblong box. She quickly read the tag: 'My love, my life, my one and only A. Thank you for making me the happiest man in the world xxx E'.

She knew that Elliot would be reading the tag she had written: 'I have waited my whole life for this moment. Love you with every beat of my heart xxx A'.

Alice let out a gasp of wonder, as Elliot simultaneously gave a low whistle and breathed, "Wow." She lifted the intricate, platinum bracelet from its box and draped it across her wrist. It sparkled as the rows of tiny, encrusted diamonds caught the light. The Art Deco design matched her engagement ring perfectly, right down to the milgrain edging. Alice bit her lip and butterflies started in her stomach as the enormity of the day suddenly hit her.

"It's beautiful, Elliot," she whispered, "I love it, thank you."

"Thank *you*. I love them," he said. Alice could hear how choked he was. She had chosen to stick with the platinum theme and had bought him a pair of solid platinum, oval, cufflinks, edged with a Celtic design. Each cufflink had a black onyx centre, in which was engraved an initial that had a platinum infill. One cufflink had the initial E and the other, an A. They had travelled up to York especially, to choose their gifts for one another, wanting them to be from a place of significance. They had also bought their platinum wedding rings from there, a month previously.

"See you in church, Mrs Barraclough-to-be," he said, for the last time.

"See you in church, Mr Barraclough," she agreed, hanging up and holding the phone to her chest, visualising his face as he waited for her in church. The butterflies were really setting in, to the extent that she thought she would throw up. Taking deep breaths, she tried to steady her churning stomach before going downstairs, head-on into the pre-wedding hurly burly.

By nine o'clock, Alice had been transformed. Celia had hired a team of hairdressers and beauticians, who worked tirelessly and methodically on the ladies; not just Alice and her six attendants, but all the ladies in the wedding party. Half of the ushers were getting ready at Sheila and John's house, with Anne there to organise them and the other half, at Charlotte's house, with Isabelle there to help. The three ladies had strict instructions to allow themselves enough time to drive over to Celia's by half past nine, for their pampering session with the team. The wedding photographer flitted between the three houses, snapping candid shots as the parties got ready.

Alice escaped to her bedroom, scrutinising her reflection in the dressing table mirror. Her make-up was flawless; she had opted for a more natural look and was pleased with the overall result. She had hesitantly agreed to the false eyelashes that Ellie and Rachel had raved about. They weren't as heavy or clumpy looking as she had imagined; in fact, their 'natural look' was indeed, just that. And the subtle shades of bronze and peach eyeshadow highlighted her eyes perfectly. She loved her hair: the style she had chosen, the 'love knot', involved her hair being swept back into a low chignon and incorporating expertly styled knots. The effect was similar to the Celtic love-knots design so often used in rings and necklaces, and suited her perfectly. Simple, pearl hair pins were inserted between the knots, and a crystal and pearl hair vine, with delicate, ivory, enamel flowers, sat across the crown of her head.

Her wedding jewellry was lined up on the table in front of her, in order of something old, new, borrowed and blue. She gently touched each item in turn: her pearl ring from her parents, her diamond bracelet from Elliot, Sheila's solitaire diamond necklace and finally, a blue and white lacy garter, bought by Ellie. She picked up the bracelet and held it up to the light, smiling at the memory of their day in York, scouring jewellry shops in the Shambles and beyond. Staring at her reflection once again, she seemed transfixed by her eyes, deep in thought. Taking a decisive breath, she sent Elliot a text.

'I need to see you. Meet me outside on your drive in five minutes xxx A'

She tightened the belt of her knee-length dressing gown and quickly pulled her fluffy bootie slippers onto her bare feet. She only had her underwear on but knew she wouldn't have time to get dressed properly. Grabbing her car keys and bag, she quietly hurried downstairs and out through the door, before anybody spotted her.

Elliot was waiting by his front door when she pulled up minutes later. He slowly hopped over to her car, not quite adept with his crutches yet. He was wearing loose trousers and a hastily thrown on jumper; traces of shaving foam in his ear and under his chin indicated what he had been doing when he received her text. She got out of the car, holding a hand up to shield her face.

"Alice? Is everything alright? Are you okay?" he asked. His puzzled smile belied his concern at her unexpected appearance.

"Yes, I'm fine. You mustn't look at me but I just needed to see you," she stammered. He let out an exasperated laugh.

"Well, how is that going to work?" He steadied himself with one hand on her shoulder, leaning heavily on one of his crutches and peered under her hand at her face. She smiled awkwardly.

"Promise not to look too much then," she insisted shyly. He inclined his head.

"I promise," he agreed. "You look beautiful," he emphasised.

"Elliot!" she squealed, "you're not supposed to see that!"

Elliot stepped back, looking at the ground, shaking his head and laughing.

"Okay, okay, I don't know that you're beautiful. I'm marrying you in a couple of hours but I have no idea what you look like," he teased dramatically, then paused. "I am still marrying you, right?"

Alice dropped her hand instantly, looking horrified.

"Of course you are! I'm sorry, I didn't mean to …" She moved to hug him then stopped herself, hesitating, hampered by tradition.

"Oh, to hell with it!" she exclaimed and put her arms around him, letting him rest his weight on her.

"Sorry, I didn't mean to worry you. Of course we're getting married; nothing is going to stop us. Surely you know that by now," she insisted, widening her eyes for emphasis. Elliot grimaced.

"It's been a hell of a week, hasn't it?" he acknowledged. He searched Alice's face, wondering what she was doing there, defying the pre-wedding protocol that she had been so adamant on adhering to.

Alice leant into the car and picked up a long, thin jewellry box, from the passenger seat. It was black, with a silver, voile ribbon tied around it and finished off with a neat bow. She offered it to Elliot.

"I was going to ask Andrew to bring this round but I wanted to see your face when you open it," she said.

"But you've already given me a present: the cufflinks? he sounded confused.

"I know but this is from Ellie, and ... something else from me, that I wanted you to have now. I couldn't wait till later," she rushed her words and he could see how her hand trembled as she handed him the box. He studied it for a moment looking thoughtful, then held it to his ear and shook it.

"No, I don't think it's an electric guitar," he sounded disappointed.

"It's really not!" she laughed.

"Hey, don't crush my dreams. I'll get better with practice," he grinned, admitting how rusty his playing was. Alice shivered and stamped her feet against the cold.

"Open it then," she urged, "we have got a wedding to get to, you know."

Elliot carefully pulled the bow and the ribbon unravelled effortlessly. Lifting the lid, his eyes lit up and an appreciative gasp escaped his lips. He gingerly picked up a stainless-steel case and bracelet watch, with a navy-blue sunburst dial, and held it against his wrist to admire it. Alice looked pleased with his reaction.

"Turn it over," she prompted. Elliot did so; the casing had an inscription engraved on it.

'I love you Dad, with all my heart. Ellie xxx'

He bit back tears, completely caught unawares by his emotional reaction. He looked at Alice, lost for words. She gave him a sheepish smile.

"She wanted to give it to you herself but knew she'd cry off all her make-up," she said. She pointed at the box.

"There's something underneath that bit of card," she instructed, stepping back and watching him intently. He lifted the card and stared at the content, holding his breath. He frowned.

"You kept the pregnancy tester from when you found out about Ellie?" His voice sounded strangled as he looked at the bold, blue, plus sign on the white, plastic stick. Alice nodded.

"Yes, of course I did," she said quietly. "But that's not it."

Elliot's head snapped up, staring at her in disbelief. It seemed like an eternity before he uttered,

"What?"

She smiled and raised her eyebrows, waiting for the penny to drop.

"When's this from, then?" he asked, licking his lips nervously.

"This morning. About an hour ago, actually. I couldn't get here any sooner, sorry," she sniffed, trying to keep the tears at bay.

He stared at the tester again, then back at Alice.

"You mean...?" He had started to shake, uncontrollably, depending totally on his crutches for support. Alice let out a choked laugh.

"Yes. I 'mean'," she said. Seeing how unsteady he had become, she rushed forward to hold him. He clung on to her arm, staring at her, fear and elation mingled in his eyes.

"We're having a baby, Elliot," she murmured, nodding, frantically breathing in through her nose in an effort to stop the tears from spilling down her face. Her make-up was immaculate and she knew she couldn't ruin it now.

"Are you sure? I mean, is this test accurate?" He needed to be absolutely certain before he could allow himself to believe it. He stared at her, the answer evident in her elated smile and sparkling eyes.

"Yes, it's definitely right. I had just assumed I was missing periods and feeling sick due to the stress of the wedding. It's been exhausting and to be honest, I hadn't really thought about it until the other day, at the hospital," she said, watching his reaction as he struggled to take it all in.

"Periods, as in, plural? How pregnant are you?" he asked, berating himself for not noticing either.

"About nine, ten weeks, I'd say," she said, instinctively touching her stomach. Elliot placed his hand over hers, wanting to connect with the life that was growing inside her. His heart started to pound as adrenalin kicked in.

"These damned crutches!" he cursed. "I just want to pick you up and run to the church right now; I can't wait another minute to marry you," he said passionately. He stared at her, loving how her face glowed with happiness. He moved to stroke her cheek but she jerked her head away, laughing in mock-horror.

"Don't touch my make-up, it took ages! And not my hair!" she shrieked, as his hand hovered in the air.

"Where can I touch you then?" he pleaded, looking helplessly at her. She pulled her sleeve up and offered him her elbow.

"Here?" she joked. He grinned and with a bow, bent forward to kiss her elbow. Her face softened. She pointed to her neck.

"Here?" she suggested. He kissed her neck. She pointed to her ear.

"Here?"

He kissed her ear. Then, with his crutches hanging redundantly from his forearms, he grabbed her waist and kissed her lips with such a passion that she lost her footing and stumbled backwards against the car, with Elliot leaning heavily against her. He pulled back quickly, putting a protective hand on her stomach.

"The baby, I'm sorry. Did I squash you?" his voice was full of concern. Alice shook her head.

"No, the baby's safe in there, don't worry," she said quietly, pulling him back towards her to continue the kiss.

"You're wearing my lipstick: it suits you," she joked, moments later as they straightened themselves up and Elliot regained his balance. The most enormous grin had spread across his face and he chuckled as he looked at her.

"I can't believe it! I just can't believe it," he exclaimed, shaking his head in delight.

"Me neither," she laughed. "Listen, I've been thinking - because I've had an hour to plan everything, you know - how about you leave work and become a full-time dad? I mean, you could spend some time doing research for that history book you've always wanted to write. Not that you'll get much free time, I have to warn you but ... I think you'll make a great dad. Correction: I *know* you'll make a great dad," she enthused, gauging his response. It wasn't what she expected. His face contorted as he struggled against but finally succumbed to tears. Letting out a strangled sob, he rocked on his crutches, staring at the ground, trying to control his emotional outburst.

"I'm sorry," he spluttered, "I just ... it's been such a crazy week ..." He tried to laugh through his tears, sniffing repeatedly. Alice held on to him, helping him back towards the house. Looking up, she saw James at the upstairs window, watching them with concern. She beckoned to him and seconds later, he was by her side, supporting Elliot and helping him back indoors. Elliot nodded, thanking him. James shot Alice a questioning look as she stroked Elliot's arm.

"See you in church. I love you," she whispered, then smiling at James, said,

"Look after him, James. He's going to be a daddy!"

His mouth dropped open in surprise and he looked from one to the other, noting Alice's joyous face and Elliot's tear-stained one.

"He *is* happy," she laughed. Elliot looked at James and nodded, feeling foolish, not trusting himself to speak yet.

James steadied him by the door and hurried over to hug Alice, beaming at her.

"That is wonderful news! Congratulations. And may I say, you are looking particularly beautiful today," he commented benevolently. Alice's face froze and she quickly shielded it with her hands yet again.

"No, you're not supposed to see me!" she exclaimed, laughing as she jogged back to her car, holding her dressing gown together to avoid it from exposing her legs. She turned and blew Elliot a kiss. He caught it in the air and patted his hand on his heart.

"Don't keep me waiting," he warned her, his grin returning and countenance restored.

"Wild horses wouldn't stop me," she called as she climbed into the driver's seat. She hesitated, reflecting for a second.

"Although, considering where we are: wild horses would be the only thing that *would* stop me!" she laughed, waving as she shut the door and reversed out of the drive.

The next hour passed in a whirl of fevered activity, the house alive with excited chatter as six bridesmaids were dressed and fussed over, each one being given strict instructions to sit and not move once they had 'been done'. They had all been growing their hair over the previous months to enable them to have matching hairstyles, and Ellie had decided, in lieu of a 'Frozen' themed wedding, that they should all have an Elsa-style, voluminous French braid. It had involved lots of curling and teasing into the desired effect, with a large, pearl, snowflake-shaped clip at the top of each braid, adding the finishing touch. Their dresses were of duchess satin, offering a heavier weight and softer sheen than regular satin, in a shade of cranberry red. Alice had been very specific with her colour choices: she wanted a rich, rustic Christmas red to contrast with the white of her dress, and to celebrate the season. Laura had been quick to find the perfect shade of cranberry; not too harsh and not too dark. The style of their dresses complimented Alice's: a floor length, A-line with a sweetheart neckline and capped sleeves, and a low back. Their bouquets were predominately white, being made up of white roses and freesias, ruby carnations and white gypsophila with a splash of red berries on thin wire stems. Threaded through the blooms, tiny, fairy lights, gave off a warm, festive glow. Alice's bouquet was much larger and predominantly red, with red and wine coloured roses, ruby carnations, white freesias and again, offset with gypsophila and red berries.

Satisfied with the results and happy that all six girls were completely ready, Celia quickly got her own outfit on and helped Roz and Sheila with their corsages. Andrew had arrived just ahead of the cars, ready to escort Alice to church, and taking their cue to leave, Celia, Roz and Sheila got into the first of the three cars. Although the church was easily within walking distance, it had been deemed too cold, even for such a short distance, particularly for Alice and the girls, in their thin dresses.

Laura helped Alice get into her dress, carefully unzipping the cover and holding it up high for Alice to admire. She had seen it so many times over the past few months, in various stages of creation, but at that moment, sitting on her bed half an hour before the ceremony, it felt like she was seeing it for the first time.

"It's so beautiful," she breathed. Laura nodded in agreement, pleased with her own handiwork. She had relished the challenge of drawing up designs for Alice, working within the parameters set: classic lines, romantic yet understated, and predominantly lace. She played on Alice's strengths, mainly her straight back and broad shoulders - a result of years of regular swimming - and had opted for a figure hugging, sweetheart neckline and an illusion back. The lace covered bodice and capped sleeves, emphasising her cleavage, were adorned with delicate swirls of pearls, crystals and embroidery, which cascaded down the A-line, tulle skirt and generous, chapel train. With clever use of embellished, lace appliqué and sheer tulle, the same embroidered swirls caressed the sides of her back, down to the base of her spine, leaving the rest of her skin tantalisingly exposed, under the tulle. So as not to detract from the dress in any way, Laura had designed a sheer veil with no added faff, bar a scattering of minute crystals, to subtly catch the light.

Alice ran her hands down across her body to smooth the dress out, lingering over her stomach, gazing at her reflection and trying not to smile at the thought of the secret she was carrying. Laura's sharp eyes didn't miss a trick. She looked at Alice, watching her face as she caught her eye. Alice's smile widened.

"No!" Laura breathed. "Are you?" she turned her away from the mirror to look at her. She didn't need to hear the words; the answer was written all over Alice's face.

"My God, you don't do things by half, do you?" she exclaimed, hugging her, carefully so as not to crease the dress. They grinned at each other, both starting to well up. Laura widened her eyes and blinked away the tears, the thick mascara feeling heavy on her lashes.

"Good grief, Alice; every time I see you, there's something new to cry about!" she laughed. "But this is priceless. Brilliant, just brilliant. Does Elliot know?"
Alice nodded.

"Yes, I told him this morning, as soon as I'd done the test."
Laura stared at her, then shook her head in despair.

"You did the test *this morning*? On your wedding day. Are you just an adrenalin junkie or something? Whatever happened to little Alice who never rocked the boat: who just lived the quiet life, hiding away in the country?" she teased.

"I woke up. Elliot found me and brought me back to life," she admitted simply, turning to look at her reflection. She radiated, bursting with happiness. Bubbling with excitement at what the future held. And right now, her future was waiting for her in their church. Taking a last look at herself and poking an errant strand of hair back into place before they carefully lifted the veil over her head, she turned from the mirror and took Laura's hand.

"Okay, let's do this. Tell them I'm ready." She drew in a deep breath and headed for the bedroom door. Andrew was hovering at the top of the stairs, waiting for them. He caught his breath, letting out a choked exclaim; a curious noise that came from not knowing whether to laugh, or cry, with surprised joy.

"Crikey, Alice," he murmured, "you look absolutely stunning." He held her at arm's length, mesmerised by the transformation in her. She could see he was struggling to not utter the words that were playing on both of their minds; how proud their dad would have been at that moment.

"So, going anywhere nice?" he joked, offering her his arm and helping her negotiate the stairs, with Laura following close behind to hold up the train.

The girls were standing in the hall, watching her descent and making noises of appreciation at her dress. They gave her a round of air-kisses, mindful of their carefully applied lipstick, before making their way out onto the drive, giggling with anticipation. The first car had returned, ready for the next journey. Marnie, Lily, Amber, and Natalie carefully climbed in, each accepting the bouquet that Andrew and Laura passed to them once they were seated. Rachel and Ellie got into the second car, and as Andrew passed their bouquets, he leant in to kiss them each on the cheek.

"My goodness, girls, you are both so beautiful. You've made this old man very proud," he said, taken aback by how grown up they looked.

"Less of the 'old', thank you," Laura interjected as she climbed into her seat. "There's plenty of life left in you yet," she teased, accepting his kiss. "See you there; look after your sister," she winked, sensing how emotional he was feeling and the effort it was taking to keep it all in check.

Andrew watched them leave before helping Alice into the third car. They took their time, making sure the train was folded carefully before she sat down. Andrew leant back in his seat and let out a sigh, clutching her hand as the car slowly left their drive.

"Alright?" he asked, watching her face. She stared out of the window, trying not to well-up as they drove along the familiar route to the church. She had a sudden flash of her younger self, skipping along the pavement on her way to see her grandpa.

"Mmm-hmm," she inclined her head.

"Only... that was a very telling wink I just got from my wife ..." he paused.

"I'm pregnant." She gave him a shy smile. Andrew laughed in surprise.

"Crikey! That's fantastic, Alice! I'm so happy for you both. More so for Elliot, if I'm honest," he admitted, grinning at the thought of Elliot's euphoria.

"Me too," she agreed wholeheartedly. He turned in his seat and pulled a serious face.

"Now, was this planned or do I need to have a big brother talk with you both about contraception? Because this is becoming a bit of a habit," he started to laugh, teasing her.

"Call it divine intervention," she shrugged happily, her stomach flipping over as the car slowed down to turn into the church.

Celia and Roz had taken their seats at the front on the left-hand side: Sheila and John on the other side of the aisle with Elliot and his two brothers. The church was filling up quickly and Celia was glad that she had accepted the suggestion of extra seating towards the back of the church. When they had sent out the invitations, Roz had reckoned with a certain percentage not being able to make it but as it turned out, everybody had.

Celia gave the young ushers an encouraging 'thumbs up', watching them politely show guests to their seats. Riley and Chris surpassed themselves; they resisted the temptation to practice moonwalking and body popping on the polished, stone floor, and instead, smiled genially at guests and chatted to the ones they recognised. The church was awash with flowers and the smell of rose, freesia, and pine, pervaded the air. Large, Christmas-inspired arrangements of fresh blooms interwoven with sprigs of pine, dominated the deep windowsills, and pedestals of similar displays greeted the guests as they entered the church. The theme continued down the aisle, with the end seat of each row having a small bunch of blooms, tied with cranberry red ribbon, attached to it. Large pedestal displays were also positioned on either side of the wide steps leading up to the altar. The whole effect was stunning in its effortless uniformity.

Celia surveyed the church with a mounting sense of achievement; she had managed to pull it off, despite all the odds. Her eyes rested on Elliot. She smiled as she watched him turn repeatedly to look at the entrance, eager to spot the first glimpse of his bride. Laura had picked out the suits that he and the groomsmen were wearing, and Celia was impressed with her choice; charcoal grey tails with a white shirt, white, jacquard waistcoat and a cranberry red, Ascot cravat. The finishing touches were a pearl tipped cravat pin, a cranberry red, pocket handkerchief, and a white, carnation buttonhole.

"They're such a good-looking family, aren't they," she whispered to Roz, indicating to the brothers in the opposite row.

"Such handsome boys," she reiterated fondly. Roz smiled and nodded. Isabelle tapped her on the shoulder, from her seat behind them.

"Laura's here," she whispered.

Laura was to be their cue to start the ceremony. She had waited with the bridesmaids for Alice and Andrew to arrive, helped Alice out of the car, and positioned the procession who were waiting to make their entrance. Once she had taken her seat next to Isabelle, Tom, and Michael, she looked over at the trio of musicians by the lectern. They were music students from the local college and were also part of the church choir. One was seated at the piano and the other two were standing, with viola and violin at the ready. Laura nodded: their cue to start playing. Elliot was on his feet instantly, flanked by James and Dan, and leaning on his crutches. He turned to the entrance, holding his breath, waiting. He had been happy to hand over all the wedding planning but had been adamant about two things: he was to choose the entrance music and he was going to ignore tradition, and watch Alice as she entered the church.

"Why would I wait with my back turned, when my bride is walking down the aisle?" he had said, "this is the most important day of my life and I'm not going to miss a single second of it."

The bridesmaids waited, giving the congregation a chance to stand and for the music to get into full swing, before they slowly made their way into the church; Ellie and Rachel, followed by Natalie and Amber, then Marnie and Lily. Lily had a basket of rose petals to scatter behind her, paving the way for Alice and Andrew's entrance.

As soon as Alice heard the first refrain of music, played on the viola and piano, she faltered and stared at Andrew as the unmistakable melody of 'Can't Help Falling in Love', reached her ears.

"Oh, good Lord; I am going to cry," she murmured. It was Elliot's favourite song and one he would sing to her often, as they slow-danced in the kitchen. Andrew gave a half-smile.

"If you think that's going to set you off, just wait till you see what Ellie and Natalie have done in there. It's a real 'Armageddon' moment," he warned her. She frowned, not understanding.

"You know, the film? The ending?" He didn't get a chance to explain; patting her arm that was linked through his, they made their way through the open doors, smiling at the sea of faces in front of them. The violin solo gave her a prickly sensation at the back of her neck and she bit her trembling lip, willing herself to look at Elliot and not to cry. He was watching her progress, with a look of utter pride. His wide smile dominated his face but Alice could see he was also struggling to hold it all together. For a second, she wondered at the wisdom of telling him about their baby before the wedding, and then she caught sight of something behind him, to the side of the steps leading up to the altar. Undoubtedly the added cause of his barely contained emotional state; three tripod easels, each holding a large, framed photograph of David, Reggie, and her grandfather, in pride of place to witness their marriage. She very nearly came undone and seeing her reaction, Elliot very nearly joined her. He reached for her hand as she and Andrew approached.

"You look beyond beautiful," he whispered, "I love you, Alice." His voice shook and his hand trembled.

"I love you too, Elliot," she whispered back, overcome with the need to throw back her veil and hug him.

"Here we go," she grinned, with a shaky laugh.

"Here we go," he breathed as they turned to face Martin, who greeted them with his welcoming smile.

"Here we go indeed," he also whispered, giving them each an encouraging nod before addressing the congregation.

"Welcome everyone, to St Saviour's church and to the marriage of Alice and Elliot. I am, personally, particularly thrilled, and honoured, to be performing the ceremony here today because Alice has been a big part of my life for some years. She is family to me. She and Elliot are both children of Brockenhurst, of our community, and have returned home to unite in marriage. Many of us thought that this day would never happen - right up to the very last minute - but with our prayers, and their devotion to each other, and against all odds, the day is finally here. And I know, for certain, that it is the start of a wonderful, joyous life together, for Alice and Elliot."

Postscript

Seven months later

It was a familiar scene: Celia's lounge and kitchen were teeming with people, dressed in suits and summer frocks, with the midday sun blazing through the large windows. Mountains of food and an abundance of drink could be found on a number of strategically placed tables, acting as beacons for thirsty and hungry guests. Celia busied herself, making sure everybody had something, and offering tea or coffee as an alternative. She paused by Elliot, to gently stroke her young grandson's podgy cheek, as he lay cradled in the crook of Elliot's arm. His skin was silky soft and pink, and he had a shock of black, fuzzy hair that covered his whole head. It looked odd on such a small baby of just four weeks. He didn't stir from his sleep at Celia's touch, perfectly content and oblivious to the lively chatter that filled the room.

"Tea?" she offered in a hushed tone, smiling at Elliot and Alice.

"Please," they both smiled back, gratefully. She noted how tired they looked; tired but happy. Elliot was, as always, impeccably dressed in a light grey suit, pale blue shirt, and charcoal tie. The terry towelling burp cloth draped across his shoulder added an interesting touch but even that didn't look out of place. Alice's blue and grey, floral summer dress complimented his outfit and her proud smile matched his. She looked less jaded than he did, with a maternal glow that seemed to wash away the effects of sleep deprivation. They chatted to their guests, patiently answering the same questions over and over, and trying not to convey their over-protectiveness when hands reached forward to touch their son's head in greeting. Cards were pressed into Alice's hand, and christening gifts stowed on the sideboard.

Left alone for a moment, Elliot looked across the room, watching the interaction between people, then turned back to Alice.

"Are you still sure about Ellie and Brad? Not being an item, I mean," he whispered with a barely contained smile. She frowned.

"Yes, of course. Why?" Her eyes scanned the room, looking for Ellie.

"I'm not so sure. They've got that look going on. Watch them," he said, nodding his head in her direction. Alice spotted her, on the other side of the room, partially masked by Rachel who, as if on cue, moved away. Ellie smiled up at Brad as he gently stroked her arm while talking to her. He leant forward and whispered in her ear, making her laugh. She touched his thigh as she whispered back. They shared a look, totally oblivious to anybody else in that moment. Rachel re-joined them, blocking Alice's view once again.

"So ... still convinced?" Elliot chuckled. Alice stared at him, wide-eyed, realisation dawning. He laughed.

"Told you. I knew it; I recognised that look, from the minute I met him," he said, feeling smug at being right. Celia appeared before Alice had a chance to comment back.

"Elliot, dear, are you ready to give a little speech? Wet the baby's head?" she suggested, holding a hand up to signal Dan and Andrew, who immediately started refilling guests' glasses. Andrew handed Elliot and Alice a glass each, and then tapped his own, to command the room's attention. That done, he bowed to Elliot, grinning. Elliot cleared his throat, glancing down at his sleeping son before addressing the guests.

"Thank you. I just wanted to welcome you all, and to thank you for coming. First off, I'd like you all to join me in a toast to our wonderful daughter, Ellie, who is nineteen today." He raised his glass to her.

"Happy birthday, my beautiful girl."

A chorus of 'happy birthday, Ellie', resonated around the room, and she did a curtsey, laughing with embarrassment.

"And I have to thank Ellie for sharing her special day with her little brother. It seemed a fitting day to hold his christening." He smiled at Alice before continuing. "Thank you all for joining us in the church this morning, and a special nod to Martin for the wonderful service," he added, seeking him out in the crowd to acknowledge him. A thought struck him.

"Godparents, where are you?" He waited for Isabelle, Tom, and Natalie to work their way across the room and stand with him and Alice. He winked at Natalie, proud of how she had risen to the role.

"So, if you have your drinks ready, I'd like you all to raise a glass to welcome David Reginald Barraclough, into this wonderful family." His words were echoed, and glasses clinked, and the chatter recommenced. Ellie came over to join them, bestowing a soft kiss on her brother's head. He still didn't stir.

"Great speech, Dad," she enthused, then noticing Alice's expression, looked puzzled.

"What?" she asked.

"Is there anything you want to tell me, Ellie?" Alice wondered, her voice pitched higher than usual. She tried to look casual but there was a smile brewing.

Ellie grinned, sensing she had been rumbled. She raised her eyebrows.

"Yes! Being nineteen is absolutely amazing!" She kissed Alice noisily on the cheek and did the same to Elliot, laughing at their expectant faces. She made to walk away, then turned back, holding up a hand as if she had suddenly remembered something.

"Oh, and just so you know," she paused for effect, "I'm sleeping with Brad, and we're in love. He's been in love with me for years, apparently. And so, we're moving in together, after the summer, for our second year at Uni. Just the two of us, no flat-mates. Okay?" She grinned, delighted at her mother's stunned face, and then without giving them a chance to respond, skipped back to Brad's side and openly took his hand.

"She gets her honesty from you," Alice said flatly.

"Clearly," Elliot laughed. "With my honesty, your beauty, and our brains, she'll go far," he smiled.

Just then, little David wriggled and stretched, briefly opening his eyes before scrunching up his face and going bright red.

"Hmmm, I think he needs changing," Elliot gave a laugh, turning his nose up at the smell. Handing Alice his glass, he made to leave the room in search of the change bag.

"It's okay, let me," she said, "he's probably ready for a feed anyway," she smiled, knowing his routine.

"Have a word with Brad: let him know we're on his side. I bet he's nervous about us finding out," she encouraged. Carefully lifting David from Elliot's arm, she headed for the stairs. Seeing her leave, Celia followed and patting Ellie's arm as she passed, asked her to fetch Alice a cup of tea.

A few minutes later, David was changed and ready for a feed. Alice propped herself up on her bed, positioning pillows to make them both comfortable before he latched on. Celia sat on the edge of the bed, watching with a maternal smile. Ellie and Roz joined them, with a tray of tea and some biscuits.

"I know you get hungry when he's feeding," Roz said, passing her a biscuit. They all perched on the bed, with identical, contented smiles on their faces, watching David's jaw move rhythmically as he fed from Alice.

"So, how was your last day? I haven't had a chance to ask," Roz wondered. Alice pulled a sad face.

"Tearful."

She had worked up until her thirty-sixth week, before her maternity leave started. David had arrived, three weeks ahead of schedule, the following week. Elliot had suggested that she take a year out, on top of her maternity leave, to give them a chance to both be at home for baby's first year. She didn't need much persuading, jumping at the chance to experience the baby days ahead, with Elliot. He was then going to be an 'at home' dad once she returned to work.

The four ladies sat in companionable silence, contemplating life's journey and the events of the past twelve months. Twelve months to the day, in fact.

"Just think, Mum," Alice said, breaking the silence, "if you hadn't insisted on sending me out for more crisps for Ellie's party, I wouldn't have bumped into Elliot and none of this would have happened. I wouldn't have told Ellie about Elliot, you wouldn't have confessed about David and your baby," she said to Roz, "and you wouldn't have found Isabelle," she said to Ellie. "And I would never have got back together with Elliot, married him, and had David."

They all nodded in agreement.

"So many positive things came out of that one chance encounter," she said quietly, locking eyes with her baby. They fell into silence again.

"So, are you saying that too many crisps are a good thing?" Ellie piped up cheekily, reaching for a biscuit.

"Yes, that's exactly what I'm saying. You can never have too much of a good thing," Alice laughed.

"Amen to that," Celia smiled.

"I think we should raise our tea cups, and toast the humble bag of crisps," Roz said. They held their cups aloft.

"To the crisps," they chorused.

"And to us," Ellie added. "Always, to us."

***

Coming soon ...

When sixteen-year-old Mary O'Shea and her parents moved from Ireland to a bustling Yorkshire village, she assumed her life would continue in the same vein despite the change in location. Awkward and naïve, with an over-protective father, she stuck to her safe routine of school studies, a Saturday job and spending time with her small circle of friends. Nothing exciting ever happened and that suited her fine. Until the day that she was thrown together with the notoriously troubled Richard White.

'***Close Your Eyes'*** unravels the tale of a dangerous infatuation; a destructive love that couldn't possibly have a positive outcome. Or could it?

Acknowledgements

As always, a massive 'thanks' to my family, Team Griffiths: Simon, Carina, Dino, Anton, Lou, Damon & Heidi. For always believing in me, propping me up with tea and biscuits, and listening to me ramble on about my world of make-believe.

Thanks to the residents of Brockenhurst, Wilmcote and York, for being so friendly and enjoying a chat. And to the RSC Stratford for always making date nights with Simon all the more special.

Huge respect to the Commonwealth War Graves Commission for the dedicated work they do to commemorate our fallen heroes.

To my Facebook 'family', thanks for all your support and daily smiles.

To Spotify, life would be so empty without your constant supply of awesome music. As a cool dude once said, '*If music be the food of love, play on; give me excess of it*' – although in my case, an excess of music makes me love it even more!

Gramps

m. P.(d.) Ellie's gramps - vicar

Patrick + Jean

Ros siblings + Celia - (Reggie (d.)) Andrew

Rachel] Riley
Scott

David
Elliot
Baradon (d.)

John (bro)

Sheila (sis)

Alice - Elliot

Ellie

Cici